Hell in the Meantime

Rod Johnson

A Josh Morgan Publishing novel.

ISBN: 0-578-58352-6
ISBN-13: 978-0-578-58352-5

DEDICATION

To my mom and dad. I miss you both greatly.

"This is the law: blood spilt upon the ground cries out for more."

- *AESCHYLUS, The Libation Bearers*

ACKNOWLEDGMENTS

None of my books would be possible without my wife Amy. Her help in editing/proofing is priceless.

PROLOGUE

Josh Morgan's decision to murder Everson Blake was why he was in this mess.

Morgan was a CIA officer. That is, until he was booted out of the Agency for his role in an unsanctioned operation to assassinate the president of the Latin American country of Terrador. The sole purpose of the hit had been to preserve a criminal alliance of U.S. intelligence operatives, drug cartel members, and Terradoran government officials. Once he uncovered the truth, Morgan upended the plot.

In the aftermath, President Trenton Weston believed that the CIA officer was paying an unduly heavy price for his role in a plot that he had ultimately foiled and intervened to keep the young man's punishment to a minimum.

Weston's and Morgan's lives intersected again when a foreign operative kidnapped the ex-Chief Executive. The president of the Holy Islamic Republic of Saudi Arabia had ordered Weston brought to the al Qaeda-ruled country to stand trial as a war criminal. During that incident, a Deputy Director of the National Security Agency had tracked the agent and Weston – to kill the former President. Everson Blake had been one of the principals in the rogue operation in Terrador and harbored a personal vendetta against both Morgan and Weston for blowing up the enterprise.

Because the current administration had turned a blind eye to the kidnapping for political reasons, Josh Morgan rescued Weston almost singlehandedly. The former CIA officer intended to turn Blake over to authorities, but the NSA Deputy Director threatened Morgan and everyone he cared about. Knowing the power the man had, Morgan saw no way out. He shot the man in cold blood. Former President Weston came to Josh's defense once again by inventing the story that Blake had shot himself rather than go to jail.

The official version of events portrayed Blake as a hero. Almost nobody knew the truth about his corruption or his intention to kill the ex-President. But Josh Morgan knew the real Everson Blake. And he had killed him.

ROD JOHNSON

CHAPTER 1

Day 1 – Sunday

The two men rose and shook hands.

"You know, your bid came in extremely low, Linus. You were the frontrunner to get the contract anyhow since your company built out the base in the first place. I don't think you needed to cut your margins so thin."

While his personal assistant began packing up the materials from the meeting, Linus Schwartz looked across the table at the Pentagon officer. "Well, I wanted to make sure our bid won. Terrador was one of my first projects for the Defense Department, so it's a bit special. Besides, our margins will be fine. Getting ramped up wasn't difficult at all. Our familiarity with the base is paying dividends in that regard."

"Well, at any rate," said General Mahoney, "we're more than pleased that you're so far ahead of schedule. As you know, we already have troops there. It was a mistake to ever abandon the facility in the first place, in my opinion. But you know how those bastard politicians are. Get a little heat from their constituents and they overreact. Those pantywaists have no backbone."

"You don't have to tell me. We have to jump through so many hoops to get any project off the ground," agreed Schwartz. "Well, good to see you, general. Thanks for meeting me on a Sunday."

"Of course, Linus. Happy to do it. I appreciate you providing this update in person. You and your company have been an important partner to the Pentagon."

The two men shook hands again, as did the general's aide and Schwartz's assistant.

The construction and engineering magnate hobbled past the door and into the hall. Once safely past the threshold, the artificial smile and good humor passed from the man. Each of these types of meetings made him feel a need to bathe himself. The disdain the man felt spread across the full military apparatus. But it never stood in the way of his reaping hundreds of millions of dollars for his company, much of which found its way into his pockets.

◆

The call from Maggie Loughlin had completely blindsided the Director of Central Intelligence. Elizabeth Parnell returned her phone to her desk. Closing her eyes, she shook her head slightly. She had known for some time that Josh Morgan's arrest was a possibility. What surprised her was the timing.

The United States had just backed away from the edge of a cliff. Everybody, logic suggested, should have been so preoccupied with the prospect of an imminent war with Russia that it would be inconceivable that this could've been anyone's primary focus.

Apparently, things had been much farther along than she thought before the events transpired that had put the two superpowers on a collision course. So, when the crisis had passed, the group that had the former CIA case officer in their sights picked up right where they left off.

"Damn."

◆

Maggie Loughlin had no clue what was going on, so she certainly didn't know how it involved the CIA Director or how she could help. But, as the officers led Josh out the door, her fiancé had made it clear: Call Betsy Parnell first; then call an attorney.

Parnell's response upon learning that Morgan had been arrested had been several seconds of silence. Maggie was near tears when she asked for an explanation, but when the DCI referred her back to Morgan, her confusion rapidly turned to annoyance.

Why, she had asked, couldn't Betsy give her some sort of an explanation when Morgan had directed her to the DCI? But Parnell insisted that she take it up with Josh. The Director had apologized and, before she hung up, suggested that Maggie call Ryan Crenshaw.

"Ryan? Does everyone know what's going on but me?" Maggie wondered aloud.

Crenshaw had been Morgan's Russian language professor at The University of Texas. The two became good friends, spending hours on the professor's porch of his home in Dripping Springs, Texas, just outside of Austin. Eventually, Crenshaw confided to his young student that he had been a case officer with the Central Intelligence Agency. He became instrumental in recruiting Morgan into the spy agency.

Maggie decided she could be angry with Parnell and get busy trying to get help for her fiancé at the same time. She dialed Crenshaw's number. After a number of rings, the former professor's voice spoke his recorded greeting. Maggie decided this wasn't something he should hear about in a message. She hung up.

Her mind was spinning. She didn't know who to call. She and Josh didn't have an attorney in Washington. The one they had used a couple of times was back in Jackson, Wyoming. But even if he weren't so far away, he wasn't a criminal attorney.

Maggie decided to call the person who had become such a good friend to Josh over the last couple of years. He had been instrumental in shaping Morgan's and Maggie's lives into what they were now. Maggie would ask for his assistance one more time. Besides, she knew he would want to know – and to help.

◆

Former President Trenton Weston and wife Alicia were already packed and ready to head back to Texas from the Washington, D.C. Four Seasons when the man's phone rang. Seeing the name, he picked up a call he would've otherwise ignored.

"Hi, Maggie. It's good to hear from you. Alicia and I..." He paused at the frantic interruption and motioned for the former First Lady to come back into their hotel suite from the hallway.

Weston sat on the sofa and listened.

"Slow down, Maggie. Arrested?"

Alicia Weston's eyes widened, and she sat beside her husband. As he listened further, the ex-Chief Executive motioned for the bellhop to bring the bags back inside.

"Do you know where they took Josh? Uh-huh. I see. Maggie, try to stay calm. I'm sure this is some misunderstanding. I'll make some calls. And Maggie..."

Weston looked at his wife and shrugged, eyes wide, and listened to his young friend as her composure completely left her. After a couple of tries, Weston was able to take control of the call again.

"Stay right there, sweetheart... I know... Yes, I understand. Yes... I'm sending someone to pick you up. Maggie... It will be all right. We'll get this sorted out."

The former POTUS disconnected and called to Secret Service Special

Agent John "Jack" Johnston, who had been on his protective detail since he left the White House.

"Jack…"

Alicia interrupted. "What is it, honey?"

"Josh has been arrested. Maggie doesn't know what he's suspected of. She doesn't know what police department or agency. She doesn't even know where they took him."

Weston turned his attention back to the agent.

"Jack, I want you to go pick up Maggie Loughlin. You know the address. Then swing back by here to pick us up. I hope to have figured out where we'll be going by the time you get back."

Alicia Weston was already donning her coat and grabbing her purse.

"I'm going with Jack."

◆

The ex-spy had been processed and sat in an interrogation room at the police station. CIA Director Parnell had come across information that suggested a plot to make Morgan pay for what he had done nearly a decade earlier. Beyond setting the events in motion that toppled a lucrative rogue organization in Terrador, the people behind it believed Morgan had killed their leader, NSA Deputy Director Everson Blake. Parnell didn't know who the current players were; only that, whether out of personal revenge or perhaps in the hopes that their Terrador apparatus might be reinstated, they were going to punish Morgan for his sins against them.

She had warned Morgan, so he wasn't caught completely by surprise when the police showed up However, he had expected the event to occur sometime later, perhaps weeks or even months down the road.

So, the former CIA operative sat in the room at the police station, wondering when help would arrive and in what form it would be.

◆

Soon after his meeting at the Pentagon, as his limousine sped away to another appointment, the CEO of Schwartz, Cannon, and Raines, Inc., placed a call to an associate in D.C.

"Everything proceeding smoothly?" Schwartz nodded approvingly as he heard that all was well. "There's no room for mistakes. Do you understand?"

Assured that his minion in the project grasped the gravity of the work he was performing for the billionaire, Schwartz hung up.

Like many successful businessmen, Schwartz compartmentalized the various areas of his life. Anybody who didn't need to know of a particular project, didn't.

For his part, Dexter Leach had served Schwartz as personal assistant for over twenty-six years, so he knew to tune out, to the extent possible, any conversations that didn't involve him. Furthermore, he never asked questions about matters that his boss undertook privately. So, while Schwartz carried on his telephone conversation, Mr. Leach, as the boss always called him, busied himself with texts to the home office, issuing directives to HQ personnel from the action items compiled at the Pentagon meeting.

Leach would've preferred a title other than "personal assistant." That was fine when he went to work for Schwartz while he was still in law school. But now he was a very young-looking forty-eight years old. The term seemed to portray him as someone performing in a more menial capacity than he was. Unfortunately, his boss was rather old-fashioned in his thinking. But the money the CEO paid his subordinate made the younger man ultimately amenable to whatever title his boss wanted him to have.

Schwartz had never married, instead satisfying his carnal and companionship needs with various involvements and the occasional live-in mistress. He was always generous to his lovers, who were generally far beneath the social status the man held. Perhaps it was because, as a self-made billionaire who grew up in near poverty in Georgia, he was more comfortable with "common" folk than with social butterflies. Any relationships that appeared to be heading toward something longer than a date or two necessitated in Schwartz's mind, and in the minds of his advisors, a written contract that outlined the "rules of engagement" for the affair, despite that an actual "engagement" was never a possibility.

Now at age eighty-two, Schwartz was content keeping to himself and hadn't seen anyone for over a decade. However, in the past, for the founder of the engineering, procurement, and construction company that bore his name, brief romantic encounters tended to be with much younger women, while any associations that carried on for a while were always with women somewhat nearer his own age. But brief or lasting, once Schwartz felt a particular woman had exhausted her ability to satisfy his needs, she was summarily dismissed, much as an employee would be. During the last twenty-five years, that task always fell to Mr. Leach, who provided a generous parting gift to each contestant for playing.

Linus Schwartz had truly loved only one woman. In his mid-twenties, Schwartz became smitten with a young woman, married, who worked at the construction company where the ambitious young man was beginning to make a name for himself. With his initiative, hustle, creativity, and ruthlessness in dealing with obstacles – even if those obstacles existed in the form of other human beings – he had impressed the business owners he worked for.

The object of his affection was a secretary at the firm. The two developed a friendship, largely from the persistence Linus showed in simply being attentive to her.

Schwartz was completely enamored with Dorothy. Many mornings, he would bring her a breakfast roll from the diner near his apartment, dismissing the gesture by saying his "eyes were bigger than his stomach." He would rush to the coffee pot anytime he saw "Dottie" heading that direction. He always carried boxes for her, retrieved things out of her reach on the top shelf in the stock room, did all the little things to make her life a bit easier.

Dottie thought Linus was charming. His acts were the thoughtful, harmless little gestures that good friends did for each other. Linus was kind and generous and Dottie enjoyed the little flirtations. He was, to Dottie… sweet. That was simply the best word for him.

One night, after a business dinner – one that Dottie's husband was unable to attend – Linus had insisted he give his colleague a ride home. She'd had a bit too much to drink, and he didn't want her to take a cab. Dottie's friend drove a short distance out of the city. In her foggy state of mind, the rider was unaware of the destination. When the driver stopped, she prepared to exit the car for the walk up the sidewalk to her small white house. Only then did she realize they were on an isolated dirt road that led into a small farmland pasture.

Linus Schwartz had seized the opportunity to have some time alone with the woman he desired. Once parked, he proclaimed his undying love for Dottie, who struggled through her tipsy mind to comprehend what was happening.

"No!" she had shouted, following it up with a more hurtful, "Don't be ridiculous!"

Completely taken aback, Dottie's co-worker grabbed both of her hands forcefully. "What are you saying? What about work? I know you feel the same as I do!"

Dorothy struggled to pull her hands away, recoiling at the man's touch. "You're crazy!" piled even more pain on the man, whose frustration was morphing into rage. "Besides, I'm married!"

Schwartz heard in her last statement the one thing he needed to further rationalize his unfolding intentions. She's married! That had to be it. She was simply being honorable, and it was standing in the way of her passion for Linus, he was sure. He knew she wanted this as much as he did. He tried to pull his love closer, but she continued to resist.

Finally, Linus pushed Dorothy back onto the car's front bench seat and kissed her forcibly. With one hand on her breast, Schwartz lifted her skirt. He never bothered to remove her panties, simply pushing them aside.

The ride home had been made up of one-sided conversation. Dorothy hung her head and sobbed, while Linus reassured her. He was certain that what she shed were tears of joy mixed with distress at her dilemma. He felt sympathy for her. How terrible it must be for her, he knew, to feel she couldn't be with him.

"I promise, honey, we'll find some way for you to get out of your marriage. We'll be together soon. I swear it. I know you love me. I love you, too, Dottie. We'll figure this…"

Before Linus' car came to a complete stop at Dottie's house, she bolted out of the car, crashing to the sidewalk. She gathered herself and stumbled toward her front door.

"Poor kid," Schwartz thought. "She feels stuck, but I'll come up with something."

Dottie never went to their workplace again. Linus bravely called her house a few times, mostly when he knew her husband should be at work. But Dottie had never answered. Two weeks later, Schwartz summoned the courage to go to her house and confront her husband with the truth – at least, *his* truth – that he and Dottie wanted to be together. He would tell her husband that he could accept that and move on peaceably, or … There were other ways that Linus could bring this to its proper conclusion.

But when young Linus got to Dottie's house, it was vacant. Peering through windows that were absent curtains, he saw some unused boxes scattered about rooms that were completely empty.

"Bastard!" Schwartz screamed aloud. He slammed his hand onto the screen that covered the window to the living room. The impact was so forceful on the mesh barrier that the glass behind it shattered, leaving scars on his right hand that he carried for the rest of his life.

Linus Schwartz, future billionaire, swore to himself that he would find Dottie and rescue her from her husband. He would make him pay for taking her away and keeping her from her true love. But his efforts were in vain.

Nearly sixty years later, his perspective regarding his relationship with Dorothy Stovall had evolved. Even with evidence to the contrary, he never let himself accept that the love was one-sided. And he never got over her. That lingering unhappiness and rage at the failed romance had been the singular event that propelled him into the man he became.

Now Schwartz was consumed with his business empire and philanthropic pursuits. The slightly stooped nature of his posture made him appear even smaller than his five-ten height. He was thinly built but possessed a bit of a potbelly that was accentuated by the vests of the three-piece suits he usually wore.

The tycoon's face was wrinkled, but no more than most people his age. Unlike many of his contemporaries, his pate was fully covered with hair. However, it was very thin, a feature made very noticeable by the tiny furrows created by his comb and the hair oil he had used since he was a young man.

Yet, despite the effects of time on his body, his mind was as sharp as any, which made him a formidable adversary in business negotiations.

Linus Schwartz had his money and his charities, and that was enough.

◆

Secret Service Special Agent Jeff Coulter, who worked alongside Special Agent Johnston in Weston's permanent detail, held open the door of the black SUV for his protectee.

Weston took a seat beside Maggie and his wife. He hesitated before launching into what little information he had.

"Maggie, I had no luck getting information from law enforcement..."

Maggie's eyes widened and she shook her head as if trying to resist what she had just heard.

"The information I got was from Betsy Parnell."

Maggie was angry, resenting that Trent had been able to get info from the CIA Director. She wondered why Parnell wouldn't have just told her anything she knew.

"First, Maggie, Betsy wanted me to tell you she's sorry for not telling you this herself..."

The secondhand apology didn't help, but at least she was getting information, Maggie thought.

"Morgan is being held at a local police station. I'm sorry to say... whew..." The ex-President took a deep breath. "Maggie, things are going to work out. This is all..."

"Trent, what is he charged with?" The question was almost a shout, and a demand.

"Murder, dear. Josh has been charged with murder."

Maggie Loughlin's prolonged silence was difficult for Trent Weston to interpret. Alicia Weston put both hands to her mouth and looked first to her husband and then to Maggie. The former First Lady spoke first.

"Trent, this has to be a mistake."

"You know something about this. Don't you?" Maggie finally said. Her blue eyes cut to Weston and through him

The ex-POTUS hung his head. He tried to make eye contact with Maggie but couldn't maintain it. Instead he looked out the window. Finally, he told her what he knew in a very hushed, very somber voice. And for the first time since the episode ended over eighteen months earlier, Maggie heard the entire story of the final events when Josh had rescued Weston from both a Saudi agent and from NSA Deputy Director Everson Blake.

She heard how, when Josh had caught up with the Arab who had taken Weston hostage, he had killed him. Then he had confronted Blake, fully intending to hold him to be arrested. But the NSA officer made a number of threats against Maggie. Furthermore, he had made it clear that his story would even cast suspicion on Weston as being in league with the Saudis. None of it made sense, but Blake had already tried to kill Josh and Maggie and had been intent on murdering the former President.

Blake, Morgan had felt, would be able to reach out from prison to make good on his threats.

"So, Josh believed he had no other choice and he shot him," Weston concluded. "He was going to give himself up and confess. I concocted the story that Blake had committed suicide rather than face a lifetime in prison."

"So this is partly your fault!?" Maggie accused. "If he hadn't been chasing you around, trying to save your ass, he would've never been in that situation!"

Alicia Weston tried to take Maggie's hand, but the younger woman pulled away. Trent Weston lowered his head a moment before returning his gaze to the window and the scene passing by them as Special Agent Johnston drove them to the police station.

The three passengers sat in silence for some time.

Maggie saw the anguish in the man. "I'm sorry. I was out of line, Trent. I know I hurt you..."

Weston looked up.

"Oh, Maggie, dear. You weren't out of line. And I'm not upset that you said that. I'm hurt..." Weston choked on the words. "...I'm hurting because you're right."

Of the three people in the SUV who loved Josh, the one who finally broke into tears was the former President.

Alicia Weston pulled both her husband and her friend close into a prolonged embrace.

♦

District of Columbia Metropolitan Police Detective Dillon Howard sat across from his prisoner in the interrogation room while Assistant U.S.

Attorney Siobhan Cassidy watched through the one-way glass from the observation room.

One part of murder suspect Josh Morgan really just wanted to come clean about the whole sordid thing regarding Everson Blake. He still believed that, morally speaking, he had done nothing wrong. Still, he *had* broken the law, and that, he knew, was a different matter. But no matter what personal catharsis he might realize by confessing and taking his chances with the legal system, his life was different than it had been when he confronted Blake. There was Maggie. She was happy in her job in the White House press department. Morgan had a job as a visiting professor at Georgetown University. And he had friends, he believed, beyond the one or two fishing buddies he'd had in Wyoming. Josh felt he had a life worth protecting.

"Your best hope is to limit the damage. Tell me what you know. I'll try to help."

Morgan smiled. The detective wanted to help? He didn't think so.

For his part, and though you'd never know it to look at him, Howard was getting frustrated. It wasn't because he hadn't gotten anything *useful* from Morgan. He could handle that. It was because he hadn't gotten *anything* from his suspect. Nothing at all. Zip. Nada. Joshua Matthew Morgan hadn't spoken a single word since he left his apartment.

"Everyone knows you killed Blake. He was unarmed, too. Probably a capital offense. This thing is a slam dunk."

Morgan folded his arms and leaned back in his chair.

Detective Howard desperately wanted a smoke. He had quit. Well, he was trying to. He realized silently that he was the personification of the old joke. "Quitting smoking is easy," he thought. "I've done it three times this year alone." Yes. A cigarette would help right about now. He reached up and rubbed the nicotine patch that was on his upper arm beneath his shirt. The patch seemed to help the physical addiction, to a degree. But the truth was, for the police investigator, as with countless others, the emotional addiction was equally strong. Holding the white stick in his hand, smelling the smoke, the mere act of succumbing to a years-long habit – all those things were as integral to a smoker as the act of inhaling. Yes, he desperately needed to light up, and the more he thought about it, the worse his desperation got.

And his anxiety was all because of this arrogant little shit and his refusal to say anything. Howard rubbed through his shirt sleeve again.

Morgan's fishing pal back in Jackson Hole, Deputy Sheriff Scott Taggart, had likewise struggled for years before finally conquering his smoking habit. Tag had acquired the same unconscious habit of touching his patch. It was subliminal, Josh thought. Anytime he got stressed, when he would normally light up, he reached for his patch instead. So, Morgan recognized the action in his interrogator and knew he was stressed. Once again, he smiled.

Assistant DA Cassidy stared through the glass, arms folded, lips pursed as her own impatience grew.

"Hi, Siobhan."

The assistant turned to her boss as he came into the room.

"Riley."

United States Attorney for D.C. Riley Maxwell always loved the brogue that his subordinate's words still possessed, despite that she had moved from Ireland with her mother some twenty years ago, after her dad had passed. She wasn't stereotypically Irish in appearance – no fiery red hair, which Maxwell would've enjoyed. It was brown. But the young woman possessed a very Irish streak of stubbornness and a love of tea that was typical of many from the Emerald Isle.

Another notable difference from the stereotype was that Cassidy was a teetotaler. Maxwell believed that her refusal to drink alcohol at department parties was the primary factor, along with her stubbornness, that had made her immune to his advances. That and the fact that she was very happily married.

He ogled her lean figure as he walked past her and let out an inaudible "whew." Cassidy saw him in the very limited reflection of the one-way glass and was about to give him a piece of her mind when he spoke.

"What's the word?"

The assistant was already looking for another job and would report him for harassment in the near future. So, for the time being, she stood down.

"There is no word," she replied.

"What do you mean?"

"Mr. Morgan hasn't uttered a solitary syllable since we picked him up."

"No kidding."

Assistant Cassidy simply nodded. In fact, she had questioned the legality of picking Morgan up for a crime committed in Texas, but her boss had insisted. "Perfectly within our authority," he had assured her confidently. She reminded herself that she would be leaving her position soon and did as she was told.

Cassidy certainly had no sympathy for cold-blooded murderers, but she was dedicated to the letter of the law. She had wondered aloud why Texas hadn't prosecuted the man. "It's political," Maxwell had told her. "Complicated."

She thought again about her pending resignation, once she found a job, and figured this case would all get sorted out. Cassidy would just let it go.

Back inside the interrogation room, Howard decided he could play the quiet game, too. He sat silently for about five minutes. Finally, he said, "Do you need to go take a leak?"

Morgan shook his head marginally.

"Water?" got the same nonverbal answer.

"You little prick! I can't help you if you don't talk to me!"

Morgan really wanted to laugh but decided that would be a bit over the top.

Howard pointed his finger at his opponent and shook it, but he gathered himself and walked out of the room without a word. He would find a cigarette somewhere.

Morgan stretched his legs, crossed them at the ankles, dropped his head, and closed his eyes. He knew he wouldn't actually sleep. And he was far more anxious than he was letting on, but the mental discipline he was devoting to antagonizing his questioner was the only thing preventing him from being overwhelmed at his situation.

He wondered how Maggie was coping. What success was she having arranging help for him?

The larger question looming in Josh's mind was whether he could even *be* helped. He was, after all, guilty.

♦

One of the agency's in-house counsel sat in CIA Director Parnell's office. The DCI had brought Ellis White up to speed on the events of almost two years ago – everything from Former President Wendell Mercer's decision to look the other way at his predecessor's abduction by a Saudi agent, to his abetting NSA Deputy Director Everson Blake's actions. The spy chief had also told him everything she knew about the final confrontation of Morgan with Blake and Al-Majeed in Texas. She left nothing out, including her decision to send CIA Officer Trevor O'Bannon to help out.

"Interesting story, Betsy. You know I can't just waltz into the police station and help Morgan in my official capacity. Right?"

"I do. What I really want to know is if there's anything you can do to justify my own actions in a legal sense. Then maybe I can step forward and help our guy out."

"Sending O'Bannon to help was almost certainly illegal, no matter how we try to spin it."

"Geez, Ellis. Don't you think I know that? I really didn't care at the time. Morgan was in way over his head and needed our help. President Mercer sure wasn't stepping up. In fact, he was in it up to his neck and… Never mind. I already told you all that. Anything you can do to help is appreciated."

White put his hands together, almost as if praying, and rested his chin on them. Betsy waited patiently as he considered what he'd heard.

"Executive Order 12333 permits the Agency to collect intelligence domestically if it has an authorized intelligence purpose. For example, if we believe someone is involved in espionage or terrorist activities."

Parnell thought for a minute. "That requires senior approval. Maybe even from the Director of National Intelligence and/or Attorney General."

"You were Deputy Director, Intelligence then. Right?"

"Sure, but I didn't authorize anyone to act, except for O'Bannon, and he was there specifically to cover Morgan's butt. I don't see how we could make the legal exception work for Roadrunner."

"Then what about for Morgan?" the counsel proposed.

"Him? He wasn't working for us."

"Wasn't he?"

Director Parnell thought of the lawyer's question as a suggestion.

"I think I see where you're going. The problem, I think, is that we'd have to show that I sent him there. Correct? And I didn't."

"Maybe you did," countered White.

"I'm sure I..." the DCI tried to correct but was stopped by the attorney's raised hand while he reviewed his notes.

"Ah, here it is. Ben Reid." White looked up at Parnell.

Betsy smiled wistfully. "Best associate I ever had, and one of the best men I've known."

Ben Reid worked for Parnell and had sent a covert message to Morgan about Weston's kidnapping because of his connection to the man. That email was the catalyst for Morgan's involvement in trying to find and rescue the former Chief Executive. Reid had been murdered for his action by some of Blake's men.

When she thought of Reid's tipoff to his friend, Betsy's sad smile transformed and produced a small laugh.

"Only time he ever really pissed me off was when he sent that email to Josh to let him know what was going on – or rather wasn't going on – behind the scenes to go get Weston. Of course, turns out he was right in doing so."

"You ordered Reid to bring Morgan into this, didn't you?"

Betsy wondered if her guest was listening. "No. I told you, Ben did that all on his own."

Ellis White, Esquire, thought to himself that, for the head of the spy agency, Parnell was a little dense. He sighed.

"But Ben Reid can't testify that he acted on his own, can he?"

The remark angered the DCI because of the seeming calloused referral to Reid's death. That is, until she finally got a clue.

Attorney White arched his eyebrows and raised his hands in a questioning manner.

"So, upon further reflection?"

"As a matter of fact, upon further reflection, I recall now. I *did* instruct Ben to bring Morgan on board."

Ellis followed up, "Then I think that makes him a *de facto* employee of yours, or at least a representative in the legal sense."

Parnell couldn't smile. She knew the logic might not hold up in court, but she had little else to work with.

CHAPTER 2

Not one soul in the Metropolitan Police Department's station could've possibly anticipated that Former President of the United States Trenton Weston would show up at their precinct. At least nobody except for U.S. Attorney Riley Maxwell. He wasn't completely surprised. The former resident of the White House was just there sooner than expected. But there Weston was, and the prosecutor was ready for him. A Secret Service Special Agent led the way, followed by an auburn-haired young lady. Then came the ex-President and his wife.

The next man in line carried a large briefcase, had an assistant, and was attired in a three-piece suit. There was no doubt he was a lawyer. The last in the troupe was another Secret Service agent.

Despite the power and prestige that being a former POTUS carried, Weston deferred to the man in the pin-striped suit. The police sergeant at the front desk was about to enquire what he wanted, when Maxwell intervened. He recognized the man that he knew would be his adversary in all matters related to murder suspect Joshua Morgan.

Maxwell held out his hand and began to introduce himself. The man in the expensive suit shook his hand but cut off the introduction Maxwell had initiated.

"Donald Summers. I represent Josh Morgan. I'd like to see my client."

Summers had been President Weston's White House counsel for the duration of his friend's only term. The two had gone to law school together. Summers was tall and thin. The man's hair would've been completely white around the sides, but he kept them shaved to match the top of his head that nature had made devoid of hair. At sixty-eight years of age, Summers was still passionate about his life and his work. He wasn't a criminal attorney, so he would likely yield to another lawyer if things progressed much further with his client. But he was one of the brightest legal minds in the country.

He had once been considered a prospect for the U.S. Supreme Court, but that never materialized.

Maxwell was a bit intimidated but wasn't going to be deterred from pronouncing his name to the man.

"U.S. Attorney Riley Maxwell," he said as he led the entourage into a conference room.

Shutting the door behind him, he continued, "Impressive firepower… for a murderer."

President Weston spoke up. "It was difficult to track down who had arrested Mr. Morgan and why."

The U.S. Attorney motioned to chairs and began to take a seat himself until he realized that no one else was doing so.

"Yes. We understand there may be some issues with this prosecution that involve national security, so we're keeping things on the QT… for now."

"Precisely what are the charges against Mr. Morgan?" the former counsel to the President continued.

"Murder in the second degree… precisely."

Everyone of Morgan's group maintained their calm, though Maggie thought her knees were going to buckle. She finally sat, along with Alicia Weston.

"I'll require a copy of the arrest warrant," insisted Morgan's legal representative.

"Of course."

"And I need to see him now. I assume you made him aware of his rights."

"We did."

"Did he invoke his right to counsel?"

"I haven't been in the interrogation room personally for the whole time, so I can't say for sure, but…"

Summers harrumphed for show. "Are you the prosecutor in this case?" He frowned for further effect.

"I am, but I can't attend to every little detail myself. I have a very capable staff."

"*Little detail?* Is that your view of the Miranda Warning?"

"I'm a busy man…"

"So am I," countered the defense attorney. "So, I need to see Mr. Morgan now. And I'd like to visit with whichever of your 'capable staff' knows what the hell is going on with my client."

Maxwell bristled at the rebuke. "Wait here."

He left the room in a huff.

Maggie was shaking, though not nearly as much as she thought.

Summers and Weston took seats along with her and Mrs. Weston.

Summers turned to Maggie and the man who had been so forceful with the U.S. Attorney suddenly became an understanding and sympathetic friend. He reached across the table to take Maggie's hand. "How're you holding up?"

"Not well, I'm afraid."

Summers patted her hand sympathetically. "Ms. Loughlin, I've seen you on TV the last few months. You are a remarkably controlled and impressive young woman. You have a presence that speaks volumes about your character. Now I need... Josh needs you to keep that amazing poker face you displayed during this whole Russia mess. These clowns need to see confidence and fearlessness from all of us. Okay?"

Maggie only nodded.

"Okay, Maggie?" Summers repeated.

Morgan's fiancée blotted at her eyes, though tears hadn't really formed. She finally smiled and said, "Yes."

"I can promise you this one thing. You'll know everything I know, or at least everything Josh lets me tell you. We'll get to the bottom of this."

Trent Weston reached over and patted his college friend's forearm.

The door opened and the defense attorney's countenance regained the severe look it'd had the first time he encountered the U.S. Attorney. He stood. He was completely surprised when, instead of bringing one of his assistant attorneys for a discussion of the interrogation, Maxwell was carrying a tray with five cups.

"It's going to be a few minutes until my associate is available. I thought I might as well bring you some coffee." The prosecutor set a cup before each of Morgan's visitors.

Then, he turned abruptly and left again.

Summers turned to his group and held up his hands in disbelief.

Maggie took the coffee in both of her hands. Alicia Weston drank hers, while her husband took a small sip and pushed his away.

Don Summers and his assistant ignored theirs entirely. The attorney paced while waiting for his legal adversary to return.

About a ten-minute wait ensued until the door swung open again.

"Here. Follow me," Maxwell instructed as he handed the paper to Summers that detailed the charges and rationale for arresting Morgan. The defense lawyer handed the document to his associate who had yet to say a single word. The prosecuting attorney wheeled about, and Summers followed.

Before the door shut behind him, Josh's lawyer looked back to Maggie and mouthed, "It'll be all right."

Then he left to see his client with his assistant, Shelley Cain, close behind and already reading the arrest warrant.

As the two men left the room, Maggie suddenly said, "Oh, my. I need to tell Marie. And the President needs to know."

Trent Weston reassured her. "I've already called the President. She'll let Marie know." Marie Ginnetti was the President's Press Secretary and Maggie's boss.

"What must the President think?" Maggie said.

"Maggie, dear, she knows almost all of what transpired with Josh. She was Vice president then. She told me on the phone exactly what she thinks. She said this is, to quote her, 'bullshit.'

"She said to take whatever time you need and to know that you have her full support. Of course, she can't take any kind of action… at least not now. This is all secret for the time being. So…"

The former President's voice trailed off as Maggie started to apologize again for blowing up at him on the ride over. He patted her arm. "You didn't say anything wrong. Besides, we're family."

Alicia Weston pulled their young friend a little closer.

◆

Maxwell led Summers and Cain toward the interrogation room. Summers peeled away to enter the observation room. Maxwell did an about-face to follow.

Along with an electronics technician whose job it was to make a video and audio record of everything said during the questioning, he saw a young woman of about twenty-eight years of age. A fifty-something-year-old man who was probably a detective, pushed past Summers to leave the room.

The young lady extended her hand. "Siobhan Cassidy. I'm an Assistant U.S. Attorney with the Homicide Division of the U.S. Attorney's Superior Court Division."

"Ms. Cassidy. I'm Don Summers. This is my associate, Shelley Cain. Did my client invoke his right to counsel?"

Attorney Cassidy replied, "Not exactly…"

"What does that mean? 'Not exactly?'"

"When our officers arrested him, he asked his wife to call an attorney."

"Ms. Loughlin is his fiancée. Was that declaration made before or after he was read his rights?"

"After… I believe."

"I believe that qualifies as invoking his rights." Summers turned to Cain, who was busily taking notes, to emphasize the importance of her boss' last remark.

"Tell me, Ms. Cassidy, did you or anyone in your office continue to question Mr. Morgan after he invoked his right to counsel?"

U.S. Attorney Maxwell spoke up. "Yes, but it didn't matter. The suspect hasn't said a word."

"Doesn't matter?" Summers looked to his associate, whom he had trained well in the four years she had worked with him. At the discreet prompt, she furiously underlined part of her transcription, which got Maxwell's attention.

Summers noticed that, whenever Maxwell spoke up, Cassidy rolled her eyes. It was slight but he caught it. The crossed arms were more obvious, and the two things combined spoke volumes.

Josh's lawyer spoke directly to Cassidy, though he was responding to Maxwell's remark. "You realize your job is to err on the side of caution. The fact that Mr. Morgan hasn't spoken to you is of little significance in the eyes of the law. He had invoked, and any further interrogation without his representative present is highly inappropriate, if not a violation of his rights."

At being ignored, Maxwell stepped around and in between his Assistant Attorney and Summers. His face was red and, despite the effort to smile, his lips quivered a bit.

"Please direct your comments to me, Mr. Summers."

The defense attorney noticed that the Assistant U.S. Attorney's eyes seemed to brighten somewhat. Perhaps she was enjoying Maxwell's annoyance as much as he was.

"Oh, I beg your pardon. You said you were in the dark about the particulars of this case and were relying on your 'capable staff.'" Summers looked over Maxwell's shoulders and offered a small smile to the man's assistant. She smiled back.

"I did not say I was in the dark. I said…" Maxwell's words stalled when he couldn't come up with a suitable substitution for his words being thrown back at him. Cassidy shook her head.

Summers had always believed that a man can largely and accurately be sized up by what the people who worked with him thought about him. Maxwell wasn't faring well.

"I realize there is no statute of limitations on murder, but there are jurisdictional limits. So, then, Mr. Maxwell, perhaps you can tell me in what area of the District of Columbia Texas is. That is, what makes this your jurisdiction?"

The U.S. Attorney's red face brightened even further.

Summers patted him on his shoulder and said, "Withdrawn," somewhat playfully. "We'll get back to that." He looked over at Ms. Cassidy. "Oh, yes," he thought. "She's definitely enjoying this."

He spoke aloud again, this time to the technician in the room. "Young man, please turn off all of your equipment. And then, all of you may leave while I speak to Mr. Morgan." His demand was understood, and his steamrolling of the U.S. Attorney was complete; at least for the time being.

Detective Dillon Howard was more composed after having two cigarettes, though his contempt for his suspect had only grown. Morgan had remained speechless since he got back.

The door opened.

"I understand you've been illegally interrogating my client."

Morgan had no idea who the man was, but he finally spoke. "Yes, he has, counselor."

The detective's head jerked around at finally hearing his prisoner speak. Josh smiled at him. Howard left the room, muttering curses that were more understandable to Morgan and his two attorneys than he thought.

'Mr. Morgan, I'm Don Summers. This is my associate, Shelley Cain."

Josh Morgan shook the man's hand vigorously. "You don't know how glad I am to meet you."

◆

U.S. Attorney Riley Maxwell sat in his office sulking, muttering some of the same words Detective Howard had used when exiting the interrogation room. He pressed the icon beside a name on his phone forcefully, as though that would somehow put his call through more quickly.

"It's me. Yes... Well, we knew he would get help. Just didn't expect this caliber, this fast. Right... Right... Of course. I'll keep you posted."

The attorney hung up. As committed as he was to this plan, he couldn't help but worry. Were things moving too fast? Did they have all their bases covered?

◆

Summers gave Morgan the rundown on his association with Weston, not only during the man's time as President, but as lifelong friends.

"How's Maggie holding up? When can I see her?"

Summers said, "She's tough, but there's no denying she's shaken. We'll try to get her in to see you in a few minutes. Until then, let's talk strategy."

As Weston's White House Counsel, Summers was aware of all the details concerning the rogue Terrador op gone bad. As Weston's close friend, he was aware of even the undisclosed elements of the ex-Chief Executive's abduction by the Saudi agent and subsequent rescue by Morgan. Therefore, he knew exactly what had transpired on the pier at Gulf Mariners Marina. Now, as Morgan's attorney, he had to figure out a strategy for the young man who was undoubtedly guilty.

"Our first plan is to make the allegations go away. If we can't, if this goes to trial… well, we'll start to plan for that, but let's hope our first plan of attack works."

Morgan nodded.

"So, Mr. Morgan…"

"It's Josh."

"Okay, Josh. I'm going to try to get Maggie in here. Shelley and I are going to confer and then I believe I'll have a call to make. Any questions?"

Morgan didn't even know what questions to ask about the case. He finally voiced his primary concern.

"I'm on leave from my new job at Georgetown. They postponed my start until next semester while I recover from…" He didn't know what his attorney knew about his role in the recent crisis with Russia. "…Well, while I recover. What does the university know about this?"

"As far as I know, nothing. The U.S. Attorney seems determined to keep this quiet. At least for now. We'll demand that he continue to do so. Anything else?"

"Just thank you. And tell Trent how much I appreciate him sending you."

Summers smiled, closed his briefcase, and stood to leave. "Bail won't be set until tomorrow morning, so hang in there."

As Summers walked from the interview room, he had a sudden thought. He turned around and entered the observation room, where he was relieved to find the video and audio recording devices still turned off and the room empty.

◆

A uniformed police officer entered the room where Maggie sat with the Westons.

"Come with me" resulted in Maggie hurriedly standing to follow. In the hallway she encountered Don Summers.

"Maggie, Morgan is fine. We talked a little strategy…" The attorney whose job it was to defend Josh Morgan noticed that Maggie's blue eyes kept looking past him down the hall where the police officer was waiting.

"You know, this can wait. Go to Josh."

The words barely left his mouth when he heard a quick, "Thanks," and Maggie rushed away. Summers and Shelley Cain walked past Secret Service Agent Johnston into where his friend and his wife waited. The pair sat and the senior attorney leaned back in his chair, removed his wire-framed glasses, and rubbed his eyes.

He took a deep breath and clicked his tongue as he organized his thoughts.

"You'll recall, old friend, your boy in there is guilty as sin."

Weston didn't react. He only said, "What can you tell me, Don?"

"Oh, Josh authorized me to tell you everything; both of you."

Summers paused and reached across to his junior attorney, who instinctively gave him the yellow pad of notes she had taken. He replaced his glasses and scanned the several pages.

"Trent, you heard what I said," confirmed Summers as he looked up from his reading. "Josh *is* guilty. You and Alicia know that. Right?"

Trent Weston confirmed with a slight nod of his head. His wife appeared bewildered. They exchanged the worried glance that parents would have if this was happening to their son. They both felt that way about Josh.

"Also, just so you know, I told him that I'd be looking for a criminal defense attorney to replace me, but that I'd continue to work his case until then. He tried to insist, solely because *you* brought me in… Apparently he has enormous trust in you – no accounting for poor judgement."

The two friends smiled.

"Anyhow, he tried to persuade me to continue to represent him because he trusts you, and you trust me. The compromise – I guess you'd call it that – is that I find a good trial lawyer and that I would sit in the second chair, if it goes that far."

The Westons' eyes brightened at the word "if."

"You think there's a chance it might not, Don?" hoped Trent Weston.

"Yes, but a slim one. Maxwell's already messed up. At least, I believe he has. I don't think it completely derails the plans to prosecute Josh; just resets the process."

"Well, any disruption in their plans is a minor victory," supposed Weston.

"Yes, it is."

Weston added, "If it goes to trial, shouldn't my testimony that Blake committed suicide pretty much guarantee a 'not guilty' verdict?"

"Josh has already ruled out your testifying. Said he won't let you perjure yourself."

Alicia Weston's eyes opened wide and her head shifted backward suddenly. She looked at her husband, who looked back but gave no further response.

"Well, change his mind. I'm already on record about what happened. That's why charges were never filed in the first place."

"Perjure?" Alicia interrupted.

Trent was not inclined to explain right now. "I'll tell you later."

"Believe me, Trent, I tried. He won't hear of it. He rightly said they have the burden to prove he's guilty. He's willing to take his chances with the circumstantial evidence."

"Foolish boy. What if it looks like it's not going well?" asked the defendant's friend.

"Josh said we'd have to change our strategy on the fly. Instead of saying he didn't do it, we'd proceed with the 'not guilty' plea, but our defense will be that he had no choice."

Weston thought about the scenario. "Self-defense? I just don't get it, Don."

"Trent, you're a lawyer so I'm not telling you anything you don't know, but there's what's right and what's legal. What stands between the two is what's justifiable. Justification is the one thing that can transform an action. The homicide doesn't suddenly become 'legal;' only justified. If this thing gets to a trial, that's what Josh says he will attest to. He's adamant that he'll testify in his own defense."

"He can't!" objected Weston.

"I told him 'no.' In fact, I told him if he insists on getting on the stand, he'd have to get another lawyer."

Alicia entered the conversation. "What about bail? We'll post it."

The attorney leaned forward and tried to avoid getting the couple's hopes up. "May not need it. At least not yet. We can't do anything until tomorrow anyhow, but I have one trick up my sleeve. Be prepared for bail, though, just in case. What I have planned will depend on the judge."

The former POTUS lowered his eyebrows and frowned. "Doesn't it always?" He took a longer sip of the coffee Maxwell had brought earlier. It was cold. Weston sneered and pushed it away.

"By the way, Trent, Josh asked me to talk to the CIA Director. Any idea what that's about?"

"I don't know. Maybe to shed some light on behind-the-scenes stuff leading up to and during the encounter. I know one of her guys was there."

Summers sighed loudly.

"A CIA officer operating domestically. This just keeps getting better. You never told me that."

The ex-Chief Executive shrugged.

♦

Maggie walked into the interrogation room. The police officer waited outside.

"I thought you'd have on one of those sexy jumpsuits."

Morgan stood and the two embraced for a few seconds.

"How are you?" they said at the same time. Each smiled, embraced again and sat on the same side of the table.

"How are you, Maggie?" Morgan took her hands in his. She tilted her head and shrugged. She didn't know how to answer.

The two sat in silence for a few seconds. Finally, Morgan lowered his eyes and began what he thought would be an overdue confession.

"Maggie, down in Texas, the thing with Everson Blake…"

His fiancée gently raised his chin with a single finger. "I know. Trent told me all about it. Why hadn't you told me?"

"What would I say? That I…" The ex-CIA officer realized there might be electronic ears listening and cut off his question.

Instead he simply said, "Looks like we'll be spending some time apart."

The couple passed the short time they were allowed mostly in silence and otherwise encouraging one another and talking about how they would get through this.

◆

The threat of disclosure about his actions when Saudi operative Fadi Al-Majeed abducted his predecessor forced Wendell Mercer from the presidency. Since that time he rarely entertained visitors but his association with his present guest went back a number of years. Linus Schwartz had served as the impetus behind Mercer's decision to go into politics. The older man had helped shaped Mercer's platform when he ran for the White House. His personal contributions and support were invaluable, but it was the Political Action Committee Schwartz organized that proved pivotal in Mercer's surprising win over incumbent Trenton Weston.

Schwartz's efforts as a bundler were instrumental in the massive amounts of dollars raised in support of Mercer. Schwartz rarely raised the money himself, instead using a team of advocates to reach out. Then Schwartz would make calls as needed to prod reluctant donors and stage events to promote his candidate. The efforts of the construction CEO and his teams of activists gathered countless numbers of donations at the maximum each state allowed and presented them in one impressive bundle to Mercer's operation.

The rewards Schwartz reaped for his efforts on behalf of the Mercer campaign were immense. So, of course, he had been devastated when Wendell Mercer had been forced to resign. Both personally and monetarily, Schwartz suffered. The embarrassment at Mercer's retirement would've been much greater had the public at large known the real reason for his departure. But in the world of business, where so much of Schwartz, Cannon, and Raines' revenues resulted in work for the U.S. military, the resignation was a setback of some significance. Projects that typically would've been sure things under Mercer began to find their way to other contractors under Mercer's successor, Sandra Hendrickson. That was the primary driver for the ridiculously low bid from SCR to restore the Terrador installation. Schwartz couldn't be sure he would get the job in the current course of awarding the contract. And he *had* to land that project.

Schwartz never truly felt the affection for Mercer that he pretended to. He thought the man a reckless egomaniac who believed that he could charm his will on anyone. The tycoon wasn't entirely mistaken about that. But Mercer's hubris made him a useful idiot, Schwartz considered, and so he treated him like a son.

Even though his usefulness was greatly diminished to Schwartz and SCR, Inc. after leaving the White House, there were ways he continued to prove valuable. The man still had connections. More than that, he had information, and "knowledge is power," as Sir Francis Bacon first said in 1597. Nothing was off the table, as far as Wendell Mercer was concerned. He would tell his benefactor anything he needed to know.

And so it was, when Mercer resigned, Schwartz was one of the first to reach out to him. The billionaire flew the suddenly former President on his jet to his private island in the Caribbean to "recuperate" from the cover-story "health issue" that had presumably driven the man from office.

In such despair over his fall from the political throne, Mercer seemed on the verge of breaking down entirely at the island compound. Schwartz literally had him on suicide watch, though the men watching over the ex-Chief Executive were discreet enough in their watchfulness that Mercer never caught on that they were charged with his survival.

Mercer remained at the mansion for almost three months. Over time, his host reduced his visits to the occasional weekend, but when Mercer had first arrived there, Schwartz spent the entire first two weeks with his "friend." The purpose was ostensibly to console and encourage Mercer. The real goal was to pump him for information about his departure from 1600 Pennsylvania. Schwartz had to know how the change in Washington would affect him and his company. But there was, more importantly, a crucial personal matter he had to find out about.

As always, the ex-politician came through for the businessman, divulging details of the entire Weston kidnapping and its resolution. He spilled his guts on things he knew to be facts, but weren't public knowledge, including his own involvement in turning a blind eye to the abduction by the Saudi Arabian agent. Mercer also provided the details about his complicity in the actions of Deputy Director of the National Security Agency Everson Blake.

Mercer even shared things he speculated were true, based on information passed on to him by investigators into the events at the Texas Gulf Mariners Marina on the Texas Gulf coast. The former commander-in-chief stated that the evidence didn't point to a suicide by Blake and that the only other possibility was that Josh Morgan, the shit, had shot him. He

ROD JOHNSON

assumed that the asshole Weston had bought into the suicide scenario and then led the effort to further cover it up. Mercer's voice practically dripped with venom at the mention of the names of the two men who had jointly ended his presidency.

Consequently, the billionaire was as much in the loop about the events and outcome of Trent Weston's ordeal and of Josh Morgan's role in ending it as virtually any other person on the planet.

Once he was confident that he knew as much about the Blake-Morgan-Weston affair as Mercer himself did, Schwartz had left him to sulk on the private island. That was well over a year ago. For the last nine months, Ex-President Wendell Mercer had maintained a private apartment and an even more private life in Washington, D.C.

Now, on this night, Linus Schwartz hoped to glean a bit more information, but primarily he wanted to get the names of people in various intelligence organizations, law enforcement agencies, and even the State Department who might be open to a partnership of sorts. The rationale given to Mercer for Schwartz's inquiries was that it would help in the reestablishment of the Terradoran military base. In truth, it was actually just another effort by the SCR CEO to identify potential friends in high places who might be willing to help with covert, though personal, projects that were underway. The scope of his plans was growing larger and more complex than the businessman had originally conceived.

As he always did, Mercer came through with some suggestions. Oh, he showed the same recalcitrance he always did when passing on information that Schwartz had no business having, even with his level of security clearance. The construction magnate always thought Mercer's reluctance to disclose names, data, and details was artificial. It was most likely intended to not only impress Schwartz with the magnitude of the info he was about to receive, but to also increase the value of it so that any future consideration from him to the ex-President would increase. It never failed to amuse Schwartz, because the imbecile puppet he had almost singlehandedly installed in the White House wouldn't get the best of him on any barter – ever!

CHAPTER 3

Day 2 – Monday

Josh's attorney had told him that he had strongly reinforced the demand to the U.S. Attorney. The case involved national security matters. Apparently, Maxwell had taken the matter seriously and had isolated Morgan. He had spent the night in his own cell in a section away from other prisoners.

He had slept surprisingly well, everything considered. And he wasn't nearly as pessimistic as he thought he should be.

He found it comical that he had been given the "D.C. Department of Corrections Inmate Handbook." It covered everything from medical screening to smoking to telephone calls. It had the rules for media access, staff contact, and use of force. No mere pamphlet, the book was thirty-two pages long. Josh had flipped through it for the part on escape. He actually found that section 110 listed the five things that are considered to be "escape," but he had been looking for more of a "how-to." Apparently, the DOC frowned on it.

Morgan's uniform wasn't exactly the same color as his Longhorns' burnt orange. It was more like that of the University of Tennessee Vols.

At about seven-thirty, a corrections officer brought breakfast to Morgan's cell, apparently to keep him out of the general population. The officer watched as he ate. At eight, other officers handcuffed and shackled the murder suspect and transported him to the courthouse for arraignment. In a small room off a hallway to the courtroom, attorney Don Summers delivered his client a suit, shirt, and tie.

"Maggie said you looked good in this."

Josh smiled. The last time he had worn this suit was on Inauguration Day. It was a very dark gray, almost black. Finishing up the knot on his teal-colored necktie, he was ready for his day in court. He presumed it would be the first of many.

"Don't get your hopes up, but we're going to see if we can't get you out of here."

"Bail?"

"Hopefully better, but maybe." The attorney smiled and patted the younger man on the shoulder.

Trent and Alicia Weston waited with Maggie in the hall in front of the courtroom. Attorney Shelley Cain stood with them but maintained her characteristic quietness. She reviewed notes while they waited for Summers.

"How is he?" asked Maggie as her fiancé's lawyer approached.

"As cool as can be. I'm surprised at his composure. Yes; one cool customer."

Cain handed her boss a printed, formal document. Attached to it was the copy of the arrest warrant that U.S. Attorney Riley Maxwell had provided the day before. Summers ran his right index finger along each line as he read the brief. He occasionally grunted an "uh-huh" or "yes" or nodded his head as he digested the work of his associate.

"Excellent" put the exclamation point on his satisfaction of the product of Cain's overnight project. "Fine work, Shelley."

Summers looked at the three pairs of eyes fixed on him that were hopeful of some explanation. They received none. The lawyer only held the legal document up and waved it toward them.

"Let's hope this works." Then to his assistant, "Come on, counselor. It's time we fire our first salvo." Maggie and her two companions looked to one another without the vaguest notion of what was taking place. The two attorneys separated. The man upon whom Morgan's fate was entrusted walked down the hallway while Shelley moved toward the doors of the courtroom and held one open for Morgan's three friends. Inside, they found the courtroom to be completely empty, except for the bailiff, court reporter, and another officer.

Shelley Cain led the trio to seats directly behind the defense table, before taking her seat there.

Momentarily, Riley Maxwell and his assistant, Siobhan Cassidy, entered the room with two other staffers. Without so much as a glance toward Morgan's supporters or Cain, they took their seats and huddled to speak in hushed voices among themselves.

Only a couple of minutes later, the side door opened again. Summers came in, followed by Josh, with a court officer ushering him along. Morgan leaned over for a hug and kiss with Maggie, which the accompanying officer allowed for a very limited time before leading Morgan to his seat beside Don Summers.

As he sat, the accused murderer looked over his shoulder for another glance at Maggie. He winked at her. She rewarded him with a nervous smile. He mouthed, "It's gonna be fine."

The exchange ended at the bailiff's announcement, "All rise."

All fourteen souls in the room obeyed and a very athletic-looking man in his late forties entered and took his seat at the bench.

◆

Miles away in Langley, Virginia, in the George Bush Center for Intelligence, Director Elizabeth Parnell sat in her corner office with CIA Case Officer Trevor O'Bannon. "Roadrunner" had been an instrumental part in the resolution of the kidnapping of former President Trent Weston. First, he collected intel on a meeting in Cozumel between a Saudi Arabian agent and a Mexican native of the Chiapas region of his country. The surrogate of Mayan ancestry would be the one who captured the ex-U.S. Chief Executive and turned him over to his Arab sponsor. Ultimately O'Bannon aided Josh Morgan when he confronted Al-Majeed and the NSA Deputy Director who wanted Weston dead.

O'Bannon had been back in the field for only seven months. He had been seriously wounded, nearly killed at Gulf Mariners Marina while going to Morgan's assistance.

"So, Trevor, just to be clear, I ordered Ben Reid to contact Josh Morgan and bring him in on our efforts to rescue President Weston."

Roadrunner was almost certain that this was a lie, but dutifully said, "Yes, ma'am." He figured if the DCI said she did, then she did. Even if she didn't.

"And you understand my clarification about why Morgan was operating domestically?"

"Yes. You believed that Deputy Director Blake was preparing to carry out a terroristic act by murdering Weston; that he was possibly aiding the Saudi operative." At the time, that wasn't O'Bannon's understanding of why he was there, but as with many ops, he wasn't given the full details of the rationale behind his role.

"Precisely," confirmed the Director. "And, of course, you were seriously injured when Morgan and Blake had their confrontation. So, you have no idea what transpired then."

"Correct." And that actually was true, O'Bannon thought.

"Obviously, the hope is this thing gets taken care of without a trial so that you're never brought into it. If you are, it will be a private testimony. And you'll testify to what you know, which is what I've told you."

"Absolutely, Director. That's all I know."

"Thanks, Trevor. Sorry to bring you back in from the field, but Morgan is one of our own."

"I agree." Roadrunner left the office with a clear and "accurate" picture of the events of one-and-a-half years ago. And he would testify to it, if needed.

♦

The judge organized a few papers as the bailiff continued.

"The court is now in session. The Honorable Judge Leonard Dunn presiding. All those having business before this court, the Superior Court of the District of Columbia, draw near, and you shall be heard."

The few people in the room sat. Judge Dunn read over the documents before him. On two occasions he looked up over his reading glasses toward the prosecution team. Finally, he looked past the legal teams and saw, in the first row immediately behind the defendant, Former President of the United States Trenton Weston.

"Well this is off to an interesting start," he said to himself. He stared at the man who once sat in the Oval Office. Weston, he noticed, stared straight back at him. The ex-Chief Executive didn't react to the judge's recognition. He did, however, possess an almost-smile. Dunn was caught completely off-guard, wondering what possible connection Weston could have to this case.

"We have before us the matter of the *People of the District of Columbia v. Joshua Matthew Morgan*." He looked at Josh, who stood with Summers and Cain.

"Counselors, please state your appearances." The other of the legal teams rose.

"Riley Philip Maxwell, your honor; prosecuting attorney."

"Good morning, Judge Dunn. I'm Donald Paul Summers, representing Mr. Morgan."

"And you are Mr. Morgan, I suppose. What is your full true name?"

"Joshua Matthew Morgan, your honor."

"Mr. Morgan, if at any point you do not understand something or are confused, please say so. Either the court or your attorney can explain it to you. Do you understand?"

"Yes, your honor."

"Mr. Maxwell, state the charges against the defendant in this case."

Maxwell rose confidently and cleared his throat. "Yes, Judge Dunn. The District of Columbia has charged Joshua Matthew Morgan with Murder in the Second-degree in the killing of Everson Blake, Deputy Director of the National Security Agency. We intend to show..."

Judge Dunn waved his hand and looked down at the brief. "You can save that for your opening statement... if there is one."

Josh's attorney tried to hide his smile. Josh looked at him and started to enquire what the judge meant, but, before he could speak, his lawyer patted him on the forearm and said quietly, "Not now."

Maxwell's eyebrows lowered and he looked at Siobhan Cassidy, who, in turn, looked across the aisle at the defense. The shake of her head was almost imperceptible. The rolled eyes were not.

Maggie started to ask Trent Weston what the judge's statement meant. The former President said, "Shhh." Alicia Weston maintained her gaze at her former attorney husband. Her eyes begged for understanding, but Weston answered them with a smile and a pat on her folded hands. He didn't know what was behind Dunn's cryptic remark, but knew it sounded good.

Superior Court Judge Dunn turned his attention to the defense.

"Mr. Morgan, have you been read your rights?"

"Yes, sir, Judge Dunn."

"And you have retained Mr. Summers to represent you?"

"Yes, your honor."

"Before I ask you for a plea, let me ask your attorney if there is anything he'd like to say."

"Your honor?" complained the prosecutor. The judge silenced him with a wave of his hand, to which Maxwell responded with upturned hands and a shrug of his shoulders. Again, he looked to his assistant, who never acknowledged him.

"I would, your honor," answered Attorney Summers. "May we approach?"

The judge nodded and motioned toward both legal teams. "I would think you'd want to."

Maxwell raced to the bench, motioning for Cassidy to come with him. Summers put his hand on Morgan's shoulder and moved him gently toward the bench. He waited for his assistant attorney to move from behind the defense's table and followed the two to speak with the judge.

"Your honor, I'm not sure what's going on here, but I take exception to this conference," objected the prosecuting attorney.

Summers waited patiently for the U.S. Attorney to finish, his hands folded in front of him.

"Your comments certainly seem to be evidence of some sort of bias in favor of this defendant," Maxwell continued.

"Careful, counselor, or I'll find you in contempt. Mr. Summers, you may proceed."

"Your honor, it is our contention that the warrant, as issued, has no merit. The District of Columbia has no jurisdiction with regard to an alleged murder that occurred in the state of Texas," the defense attorney declared.

The prosecutor interrupted. "Judge, Deputy Director Blake was a law enforcement officer, making this murder a matter of federal jurisdiction."

"To my chambers." Judge Dunn slammed his gavel, the bailiff ordered, "All rise," and the group of trial lawyers and the defendant followed the judge out of the courtroom.

It was evident to Maggie, Trent, and Alicia that Maxwell was clearly agitated, though not even the former lawyer among them knew why. Each wondered what was behind the conference that was about to get underway in Judge Dunn's office.

"Trent?" asked his wife.

"Don't ask me, but I'll say this: The fact that the prosecutor is upset has to be a good thing."

♦

Judge Dunn hung his robe on a coat rack behind his desk and sat down. Everyone else remained standing.

Don Summers began his dispute of the legitimacy of the charges.

"Your honor, as I stated in the courtroom, this act took place in Texas and this court has no jurisdiction there. Furthermore, no crime was committed at all. No charges were ever filed there because Texas law enforcement officials, including the Texas Rangers, declared it a case of suicide. FBI special agents looked into it, too, due to the fact that the victim, Deputy Director Blake was a federal official. The Bureau decided at the time that they had no jurisdiction concerning the suicide…"

Maxwell tried to interrupt, but Dunn raised his hand in the generally accepted gesture for "halt."

"The position of the Bureau was that their only area of investigation was of a Saudi agent and his actions in the United States."

Prosecutor Maxwell bullied his way into the discussion. "Judge, the jurisdiction of the U.S. Attorney's office isn't limited by state boundaries in the same way as state attorneys. My authority to prosecute is undeniable, based on two indisputable facts. First, Blake was a law enforcement official, which makes this a federal crime. And two, he lived in Washington, so the crime was, in essence, also committed here.

"Judge, I demand you…"

"You *what?* You'd better watch your step, counselor!"

Maxwell's face was flushed, but not from embarrassment. How dare this judge question his authority? But he decided he should shut up.

"Maxwell, your arguments about this being a federal crime are very thin. But they are moot. Look at your paperwork. The warrant is drawn up under the auspices of the Criminal Division of the Superior Court of the District of Columbia. This *isn't* a federal warrant."

"Your honor, if I may," resumed Don Summers, "there is another issue. Mr. Maxwell lacks any admissible evidence. There is only one witness to this event, and he is already on record as stating that Blake killed himself."

Morgan looked at his attorney with some displeasure for defying his instructions to leave Weston out of this matter.

"We have evidence to substantiate the murder charge, your honor. It deals with angle of entry of the bullet, lack of powder burns, absence of gunshot residue on Blake's hand…"

Summers interjected. "None of the investigators came to that conclusion."

"The investigators were all swayed by the fact that the witness was a former president."

Judge Dunn was stunned. The specifics of the shooting were never made public since they dealt with national security, so he had never heard that.

"Well, you've got to admit, Riley, that's a damned credible witness. And where did you get your information? None of the details were ever released and…"

The defense and prosecuting attorneys began to bicker over the facts.

"Gentlemen! Gentlemen, that's enough!"

The two attorneys stared each other down until the judge spoke. "Is there a motion somewhere in this mess?"

Shelley Cain handed the legal paperwork to her boss, who, in turn, handed it to the judge and a copy to Maxwell.

"Your honor, this is our motion to dismiss."

Dunn set the folded document on his desk and tapped his fingers on it. "You know, I can almost rule on this right now." Then to Maxwell, "Counselor, this is the damnedest screwup I've seen in a long, long time – maybe ever. You may all return to the courtroom. I'll be there shortly to announce some decisions about this."

On the way out of the judge's chambers, Morgan grabbed his attorney by the arm.

Summers knew what was coming and turned to face his client, who stuck his right index finger in his lawyer's chest.

"I told you to keep Trent out of this!"

"Well, no you didn't, Josh. Not exactly. You said you wouldn't let him testify. You said you wouldn't approve of his perjuring himself. Besides, I didn't bring him up. Maxwell did."

"Shit! Are you ever the lawyer!? You had to know this could happen. And with Trent sitting right out there in the courtroom, he knows which 'former president' Maxwell meant."

"Josh…" Summers took a deep breath. "I'm sorry. Yes, I knew this might happen. I even hoped it would. It was a powerful moment for you."

Josh began to calm down and took a deep breath of his own.

"Josh, Trent told me to put him on the stand. He said you're family and that he'd do whatever he could to help."

Josh's face began to flush again, and his finger rose toward the attorney's chest.

Summers calmly and gently stopped the young man's arm from rising.

"You have my word that I'll never put Weston on the stand. I don't think you understand that I can't. Since I know he's lying, I'd be suborning perjury."

Morgan felt a momentary relief until Summers continued.

"What you – and Trent – have to worry about is Maxwell calling him as a witness. Since they're so sure that he's lying, they'd be smart to get him in the witness box and make him confirm his story, or admit he lied. But we'll worry about that later. There are a lot of things that will have to happen before we get that far."

Summers leaned his head toward his client. "Okay?"

Morgan nodded meekly.

Once they were back in the courtroom, the participants in the conference with Judge Dunn were a study of contrasts. The four members of the prosecution team had their heads together, whispering, and occasionally staring at the defense team and their client. Riley Maxwell was explaining the content of the meeting with his two staffers who hadn't been there.

Summers and Cain were animated, speaking with one another with smiles. They never cast one glance toward their legal opponents.

Josh had turned his chair to the side so he could see Maggie and the Westons, and was trying to interpret what he'd just witnessed, when he heard, "All rise!"

Everyone did; then sat when they were permitted, after the judge had taken his place on the bench.

Judge Dunn chewed on one of the earpieces of his glasses, head cocked, and eyes cut upward, as if was seeking some sort of divine word. Or maybe he just wished he were somewhere else – anywhere else. He massaged his eyes with his thumb and index finger. In time, he set his spectacles down.

"Ladies and gentlemen, this is a highly irregular situation. The defense has made a motion to dismiss. As I told everyone in my office, I could almost make my ruling now. But in the interest of justice, I'll defer my decision.

"Mr. Maxwell, Mr. Summers, I'll hear oral arguments about this motion Wednesday at 9:00 AM and will make my ruling then."

The judge pointed at Maxwell. "Counselor, you'd better be sure you get your ducks in a row. You have a little over twenty-four hours."

Summers spoke up. "Judge, regarding bail..."

The judge motioned him back into his seat. "We'll get to that. First, in a few minutes I'm going to adjourn this hearing without asking for a plea from Mr. Morgan. Mr. Summers..."

"Yes, your honor," said the defense attorney, rising.

"I want to see all of the police reports from this shooting. I know this is normally brought out in the trial, but I'd like to see it for my ruling. I'll need it by 1:30 PM tomorrow to assist with my consideration."

"With all due respect, Judge Dunn, that's an awful lot of material to gather in less than twenty-four hours."

"Then you'd better get cracking. Besides, I suspect you already have it."

Summers stifled his smile. The judge was correct.

"Mr. Morgan, would you please stand? Under these circumstances, I see no reason to hold you..."

Josh, Maggie, and the Westons were all expecting the dollar figure that would represent his bail. Instead...

"I'm releasing you on your own recognizance."

Maxwell slapped his fist on his table with enough force that Judge Dunn heard it. The judge turned his eyes toward the man, but otherwise ignored it.

Morgan looked over his shoulder to Maggie, who was sitting between the Westons and receiving hugs from each.

"You will need to surrender your passport, of course..." The judge didn't know that Morgan had two duplicates identifying him as a Russian and a Spaniard.

"...and you'll be required to wear an ankle monitor."

Maggie reached into her purse for Morgan's passport – his real one. She had brought it since Trent Weston had told her that it would be needed in the event bail was granted.

Judge Leonard Dunn looked a last time at President Weston and adjourned the proceedings.

After a little over one hour, Morgan appeared with his attorney, fully processed for release and wearing his monitor.

Josh and Maggie hugged. Alicia Weston placed a small kiss on the young man's cheek and gave him a hug. Trent Weston pulled him into a tight hug, too, and patted him on the back.

♦

"Thank you for seeing me on such short notice." Attorney Don

Summers shook Director Parnell's hand and sat.

"Well, Morgan is one of ours." Parnell sat across the conference table from the defense attorney in the small conference room off her office.

"One of yours? That's not how Josh explained things to me."

"He doesn't have authorization to disclose that."

Summers squinted and tilted his head. "I don't understand why he would withhold anything. I'm bound by confidentiality rules."

"These aren't your typical secrets," the DCI asserted.

The lawyer opened his briefcase and retrieved a notepad.

♦

"Lovely," observed Maggie Loughlin. "Maybe you could get me a matching one for my next birthday."

"Well, that spoils my surprise," complained her fiancé with a grin as he lowered his pants leg to re-cover the ankle monitor. The couple snickered.

"You know, the best thing about this is that I can go anywhere I want to… so long as it's within our apartment," he said sarcastically, sweeping his hands around to point out the walls of their home.

"At least it's better than being in jail. Right?"

Morgan pulled Maggie up against him on the sofa. "Anywhere with you is the best place on the planet."

Maggie laid her head on Josh's shoulder and smiled. The pair sat without words for quite some time. Finally, Maggie asked the question that had been bothering her since her ride to the police station with the Westons.

"Josh, why didn't you tell me the whole story about what happened with Blake? Didn't you trust me?"

Morgan delayed his answer so long, Maggie leaned around to see if he was asleep. She could see the wheels turning and decided to give him some time. She felt like she needed to fill him in.

"You know, Trent gave me the whole story. I know everything; at least, I think I do. So, you don't have to explain anything, except why you felt you couldn't tell me."

Morgan lowered his side of the recliner sofa and sat up. Leaning forward, he rested his forearms on his knees.

"I didn't want to worry you," he finally replied without looking at his fiancée.

"But it was already done. What was there to worry about?"

Eventually Josh turned to Maggie and took her hands.

"First off, I think you would've been frightened about what took place; sort of in hindsight. But mostly…" Morgan pulled away and rubbed his hands together. He couldn't quite bring himself to look at her and shifted his gaze away. "Mostly I worried about exactly what is happening now. I knew this was always a possibility. You would've figured it out, too, at some point. I didn't want you having this thing hanging over your head."

Maggie gently turned Josh's face toward hers and retrieved his hands.

"Sweetheart, look at me," she insisted, as Morgan tried to lower his eyes. He finally looked up.

"Josh, whatever affects you is my concern, too. Anything that goes on, we're in it together." She pulled his head to her chest.

"So, you just figured you'd carry this load alone?"

Morgan straightened up and put his arm around Maggie. "To tell you the truth, after about a year, I thought the whole thing had gone away. That is, until I met with Betsy."

Maggie wriggled her face at the Director's name. She was still a little miffed that the DCI hadn't been more forthcoming when she had called her to let her know about Morgan's arrest. Shortly, Morgan's implication sank in and Maggie sat up.

"What? Betsy warned you about this?"

"Yes, when Ryan was here. He had a meeting set up with Betsy. That's why he was here. She had asked him to bring me to her office. She explained to me that someone was trying to stir things up.

"Remember when Trent was first kidnapped, and I told you my life story? I told you about Terrador, Blake, and the whole mess that led to my getting cut loose from the Agency? This current thing is related to that. At least according to Betsy. Someone is trying to get me out of the picture. Maybe Blake's old friends."

"Why, Josh?"

Morgan shook his head and walked to the picture window where, it seemed, he did a lot of his thinking.

"No idea. Revenge, maybe. Could be just plain old payback. I don't know."

"And you didn't think you should give me a heads-up then?"

"Sweetheart, that's when this whole thing with Russia was blowing up; pardon the pun. I had a little bit going on at the time."

Maggie wanted to be mad but decided she could save that for later. She snuggled up against her fiancé and they stared mindlessly at the cityscape before them for a while.

♦

"So Morgan isn't on the Agency's payroll anymore? You just sort of bring him on as – what – a freelancer from time to time?"

Parnell nodded. "Exactly."

"I suppose the whole thing with Trent's kidnapping is the only such time you've used Josh's services," Summers said, expressing a large dose of skepticism about the explanation he was getting from the CIA Director.

"Not at all," the Director clarified. "It was the first time, but, as a matter of fact, I sent Morgan to Russia during this crisis over the bombings here." She sat with her hands resting on the conference table.

"Russia?"

"I'm afraid that's all I can say about that."

Morgan's defense attorney scribbled on his notepad as they talked, glancing up now and then, until he thought he had the Director's entire statement down. He finally put his pen down and removed his glasses. He rested his forearms on the table and looked directly at Elizabeth Parnell. Despite his background as White House counsel and his prowess as a tough, relentless attorney, this was one stare-down he wouldn't win. After what seemed like a silent eternity, he finally blinked and turned his eyes toward his notepad.

The lawyer replaced his glasses and looked at his summary for a few seconds before propping the spectacles on his forehead.

"So, let me make sure I understand this. You instructed your staff member Ben Reid to covertly fill Josh in on the intel concerning President Weston's abduction. Why didn't you just call Morgan in yourself? Why the secrecy?"

Without hesitation, Parnell said, "There were some extenuating circumstances I'm not at liberty to divulge." She didn't know that as Weston's former counselor and lifelong friend, Summers was aware of those circumstances.

"And Reid can't corroborate this because he was…"

Parnell completed the sentence with a sadness that wasn't manufactured. "Murdered. Yes." Betsy looked down and fidgeted with the pencil on her own pad on the table. She returned her attention to her questioner, waiting for him to continue.

"And you enjoined Josh in the operation because he was acquainted with Weston?"

"Yes."

"But Josh wasn't a field guy."

"He wore many hats. His involvement in dismantling a rogue operation and preventing an assassination in Terrador proved his ops abilities."

"And the reason for sending him after Blake was your suspicion that the man was in league with the Saudi agent Al-Majeed."

"Yes," Parnell confirmed. "As I explained, Executive Order 12333 gives CIA the authority to operate domestically when we're gathering intel about someone suspected of conducting terrorism-related actions on our soil."

The attorney looked at his notes again. Parnell remained silent.

"But you didn't stop at gathering intel."

"What were my guys supposed to do? Not shoot back?"

"And Josh Morgan, who had been out of the game for some years, was the best guy for that operation."

"I believe the results speak for themselves."

The attorney suppressed a smile. He knew he couldn't argue with that.

"You've laid out a compelling case that Morgan was acting legally within the U.S. That certainly resolves any basis for accusing him of acting outside the law individually or in violation of the so-called 'leash law' that prohibits CIA ops on domestic soil. I'm not sure if that's relevant here, but it's good to know."

DCI Parnell knew that the group that was out to get Morgan had another bomb to toss at him – treason. So, she was already laying the foundation to dispute that accusation.

"One last thing – just to be clear, Josh Morgan *didn't* shoot Everson Blake?"

"To my knowledge, he shot himself. That's what the only living eyewitness says. And that was the conclusion of the only agencies or law enforcement organizations that looked into it."

"But their conclusion was based solely on Weston's testimony. What if he was lying?" The attorney tried to gauge what the DCI knew from her reaction.

"Why would he?" gave away nothing of the Director's knowledge.

"That's quite a story."

Parnell remained silent.

Morgan's' defense attorney pondered all that he'd heard. He knew from his friend Trent Weston that Morgan had shot Blake. "And that's the God's-honest truth?"

"I'll testify to it," pledged the CIA's Director.

Don Summers realized that her answer wasn't really what he'd asked.

.

CHAPTER 4

"Thanks, Ryan, but I don't think you need to come. Really, I appreciate it, but let's see how this begins to shake out. Then maybe you can."

Ryan Crenshaw reluctantly accepted his former student's insistence that he not fly to Washington to support him. He moved on to the subject he'd really called about.

"Betsy called me, Morgan."

"Oh? My attorney is meeting with her as we speak."

"I need to fill you in on what she's telling him, son."

Morgan was pretty sure this was going to go down a path he hadn't wanted.

"Shit," he said to his caller. "And she couldn't tell me herself?"

"Now don't be upset, Josh. She called to use me as a sounding board. At first, I had the same reservations you're probably going to have but I came around. I thought I might be more persuasive." Then Crenshaw related the whole narrative Betsy had constructed to tell the attorney in Morgan's support.

"So, Betsy instructed Ben to let me know about Weston's kidnapping and ask for my help? Bullshit!"

"How do you know, she didn't?"

"Dammit, Ryan!" Morgan looked at Maggie, who had no idea of Crenshaw's end of the conversation. She just knew her guy was really pissed.

The ex-CIA officer bit his lips and scratched his chin a moment. Finally, he rubbed his hand through his brown hair.

"And I was operating under the authority of the Agency?"

"Why else would Betsy have sent O'Bannon to your support?"

Morgan slapped his forehead a couple of times in frustration as he tried to digest this tale.

Crenshaw realized Morgan wasn't going to answer his question. "Morgan, this is the backstory that Parnell is going with. There isn't one thing that contradicts anything you know. And you won't have to say you know, but it's important that you get on board with it."

"I don't see why. The rationale for my being with Blake doesn't have anything to do with whether I shot him or not."

"Treason, Morgan. Remember that? Betsy's warning to you included the possibility that you would be charged with treason or misprision of treason. Betsy's laying the groundwork to show you were acting in support of the government; not against it. For heaven's sake, man! Have a little gratitude!'

Morgan collapsed on the sofa and massaged the back of his neck.

"Son, for all you know, Betsy is telling the absolute truth. You don't know anything to suggest she isn't. Think about it."

Morgan began to come around. "Ryan, I appreciate it. I really do. I just don't want anyone getting into trouble because of me."

"We won't."

"I hope not."

"We *won't*."

"Okay."

"Okay. Now, go love on Maggie some. Give her our best."

♦

Attorney Don Summers was reviewing the documents he had collected from all the agencies that had looked into Morgan's actions in Texas with regard to Weston, Blake, and Al-Majeed. Shelley Cain had done an excellent job acquiring them and organizing them, particularly in such a short amount of time.

He suspected that everything – well, most of what the CIA Director had told him was fabricated, but he didn't know. And since he didn't know for certain, he decided that he could use the information without suborning perjury. He wasn't clear on why everything Parnell had told him mattered. Maybe she was just being thorough, he supposed. It obviously added some credibility to the young man. Well, it would for any juror inclined to think service in the intelligence community was an honorable thing. For anyone who didn't... Summers knew he had to keep such people off the jury in the first place.

What nagged at him was the feeling that there was even more to the story than he knew. And as an attorney, he didn't like being kept in the dark by a client.

♦

43

U.S. Attorney Riley Maxwell was beyond worried. His sponsor in the plan to get Josh Morgan sidelined had been very clear. He wouldn't permit mistakes such as the one he had made by filing the charges under the auspices of the District of Columbia Superior Court. The correct path would have been by way of a federal warrant through Maxwell's office as attorney for the United States of America as a whole. It would've been a minor distinction, and one that would've drawn scrutiny anyhow. But it might have held up long enough to keep Morgan in jail longer – or at least restrict his movements. The feeling among Maxwell's associates was that the circumstantial evidence wasn't enough to get a conviction. However, it would be sufficient to get the ball rolling. That would've dragged things out.

But Maxwell had screwed up royally. And the botched effort had drawn enough attention to the attempt to get Morgan that it might be difficult to recover.

It was late and he and his assistant, Siobhan Cassidy, were the only ones left in the office. He sipped water from the paper cup he had filled at the water cooler in the common area outside his office. If there was one thing that always calmed him down, it was sex. And screwing Cassidy would immediately get his mind off things. He tossed the paper container into the trash and gazed through the glass pane in the door to Cassidy's office.

The young attorney was completely focused on her work. Maxwell took his coffee cup from the credenza that held the maker and all the ingredients for brewing for his office staff. He turned his back away from his assistant's view and filled the porcelain mug with the amber liquid that was in the flask that was perpetually in his pocket. He took a drink of the whiskey and returned his gaze to Siobhan. In his mind, he lifted her to her desktop, she kissed him passionately while he laid her back onto the wooden surface. Then mentally he caressed her breasts before removing her panties and dropping his pants to step between her open legs and insert himself.

Another drink of the whiskey made the fantasy more real. He had already had some of the liquor in his office to steel himself for his uncomfortable phone conversation.

Cassidy looked up from her work and saw her boss staring at her. When she stood and moved toward the door, the man became more aroused. However, when she closed the blinds on the glass in the door, his fantasy was shattered. In its place, an anger began to simmer. Riley Maxwell decided at that moment that the young woman who worked for him wanted him, whether she knew it or not. And she would have him tonight, whether she consented or not.

The attorney walked to Siobhan Cassidy's office door, where he paused momentarily to finish the liquor in his cup. He walked into her office and set the cup on the bookshelf beside the door.

"Siobhan..."

The young Irish lass' look of disdain further powered his anger – and his desire.

"Siobhan, would you get the Thompson file for me?" Maxwell couldn't recall what that case was about; only that it was one she was currently working on. She always kept the folders with the documents for current cases in a cabinet behind her desk.

Without a word, Cassidy rose and turned to the cabinet. Maxwell stepped behind her and prepared to reach around her for her breasts, but, sensing his approach, Siobhan turned. Stunned by her boss' nearness, she recoiled and stumbled against the file drawer she had just opened. As Maxwell attempted to reach for her, the young attorney spun out of his way but found herself pinned against a wall by the pursuer. Never one to do anything halfway, the lass skipped right past words and even a slap and delivered a solid punch to the attacker's right jaw, followed by a knee to his balls.

Maxwell gurgled an unintelligible expletive and clutched himself. Foolishly believing she had gotten the upper hand, Siobhan Cassidy stepped toward Maxwell and began to raise her finger. The man flung his right arm up, the back of his right fist savagely punishing his assistant's face. He grabbed her neck with both hands.

"You bitch...," he began before the potential implications of the moment penetrated his rage. The sight of the young woman's body slumping into the wall upon his release of her neck, coupled with the pain and fear he saw on Siobhan's face created a growing panic. Maxwell reached to help her up. She scrambled away on the floor, lifting her hands to cover her face from what she assumed would be a further attack.

"Siobhan, I'm sorry. You have to understand. I've had some whiskey and things just got away from me. I always felt you..."

"You arrogant bastard!!!" the brown-haired attorney screamed.

"But, it's just that I've always been attracted to you and..."

"You're history, you fucking reprobate. You'll never work again! Ever! I'll see you go to jail..." Cassidy was shaking her finger at her assailant, any fear she'd felt was replaced by a fury that wouldn't be contained.

Maxwell stepped toward her again. "Siobhan, listen..."

Emboldened by the panic she was seeing on Maxwell's face, the woman stepped toward him, fist drawn back. Maxwell was silent as he retreated to a position that put her desk between them.

Keeping a wary eye on her soon-to-be ex-boss, Assistant United States Attorney for the District of Columbia Siobhan Cassidy grabbed whatever she could of her personal belongings from the desk. She lifted her purse and briefcase from the floor beside it and clutched the aggregate of items to her chest. She turned to back out the door, somehow managing to keep her right index finger free enough to wag at the would-be rapist.

"Siobhan... Ms. Cassidy..."

"You're toast, Maxwell!"

◆

It had been a tumultuous several years for the small Latin American country of Terrador since its dictator had been deposed. During the time Juan Castañeda had been the self-appointed *El Presidente*, the island nation had suffered while the dictator and his associates prospered. The U.S. government had invested billions of dollars in building the military base and direct financial aid to the government. Of course, there was a catch. The sole purpose of the improvements in the nation's infrastructure was to support a base of operations for U.S. intelligence and covert forces in the fight against the socialist guerillas gathering strength in the nearby Central and South American countries.

Castañeda had benefitted further by turning Terrador into an offshore banking center and safe haven for international drug traffickers. Cartel leaders vacationed there. Some had homes. For the most part, the U.S. hadn't cared what the man did, as long as he allowed the base to remain.

The corruption of Castañeda and his business partners, many of whom were from U.S. intelligence agencies, finally fueled enough anger that the citizens overthrew the dictator in a bloodless coup, led by Miguel Salinas. Shortly after the overthrow, the Terradoran people installed Salinas as their first democratically elected leader.

Salinas was the man then-CIA officer Josh Morgan was supposed to see assassinated. The outlaw element of American intelligence who had worked alongside Castañeda needed him back in power. They missed the hundreds of millions of dollars in riches being lost as a result of Salinas' reforms. Morgan's inexperience and naiveté made him the perfect choice to act as a liaison between the former dictator's men and the U.S. officials in getting the job done.

However, Morgan's instincts had told him something was wrong, and he managed to disrupt the plan. Still, his role in the almost-assassination cost him his career and started the downward turn of his life. The descent continued until he found a new purpose in tracking down Trent Weston when he had been kidnapped. And he found new meaning in his life when he met Maggie Loughlin.

The plot to kill Miguel Salinas had occurred one year into his first term. The charismatic young president fulfilled his promises to clean up the country, making it a hostile environment for the traffickers. But at the same time, public outcry in the United States over the involvement of American forces in foreign countries created enough pressure that the government withdrew its presence. And when the special operators left Terrador, so did the American dollars. The infrastructure fell into disrepair and the economy collapsed.

Salinas narrowly won reelection, but popular support continued to wane until nothing remained of the small nation's experiment with democracy. For the past year, after he completed his final term as president, the man who had given hope to the people was living in virtual exile in Costa Rica.

Current *Presidente* Álvaro Abellán, who won the office after Salinas, held few of the ideals of his predecessor. The Terradorans elected him primarily because his challenger on the ballot was Carlos Castañeda, brother of the former dictator. Cartel leaders had killed Juan not long after he was deposed. He had tried to exert influence over cartel operations in the South American country to which he had moved after his overthrow. The cartel didn't share his view of his supposed authority.

But business was business and the drug traffickers didn't carry their animosity for the older Castaneda to the younger one.

Defeated in the polls against Abellán, Carlos was nevertheless undaunted in his pursuit of the leadership of Terrador and had struck a bargain with his brother's former business partners.

Simultaneous to the unfolding plot of the cartel members to reassert themselves in Terrador, unrest in Venezuela and other Latin countries was creating interest among the United States military and intelligence to quietly engage the Abellán administration. The U.S. was promising renewed aid to his young administration in exchange for reopening his country to operations there.

Like many Central and South American countries, Terrador had long embraced American baseball as a pastime. So, while it was possible that some knew who Yogi Berra was, it was unlikely they had heard his Yogi-ism and therefore wouldn't understand its relevance to their circumstances.

It was like *déjà vu* all over again.

♦

"Josh, my conversation with the CIA Director today was very enlightening. She gave me a lot of information about what happened between you and Blake. Actually, about the whole situation. She told me a lot more than you did."

Josh knew from his conversation with Ryan Crenshaw what Betsy was going to tell Summers, but he didn't want to be a part of furthering the fabrication. He remained silent.

"I don't take it very well when people hold things back from me."

Neither did Maggie, who suddenly suspected that Josh was again withholding information from her. She gave him a long stare. Morgan looked away.

"You have to understand, Don, that I didn't know how much I was allowed to disclose about the..." – how he hated to use the word because of what it implied – "...about the *operation*."

Maggie understood that the term implied an official sanction. She had never understood her fiancé's actions to be anything other than that: *his* actions.

"Be that as it may, Josh," the attorney rebutted, "you're on trial for murder. I would think a little frankness, some full disclosure would go a long way toward helping me help you."

"Yes, sir. You're right."

"What I don't understand is that almost none of it seemed relevant to your dilemma because Director Parnell insists that Blake killed himself. That's contrary to Trent's account to me, irrespective of his public narrative – and yours. But if that's true, you're off the hook. Aside from that one bit of information – and, of course, she wasn't there, so she can't say firsthand – everything else was just a justification for *why* you were there. I don't get the connection. Why is that important for the accusation that you murdered Blake? Seems to me, why you were there wouldn't matter. Either you killed him, or you didn't."

Josh decided to come clean about the whole mess he was in – how the murder charge was the tip of the iceberg.

He knew that Trent Weston had gotten the story from Parnell and had passed it along to Maggie on the drive to the jail. But he didn't know how much detail Betsy had provided, so some of this might be new ground for Maggie. Josh looked at her, sighed, and tried to smile. He turned back to his defense lawyer.

"Don, if the murder charge doesn't stick, the guys who are behind this are going to hit me with an accusation of treason or misprision of treason."

Summers was totally unprepared for the revelation. Nobody spoke for several seconds. When the attorney did, he only uttered one word.

"Treason?"

"Yes. They're going to charge that I was working with Blake. Or, possibly that I knew what he was doing and didn't do anything to stop him."

Morgan saw that Maggie wasn't in the least surprised. So, she and the Westons knew the whole story.

"Treason," Summers affirmed. This time it wasn't a question. "Why in the world wouldn't they go with treason first? Leading with the murder charge is a little like hitting something with a flyswatter when you had a sledgehammer."

"Here's the best I understand. I get charged with treason or misprision first, Trent Weston completely refutes that by his testimony that I was actually trying to rescue him. I wouldn't have been doing that if I'd been acting with Blake. The same argument holds if I was aware of what Blake was doing but didn't try to stop him. Trent's story crushes theirs."

Summers was beginning to understand. "So these – whoever they are – who are trying to get you on something have a huge problem with Weston's testimony. They have to discredit him."

"Yes. If I get convicted on the murder charge, that will mean Trent lied. If they still wanted to go after me for treason, his testimony would be irrelevant since my murder trial would've established that he lied. His description of events wouldn't matter. Of course, I don't think they'd go after me for treason if I'm convicted for killing Blake because…"

"Because you're already in prison; likely for life."

"Right. And in the event that I'm acquitted, they believe Trent would've testified in the murder trial, and they might've succeeded in punching enough holes in his story so as to discredit him. You know, through forensic evidence that they believe casts doubt on his testimony. That opens the door for their treason theory."

Maggie had indeed heard the scenario from Trent but hearing Josh describe it so matter-of-factly, as though he was describing plans for a home project, was unsettling.

Morgan continued. "I think Parnell's background is meant more to prepare for the possibility of a treason charge than it is to address murder. It gives me an official reason for being involved."

The defense attorney donned his glasses and flipped through the yellow pages of notes he had taken during his conversation with Parnell. He moved his finger along beneath the lines of scribbling as he refreshed himself about everything the Director had said. After he finished, Summers set his spectacles on the dining table around which the trio was sitting and leaned back.

"I think I understand. The people setting you up will say that you were on that pier to help ensure that Blake is successful in seeing Trent dead, or at least spirited away from trial as a war criminal. And if you were trying to help him, why…"

"Why would I have killed him? Maybe to cover my own ass. By that point, everything had gone to shit. But it really doesn't matter. They think they have enough shit to throw against the wall that some is bound to stick."

Morgan was prepared to continue but his attorney prevented him with a single raised finger. Summers looked toward the ceiling. He obviously had his thinking cap on. Finally, he broke the silence.

"So, the DCI's version of events clears up one thing, creates another problem, and then solves it."

"I don't understand?" Maggie said.

"The initial thing it addresses is why Morgan was in the middle of this. By acting in some quasi-official capacity for the CIA, it gives him a legitimate rationale for being involved."

Maggie was beginning to get it. "You're saying that he wasn't just some rogue citizen in the middle of something where he didn't belong."

"Yes. And that damages any theory that he was down there as a traitor. Unless, that is, the CIA itself was conducting a treasonous operation."

"So, what's the problem it creates?" Maggie followed up.

Morgan answered. "CIA can't operate domestically. At least, generally speaking. There are only very limited scenarios where it can."

"And Betsy's story addresses that?"

"It's not real strong, Maggie, but, yes. Her explanation solves that problem. She said…" Summers glanced at Morgan and shook his head slightly. "…that the Agency suspected Blake was acting in a terroristic capacity; either alone, or with the Saudi."

"So, that makes it legal for the Agency… if they're trying to capture a terrorist," speculated Maggie.

"That's the tricky part, Maggie. Technically, the CIA can only be involved in collecting intel about the supposed terrorist threat. And that's what Betsy says Morgan was doing."

Maggie furrowed her brow below her auburn hair. Her blue eyes shifted to Josh, then back to his attorney.

"But he wasn't…"

Summers cut her off with two raised palms. "Stop, please!"

He didn't want to hear any explanation that contradicted what the CIA Director had told him.

"Not another word."

Maggie understood. She didn't exactly like it – neither did her fiancé – but she got it.

Summers got things back on track for the here and now.

"But, first things first. Tomorrow afternoon is my deadline to deliver to Judge Dunn all the information my office has collected about the entire spectrum of events regarding Josh, Weston, Blake, and the rest of the parties involved. You can bet Maxwell will have a lot of information that he thinks supports his story and undermines ours. But, none of that matters for the oral arguments on Wednesday. The only topic to address is whether Maxwell filed the charges under the proper jurisdiction.

"Not to get too far ahead of ourselves, but that should be a slam dunk.

No promises."

"So, if none of the details about the operation matter, why'd Dunn ask for them?" enquired Maggie.

"Maybe he's just curious," laughed Josh. Maggie chuckled, too.

Summers smiled but he added, "You could be right, Josh. Judges aren't immune from being nosy. He may just wonder what a former president has to do with all of this. As a practical matter, Judge Dunn might be just covering every base in case his ruling is appealed."

"You think they'll appeal?" Maggie quizzed.

"No. I think this is clearly an error by the U.S. Attorney. But, rest assured, he'll come back at you… correctly."

"So, I shouldn't get used to my freedom then. Anyone got a 'get out of jail free' card?"

Nobody laughed.

As Morgan's attorney began to gather his things to leave, some thoughts continued to nag at him: Why would the federal attorney go to this much trouble to try cases that he almost certainly couldn't win? And while he understood the logic of leading with the murder charge to discredit Weston, one thing didn't make sense. If they proved that he lied, they would likely win the case. Then the treason charge would just be piling on. Was it just for show?

Furthermore, the treason accusation was basically a farce. Could Prosecutor Maxwell actually think he could win?

"It's almost as if the entire purpose is to engage Josh in a long, drawn out process for no reason other than forcing him to deal with it," he said to himself.

There had to be something else at work here, Summers concluded.

◆

Former U.S. President Trenton Weston and the former First Lady were ready for bed at the Washington Four Seasons Hotel where they had stayed since a few days before Inauguration Day. That was nearly three months ago.

The husband was sitting on the edge of the bed, rubbing his eyes and flexing his arm.

"Are you okay, honey?"

"Just slept wrong on my arm last night, I guess. It's a little weak. It's been like this most of the day. Plus, I have a headache. I think I'm just very tired – and worried. Stressed out over Josh."

Alicia felt she had waited long enough for her husband to address something that was nagging at her. She had decided he wasn't going to initiate the conversation.

"Sweetie...?"

The ex-POTUS always hated when his wife used a term of endearment without the appropriate sugary sweet tone of voice that should accompany it. Her current tone was no different than if she'd said, "Hey, you."

"About the perjury?" he guessed.

"Yes," she answered. Alicia wasn't so much angry as she was confused.

The ex-Chief Executive pulled her to the edge of the bed and to a seat beside him. Weston rubbed his eyes. Then he flexed his shoulder some more.

"Of course, you know the official version of Everson Blake's death was that he shot himself. That story was my doing. I made it up to keep Josh from admitting what really happened; that Blake was unarmed, and Josh shot him."

Alicia Weston's hands flew to her open mouth. Her husband avoided his wife's eyes. She, too, stared straight ahead.

"I thought Josh shot him in self-defense. And I thought that the CIA or some other agency made the suicide thing up? You know, to cover up what Blake was really doing."

"You never heard me say that."

"You're saying that nobody in the government knows the truth?"

The wait seemed interminable before her husband pursed his lips and gave his response. He looked at his wife and shook his head.

"Almost nobody other than Josh and I know what really happened."

Alicia Weston had never questioned her husband at any length about the events at Gulf Mariners Marina. Trent had come home safe and that was all that mattered. And he never offered details. So, when he had told her that Josh had shot Blake, she simply assumed that everyone knew and had decided to cover it up. She had first heard the suicide conclusion in hearings that ended the investigation.

"Blake had tried to kill Josh by exploding the boat he and the Saudi were on. Josh jumped off just before the blast. Then Blake searched for Josh up and down the dock; again, to kill him. The man had pistol-whipped me, and... Anyhow, when Josh got the drop on him, he was prepared to turn him over to authorities.

"But Blake goes on this diatribe, threatening Maggie, you, me. He made a strong case that he'd avoid jail. Or at least that he'd be able to reach out from prison and make good on his threats. Alicia, the man had resources at his disposal. Josh believed him. I'd have believed him, too. He was so damned smug."

"So, Josh shot him? In cold blood?"

"He felt it was his only option. I think he was right."

Alicia rubbed her entire face as she came to accept what her husband had said. "And you invented the suicide story?""

The answer was strained, but immediate.

"Yes, it was my idea."

Alicia looked up, eyes wide with shock.

"I couldn't let Josh confess to the whole thing – not after he saved me. And now he won't let me repeat it. He won't let me testify; not even to save him."

The pair sat in silence for a few moments. Weston finally expressed his hope to his wife, "Maybe it won't come to that."

The former First Lady of the U.S. took her husband's arm in hers and laid her head against his shoulder.

"But I'll tell my story, whether he wants me to or not. He can't go to prison for saving me," Weston vowed. "I owe him my life, sweetheart."

"Whatever you think is best, Trent. Whatever you need to do. This is Josh."

♦

Attorney Riley Maxwell was at his desk, pouring another shot of whiskey. It was his second since his protégé had left, and fourth overall since before their – well, disagreement.

Maxwell fumbled his cell phone until he finally managed to access his contacts and touch the number he wanted to call.

"Mr. Maxwell," the distant voice greeted.

"Yes, sir," Maxwell answered. "I'm, uh... I'm afraid we might have another problem. Well, rather, *I* have a problem It shouldn't affect you or our plans."

His statement was greeted with dead silence on the other end of the call. Finally, the recipient replied in a low, calm voice, "Go on."

"Well, sir, mmm, how do I put this. Uh, one of my subordinates and I have had a situation."

"Who? And what sort of situation?"

"Siobhan... uh, Ms. Cassidy... my assistant. We were working late and I, uh, well... turns out she wasn't as horny as I was." The U.S. Attorney let out a small, forced laugh.

"Go on." The other man on the call waited for more information.

"Well, sir, we had a bit of an altercation... just an argument, really. I... What? Sir?" Maxwell winced at the query that had interrupted him. He scrambled mentally for an answer that wouldn't sound like as much of an indictment as he knew it was going to be.

"Well, she sure as hell knocked the shit out of me. She... Uh, huh. I know that's not what you asked, sir. I... Well, I might have hit her. I mean, I'm sure she's not really hurt or anything, but...."

Another question came from his associate. Then, "Yes, sir. Well, she left…"

Maxwell felt the severity of his actions collapsing on him. "No. She just left. But she made some threats… Uh, huh. Yes, I guess you're right. I suppose it does affect you."

His collaborator spoke for a few seconds.

"Yes. Thank you…" Attorney Maxwell finished his sentence, even though the man he had called had already disconnected the call. "… Mr. Schwartz."

CHAPTER 5

Day 3 - Tuesday

The day started off like any number of others since Josh and Maggie had been together. Maggie slept in – a little. She had gotten into the routine typical of most of the West Wing staff in the White House. When she rose and wandered into the kitchen, her fiancé was cooking what he referred to as a "Texas" breakfast: bacon, fried eggs over-medium, and biscuits. The only thing that made it different from what he had enjoyed as a child at his granny's house was that, unlike Ellie Houston, Morgan didn't make the biscuits from scratch.

Maggie found it a bit amazing that Morgan whistled while he cooked, as though he hadn't a care in the world. She thought he acted as though they were enjoying just another lazy, carefree day.

"Morning," greeted Morgan as he finally looked up from his culinary endeavor. Maggie nestled in beside him without a word and rested her head on his shoulder. He stretched his left arm around her while turning the eggs with his right hand. That done, he pulled her around for a more affectionate embrace. "Sleep well?"

"Not especially," Maggie answered.

Josh turned his attention back to his cooking, taking the frying pan of thick-slab bacon from the burner and hurriedly using tongs to scoop the slices onto the serving platter. Maggie took the bacon to the dining table. Already there were his orange juice, her cranberry juice, salt, pepper, honey, and butter. By the time she returned to the kitchen, Josh had the eggs on plates and was sliding the sheet of biscuits from the oven.

Maggie poured coffee for herself, refreshed Josh's, and lifted the plate that had one egg and a single biscuit from the counter and walked back to the table with her cup in her other hand.

Her apparently happy-go-lucky fellow followed with his coffee and two eggs and three biscuits, whistling all the way. Maggie watched him put far too much butter on two of the biscuits. She was always amazed that his cholesterol was consistently low at his check-ups, given the diet he so heartily enjoyed. The third buttermilk biscuit was reserved for honey, which dripped messily over the edges onto the plate. Morgan would sop up the excess after he was finished with everything else, just as his grandfather always had.

Morgan assumed Maggie's stare was due to his whistling at the table, so he stopped, with a "sorry." He put three slices of bacon on his plate. The fourth never made it that far.

"Mmm. I'm one good chef," he proclaimed, pronouncing the word with an actual "ch" sound instead of properly with a "sh." He noticed that his fiancée's stare lingered.

"What?"

"Why are you so happy? How can you eat?"

The man of the house answered with a shrug and then, "I'm hungry." He pointed at Maggie's plate with his fork and, through a mouthful of breakfast, said, "That's getting cold. Eat up."

Maggie was almost mad at his display. She was practically sick with worry, and he apparently couldn't care less about his predicament. Or, at least, that's how he acted. Feeling her eyes begin to moisten, she pushed her plate away and started for the bedroom to change out of the t-shirt she always slept in. Morgan caught her hand and pulled her to him. He had the good sense not to ask what was wrong. Pulling her into his lap, he let out a long sigh.

"I'm sorry, sweetheart. I know this is tough on you."

"Me?" she replied incredulously. "What about you? You're acting as if nothing's going on. And I… I was completely blindsided by this. I had no idea what happened with Blake; about what you did. I never knew this whole thing was even the remotest possibility."

After a lengthy pause, Morgan apologized – again. "I know, Mag. I should've told you a long time ago."

The deep sigh belonged to Maggie this time.

"It's really not that, Morgan. It's just that…" She wiped at her eye with her thumb. "Josh, goddammit! This is your life. This is our life together. What am I gonna do if…?" Her words stalled, as though saying them would make the possibilities more dire, and more likely.

Morgan eased her from his lap into one of the other chairs at the table. He took both her hands in his and, while he looked at her, she merely looked down. He gave her a moment before reaching up with his right hand. His gently touched her cheek and then brushed auburn strands away from her eyes.

"Don't ever think I don't worry about being taken away from you, Maggie. You've saved me. I've never been as happy as I am now; as I am with you. You're everything to me. So, please try to understand where this is coming from."

He brushed his own dark brown hair back and resumed.

"In a way, I'm glad this has happened. I've always had an uneasy feeling that my history with Blake wasn't over. And if it isn't, it's the last thing from my old life that's still hanging over my head – over our heads. This is my chance to finally be free from all that. If we're ever going to have the life that I think we both want, then I've got to see this thing done with. Do you understand?"

The auburn hair bobbed as Maggie nodded.

"So, however this plays out – and I have every confidence that things are gonna be fine – either way, it'll be over."

Maggie returned to Josh's lap and leaned her head on his. She reached to her plate, retrieved a biscuit and took a bite.

"It's cold," she said with a smile.

Josh took the bread from her and opened it. He placed two slices of bacon on it and folded the biscuit over.

"Here. This'll be great, even if it's not piping hot."

Maggie took a bite and the two sat in silence for a few minutes before adjourning to the bathroom to dress for the day.

♦

"So, you're saying there's not a thing I can do?"

"I'm afraid not, Madam President. At least, not in any official capacity," Attorney General Craig Jensen advised.

POTUS Sandra Hendrickson stared at the man.

"Ask your husband, ma'am. He'll tell you the same thing."

"He already did," the President lamented. Her husband Adam was a former Deputy Attorney General. "It's just that Morgan has served his country – twice now – when he didn't have to. He put his life at risk. He's already paid a big price physically, and emotionally, I suspect; and now this."

The Chief Executive tapped her fingers on her desk and brushed at her increasingly graying hair. Jensen felt he should speak, but after almost thirty minutes of discussion about Josh Morgan, he had nothing to add.

"You can't instruct this... this..."

"Maxwell. Riley Maxwell."

"...This Maxwell to stand down?"

The attorney general was a little annoyed. He felt he had already answered that. "That would be completely in..."

"I know. Completely inappropriate. I'm sorry, Craig. Bear with me. I'm just frustrated and thinking aloud."

"Yes, ma'am."

POTUS tapped her fingers some more. Finally, resigned to the fact that her hands were largely tied, she concluded, "Here's what we can do. I want your investigators to look into every aspect of the charges against Morgan. I'd like you to personally keep an eye on this and update me regularly with its progress."

The AG balked. "Are you sure that's a good use of my department's time? Or of mine?"

The intensity of the President's eyes convinced him she thought it was.

"Can I file an *Amicus Curiae*? Not as President, but personally?"

"Ma'am, I don't think you can separate yourself personally from who you are politically. A 'friend of the court' briefing from Sandra Hendrickson would be indistinguishable in the eyes of the law as one typed out on official White House stationery. Most likely, it would be considered highly prejudicial and disallowed."

"Talk with President Weston. I know he'll be doing everything he can in support of Morgan, beyond just his role in the matter. See how we can help him support the young man. Stay under the radar, Craig."

Attorney General Jensen wasn't sure how to fly under the radar on this. As one of the four cabinet members considered to be the most important, he was fully informed of the role Josh Morgan played in the just-past crisis with Russia. So, he understood Hendrickson's interest in the proceedings against him. But he didn't understand her willingness to put herself at risk. The AG was sure her political capital could best be spent elsewhere. And if her efforts were discovered… Well, he wasn't sure what legal jeopardy it might create for her. He would do some research on that. And he would do it personally. Despite the President's orders to involve his staff in this matter, Jensen knew the smaller the circle of players, the better.

Jensen was unaware of the full extent of Morgan's role in finding and rescuing Former President Weston and, therefore, of bringing the Wendell Mercer administration to an end. Beyond the fact that it had propelled Sandra Hendrickson into the Oval Office, the AG couldn't know of her personal disdain for her predecessor, based solely on the corruption she had witnessed while serving as his veep.

So, he would look into the current matter. He would talk to Weston. He would reach out to anyone else he thought would have knowledge of the details of the case against Josh Morgan. But he would do it in a way that most strongly shielded President Hendrickson from danger, politically, and perhaps even legally. He was certain she needed to be protected from herself.

The first thing Jensen would do was to look into the online files concerning the *District of Columbia v. Joshua Matthew Morgan.*

♦

Defense Attorney Donald Summers was looking over the reports in his client's files. They were identical to the ones that his assistant Shelley Cain was simultaneously delivering to the law clerk for Federal Judge Leonard Dunn. All of the findings were consistent in one regard – and it was an important one. The conclusion of each investigation and the compilation of interviews was that Everson Blake had killed himself with a bullet shot to his chest. The interviews included those of the marina's office workers who had interacted with Saudi Fadi Al-Majeed. They had attested to his presence at Gulf Mariners Marina. There wasn't much left of him after the explosion of the twenty-eight-foot cruiser he was on. The statements only served to add to the characterization of the events that set the stage for why Josh Morgan, NSA Deputy Director Everson Blake, Former President Trenton Weston, Blake associate Mark Sanders, and CIA Officer Trevor O'Bannon were at their facility. Neither marina employee was present at the time of the confrontation between Blake and Morgan.

Summers saw that the only piece of evidence that seemed to enter into the suicide conclusion was the testimony of Weston, who was the only eyewitness to the final events of the night. But Weston, after all, was the one who had been abducted, the only one alive who was involved. O'Bannon was unconscious when Blake allegedly killed himself. The only one who was conscious was a former Chief Executive of the United States. That last fact carried a lot of weight in the final analysis for the local police, the Texas Rangers, and, finally, the FBI.

And that was a very good thing, Summers decided, because the physical evidence made the official conclusion somewhat dubious. The attorney knew the whole story, including, regrettably, that Weston had lied about the events. In a trial, that would almost certainly not hold up. So, in the end, Summers knew that his best hope was to keep the case out of court. That should be straightforward, given that the case had been disposed of by investigators soon after Morgan had shot Blake. However, there were things in play that would complicate matters. And one of those things was the pressure by powerful individuals, as yet unidentified, who were pushing this thing forward.

Summers leaned back in his chair and pushed his glasses onto his forehead. The lawyer massaged his temples. Just as he began to mentally walk through his day, his administrative assistant opened the door to his office and peeked in.

"I'm sorry, sir."

Erin Hamilton had worked with Don Summers for over ten years. She had the same sixth sense about things that Radar O'Reilly did on M*A*S*H reruns and always seemed to be a step ahead of her boss. Ms. Hamilton was extremely capable, handling preemptively almost all of the matters that came to her boss and exactly in the manner Summers would. She never interrupted him unless it was necessary, and she never opened the door to his office unless it was an urgent, or very unusual matter. Summers knew that and valued it, so he never turned her away.

"Come on in, Erin," Summers invited with a wave of the hand.

Hamilton stepped just inside the doorway of the well-appointed, though messy, office.

"Don," she started. Summers insisted she call him by his first name when clients weren't present. "Don, I have Siobhan Cassidy on the phone. She's the Assistant U.S. Attor…"

"Sure, Erin. I know who she is. What does she want?"

"Well, she says she has some information about the Morgan case. It's for your ears only, she says."

"Well, I'm sure it's just some matter of discovery that they have to pass on."

"I would've thought so, too, Don, but she made it clear that she was calling entirely on her own. Maxwell doesn't know."

Neither attorney nor assistant said anything for an extended time. Finally, Summers ended the silence.

"I've only spoken with her a couple of times, but she's bright and has a great reputation. She's got to know that passing on case-related information is at best highly inappropriate, and, at worst, illegal."

The pair paused. Summers reached for his phone and pressed the button by the flashing light. As he did, Hamilton retreated from his office, closing the door quietly behind her.

"Ms. Cassidy, how are you? I understand you have something to discuss with me about Josh Morgan's case. You know we're on very thin ice here. Right?"

A shaky voice on the other end of the conversation provided her guarantees. "Yes, sir. I assure you this has nothing to do with the details of the case. Nor does it relate to anyone involved. At least, not officially." She waited.

Defense counsel for Josh Morgan struggled for what that might mean. He could think of nothing.

"Okay. Go ahead, Ms. Cassidy, but be forewarned. If I begin to feel uncomfortable with where the conversation is going – even if it's just getting a little into gray areas – I'll have to cut you off."

"I understand. Mr. Summers, I left my position with the District

Attorney's office last night. Why doesn't matter..."

"Uh, oh. It might," Summers worried silently. "Is this some sort of revenge disclosure because of personal animosity?"

His caller continued, "There is some person – I don't know who – behind this prosecution. Someone very wealthy."

Summers removed his glasses from his forehead and straightened up in his chair but said nothing. Finally, he leaned forward, propping his elbows on his desk.

"I'm not sure what that means – 'behind' it," he finally replied. "What's the person's interest in the case?"

"Mr. Summers, there are some things going on that I believe represent ethical violations by Maxwell's office and are illegal."

Summers stroked his chin. "Why don't you go to someone in your office? Or better yet, the police?"

"I can't." Cassidy then blurted out, "Maxwell assaulted me last night."

"Woah, woah, woah! I don't need to hear this, Ms. Cassidy," he countered, simultaneously waving his free hand in objection and standing up.

"I'm sorry. It's just that, someone has been pulling the strings behind the scenes on a number of cases for a few years. Maxwell's in his pocket. People related to some of our cases have disappeared. Witnesses have reversed course on their testimony. Sir?"

Summers was becoming more certain that he didn't need to know anymore, but, despite his reservations, he answered, "Yes, Siobhan."

"I think I'm going to need legal representation at the very least." Summers could hear the gulp and the crack in her voice.

"And, at worst... well, it could be a lot worse. Will you help? Can we meet?"

Summers sat down abruptly. His gasp was audible to his caller, he was sure, as he calculated how to proceed.

"Tell you what; we can meet, but only so I can provide you some off-the-record advice. I'm going to limit you on what you can say, and then I'm going to refer you to someone else. Okay?"

"Yes, Mr. Summers."

The pair arranged a meeting place and time. Ordinarily, with something of this nature, the attorney would send one of his team of investigators to such a meeting, or possibly Shelley Cain. This time, he felt he should go himself. There was much about this that concerned him – not just the implications, but Cassidy's accusations themselves – and he felt he should keep them to himself for now, no matter how much he trusted his staff.

"Thank you."

"Don't thank me yet. There might not be anything I can do except provide a name."

"I understand."

"Do you?" Summers wondered as they hung up.

◆

In another part of the city, Federal Judge Dunn was reading the case files and coming to the same conclusion as the defense attorney. Investigators had given little attention to physical evidence and the judgement that Blake had committed suicide rested almost solely on Weston's testimony. However, the credibility of Weston as a man and as the victim in the sordid affair was compelling. At least now Dunn understood the former President's presence at Morgan's hearing.

But the weakness of the physical evidence and the power of Weston's eyewitness account was of no concern with regard to the oral arguments the judge would hear on the following day. All that mattered was whether U.S. Attorney Riley Maxwell had properly filed the papers to arrest Morgan. And for Dunn, that much was settled in his own mind. Still, like Summers had wondered some miles away, who had the clout and the personal interest to dredge this up after all this time? And why?

◆

"Thank you for your time, President Weston. I have to ask you if we can keep this conversation completely off the record."

"I understand, Mr. Jensen. I suppose this is about Josh Morgan."

"It is. President Hendrickson is desperate to do something to help Mr. Morgan, but I can't see a way for her to do so; either as President or personally."

"Then, what can I do for you?"

"POTUS suggested that you might provide some insight into why this case is being brought against him."

"Can you be more specific?"

"Yes, sir. I know that Morgan was instrumental in resolving the recent tension with the Russian Federation. The President was more than candid when she admitted to being premature in her decision to… well, let's say escalate the confrontation. And I know of your role in getting to the truth, too. She feels like she owes Mr. Morgan."

"Then…?"

"But, with regard to Mr. Morgan's current situation, she said that there is more to the generally accepted version of your rescue and the death of Everson Blake. But she wouldn't give the details. She said that it was your place to disclose them, and only if you wanted to."

Former President Weston thought of his options for a few moments. He decided that the only version was the official one – at least for the Attorney General and at least for this point in time.

"Josh Morgan rescued me from the Saudi government's agent. Everson Blake was also intent on killing me and Josh prevented that. He confronted Blake, who decided that the writing was on the wall. Local authorities were closing in and he wouldn't be able to explain trying to kill both me and Josh. He wouldn't be able to explain the deaths of his associate Sanders or CIA Officer O'Bannon, whom he assumed was already dead. So, rather than face the music, he killed himself."

This summary was different than his account to the investigators in Texas and the FBI, but only slightly.

Attorney General Jensen was puzzled by what he considered to be a well-rehearsed elevator speech. "I'm not sure that helps me with regard to Mr. Morgan's present circumstances."

Weston thought, "It wasn't supposed to." Then he continued his narrative.

"Perhaps this will. I can't really tell you the 'why' of my young friend's current dilemma. But I can tell you the 'who' likely dates back to the time immediately before and during my presidency. Before I was elected, our military and intelligence operators had a significant presence in Terrador. Some abuses of our situation there and in other countries led to sufficient public outcry that we decided to pull out of some countries, including Terrador, and significantly reduce our presence in others. I fully supported those decisions.

"During my time in the White House, some of the rogue element who had profited in Terrador tried to destabilize President Salinas' administration to recover their influence there. Our Mr. Morgan was instrumental in foiling that plot. You see, he's got a history of doing the right thing, even when he gets hammered for it.

"I would suggest you look into what might be going on in Terrador now; you know, see if there's anything to suggest there might be some new efforts to restore the old drug trafficking network. If you need more information, you should contact the CIA Director. Parnell can decide how much you need to know, if anything, and perhaps assist you."

On the other end of the phone conversation, the AG was rubbing his forehead. He was getting more questions than answers. He flipped his pen a couple of times.

"Director Parnell?"

"Yes." Weston knew that she had warned Josh that some parties unknown were coming after him, but even she didn't know who or exactly why. But, the ex-POTUS decided, she could determine whether to read the attorney general in.

"Thank you, Mr. President," Jensen said. Silently he added, "For nothing."

The head of the Department of Justice's mind was spinning. The President had suggested he talk to Weston. He believed the implication was that he would offer a different version of events regarding Morgan and Blake. Instead, the old man hands him off to Director Parnell, pointing him to some operation in some piddly-assed Latin country that ended over a decade before.

Jensen had barely started looking into the thing with Morgan, but he was already weary of it. As chief legal representative for the U.S., he should follow POTUS' orders. But for the very same reason, he should insist she back off any involvement with the murder defendant, whom he was beginning to suspect was a former intelligence officer.

He elected to contact the DCI, primarily to be able to tell his boss that he'd followed Weston's lead. Then, unless he discovered some overwhelmingly convincing rationale for continuing, he'd bail and simply monitor the court proceedings.

◆

Attorney Donald Summers looked at his watch again and rose from the bench along the edge of the Reflecting Pool. He paced briefly. Finally, he called the private cell number Siobhan Cassidy had given him during their earlier phone conversation.

"Straight to voicemail," he observed silently in relief. "Must've gotten cold feet. Can't say that I blame her."

He paced two more minutes and called again. Same result.

"Yeah," he concluded again, "she either rethought her accusations or decided to go another route."

The veteran attorney knew he should've been skeptical of her story. But there was something in her desperation, in her very matter of fact telling that rang true. Her tale lacked the embellishment that a fabrication would've carried. The need for payback or even just to show her strength in some undisclosed dispute would've certainly led her to make the story more dramatic. Her tone, despite the obvious emotion from time to time, didn't exhibit the same level of hysteria a pretender would've manufactured to convince a listener.

No, there was something about Siobhan Cassidy's call that sounded honest and credible.

Nevertheless, he didn't have time to dillydally while the Assistant D.A. made up her mind whether to proceed. Five more minutes and he was outta there.

♦

For all his bravado for Maggie's sake, Josh Morgan was terrified about his ordeal. It wasn't so much the murder charges, or even the threat of being accused of treason, it was the matter of who was behind them. He had experienced firsthand the power that Everson Blake had wielded and was lucky to be alive after his last dealings with the man. These people were bound to have as much clout since they were able to keep their identities unknown to even the Director of the CIA. And what resources did they have at their disposal? They had already been able to persuade – or force, Josh realized – U.S. Attorney Maxwell to come after him.

Morgan had been honest with the woman who was sleeping beside him about being glad to get this over with. But the truth was, he had become convinced, particularly in light of Blake's death, that it was *already* over eighteen months ago. It was only when Betsy had pressed him about the truth in Terrador and then explained to him that some of Blake's old cronies were out to get him that Morgan came to believe he still had something to fear.

So, as the dimness of the bedroom nightlight illuminated the sleeping figure of his fiancée, Morgan snuggled in tight behind her and laid his arm over her waist. Her soft moan and the whisper of "I love you" comforted him yet made him fearful as he considered what lay ahead – for both of them.

CHAPTER 6

Day 4 – Wednesday

There had been an uncharacteristically late dusting of snow overnight, but it was almost completely gone. A few white specks remained in the shadows and in the recesses of the hedges. It was the beginning of April and the cherry blossoms were nearing their peak bloom. Only a couple of weeks earlier, Josh and Maggie had discussed how much fun it would be to walk the full loop around the Tidal Basin to take in the spectacle. The petals were already well past their white stage and were fully pink, and vibrant.

Problem was, Josh's ankle monitor came with instructions to remain at home, unless he was at the courthouse or on his way there or back. President Hendrickson had invited him and Maggie to have a dinner with her family in the private residence of the White House in appreciation for his help in defusing the Russia crisis. Morgan supposed that was out for now, and maybe for twenty to life.

He and Maggie were dressed and ready when the driver that his attorney had sent arrived at their townhouse. The couple had sat quietly through a light breakfast, awaiting their departure to the courthouse and the oral arguments considering the validity of Morgan's arrest. Every attempt at small talk was fruitless. Though Josh didn't appear nervous outwardly, Maggie saw that he was devoid of the same carefree demeanor she had witnessed the day earlier.

For his part, Morgan appreciated the fact that his sweetheart was largely composed. Selfish though it was, when she was coping better, it was easier on him. So, when their ride showed up, the pair walked out, arm-in-arm and smiling, into the brisk sunny day that lacked the foreboding that a dreary, rainy day might have inspired.

◆

AG Jensen resented doing interview work that he would've ordinarily delegated, but it was hardly appropriate to send someone else when the interviewee was the Director of Central Intelligence. Elizabeth Parnell had told Jensen that she would be at the Capitol for an Intelligence Committee meeting after her standing morning briefing with President Hendrickson. She offered to meet with the AG in one of the conference rooms at the Congressional headquarters between the two appointments.

He sat alone in one of the many meeting rooms outside the Senate Chamber in the north wing of the U.S. Capitol. The attorney general was normally patient, except the demands of his position made time a precious commodity. Jensen was relieved when Parnell showed up right on time.

The tale DCI Parnell told him was a fitting one, since it came from the head of the CIA. Full of intrigue and an almost novelesque plotline, it sounded more fiction than real. And once again, its main character was Josh Morgan. The man, it seemed, had a gift for being right in the middle of dangerous and controversial situations. But he had the ability to maintain a moral compass when other, more seasoned individuals in all areas of the government overreacted. When others were being fueled by emotion, Morgan acted on logic. The chief lawyer for the United States found himself becoming more sympathetic to the ex-CIA officer's plight than he wanted to be. He understood a little better why POTUS felt the young man deserved her help.

"So, basically, Director, you're telling me that your boy mucked up an assassination attempt in Terrador, almost singlehandedly rescued President Weston, and stopped a war with Russia?"

"Well, he wasn't my 'boy' at the time. Nor does he work for me now, at least not full-time; but, yeah, that's pretty much it."

"Sounds like spy movie stuff," observed the AG.

"It does, but that's the truth."

"And now, some of the bad guys from his past are back to get him?"

The DCI only nodded.

"And you don't know who, how, or exactly why?"

"Right."

"Jeez!"

The Attorney General of the United States shook his head in disbelief. He had agreed that he wouldn't take notes, but he was unlikely to forget what he'd heard. Plus, there were no real specifics of the plot against Morgan that would be of help to him. The only thing he got was a general sense of who the man was and why he inspired such devotion among important people.

"So, Director Parnell, did Deputy Director Blake really kill himself?"

"Mr. Jensen, I'm prepared to testify by sworn affidavit that I instructed my employee, Ben Reid, to involve Morgan in the hunt for Weston. I will further swear that whatever actions Morgan undertook were under the auspices of the Central Intelligence Agency. As to what happened on that pier... I wasn't there and can't say. And President Weston says that Blake killed himself."

As Don Summers had when he had met with the CIA Director, Jensen realized that the woman hadn't answered his question. And as Morgan's defense attorney had, the AG simply left it at that.

♦

Just as it had been at what was supposed to be Josh's arraignment, the courtroom was empty except for the parties involved. President Weston wasn't even allowed this time. It took some persuading since they weren't yet married, but the judge relented and permitted Maggie to attend.

As he made his way to the defense's table, Josh's attorney, Don Summers, noticed that Siobhan Cassidy was absent from the prosecution's table. In her place sat another young attorney. He had taken a couple of steps past the Maxwell team when he backtracked. He extended his hand to Riley Maxwell, who stood.

"Counselor."

"Mr. Summers," answered the U.S. District Attorney.

"Where is Ms. Cassidy this morning? Off on another case?"

Riley Maxwell flinched and stuttered, "She's... well, she's no longer on this case."

Then, in a manner completely out of character for the defense attorney and behaving in the way that was abhorrent to him, he leaned in and remarked to Maxwell quietly enough that only he could hear.

"Too bad. She's quite a looker. Wouldn't mind some of that, if you know what I mean."

He hated himself for the comment, but he wanted to see the man's reaction. The ploy worked. Summers didn't see the glint of agreement in Maxwell's eyes. Neither did he see a sense of disgust that any decent man would've felt at the lewd implication. Instead, he saw U.S. Attorney Riley Maxwell drop his head and look away. His complexion became immediately flushed, face red and splotchy. He literally gasped a breath, clearing his throat, barely getting out the words, "If you'll excuse me, I have to speak with my team."

Summers continued to his table, still gazing at Maxwell, who cast a distressed look at him, but immediately turned away from his legal opponent's stare.

Josh Morgan put his hand out to his attorney, who was oblivious to it for a moment. Eventually, he woke up to the greeting and grasped Josh's hand enthusiastically and greeted Maggie, too, before taking one more look at Maxwell.

No sooner had Summers settled into his chair and removed his documents from his briefcase than the bailiff invoked the standard instruction to "all rise" and all rose. Judge Dunn proceeded to his bench. Defense lawyer Summers observed that Prosecutor Maxwell had regained his composure from the query about Siobhan Cassidy but that his face was a mixture of anger and a sense of knowing. The apparent confidence puzzled Summers because despite Maxwell's mistake in his filings for Morgan's arrest, the defense attorney knew his legal opponent wasn't stupid. The prosecutor had to know that he was about to get shit on. And if that were true, why did he seem so self-assured?

Judge Dunn stated that he had read the briefs presented by each side and instructed the prosecution to begin.

While U.S. Attorney Maxwell waxed eloquent about the legal justification for arresting him, Josh Morgan wondered why his lawyer never raised an objection. It worried him because Maxwell was citing case after case and precedent after precedent that convinced even Morgan that the D.C. attorney had the legal authority to arrest him.

Defense Attorney Summers sat without expression behind the desk for a few moments after the prosecutor had concluded his remarks, scribbling notes. Finally, he laid his pen and glasses aside and presented his client's case.

"Your honor, Mr. Maxwell has based his entire case on two primary points. And *neither* is factual." Summers looked at his adversary, who still had an unjustified – Summers thought – look of contentment. It threw Morgan's defense attorney off for a moment.

"First, he has stated that National Security Agency Deputy Director Everson Blake was a law enforcement official, allowing his alleged murder to fall within the scope of federal prosecution. The NSA is *not* a law enforcement organization. It is an intelligence agency. In addition, Mr. Blake's role within the organization was more accurately that of a manager."

Summers put his thumbs through his suspenders and paced momentarily, staring at Maxwell, who was leaning back in his chair with his fingers intertwined beneath his chin. From a door on the side of the courtroom, four men entered. One whispered to Maxwell while handing him a folded form. The attorney set it on the table before him without opening it.

Judge Dunn slammed his gavel forcefully and demanded, "What is the meaning of this? These are closed proceedings!"

Maxwell stood. "These men are the arresting officers and are here as witnesses, if needed."

Dunn glared at the U.S. Attorney for several seconds before finally turning again to Summers.

"Continue."

The light came on for Don Summers, who suddenly knew exactly what was coming. He looked over his shoulder toward his client.

He continued, "However, his position with regard to jurisdiction is a Catch 22. Mr. Maxwell filed the arrest warrant under the auspices of the District of Columbia's Superior Court. That is, the warrant was granted for the arrest of my client on the grounds of local jurisdiction. Given that the alleged crime was committed in Texas, Maxwell's office has no authority to arrest.

"And if the alleged crime falls within the jurisdiction for a federal crime, the papers were incorrectly registered and are without merit. I move that the charges be declared such and be dropped, and my client released."

Judge Dunn waited, giving the prosecution the opportunity to object. Maxwell offered no complaint. He was reluctant to proceed without allowing the U.S. Attorney ample time to rebut, but Dunn finally pronounced the decision he had already made. He had, in fact, come to his conclusion prior to the hearing.

"If there are no objections to the motion..." Dunn looked at Maxwell questioningly one last time.

Behind the defense table, Morgan turned to look at Maggie on the bench seat behind him. The fiancé and fiancée smiled expectantly.

"I find that the arrest warrant was without merit. It can have no merit as a local matter for a crime committed in Texas. Neither can it be enforced as a matter for federal jurisdiction, since the attestations on the documents identify it as a crime local to the District of Columbia.

"I find the arrest to be illegal. The defendant is free to go. This hearing is adjourned."

Judge Dunn raised his gavel to strike it.

Before he could complete the act, as Morgan and Maggie reached to embrace, the four men seated behind the prosecution's table were already moving toward the defendant. Before they could reach Morgan, Don Summers put his hand on his client's shoulder and said, "Josh..."

One of the men spoke, "Joshua Matthew Morgan..."

Josh and Maggie turned toward the voice. Josh recognized the man from his townhouse. He exhaled deeply and turned away from the man. He placed his hands behind his back. Maggie looked past Josh at the four men, one of whom began to apply handcuffs. Then her blue eyes turned to Don Summers, who could only shake his head.

"I couldn't have imagined it would happen this fast," he said, not understanding how Maxwell could get a federal arrest warrant for Morgan before the ruling had come down on his initial warrant. Summers had already begun planning his argument based on double jeopardy, so he was stunned when the arresting officer continued his Mirandizing.

"You're under arrest for the crime of high treason against the United States of America…"

Maggie collapsed on the bench, her hand to her mouth, incapable of words beyond, "No!"

Judge Leonard Dunn was as astonished as anyone in the courtroom. "My chambers! Now!" he screamed.

"Sorry, your honor," rebuked Maxwell, with no small measure of satisfaction. "You have no jurisdiction in the matter." Dunn's hands dropped to his sides at the realization that the prosecutor was correct.

"Take care of Maggie!" Morgan pleaded to Summers. Defense Assistant Cain moved around the railing to their client's fiancée and placed her arm around her shoulders.

Riley Maxwell extended his hand to his legal competitor and said as insincerely as possible, "Congratulations on a great win, counselor. Welcome to Round Two."

The prosecuting attorney followed his investigators as they led their prisoner out. His laughter was muted, but it stung Summers. He felt conquered. He had failed to anticipate that they could move on the separate charge of treason as quickly as they did. It happened even though his client had warned him of their intention to use the federal charge as a backup plan.

◆

"The man we honor today is no stranger to us, but allow me a few moments to remind each of us of the story of his rise from the so-called 'wrong side of the tracks' in a small Georgia town to one of the most respected businessmen in the world; from a childhood of poverty to a man with the capacity and the compassion to donate millions to those in need.

"Linus Schwartz represents what is best about our country; the means and the will to build hospitals, fund charities here and abroad, and to lead by example in lifting the forgotten in our nation to their own heights of achievement.

"Mr. Schwartz worked his way through college and began his career in a small construction firm near his hometown. In six years, he was named general manager, and, in his seventh year there, he bought the company from his boss upon his retirement. However, it was in the acquisition of an engineering company that our guest found his calling. Combining design with building, and serving as general contractor of his enterprise, he increased revenues to the extent that further acquisitions were possible. His investments built his personal portfolio so that he could take on the role of benefactor to thousands through his philanthropy..."

While Washington, D.C.'s mayor continued his tribute to Linus Benson Schwartz, his personal assistant Dexter Leach came onto the stage to whisper in the guest of honor's ear. Mr. Leach had no understanding of the communication. He merely said, "Mr. Lammers wants you to know it's done."

Linus Schwartz smiled and turned his attention back to his glowing introduction and the conclusion of his rags to riches life story.

"Most recently, Mr. Schwartz acquired through merger the Cannon and Raines conglomerate, making SCR, Inc., the largest company of its kind in the world.

"We are privileged to honor Linus for his philanthropy. Our government, particularly our national defense, is fortunate to have him as a business partner. And I am blessed to be able to call him my friend. The world is a much better place because of this man."

The billionaire philanthropist rose and hugged the mayor. Then he waved to the standing crowd in the ballroom of the hotel with a cane in his hand. Lowering the ornate walking aid to the floor, Schwartz began his walk to the podium.

♦

Former President Trenton Weston and his First Lady Alicia, having not been permitted in the courtroom, had waited on benches outside the doors. The husband felt no better than the night before and was giving in to the wife's insistence that he see a doctor.

When the double doors opened, the former first couple rose to meet their friends. The Westons looked hopefully for Josh in the group, but he wasn't there. Maggie was pale and her eyes moist, but not flowing with tears. The Westons were troubled at the sight of Donald Summers, who appeared demoralized.

"They've arrested Josh for treason," reported Shelley Cain on behalf of her mute boss.

As with Josh, Maggie, and Summers, Weston knew this was a possibility. But like all, they were unprepared for the swiftness. Trent Weston fell back to the bench along the wall, one hand over his mouth and the other pushing through his hair. His breathing became heavy, increasingly labored as he leaned backward. Alicia Weston's alarm at the sudden frailty of her husband was palpable as she gasped, "Trent! Honey!"

All eyes turned to the former President now. Summers and Maggie helped the ex-First Lady as she laid her husband down on the bench. She knelt on the floor beside him. Shelley Cain began to dial 911, but Secret Service Agent Jack Johnston in the hallway had beat her to it and was moving to Weston to attend to the man. The elderly man grasped one wrist with the other hand and stared through wide eyes at Alicia, unable to speak.

"Tell Josh!" Maggie yelled to Summers. He ran down the hall, torn between remaining with his lifelong friend and informing another of Weston's friends about the emergency.

Secret Service Agent Jeff Coulter ordered a line of bailiffs to surround the ex-Chief Executive to shield him from the prying eyes of others crowding around for a look. Most were already snapping photos with their phones. Coulter pushed the onlookers back with the detached, forceful presence his job required. But, inside, his and his agent partner's hearts were racing. Weston was more than an assignment.

Alicia Weston's face contorted with concern. She stroked her best friend's hair and whispered in his ear.

"There, there, my love. You'll be okay. Everything will be just fine," she assured, although she wasn't sure it would.

Trent became motionless, except for his eyes, which shifted toward his wife.

◆

Josh was still being processed when he saw Summers dashing down the hall.

"It's Trent! I think it's a stroke!"

Josh pulled at the men beside him. They slammed him to the ground, where one got on his back.

A prolonged scream of "no" bounced off the walls of the corridor. Morgan continued to strain against his captors. A fist to the head of Trent Weston's friend slammed his face to the tiled floor. He struggled for alertness until the hand repeated the action, and he fell unconscious.

Donald Summers shouted, "Stop it! I'll have your fucking job for that! I'll have you fucking arrested."

One of the other plainclothes officers stood in the attorney's face. Summers tried to push him away, but the man spun him around and shoved him down the hall.

Summers looked over his shoulder past his escort at his client. He was motionless. He spun around and pointed down the hall at Morgan. "You get him a doctor! Goddammit! GET HIM A DOCTOR!"

The officer shoved Summers into a small holding room and slammed the door. Weston's college classmate pounded on the door furiously, not with any thought that he could prevail against it. It was rage – and worry. He finally collapsed into a chair.

Realizing he still had his phone, the man tried to decide who to call. Suddenly he dialed a number that he hoped was unchanged. Hearing the voice answer, he shouted.

"This is Don Summers! I was legal counsel for Trent Weston! He's sick! Would you tell President Hendrickson? Please! It's serious!"

It took some time while the people at the White House argued how to respond to this call. Finally, a male voice spoke.

"This is Noah Chandler. With whom am I speaking?" Summers had met Chandler a few times and quickly recounted what had happened, both to Weston and to Josh. There was another delay. Don Summers frantically paced; stroking his hair one moment; pounding his forehead the next.

The silence was infuriating. When it ended, Weston's friend and Morgan's defense lawyer heard, "Mr. Summers, this is Sandra Hendrickson."

♦

The island of Terrador was slightly smaller than Iceland. And like the Nordic nation, it had only one city. Terradora contained around eighty-five percent of the country's total population. The balance of the citizens lived in the three small villages on the eastern coast. The remainder of the island was dense jungle except for an installation near the western coast that had been built by the United States over two decades before.

The central feature was the pair of enormous airstrips that intersected at something less than ninety-degree angles. In the years of greatest activity, military aircraft, many unmarked, came and went mostly during the nighttime hours.

Until recently, Joint Base Terrador, or JBT, suffered from disrepair. The decay was inherent in the neglect that resulted from the abandonment about ten years earlier. The U.S. departed the facility, largely because of the abuses of mostly intelligence personnel and contractors that became public. The Pentagon and other American operators had struggled to find other locations and means to serve the nation's interests.

Over the last year, though, the U.S. had begun to quietly rebuild its base and its presence in Terrador. As a result, the local economy had begun to improve, to a degree. *El Presidente* Álvaro Abellán wasn't the idealist his predecessor was, but he was an opportunist of the highest order and politically astute. He publicly claimed responsibility for the renewed flood of U.S. dollars.

Abellán was, however, an honest man, even if he was without the energy or intelligence to put the increased *dinero* to its best uses for his people. So, within his administration, two factions were at work at cross-purposes to each other.

One group wanted to push forward the programs and ideals fostered by the previous president, Miguel Salinas. Those initiatives promoted assistance to the impoverished people who had borne the brunt of the economic collapse that occurred when the U.S. pulled out.

The other consortium simply wanted the money themselves. As associates of the man who had lost the most recent presidential election to Abellán, they intended to overturn the results of the vote in any way they could. They had already contacted figures who had led the creation of the organization that had profited from past corruption. Dictator Juan Castaneda had built an empire of drug trafficking and money laundering. While the infrastructure grew to serve legitimate goals, sleaze and exploitation were growing along a parallel track.

Both of the current factions had one thing in common. Each possessed the potential to undermine Abellán's popularity and endanger his position as president of Terrador.

In the U.S. Embassy in Terradora, CIA Station Chief Arthur Flynn wondered at the sudden attention his office was receiving from not just Langley, but also other agencies. Liaisons from the National Security Agency and the State Department had made several inquiries about progress at the airfield. It wasn't as if they lacked their own personnel in-country, so, he wondered, why were they asking him? He had exactly two officers reporting to him, so there wasn't much room downstream to delegate. Flynn had a reasonably amicable relationship with his NSA counterpart inside the embassy, considering the animosity that often existed between the man's agency and CIA at higher levels. And he was very friendly with the ambassador and her staff. But regardless of his relationships with his peers within the compound, it was odd to him that he was getting requests for reports directly from *their* superiors. He had cleared the matters with his own bosses in Washington and had received instructions to cooperate with all requests.

But it was peculiar.

CHAPTER 7

Josh Morgan awoke before they lifted him off the tile floor. With only mild aftereffects from the blows to his head, he received medical care from detention personnel. Morgan begged for information on his friend, Trent Weston, but none was forthcoming.

By the time the detention officers led Josh to a cell, the former President was well on his way to Walter Reed Medical Center. Although there was no reason to suspect any foul play with regard to his episode, additional Secret Service Special Agents were called to his side. Both Johnston and Coulter rode in the ambulance with Weston and his wife. Two agents arrived to retrieve the ex-President's detail's SUV, while others awaited his arrival at the hospital.

Inside the medical transport, EMTs were tending to the former White House resident. He was stable, but still very much in danger. As she had for as long as she had known her husband, Alicia Weston maintained a brave face speaking words of comfort and confidence. Inside, she was a mess. Her mind raced with all the possibilities, including her worst fears.

♦

At 1600 Pennsylvania Avenue, Secretary to the President Brianna Washington led the Attorney General into the Oval Office.

"Afternoon, Craig. Thanks for coming over on short notice," POTUS said.

Craig Jensen almost laughed to himself. In what situation would he *not* drop everything and come when beckoned by the President of the United States. Still, politeness was often sorely missing in the discourse between some politicians and their "minions." Sandra Hendrickson had always treated her entire staff with respect and courtesy. She was a strong, courageous woman. Furthermore, she possessed an appreciation for hard work and the sacrifices her staff made, not only for the country, but for her personally. She had fought her own way through the glass ceiling to rise to the highest office in the land and had been instrumental in further shattering it for other women. But one of the things Jensen most admired about Hendrickson was that she never had a personal agenda for hiring and never showed favoritism when making selections for her administration. The best person always got the job. Period.

Another of POTUS' traits was her fierce loyalty. She had remained largely silent during some of her predecessor's escapades, despite the fact that Mercer's exit from the presidency would elevate her to the role of Leader of the Free World. His personal indiscretions weren't matters that would have ever led her to rat the man out. And while she disagreed with many of his decisions about reopening relations with The Holy Islamic Republic of Saudi Arabia in the months leading up to Trent Weston's abduction, she publicly stood by his policy decisions. However, his role in how the kidnapping played out was another story. Had she known the extent of Mercer's involvement, she would've gone to the proper authorities to expose it. That was almost certainly the reason President Mercer had left her out of the loop once he had made his deal with now-deceased Saudi President al-Hashimi and domestically with Deputy NSA Director Everson Blake.

Jensen knew that her loyalty was once again about to be on display, and that her decision would be made with complete disregard to the impact it would have on her personally and politically. Hendrickson always did what she believed to be right. Even when Jensen disagreed – maybe not disagreed but thought a course of action wasn't worth the political fallout – he never considered that she was doing it for any reason other than her confidence that it was right.

Sandra Hendrickson had made some impetuous moves over the last few months that led to a near-war with the Russian Federation. However, she eventually tossed her personal blinders aside and corrected her mistakes. And the AG knew who the man was who had most assisted in avoiding a nuclear engagement with the Russians. He was about to benefit from POTUS' sense of obligation. She always came to the aid of people who believed and behaved as she always tried to do. Her action would never be made public, but some in the government and law enforcement would know and would likely leak the story. But Jensen knew Hendrickson wouldn't care. It was the right thing to do.

Jensen sat down when motioned to a chair.

"So, what have you got for me, Craig?"

"Ma'am," he said, handing her a briefing packet, "I began having staff work on this yesterday at your direction after our meeting. It's not in a polished, final form yet, but it's close enough that I believe we can have it done in a couple of days."

President Hendrickson donned her spectacles as she began to read, and said, "By first thing tomorrow, please."

The AG knew that, despite the "please," it wasn't a request.

"Yes, Madam President."

Jensen waited politely as the President scanned the several page document. He always appreciated that she was so willing to trust her advisors. Her temperament seemed to be completely devoid of the need to change things just because she could. And that made Jensen unoffended when POTUS made changes or offered suggestions.

After some minutes of review, Hendrickson handed the document back to her Attorney General.

"That looks good. Very good, indeed! Thank you. Please look at my note and see if there's anything you would have an objection with."

Jensen took his turn pouring over the pages and, as usual, he saw that his boss' comments and alterations were not about the substance of the paper. Her changes personalized some matters and added some force to others. The Attorney General wouldn't have added them without personal direction from her. He noticed that, near the end of the text, Hendrickson had changed "the President *requests*" to "the President *directs*."

"Excellent, ma'am." Jensen meant it.

◆

At Former First Lady Alicia Weston's request, one of the two Secret Service Special Agents who came to get her husband's detail's vehicle stayed with Maggie Laughlin.

Agent Joy Griffith was normally assigned to the current President's detail, but in light of the undetermined nature of President Weston's affliction, she was reassigned temporarily, rather than draw from the pool of agents that often worked second tier assignments.

Griffith had met Maggie briefly when the young woman had begun her job in the West Wing. She felt like she knew her a little better, though, from seeing her on TV during the briefings and press conferences throughout the confrontation with the Russians.

As she approached Maggie, the sight of her sitting alone on the bench outside the courtroom nearly broke her detached, professional heart.

"Ms. Loughlin…"

Maggie looked up momentarily to the source of the greeting, wan and seemingly undone by the events of the last few days.

"Yes? Oh, hello, Agent Griffith." She started to stand as she extended her hand.

"Please, don't get up, ma'am."

"Call me Maggie."

"Thank you, ma'am, but I'm not allowed. We can stay here as long as you like. My partner, Agent Marchman is parking and securing our vehicle just outside and will be in momentarily. Once he's here, if there's anything you need – anything at all – I'll see to it personally or arrange for it."

The smile on the auburn-haired woman's face was weak and obviously unfelt. There were faint streaks beneath the blues eyes from tears that were shed some time earlier. Yet, aside from the thousand-yard stare, Ms. Loughlin seemed remarkably composed.

"Can you update me with things here, Ms. Loughlin?"

"They've taken Trent, uh, President Weston, to the hospital," Maggie said, suddenly embarrassed. "But you know that." She shook her head slightly and lowered it.

"Mr. Summers, my fiancé's attorney called me. He is down the hall raising hell with the detention center administrators, although he didn't tell me why. So, I've just been sitting here." Suddenly the Principal Deputy Press Secretary seemed on the verge of losing her composure. But as suddenly as the break in her façade had appeared, the woman pushed it aside.

Maggie stood as she saw Macarthur Marchman approaching, who was doubtless Griffith's partner. Secret Service Agents were deliberately obvious – at least, most of them.

"I haven't met you. I'm Maggie Loughlin."

Mac Marchman took her hand, as he removed his gold Ray Ban Aviator Classics and put them away.

"I'm Agent Marchman, Ms. Loughlin. I'm sorry for your circumstances, ma'am."

Marchman was one of the younger, more junior agents assigned directly to the White House. Tall and lean, he looked more like an accountant than a presidential protector. But, like all of the agents surrounding the President and her family, Marchman was capable of sudden, fierce violence should it ever be required. And though all the professionals in the Secret Service were extremely intelligent, Agent Marchman was well above average. He graduated from MIT with a degree in astrophysics. He immediately went into the Navy, where he served as a SEAL for seven years. He entered the Secret Service upon leaving the Navy. Prematurely gray hair had replaced the formerly red mop on the Iowan, who was only eight months into his assignment in the White House protective detail. Marchman had distinguished himself in his time in a field office. His five years at

Brooklyn's Adams St. location was shorter than the typical six to eight years of field office work. Approaching his thirty-sixth birthday, he had already seen and done more than most men twenty years his senior.

As Maggie and her two protectors began to discuss what she should do next, attorney Don Summers approached, cell phone to his ear. Maggie, Marchman, and Griffith stood silently while Summers finished his call. When he did, he and the two Secret Service agents exchanged brief introductions.

"Maggie, Josh is fine – at least physically. President Weston – well, that's another story. The EMTs got him to the ER. Trent's stable but still in grave condition." The lawyer was visibly shaken at his lifelong friend's condition. He paused to collect himself. "I'm not sure when we'll know more."

He turned to Maggie, "Now about Josh. His head's sore from some roughing-up, but mainly he's just concerned about Trent. He's beside himself that he can't be with him. On another note, I just received an intriguing phone call from President Hendrickson's Chief of Staff, Noah Chandler, about Josh's situation."

Maggie's eyebrows raised at the thought that the White House might weigh in on the case.

"What did he have to say?"

Summers took Maggie's arm and sat her down on the bench outside the courthouse where her fiancé's proceedings had taken place and where she had sat since Trent Weston's collapse.

"Chief Chandler didn't say exactly what it was about; only that he and the Attorney General want me – well, us – to meet them here at 12:15 tomorrow. They've arranged a meeting with the judge for Josh's treason case."

"I didn't know his judge had been determined yet."

"Just found out, Maggie. His name is Byron Caldwell. He's about to retire, so this case could be his last hurrah. He's a fair man, so we could've done worse. But back to Chandler and AG Jensen. I believe they may be going to file an *Amicus Curiae*, a 'friend of the court' briefing."

Maggie felt a sense of excitement she hadn't felt since the announcement by Judge Dunn that Morgan's murder charges were being dismissed. Of course, within seconds of the order, he had been arrested for treason.

"The President is filing it?" Maggie hoped.

"Well, I can't imagine she would do so herself, considering the political implications…"

Maggie was overcome with a wave of bitterness as she heard that political matters would keep POTUS from going to bat for Morgan after he had done so much for her in regard to the Russian crisis. She managed to hold her tongue.

"... so she's probably having the Attorney General file it on behalf of the government, rather than doing so personally. I'm sure they'll position it that there were extenuating circumstances that warranted his actions; those being national security issues."

"You talk like Josh is guilty, Mr. Summers," Maggie charged.

"I'm just saying that, politically, it might be smart to admit to the actions Josh is charged with, and then explain why they weren't treasonous in these circumstances."

"Politically?" Maggie exploded. Even the two Secret Service agents appeared to be a little embarrassed. "There's that damned word again. *Politically!*"

Maggie stomped a few steps away before turning back to Josh's attorney, finger pointing in his face.

"All you people – you politicians; you lawyers..." Her condemnation couldn't have been worse if she were speaking about drug dealers. "You talk like this is all just a chess match with inanimate pieces. There's a person at the middle of this. Josh!"

A few drops of moisture escaped Maggie's blue eyes, but Summers was pretty sure they weren't from sadness. She was pissed. He reached for her arms and attempted to direct her to sit beside him. She folded her arms and moved additional steps away. The attorney simply waited until his client's fiancée spoke again.

Maggie turned to face him. When she finally spoke, it was more controlled, but her arms were still folded. And her face was still red.

"I'm sorry for the tone, but that's how this thing feels." Finally, she took a seat beside Summers.

"I know it does, Maggie. It *is* a chess match, but, believe me, I never lose sight of the people affected by it. It may work to Josh's benefit to depersonalize it. The less it seems to be personally motivated – whatever happened – the harder it would be for the treason charge to stick. After all, if he didn't expect a personal benefit, whether monetarily, ideologically, anything, it would be difficult to convict him *personally*. What would his motive have been?

"Furthermore," Summers continued, "he's already been cleared of the murder charge, even if on a technicality. That carries some weight. And, Maggie..."

Summers took her hands in his and turned her to face him.

"The White House's intervention, regardless of how it's framed and whatever the motivation... it will carry a lot of influence."

Maggie finally nodded. Her expression softened. Inside her purse, her mobile phone rang. She grabbed it quickly, anticipating some word about Trent Weston. Instead, the caller ID displayed another name. She pressed the "connect" icon.

"Maggie, this is Marie." Maggie already knew that from the display, but the sound of Press Secretary Marie Ginnetti, her boss in the West Wing, elevated her spirits and provided some measure of comfort. Maggie stood and moved a few steps away for privacy, followed by Griffith and Marchman. The conversation was brief but was filled with words of assurance and confidence from her superior and friend. Finally, Ginnetti said, "I have someone here who would also like to speak with you."

After a momentary delay, President Sandra Hendrickson spoke.

"Maggie," she began, before likewise offering her sincere, Maggie believed, belief that things were going to be fine. Her closing words were a promise of support, ending with, "You just never know what help might be on the way."

Maggie put the phone away and returned to Don Summers, who was back on his phone. His expression was troubled, so the young woman feared the worst.

"Trent?" she asked. Summers nodded.

"It doesn't look good, Maggie."

♦

Alicia Weston had feared for her husband's life when he was taken from *el Aguila de la Amistad* in northern Mexico. Until she got word of his safe rescue by Josh Morgan, she was terrified for his safety. But, in her heart, she always felt he would come back to her. At that time, she just didn't *feel* like a widow.

But now, looking at him in his hospital bed, connected with all sorts of devices, tubes, and cables, she felt like she'd had her last conversation, her final meal, her last everything with her husband of over forty-five years. Trent Weston was the only man she had ever loved. Their love grew stronger with every year. Unlike the way many long-married women described their husbands, he wasn't *still* the same dashing young man she had fallen in love with. He was much more.

The former First Lady watched through the glass into her husband's room where a team of doctors and other medical professionals attended to the former President. Turning away from the observation window, Mrs. Weston took stock of how far removed from Washington she and her husband had become. There were no personal friends at the hospital except for Maggie, who had arrived a few hours earlier and was holding her friend's hand. In truth, they had no real friends in the District. The only other people with the ex-First Lady was a swarm of secret service personnel.

A hand brushed her lightly on the shoulder. She turned to see Dr. Lawrence Murray, the ex-President's personal physician. He gave Alicia a hug.

"Larry, I'm so glad you're here," Alicia sobbed. The two held their embrace for a few seconds until Alicia Weston abruptly composed herself and said, "Now, go see Trent." She turned his shoulder so that he faced the door to the hospital room, and he obligingly headed that way.

Dr. Murray had gotten a brief rundown of his friend and patient's condition from Dr. Edwin Armstrong on his flight to Washington from Frisco, Texas. The attending physician was so accommodating that Dr. Murray himself had cut him off, knowing that he was keeping the Walter Reed doctor from his patient.

Alicia's eyes followed him as he walked into the room. He shook hands with Dr. Armstrong and the two men stood facing the heart monitor and chatted. Shortly, Dr. Armstrong gave Murray the patient's chart. Larry flipped it open and scanned the file before handing it back. Murray's body language seemed to demonstrate that he was confused by something. Hovering over Trent Weston was a doctor the patient's wife hadn't met. She had arrived about a half hour earlier and walked into the room without introducing herself or even greeting Alicia Weston. Mrs. Weston wasn't offended. She preferred that everyone be with Trent rather than waste time on pleasantries. The woman spoke to one of the attending nurses – Alicia couldn't tell what she said – and the nurse retrieved the chart from Dr. Armstrong and handed it to the female doctor.

She traced some of the text with her finger as she read. Then she placed her stethoscope over the patient's heart and listened. Finally, she read something on the laptop on the table beside the bed. She took a long look at Trenton Weston and began to type her own notes in. Once finished, she consulted with the two other doctors in the room. Dr Armstrong was obviously introducing the woman to Murray. Then she began to speak. As she did, Dr. Murray furrowed his brow, looked at his friend in the bed, and turned to look at his friend's wife. As soon as he made eye contact with Alicia, he offered a very weak smile and turned back to his discussion with the other MDs.

Finally, the three physicians emerged from the room and addressed Alicia Weston.

"Mrs. Weston," started Dr. Armstrong as the third doctor extended her hand, "this is Dr. Mia Palmer. She's a Medical Toxicologist…"

Mrs. Weston's head turned toward her husband's doctor.

"Toxicologist? I'm afraid I don't understand."

"Mrs. Weston, let's have a seat," encouraged Dr. Palmer. She took one of Mrs. Weston's arms while Dr. Murray took the other. Alicia Weston's head bobbed back and forth between her escorts, who had to support her somewhat as her knees suddenly went weak.

♦

District Attorney Riley Maxwell opened the door to his apartment with his free hand. The other held his whiskey, and an arm clutched case briefs against his chest. It was late. He was tired. But he had things on his mind.

"Mr. Lammers, I...."

The man pushed past him.

"...didn't know you were coming," he finished. Oskar Lammers, troubleshooter for Linus Schwartz, sat on Maxwell's sofa. The prosecutor in the case of *The United States v. Joshua M. Morgan* began to shuffle papers around in an attempt to tidy up.

Lammers pointed to the glass in Maxwell's hand. The attorney stammered as he came to the wrong conclusion.

"Oh, here. Let me get you one," he offered and started for the bar.

"No. I was suggesting that perhaps you didn't need one either – with so much riding on your performance."

Mentally, Maxwell disagreed. "You have no idea how much I need this," he thought, "especially now that you're here."

He said nothing but moved to the counter and set down the glass containing whiskey over ice. He wiped the moisture on his fingers from the sweat on the glass on his pants. He felt certain that his brow was sweating equally. Mr. Lammers was an intense presence.

"You really mucked things up with your assistant. Mr. Schwartz isn't pleased."

The silence hung in the air as Riley Maxwell scrambled for something to say. "I... I, uh... I'm sure..."

"It's taken care of, Mr. Maxwell."

The attorney for the District of Columbia and the United States breathed a heavy sigh and his shoulders sagged. Exhaling even more greatly the second time, he put his left hand over his mouth and hyperventilated a few times. After his labored puffing ended, he sat down at his bar counter.

"Oh, thank you. Oh, God. I knew Siobhan could be reasoned with."

Maxwell's words came to an abrupt stop at the sight of Lammers' cocked head and arched eyebrows that accented the piercing glare below them.

"Oh, my. Oh, oh, my." Riley Maxwell rubbed his forehead with both hands and pushed them up onto the top of his head. He stood and paced, keeping his left hand on his forehead and pressing his right into his waist. Finally, he rested both hands on the bar. His head hung onto his chest. Finally, he turned to look at his guest.

"Why did you...? You didn't need to..."

Lammers interrupted without uttering a single word. He leaned toward Maxwell and put both hands on the coffee table before him. The slow tilt of his head toward the prosecutor stopped his words dead.

Lammers stood and walked to Maxwell and placed his hands on the man's shoulders. He leaned toward Maxwell and said very calmly, "This is on you, Mr. Maxwell. This is important to Mr. Schwartz. He doesn't expect complications from you. And he's not a forgiving sort of man."

With the last word, Lammers patted Maxwell's right cheek. It wasn't forceful, but the mental impact nearly knocked the man's legs out from under him.

"Mr. Schwartz said things blew up on you in court."

"There was a snag, but I immediately went to Plan B." Maxwell managed a crooked smile, but Lammers didn't accept the confidence the attorney intended to portray.

"'Plan B,' as you call it, was exactly that. It was the second wave. Your blundering put it into play far too quickly. Morgan's team needed to be occupied with defending against the initial charge for some time before you hit them with the treason thing. It would've been an unexpected bonus had he been convicted of killing Mr. Blake. Now, you've fixed it so that they really only have to deal with the one charge. Mr. Schwartz didn't care much about the verdict in the murder case. That's why we didn't care who the judge was. It was only about an extended length of time and presenting a crisis for Mr. Morgan. He anticipated that it would be a complex matter to adjudicate."

"It won't be a problem, Mr. Lammers."

"It's already a problem, Mr. Maxwell. Plus, a source told us the White House is getting involved."

"We always knew they might."

Lammers wasn't pleased with the implied correction and the sense of lack of concern in Maxwell's voice.

"Not when it was a murder case. But now that your clumsy handling has made it about treason already, Hendrickson no doubt feels there is a plausible rationale for her to lend some support. It was never supposed to go this fast, Mr. Maxwell."

Lammers' German accent had mostly disappeared since he moved to the United States at age eight, but there was enough of a hint of it that it added an exclamation point to almost everything he spoke, particularly when he spoke so deliberately and intensely.

The attorney pulled away and walked to his dining table, where he took a seat. Lammers took the whiskey bottle, which was still two-thirds full, from the counter in the bar. He unscrewed the lid, turned the bottle downward, and poured the remaining liquid into the sink. As he did, he waved his left index finger side to side and shook his head. Maxwell got the message.

"No more complications. Understood?"

Riley Maxwell bobbed his head up and down but never looked up.

As Oskar Lammers left the apartment, he paused in the doorway and turned his head to Maxwell.

"Oh, and get a good night's rest." The words carried a stronger accent – deliberately, Maxwell thought. It made them a bit more menacing.

Maxwell sped to the door and peeped out the viewer. Once he was certain Lammers had turned the corner in the hallway, the DA pivoted and leaned backward against the front door. He finally turned the deadbolt, went to the bar, collected another bottle of whiskey from beneath the counter, and poured himself another drink – neat and almost to the rim of the glass.

♦

Josh Morgan was settled into his cell. It was a different one from the one he'd occupied earlier. They had removed his ankle monitor. He was back in his prisoner overalls.

He lay on his bed. His cell was isolated, as it had been earlier, due to the possible national security issues involved in his case. Don Summers had told him as much as he knew about Trent Weston's condition, which wasn't much. It relieved Josh to hear that Maggie had gone to the hospital. He was afraid she would want to stay with him at the jail, but there was really nothing she could do. And, if she saw him at all, it would've only been briefly.

Morgan had a bond hearing set for tomorrow but didn't know what to expect. Summers had told him that the very nature of a charge of treason made flight too risky, so bail was likely to be denied.

Josh had a number of questions he wanted to ask his defense attorney. How long would the trial last? In other words, how long would he be in jail, if bail was denied? What were his chances? And so on. But he knew that Don Summers, owing to his lifelong friendship with Trent Weston, wanted to be with the man – or at least with Alicia.

Josh wanted to be there, too. And beyond his inability to do so, he would also have no way of hearing about the condition of the man who had done so much for him and who was such a friend.

Morgan had only one choice of reading material, so he opened the "D.C. Department of Corrections Inmate Handbook" to see what humorous things he could find the second time around.

CHAPTER 8

Dr. Mia Palmer had suggested that the group, including Secret Service Special Agents Johnston and Coulter, move to a more comfortable and more private location than outside Trent Weston's room. Don Summers sat on one side of Alicia Weston, who was on the sofa in a lounge off the nurses' station. Maggie stood behind the former First Lady. Of course, the entire area had been cleared of other patients and nonessential medical personnel

Dr. Palmer took a breath and began.

"Mrs. Weston, we aren't completely certain, but it appears your husband is suffering from the effects of a type of toxic substance. The type..."

"Someone poisoned Trent!" Mrs. Weston's left hand flew to her mouth. Her right hand fell to her lap, where Don Summers took it. The woman's tears wouldn't be held at bay this time.

"Now, now, Mrs. Weston," the toxicologist said, placing her own hand on the lady's shoulder. "Having a toxin in his system doesn't necessarily mean someone poisoned him. There are a number of naturally occurring toxins. Most are tightly regulated now. Some can't be obtained, at all.

"Others are byproducts of manufacturing processes, too, so we'll need to ask you some questions about where President Weston has been lately. And though it's a difficult time for you, we have to get started now."

Alicia Weston dabbed at her eyes with her tissue and calmed herself. She nodded her agreement. A nurse handed Dr. Palmer a checklist, which she opened to begin her questions.

"Dr. Palmer, before we begin, what can you tell me? What type of poison is it?"

"Ma'am, this appears to be similar to something called methyl iodide. It's been known to mimic strokes. Despite how things looked, Dr. Armstrong questioned a stroke diagnosis very quickly, due in large part to the excellent health of your husband. His physicals have never shown any markers for that possibility. Those things don't rule out a stroke completely, but, along with other factors, they led Dr. Armstrong to consider other causes. Specifically, he began to look for things that might mimic one. That, in turn, led to the discovery of the toxin in your husband's system."

Alicia Weston couldn't look up.

"Of course, the medical team continued to investigate the possibility of a stroke. Their examinations showed that President Weston had indeed had one, in addition to the poison in his system. Needless to say, we're perplexed. But the discovery of the substance allowed us to begin treating your husband for more than a stroke. Had Dr. Armstrong delayed exploring other causes, your husband would be dead already." Dr. Palmer regretted adding the word "already" as soon as she said it and tried to move hurriedly into her next words. But the look on Mrs. Weston's face made it clear she had understood the significance of the slip.

"As opposed to sometime soon?" the ex-First Lady said.

"I'm sorry. That's not what I meant."

The delay in Dr. Palmer's resumption was awkward. She finally decided there was no way to gracefully move on, so she simply proceeded.

"In most cases, methyl iodide is absorbed through the skin, but an examination of your husband showed no signs of burns or other similar skin irritation."

"I don't know what that is, doctor," said the patient's wife, clutching Don Summers' hand a little tighter.

"It's used in the manufacture of some pharmaceuticals and pesticides. Short-term exposure through inhalation can affect the central nervous system. It can also cause irritation to the lungs and skin. Acute inhalation exposure can induce nausea, vomiting, vertigo, ataxia, slurred speech, drowsiness – those are some of the symptoms we saw in your husband, and what led you and the responding EMTs to think he might have had a stroke."

"Is it fatal?" worried the former First Lady aloud.

"In cases where the symptoms have progressed to what we're seeing in the President, the outlook is uncertain. But we're working on it. Don't give up hope, ma'am."

"I don't understand how Trent could've gotten this. Not by accident, at least."

"That's part of what's puzzling us, too, Mrs. Weston. Has he toured any manufacturing facilities recently?"

"None. We've been here in Washington for several weeks."

"Has he eaten or drank anything for which the preparation was unknown?"

Alicia Weston's head popped up. "Doctor, I'm not stupid. Now you're talking about poisoning."

Dr. Palmer cast her eyes downward, "Ma'am, we're considering everything."

"To answer your question, not really." She paused while she reconsidered. "Actually, all the time. We eat out. We have room service, too. I mean, how can we not? It's not like we're still in the White House."

CHAPTER 9

Day 5 – Thursday

The morning was uneventful for Josh Morgan. He had taken breakfast in his cell. He had asked for and received some magazines – very old magazines – but at least they helped him pass the time. Nevertheless, he had exhausted the two that the guards had delivered to him, reading each cover-to-cover, whether an article interested him or not.

The detention officer who brought his lunch around 11:40 informed him he had ten minutes to eat before a group of four officers would escort him back to the courthouse for his bail hearing. Morgan thought it odd. He wasn't supposed to be there until 1:30 PM.

He doubted that he would hear anything other than "remanded without bail."

"At least my field trip will get me out of here for a bit," the prisoner said aloud, though there was nobody near enough to actually hear him.

He lifted the cover off his lunch and saw the processed meat, cold green beans, mashed potatoes, and a roll. Morgan lifted the roll and tapped it on the edge of the plate.

Dropping the piece of bread back onto the platter, Josh thought, "Ten minutes will be about nine-and-a-half more than I need."

He pushed the plate away and sipped the unsweetened tea. He was too anxious to eat anyhow. The unappealing fare before him just made it easier. The "traitor" was, of course, concerned about himself, but his main thoughts were about his former-president friend. Occasionally, people are reminded just how dependent they are on technology. During the time in his jail cell, Josh had silently considered that he might gladly endure forty lashes for use of his phone for fifteen minutes. He thought he was joking but wasn't sure.

♦

The ride to the courthouse was brief. Morgan was led into an anteroom where Don Summers delivered his coat and tie.

"How's Trent?" were the first words that Morgan said.

He noticed that his attorney blinked a couple of times and that his answer was slow in coming. When the reply came, it was with the lawyer's head still dropped initially, and, when he raised it, the smile was as weak as his words.

"It's not good. Not good at all. But let's get our heads in the game…" Summers' words trailed off and he looked into his briefcase. Morgan thought the action was only to provide an excuse to direct his attention away from his client. Josh stared at the man for several seconds, trying to get a sense of what was going on in his mind. Summers looked up once. But once he caught Morgan's eyes, he immediately returned to shuffling the papers in his satchel.

"And Maggie?" Morgan finally asked. Summers looked up.

"She's here. She's holding up as well as could be expected. Your girl's a strong young woman." Summers' smile was genuine this time, Morgan thought.

Morgan's detention officer escort removed the restraints from his hands and feet. He stepped outside the door, but left it cracked. The officer had already gone through the dress clothes and had found nothing.

When Josh signaled that he was ready, the officer returned, with Don Summers in tow. Summers was on his phone, finishing his call with, "I understand. I know he'll be grateful."

The defense attorney exhaled a muted "whew" and patted Josh on the back. "There's been a change of plans, Josh. That's why you're here earlier than scheduled."

Morgan's eyebrows went down and his head tilted. He was curious but Summers didn't seem inclined to elaborate. He figured the answer would come soon enough.

♦

Alicia Weston sat alone at her husband's side. Johnston and Coulter waited outside the room. Former President Trenton Weston had lain in his hospital bed, stirring only occasionally. When he did, his movements were very slight, and he never spoke. He only turned his eyes and tried to smile past the ventilator.

Mrs. Weston began to stand when Dr. Palmer came in. The toxicologist placed her hand gently on the former First Lady's shoulder. "Please, don't get up." Past Palmer, her husband's personal doctor, Lawrence Murray, was speaking with the two Secret Service agents outside the room

Mrs. Weston saw Jack Johnston's shoulders sag. He and Jeff Coulter exchanged a glance that would've been meaningless to most people, but which their protectee saw as something beyond concern.

Dr. Murray came into the room and, after a brief hug, stood behind his friend's wife. Neither spoke.

Dr. Palmer listened to her patient's heart and lungs through her stethoscope. She pressed on this part of the ex-President's body and that. She gathered the clipboard that was the man's medical chart. Of course, the paper version was only an intermediate step in the charting process. It was the place where notes could be written by hand until they were transferred to the permanent repository of his record, the hospital computer. Palmer scribbled some notes.

The doctor brought a chair alongside her patient's wife and sat down. When she placed her hand on Mrs. Weston's in her lap, the woman's gut wrenched in apprehension. Alicia Weston had the sudden realization that, while the doctor assumed that she was providing some sort of support with the personal touch of hand to hand, such gestures mostly communicated that some piece of bad news was forthcoming. She was correct.

"Mrs. Weston, mainly from urine and blood samples, we've confirmed that the toxin is indeed some sort of derivative of methyl iodide. It's unlike anything we've seen before. Our examination of your husband's bowels shows traces there. His lungs are largely unscarred. The damage to them seems to be from the toxin itself, rather than its inhalation. We have scoured every inch of the President and found no sign of direct contact. We are left to presume that..."

"That he ingested it," Alicia Weston finished.

The doctor nodded.

Outside the room, the wife saw Secret Service Special Agent Jack Johnston watching through the observation window. She saw his personal uneasiness increase somewhat at the sight of her nearly breaking down. She smiled at the man who was at their beck and call and who had, while keeping her and her husband safe, almost become a family member, despite the personal detachment that his job required. Beyond him, Mrs. Weston saw, Agent Coulter was on the phone.

"How he ingested it is considered now to be..."

"Deliberate," Alicia finished the doctor's comments correctly a second time. Again the toxicologist nodded. The two sat in silence before the doctor resumed disclosing her findings.

"As you must know, a deliberate poisoning was always a possibility. In fact, we suspected it as soon as we tentatively ID'd the toxin. But given that methyl iodide is so tightly controlled, obtaining it would be extraordinarily difficult. Someone would need to have access to a pesticide factory, or some other chemical facility. We don't know."

Alicia Weston wiped away the single tear that was trickling down her cheek with her tissue.

Dr. Murray finally spoke, "Alicia, I've just let your Secret Service detail know of the diagnosis and of Dr. Palmer's suspicions. I suspect the call Agent Coulter is making is to his director. They'll obviously inform other agencies – the FBI, DHS, and so on."

Mrs. Weston nodded and reached to pat her husband's personal doctor's hand that was on her shoulder. His eyes were moistening.

"Alicia, who would do this? Do you have any idea?"

The patient's wife thought of her husband's kidnapping by the Islamic Saudi government for the purpose of conducting a sham trial for war crimes. She considered the former President's part in stopping a Saudi plot to start war between the United States and Russia. But obligation of confidentiality or not, Doctors Murray and Palmer couldn't hear about that.

"I think I'd better leave any speculation to the authorities," she said.

Alicia Weston suddenly realized that Trent's eyes were open – somewhat – and that his head was turned toward the conversation – somewhat. She rose quickly and moved to his side.

"Honey, have you heard this?"

Trent Weston could only nod. Weakly, he raised his right hand to the extent he was able and pointed to the ventilator.

His open eyes and movements might have given hope to Weston's wife, but for the dire prognosis she'd just heard.

Dr. Palmer spoke. "I'm sorry Mr. President, we have to leave it in. You've been semi-comatose already, so we've given you little in the way of sedation. If you'd like, if the ventilator is too uncomfortable, we can induce a coma."

Weston's eyes widened and he shook his refusal with his head.

♦

Instead of the courtroom, Josh Morgan found himself at the door to the judge's chambers. As Don Summers opened the door for him, he entered to find, sitting across from Judge Byron Caldwell, Presidential Chief of Staff Noah Chandler, Attorney General Craig Jensen, and another man and woman he didn't know. He presumed them to be aides.

Chandler was the first to rise. He shook Morgan's hand vigorously, smiling genuinely. AG Jensen likewise rose and offered his hand. Josh had met him recently when he was debriefed about his actions during the tensions with Russia. The aides introduced themselves, too, but Morgan paid little attention to their names.

The aides gave up their seats for the defendant and his attorney and moved to a place behind them along a wall covered with bookshelves.

Judge Caldwell began the meeting.

"As you know, everything said here is a matter of official record."

Morgan heard the clatter of pecking on a keyboard by a court reporter he hadn't noticed.

"I received your brief this morning at my house and have read it…"

The Chief of Staff raised a single finger to stop the judge in midsentence. Simultaneously, Chandler retrieved his vibrating phone from his pocket.

Judge Caldwell was beyond irritated but figured the President's righthand man deserved some latitude. The judge waved the court reporter into inaction.

"Of course." Those were the only words Chandler uttered before putting his phone away.

"Your honor, another person has arrived for the meeting."

Caldwell huffed, "Of course. Would you like to move the proceedings to Capital One Arena? It's much roomier. Perhaps we could sell refreshments. Or even…"

The sarcasm came to an abrupt halt when everyone else in the room stood for President Sandra Hendrickson, who entered the room. Following her were Maggie and Secret Service Agent Joy Griffith, who had returned to the President's protective detail after her brief time at the hospital with Maggie.

Josh and Maggie didn't embrace. They just held hands briefly across the back of Josh's chair.

Finally, Judge Byron Caldwell rose.

"Madam President, I…"

"Don't let me interrupt, your honor."

The President's chief surrendered his chair to his boss. In what had to be a deliberate show of support, POTUS leaned to Morgan and hugged him.

"How are you, Josh?" Hendrickson said, though she didn't allow time for him to reply. Everyone who had chairs sat and the President whispered to Josh.

"You're about to owe me, Josh. Or let's just say this evens things up."

Josh wondered at the comment, hoping that the White House was about to provide some legal support for his trial.

"Judge, please proceed."

"Of course, Madam President," Caldwell said with a nod. A single hand waved the court reporter back to work.

◆

Former President of the United States Trenton Weston and his First Lady were alone in his room. He faded in and out. Trent seemed to be suffering little pain, Alicia thought. The ventilator appeared to be more troublesome than his condition. The endotracheal tube required discipline on the part of the intubated patient to keep from ripping it out. The amount of sedation Weston had needed up until now was somewhat minimal, considering that he was largely unconscious on his own. Dr. Palmer had tried to insist – more accurately, demand – that her patient be placed in an induced coma. Alicia Weston forbade it, citing her husband's refusal earlier. Should he begin to rebel against the tube and try to extract it on his own, she would allow the heavy sedation.

However, more than her husband's objection to the medication, Alicia Weston felt that the moments she had with him were precious.

At the sound of the door opening, the patient's wife turned to see Dr. Palmer and two others she hadn't seen. Fearing she was going to try to impose her will concerning the sedation, Mrs. Weston began her objection.

"Doctor, I've told you…"

"Here's the deal," the doctor interrupted. "Given the absence of any real trauma to the President's lungs, I'm willing to see how things go without the tube. We'll remove it and see how he does with an oxygen mask. If he does well with that, I'll change it to nasally-fed. Any issues at all – I mean, even the slightest complication – the tube goes back in and I sedate to coma-level. If you refuse, you'll have to get another doctor. Do you understand?"

"That's more than fair, Alicia" added Dr. Larry Murray, as he entered the room.

"Of course. Thank you, doctor," Mrs. Weston agreed gratefully.

In the periphery of her view, she saw the right thumb of her husband go weakly up.

Dr. Armstrong arrived and said, "Ma'am, would you please wait outside?"

Mrs. Weston obliged. Dr. Murray turned to his friend in the hospital bed. Weston's eyes were closed.

"Trent? It's Larry, pal."

Weston never opened his eyes, but he provided a barely noticeable nod and squeezed his friend's hand.

"Hello, my friend. We're gonna try to make you a little more comfortable. Then we'll work on getting you out of here. The stripers are biting up at Lake Texoma. A few have our names on 'em."

Weston smiled to the extent he could with a tube stuck down his throat.

"President Weston, it's Dr. Armstrong. We're going to sedate you for just a few seconds while we remove this tube. Then we're going to wake you right back up. Given that you've already got some sedatives in your system, this brief commitment to more might make it harder for you to continue to have the little episodes of awareness. Squeeze my hand, if you understand."

The response was slow in coming, but when he had received it, the doctor continued.

"You're going to have a bit of a sore throat for a while. And you understand, even the slightest problem will necessitate replacing the tube and sedating you heavily, just as we told Mrs. Weston."

The patient's eyelids cracked slightly, and he cut his eyes toward the doctor. He squeezed his hand.

"See you back here in a few seconds, pal," assured Larry Murray.

An anesthetist inserted the needle of the small syringe into the port of the intravenous tube where it was attached to the back of his left hand and pressed the plunger. Weston's hand immediately fell limp and he was out. The team removed the tube and the anesthetist injected the contents of his second syringe into the IV port while he listened to the patient's heart. The ex-President didn't stir but the doctor nodded and removed the earpieces of his device.

Larry Murray motioned through the glass to Alicia, who returned and took her husband by the hand.

◆

"Attorney Jensen, I believe you were about to provide an explanation of the administration's position."

"Yes, your honor."

Morgan immediately felt better. He wasn't sure what the cavalry would be able to do exactly, but at least it was here.

◆

Alicia Weston was nodding off slightly when she heard a very weak, "Love you, sweetheart."

The voice was raspy and low, but it was music to her ears. She caressed her husband lightly, brushed his hair back, and kissed him on the forehead.

"Call doctor. The poison one."

Alicia smiled and nodded at her husband's characterization and leaned out the door. But her husband's request made her nervous.

"Jack, would you mind fetching Dr. Palmer, dear?"

Once she returned to her husband's side, the quiet voice spoke again. "Don't… don't think… going to beat this."

"Nonsense, Trent. You're as strong as an ox. This…" She looked into her husband's barely open eyes and felt on the brink of an uncontrollable breakdown. Even in his weakened state and with half-closed eyes, Trent was able to convey that look he always used to communicate that it was time to cut through the BS.

Mrs. Weston finally agreed with a nod.

"I know, sweetheart."

The former POTUS smiled and did what only his wife would recognize as a wink. Then he nodded off to sleep.

♦

Attorney General of the United States Craig Jensen didn't bother handing out copies of the paperwork, which Morgan assumed to be a friend of the court document. The President and Chandler knew what it said. His aides had helped prepare it. Jensen had already given Defense Attorney Don Summers a copy. And Morgan would have to learn of the contents from the AG's presentation.

"You honor, it is the position of the Justice Department of the United States that the charge against Joshua M. Morgan is without merit, both in substance and as a matter of law."

"You go, man," Josh thought.

"While it is true that a member of the U.S. Attorney's Office filed this charge, it doesn't represent the will of the Attorney General or the Department of Justice."

It was at this point that Morgan finally noticed a glaring absence. He moved his eyes around the room and, sure enough, the prosecuting attorney was nowhere to be seen. Neither was any representative of his office. He was trying to come up with some reason when he was brought back to the conscious world by the word "treason."

"Treason," declared Jensen, "is arguably the most serious of all crimes in our country. It represents a crime not against a single person, nor a crime against the government alone. It is a betrayal of all of our citizens of our country."

The AG waxed eloquent for a couple more minutes. Josh decided there was some unwritten rule – or maybe it actually *was* written somewhere – prohibiting attorneys from getting straight to the point.

"Rather than discussing possible motives or whether, indeed, Mr. Morgan actually committed acts that could be defined as treasonous, I would like to speak to the elements that would justify a verdict of treason being handed down."

Judge Caldwell offered a small smile to the President, perhaps as an apology for the interruption, and said to Jensen. "You're aware, Attorney General Jensen, that we aren't as far along as a trial yet."

"Yes, judge. But this is leading to a specific point."

"Proceed then."

"Thank you, your honor. Treason is a difficult charge to substantiate. Intentionally so. Fewer than thirty people have ever been charged. Title 18 of the U.S. Code, Section 2381, covering crimes and procedures deals with this crime in Chapter 115. The criteria are strict and deliberately narrow, so as to prevent frivolous accusations and charges levied solely for political or personal reasons.

"Article III, Section 3, and Clause 1 of the Constitution says, 'No Person shall be convicted of Treason unless on the Testimony of two Witnesses to the same overt Act, or on Confession in open Court.' Whereas Mr. Morgan has not confessed to the crimes, we must rely on the testimony of two witnesses to the same specific action.

"Your, honor, they do not exist. Not simply because Mr. Morgan has committed no such treasonous act, but as a matter of record, the supposed traitorous acts are matters of speculation only. The arrest warrant does not offer any specific acts but rather a series of activities in the pursuit of Former President Trenton Weston.

"When he is able, President Weston himself is prepared to testify to the intervention of Mr. Morgan in his rescue from an agent of the Holy Islamic Republic of Saudi Arabia. Many of the facts of the events surrounding President Weston's abduction will never be made public because they relate to matters of national security."

Jensen spoke for another few minutes, covering more technicalities surrounding the charge of treason.

"Now, as a matter of a possible second charge, misprision of treason, which we believe could be offered as a subsequent indictment when, as we believe it will, the charge of treason is dismissed or results in a not guilty verdict, we would like to be preemptive."

Morgan had read CIA Director Parnell's notes about both treason and misprision, so he was able to follow some of the AG's explanation.

Jensen argued, quite legitimately, Morgan believed, that the very circumstances of his involvement in Weston's rescue, made it impossible that he knew of the activities of Al-Majeed, Blake, Sanders, and others, but decided to do nothing about it. If he really wanted to facilitate the treason of the Arab and the NSA Deputy Director, he would've simply stayed home.

"Mr. Jensen, you have said that there are matters of national security involved. These matters are to remain classified, you say?"

"Yes, your honor."

"Then how are those facts going to help the defendant?"

"Just what I was beginning to think," Morgan considered, and his hopes began to fade. He knew that the weight of the administration's support would be helpful but would not absolve him.

The judge continued. "Thank you for the introduction to 'Treason 101,' Mr. Jensen, and the explanation as to why you believe Mr. Morgan is innocent. I fail to understand why you insisted DA Maxwell not be here. This will all go into the official record, but I'm afraid that, without substantiation, it will do little to sway me."

"Perhaps this will, your honor," said President Hendrickson, as she handed a pair of identical documents to her Attorney General. Jensen kept one and gave the second to Judge Caldwell.

POTUS stood as she spoke.

"Judge, by presenting this to Attorney General Jensen, I am instructing him to forward it to the Office of the Pardon Attorney, within the United States Department of Justice. I have consulted with Mr. Jensen, who assisted me in its preparation. It declares my decision to exercise my authority under Article II, Section 2, of the U.S. Constitution in granting a full and unconditional pardon to Mr. Morgan."

Mr. Morgan's head shot toward the folded piece of paper and then to the President, who was attempting to hide a smile. Morgan looked at Maggie, who was exuberant.

Judge Caldwell appeared dismayed. Perhaps, Morgan thought, he was let down by the disappearance of his chance to administrate this trial before he retired. He opened the folded document, took a cursory glance, and looked first at Morgan. His eyes turned next to the President, who was still standing. Finally, Caldwell returned to the document and read, mumbling the words to himself as he did.

"Be it known, that this day, I, Sandra M. Hendrickson, President of the United States, pursuant to my powers under Article II, Section 2, Clause 1, of the Constitution, have granted unto Joshua M. Morgan, a full unconditional pardon for all offenses against the United States which he has committed or may have committed or taken part in during the period from…"

The dates following the declaration of clemency covered the period prior to the unfolding of the events in Terrador that led to Morgan's dismissal from the Central Intelligence Agency and ended with today's date.

"President Hendrickson, this goes back a long way."

POTUS looked to her Attorney General.

Jensen took over the discussion and Hendrickson seated herself again.

"Your honor, if I may, there are incidents in Mr. Morgan's past that relate to matters of national security…"

The judge's eyes flashed, and he leaned forward. "If I hear the words 'national security' one more time…"

Now it was Craig Jensen's face that reddened.

"What troubles you is irrelevant, judge. In 1867, *ex parte* Garland, the Supreme Court held that the President's pardoning power is 'unlimited.' They further held that…"

"I don't need your history lesson, Jensen."

"It appears you might, judge. The ruling further held that the President's power to pardon 'extends to every offense known to the law, and may be exercised at any time after its commission, either before legal proceedings are taken, or during their pendency, or after conviction and judgment.' So, I'll skip to the heart of the matter."

The judge's face was beet red by this time as he tried in vain to interrupt. As the AG continued, Caldwell barked at the court reporter to stop transcribing and pointed to the door. The man stopped typing and gathered his belongings. He escaped the tension-filled room with his head hanging.

Surprisingly to Josh, it seemed that, the angrier the Attorney General got, the lower the volume of his voice. The intensity was overwhelming, regardless.

"The President doesn't owe you diddly in the way of explanation…"

"'Diddly,'" Morgan thought, becoming a little amused as Caldwell was obviously fighting a losing battle. "Now there's a highly technical legal term."

"Her powers to pardon anyone at any time for anything are unquestioned. Josh Morgan is absolved of any crime he may or may not have committed. Neither you nor anyone else can change that."

"Anything else, your honor?" President Hendrickson asked in a calm voice that nevertheless seemed to dare the judge to object further.

Judge Byron Caldwell tried to speak, but nothing would come. His forefinger rose slightly, but he apparently thought better than to point it at the President of the United States or her legal representative, so he lowered it. The jurist's face had changed from crimson to ashen.

"This isn't over" finally escaped his lips. Morgan and everyone else in the room wondered why Caldwell seemed to be taking this so personally.

Hendrickson stood and placed both hands on the man's desk, causing his torso to lean backward.

"Yes, judge. It is."

Caldwell looked away, unable to maintain eye contact with Hendrickson.

"Nothing?" she said. "Good." She stepped away from the judge's desk.

"Now, here's what we expect. You're going to write an order to release Mr. Morgan from custody… right now. Should you choose to fight this, you will lose, and you know it. Luckily for you, you won't appear like the fool you are because this proceeding will never see the light of day. You utter so much as a single word publicly, we will charge you with whatever we can for disclosing classified matters of national security… anything we can think of."

"But I don't really know any facts about these so-called 'classified' matters."

"So, there really should be no reason for you to say anything at all, then. Should there?"

POTUS whispered to Josh as she shook his hand.

"Are we even?"

Morgan stood as he placed his left hand over his right in shaking President Hendrickson's.

"Thank you" was all he could say.

Hendrickson looked at Maggie, who was also standing now. "We hope to see you back at work soon but take all the time you need." And with that, President Sandra Hendrickson gave Principal Deputy Press Secretary Margaret Loughlin a hug.

The nation's Chief Executive left the room. Chandler and Jensen stayed behind. The Attorney General handed Caldwell an already-prepared document granting Morgan's release.

"I know it's not on your letterhead, but it should suffice."

Judge Caldwell turned his head away, shook it slightly, and signed the document.

"Thank you, your honor."

Defense Attorney Don Summers took his client by the arm to lead him from the chambers. "Come on, Josh. Let's get you out of here."

Morgan put his arm around Maggie's shoulders and the entire entourage left the room.

Caldwell leaned back in his chair and put the pen to his mouth. After two or three minutes, he set the pen down and took his cell phone from his pocket. He was about to press the name of the person he needed to call, when he decided he needed a little more time to think before addressing that matter.

◆

Former President Trenton Weston was asleep again. He had been in and out for the entire afternoon. His wife couldn't decide if it was unconsciousness or slumber. Alicia had dozed on a couple of occasions, but nothing more. She was looking at her husband when his eyes opened for the latest time. Earlier, Dr. Palmer had authorized the change of the administration of oxygen from a mask to nasal.

Palmer had explained to Mrs. Weston that, despite his moments of alertness, her husband's condition was grim. And, indeed, Weston's speech remained slurred, though intelligible. He had little ability to move. He could turn his head slightly and move both hands to some extent. That was all.

When he spoke, Alicia would lean her ear to his mouth so that she could hear better, and also to prevent him from having to try to speak more loudly.

Weston had, in essence, begun to say his goodbyes to his wife a couple of times. Aloud, she dismissed it, telling Trent that he wasn't going anywhere. Silently, however, she felt they were fighting a losing battle. She maintained her composure during her husband's brief moments of awareness, saving her tears for his more prevalent periods of sleep.

When Alicia Weston saw Trent's eyes shift toward the window to the hallway, she shifted her gaze to join his. Looking back at them through the glass were Josh and Maggie. Neither was able to make their meager smiles look sincere. Alicia Weston motioned at them to come in.

The question, though unspoken, was obvious in the former President's eyes.

"I escaped," Morgan informed him with a grin. "Left a note saying I had to see a friend."

Weston managed to squeeze his younger friend's hand.

Morgan explained briefly and without a lot of detail, the pardon by President Hendrickson. Trent's lips moved but Morgan couldn't understand. He leaned closer and heard the repeated words, "Right thing. Proud of her."

Maggie and Alicia stepped to the hallway to leave their two men alone. Maggie explained that Chief Chandler had updated them on Weston's condition on the drive to the hospital, including the now inescapable fact that the man had been poisoned.

The news would've sent Morgan into a fury, had he not been so crushed. He was uncertain whether the Saudis were behind yet another attempt on the life of the man they despised more than any other. He simply didn't know. But in the presence of the ex-Commander in Chief, Josh managed something close to a good humor.

"You get hold of some bad fish, or something?" Morgan almost choked on the words. Weston's eyes begged him closer.

"Or something." The words were barely understandable.

"Why don't you get some rest now, my friend?"

A low, scratchy "no" was his answer.

"Right. You've probably had enough rest." Morgan knew the man's waking moments were largely out of his control anyhow.

A couple of incomprehensible sounds emerged from Weston's mouth. Morgan leaned in again.

"Waited for you."

"I don't understand, Trent."

Over the next several minutes, Josh's dearest friend managed to carry on a conversation. It was a laborious effort. The two men who had saved each other in ways literal and figurative spoke in affectionate terms, sharing their mutual love.

Through the window, Maggie's heart broke as she watched Josh struggle to hold it together as he laid his head almost atop Trent's chest to hear. She could see Josh nod frequently. Interspersed with his periods of listening were times when he moved his mouth to his friend's ear to speak. At one point, Josh rose suddenly and looked away. Weston's hand pulled weakly at Morgan's and Josh moved to listen again.

♦

Federal Judge Byron Caldwell hung up the phone after delivering the bad news of Josh Morgan's pardon. The listener remained largely silent during the disclosure, but the jurist could feel the seething rage in the absence of words.

The judge picked up the phone again to tell his senior clerk that he would be going home early.

♦

Alicia Weston's younger sister had arrived at the hospital shortly after Josh and Maggie. As a Baptist missionary, it was no small feat to arrange for her return from Sub-Saharan Africa. Ten years junior to her sister, Emma Gray had never married and had devoted her life to serving God. She and Alicia shared a connection that only sisters could, trite as that expression always sounded.

The pair rejoined Maggie at the window. However, watching the scene inside the hospital room made all three women suddenly feel as though they were invading the privacy of the two friends inside. They moved away.

Inside the room, neither Josh nor Trent had said anything for some time. Thinking the patient had fallen asleep, Josh sat silently beside his bed. Once again, Trent squeezed Josh's hand, the cue to lean in for his words.

"Yes, Trent."

"I love you, son." The words were as clear as they could be.

Josh choked at his reply. "I love you, too, Trent. More than you'll ever know."

"Oh, I know."

Neither spoke for a brief moment. Finally, Trent did.

"Would you mind getting Alicia? I'd like to spend some time with that beautiful woman." The words were the clearest he had managed since his ordeal.

"Of course." As Josh started to rise, the soft tug at his hand brought him back to Weston's lips.

"And don't watch. Might be smooching." The smile from the older friend was apparent, despite his frailty.

A pause and then, "Goodbye, son."

"I love you, Trent."

The tears were filling Josh's eyes before he made it out of the room. After telling Alicia Weston that Trent wanted to see her, he was sobbing irrepressibly. Maggie moved to his side.

"Josh?"

Her fiancé couldn't get words out.

"Josh, what did he say?" Maggie glanced through the observation window to see Alicia leaning over Trent's face, smiling at his words.

"He… He told me to take care of you. And he told me to let you take care of me." He grabbed a tissue from the nurses' station. "And he asked me to take care of Alicia. Then…"

Josh put his hand over his face and lowered his head.

As nurses and doctors rushed from their various locations toward Trent Weston's hospital room, Josh finally got the words to come.

"Then he told me he loved me. And… said goodbye." He watched the medical personnel turn into the doorway. Maggie led Josh to a chair where he laid his head on her shoulder and cried. Maggie pulled him close and joined him.

CHAPTER 10

Oskar Lammers sat silently across from his boss, waiting for orders. Linus Schwartz pursed his lips, shook his head, and slammed his fist on his desk.

"Incompetent fools!"

The billionaire looked to his personal assistant and raised two fingers. On cue, Mr. Leach moved to the bar and poured two Scotch and waters. He delivered one to each of the men. Dexter Leach rarely drank – he was on call to his boss twenty-four/seven – and never in the presence of Schwartz.

Schwartz held his glass slightly aloft toward Lammers, who returned the gesture.

"Not that we have anything to toast," the eighty-two-year-old philanthropist lamented. He took a sip of the amber liquid.

"So, wh..." The look from Schwartz shut Lammers down in mid-question.

Finally, "I don't know yet. I've always had contingencies. I never thought the charges against Morgan would stick. Just wanted to make his life as miserable as possible."

The man took another drink and tapped his right fingers on the desk. He brushed at his thin strands of hair, before rubbing the back of his neck.

"Maxwell and Caldwell – the fools – have been a disaster. Unfortunately for him, one of them is about to suffer a tragedy. The other merely needs to receive a reminder of why he must remain loyal to me."

Schwartz directed his eyes to Lammers, who nodded, and took another drink.

"Damn those two. I'm going to have to accelerate my timetable."

The man handed his empty glass to his assistant.

"Another?"

"No, thank you, Mr. Leach." Schwartz leaned on his cane to rise and walked to his bookshelf. Sliding a copy of *The Last of the Mohicans: A Narrative of 1757* outward resulted in a section of the personal library projecting forward and sliding to the side. Schwartz leaned toward the now-exposed safe and tapped in a code. The door cracked. The man pulled it fully open and retrieved a large envelope. He opened the flap to assure himself of the contents, closed it, and handed it to his German fixer.

◆

At the hospital, sisters Alicia Weston and Emma Gray huddled in a small room off the wing of Walter Reed Hospital where their husband and brother-in-law had passed away about an hour earlier. Mrs. Weston's tears had slowed to an occasional sob. Morgan had steadied himself enough to be of some support to his newly widowed friend. Maggie had struggled to balance comforting Josh with allowing her own grief to express itself.

Outside the waiting room of mourners, the Westons' protectors, Johnston and Coulter, stood stoically, though their eyes were red, as well. Each Secret Service agent had allowed himself the momentary indulgence – unspoken and independently – to wonder at their future before returning their thoughts to Mrs. Weston and their attention to their job. And, again independently, both Johnston and Coulter had decided that, given the chance, he would maintain his assignment with the former First Lady. It would never be the same, but each knew he would remain.

Special agents from the FBI were already on their way before Trenton Weston passed, to begin an investigation into the suspected poisoning of the ex-Chief Executive. Additional Secret Service agents were arriving, too.

About thirty minutes after President Weston's death, President Hendrickson had called the former First Lady. They spoke only briefly; just long enough for POTUS to extend her condolences and to make the offer to Alicia Weston to stay at the White House for as long as she liked.

The widow thanked the President for her offer and said she would consider it but felt like she would rather remain at the hotel.

After calling President Weston's death, medical staff had allowed Mrs. Weston some time alone with her husband, before moving him to a private examination room. An autopsy was necessary, due to the suspected foul play. No authorization was needed, so the staff began almost immediately after Weston's death. They would inform the widow about the procedure after some time had passed. Trenton Weston's personal doctor from the President's adopted hometown of Frisco, Texas, was present throughout the process. The hospital's medical examiner was technically in charge, but practically speaking, the autopsy was led by forensics specialists from the FBI and Secret Service. As a renowned Medical Toxicologist, Dr. Mia

Palmer was present to direct the collection of blood and tissue samples for her examination.

Dr. Murray, Trent's doctor and friend, offered to inform Alicia of the autopsy results, although he would be careful to avoid the term, substituting "examination" for it, instead.

The most offensive of all the necessary actions to everyone involved would be the interview with the deceased President's wife. The longer the delay, the less likely it would be that she would recall details of their last few days that might be critical to their investigation. Mrs. Weston would have a difficult enough time anyhow, everyone knew.

Josh Morgan stepped out of the waiting room alone and sat in another area down the hall. He had lost a man whose importance in his life was equaled only by his father and grandfather. Despite the intensity of his grief, the ex-CIA officer couldn't help but turn his thoughts to who had killed his friend.

After he had rescued Weston from Saudi operative Fadi Al-Majeed and following the subsequent resignation of Wendell Mercer, new President Sandra Hendrickson had laid the law down to Saudi President al-Hashimi. At that time, Morgan had thought that any plots by the Saudi Arabian government had ended. Then, the near war with Russia turned out to be a product of Saudi activity. So, could it be that they were behind the assassination of his friend? Josh's mind revolted at his first use of the word – *assassination*.

And, whoever it was, how did they pull it off?

On the other hand, Betsy Parnell accurately foretold his own legal predicament, Morgan realized. She had stated with some confidence that some of the old players from the unsanctioned plot to kill the Terradoran president were behind it. Morgan had reflected on that at some length while in jail. He decided, maybe they were, and perhaps they were even behind the poisoning of Trent Weston. But he couldn't quite comprehend why they would come after him now. The Director of the CIA had withheld from Morgan the fact that the U.S. was reopening its base in Terrador.

Nothing made sense. Morgan couldn't come up with a single scenario or group who would've pulled this off. But he was equally confused as to why Everson Blake's cronies would have any reason to arrange his arrest for matters that happened between him and Blake. Apparently, they did. His best working theory was that the same people behind the charges against him were guilty of killing his friend. But his gut told him, even if they were associates of Blake's and involved in the Terrador fiasco, there had to be more to it than that.

Morgan's thoughts were interrupted by a tap on his shoulder. He stood at the sight of Alicia Weston.

Mrs. Weston hugged Josh tightly.

"Josh, you were a son to Trent – and you are to me. You've done so much for us."

"No, ma'am. Anything I've done pales in comparison to what Trent – what both of you have done for me."

"We'll argue about that another time, dear." Mrs. Weston patted Josh on the cheek, which she followed with a kiss. "I'm heading back to the hotel. That's where all our things are. Jack has arranged with the hotel to let Emma and me enter through the back. They'll let us ride to our floor on the service elevator. I don't know if I'll stay there, or not."

"I'll call and check on you, Alicia."

"I know you will, dear. Do you mind if I steal Maggie away from you? I know you need her, too, but…"

"Not at all." Then turning to Maggie, he saw her discreetly and silently mouth the words, "Are you sure?" He nodded.

"I'll catch up with you later, sweetheart."

This time, it was Josh who initiated the embrace with the widow. Then a longer, more intimate embrace with Maggie.

"Call me if you need me, Maggie."

"I will. Love you, Josh."

◆

Outside Jackson, Wyoming, Deputy Sheriff Scott Taggart surveyed the barely recognizable Audi that was being dragged up the embankment. He had just heard the news of President Weston's death.

"Now this," he muttered aloud. "As if Maggie didn't have enough grief."

He watched the driver of the wrecker pull the smashed-up sedan to the road.

Tag pulled Maggie's number up on his phone but thought better of it, and called Josh.

◆

Hundreds of miles away Josh Morgan looked at the display on his vibrating phone and saw the name of his fishing buddy. He had declined to answer a few other calls over the past hour or so but picked up this one immediately.

"Hey, pal. Guess you're calling about the news about President Weston."

Morgan listened without a word until Tag had finished with his revelation.

Finally, he simply said, "Oh, shit."

Another few words came from his caller. Then Josh said, "Okay, Tag. Thanks for letting me know."

The native Texan who had lived in Wyoming for years before he and Maggie moved to Washington, sat down. He placed his phone in his pocket and leaned forward, resting his forearms on his knees.

"How am I going to break this to Maggie?"

◆

Linus Schwartz looked over the statements that detailed the financial condition for some of his holdings. Many held contracts with various arms of the federal government. In addition to SCR, his companies represented an array of industries, including SCR Instabuild Structures, Schwartz Agricultural Treatments, Volumetric Advanced Chemical Solutions, Megatrax Construction Equipment Manufacturers, and many more. The products served a wide range of military and industrial applications.

Sitting alone in the executive suite of his apartment, the man pulled out a faded, color photo of a young boy. Of course, he had a Photoshopped digital form of the same picture on his various electronic devices. But true to his preference for the old ways and days, he favored the original paper version of the candid shot, creases and all. He rubbed the first two fingers of his hand over the almost-smiling face. The ruddy complexion of the about nine-year-old seemed to fit. His striped t-shirt and jeans were typical of the times.

"If only I'd known sooner. How different your life would've been. How different both our lives would've been."

The elderly man's thoughts turned back to his love, Dorothy Stovall. Foremost in his mind was the revelation that came his way a dozen or so years ago. Schwartz never gave up on his efforts to find Dottie. Over three years after the Stovalls had moved away, Schwartz had employed a total of four investigators to locate the love of his life. The costs associated with the search nearly bankrupted him. That was long before he began to acquire his riches.

"The news isn't good," the final private investigator had told his client one day at the end of the third year of efforts. The PI informed Linus Schwartz that Dottie had committed suicide about eighteen months after she and her husband had moved away from the town where they and a younger Linus had lived.

Linus had taken the information from the investigator. He was heartbroken, but never showed any emotion as he paid the man for his services. Dottie's husband's address was included in the report. Off and on over three weeks, Linus had staked out the man's home. He never caught sight of him. That only fueled his rage at him for having taken his Dottie away; for driving her to kill herself. Schwartz passed many evenings waiting to confront him. Over the short period of time, he had even convinced himself that Dottie hadn't taken her life. Her husband had killed her, he was certain.

In his modest sedan, Schwartz would drink and wait; wait and drink. Some nights, after dark, he would sneak to the house and peer into its windows. On one such night, he was astonished to see a man sitting in an easy chair, in darkness but for the light in an adjacent room. The dim glow was insufficient to identify the man with certainty. That is, until he struck a match to light his cigarette. Without a doubt, the man was Marvin Stovall. Suddenly, Schwartz found himself knocking through the door into the room where his love's killer sat. Stovall barely moved, inert from an excessive amount of liquor.

"Who the hell are you?" he had muttered.

"I'm the man who's gonna kill you, you son of a bitch." Before Schwartz had completed his sentence, he was on the man, hands around his throat. The pathetic drunk could muster no resistance, and the attacker was filled with such unrestrained fury that he lifted the object of his hatred off the chair as he strangled him.

Finally, both tumbled to the wooden floor, where Schwartz reengaged. Stovall had gurgled for the first moments of the encounter, until the attacker managed a grip around his throat sufficient to cut off all air. Stovall's eyes had rolled back. He eventually tried to fight Schwartz off, but his efforts came too late in the one-sided battle. Stovall finally succumbed, but in his rage, the forlorn man who had loved Dottie so much had beaten the pitiful man's corpse about the head repeatedly. Finally, atop the dead man, Schwartz lifted Stovall's head and slammed it into the floor.

With a good deal of emotional release, Schwartz had risen and sat in the same chair from which he had lifted Stovall. Staring back at him from the hallway had been a boy of about two. Schwartz's satisfaction at having disposed of Dottie's husband immediately exploded into panic at the sight of the toddler gawking at him. The child was filthy and was holding a baby bottle of milk, though he was past the age when most children were weaned from one.

The future billionaire's first thought was to kill the boy, too, but he wasn't able to manage it.

"What's your name, boy?" he had asked repeatedly, but the boy never answered. He had only continued to suck the baby bottle and gaze back at Schwartz, emotionless.

The murderer had grabbed the boy up those years ago and rushed him to his car. The child never made a sound. Schwartz backed the sedan into

Stovall's drive. He left the boy in the automobile and opened the trunk. Running back into the house, he had straightened up the crime scene and carried the corpse out to his car. He had slammed the trunk shut and taken another drink of whiskey. When he looked at the toddler in the mirror, the child's reflection had only stared silently back at him

Linus Schwartz summoned some calmness on that long-ago night and had driven to a Catholic church and, finding the doors open as he expected, shoved the boy in. He had honked the car's horn until a light came on. Then he drove the seventy miles back to his own town. Leaving the body in the trunk, he had gone into his small house and lain on his bed.

That night, Linus Schwartz fell asleep, resting peacefully without regret for what he had done.

The morning after he had killed Dottie's husband with his bare hands, he had driven to one of his company's construction sites where he knew a concrete pour was scheduled. None of his boss' workers were surprised when Schwartz took his turn with the cement truck. He had always been hands-on. And all had been grateful when he sent them off on a break. Then he deposited Marvin Stovall into the forming concrete slab that would be his tomb.

Overcome with the flood of memories, and propelled back to the present, the octogenarian moved from his desk to the kitchen in his suite. The recollection had made him thirsty. He poured himself a glass of water and sat at the dining table.

He had never felt an ounce of guilt about killing the bastard but had never killed again. He left all his dirty work to his hired associates now. The latest in the line of employees was Oskar Lammers.

Schwartz had been astonished that he never heard from the police. Apparently, not a single soul in Stovall's neighborhood had seen him come or go. Or, at least, none had gotten his license number. And apparently, the child hadn't been able to identify him, either. It had taken about a year for him to become fully confident that he had gotten away with his crime.

Schwartz drank the remaining water and went to the restroom. It was early, only about eight-thirty, but the torrent of memories had exhausted him.

The recollection of his hands around Stovall's neck and the panic in the man's eyes were still crystal-clear after all these years. It always gave Schwartz immense satisfaction, even though his understanding of the events surrounding Dottie's death had evolved.

A dozen years earlier, the already elderly philanthropist's curiosity had gotten the better of him. He had to know more of Dottie's story. With the advances in technology, specifically the Internet, it had taken a new investigator less than two days to locate Dottie's sister Deirdre. Linus had never known she had a sibling.

Linus' driver had taken him to Deirdre's house. After some hesitation, the now-wealthy man walked alone to the porch of the modest house and rang the bell. He had stood, hat in hand, as the door creaked open. An elderly woman had appeared before him, with a nasal cannula, pulling her oxygen bottle behind her on wheels.

"Who the hell are you?" the obviously ill woman had barked.

"Deirdre, I'm the man your sister loved."

The woman had glared back that day, her eyes questioning his statement. She had been without a single clue of his identity.

"What the hell are you talking about?" she had demanded in an equally severe tone.

"I'm Linus. Linus Schwartz, ma'am."

Deirdre's eyes had grown suddenly wide, and she fell back from the screen door, barely able to keep her balance. Schwartz had rushed to assist, but the woman had flailed at him, trying in vain to keep him away. Coughing explosively, she had finally relented and let her unwanted visitor help her to her couch. Schwartz had run to the kitchen, returning with a glass of water.

Deirdre's eyes could've bored through steel that day. Her obvious hatred of him had baffled the man who had sought her out. Surely, Dottie had told her about him.

"Dottie and I worked together. We were in love."

Deirdre's coughing resumed and she put a tissue to her mouth. When she could speak, she had said, "Is that what you called it? In love? You raped her, you bastard!"

Schwartz's mind had reeled at the words.

"Raped? No…" He had searched for some way to make her understand. The only logical thing had come to him. "Maybe she told her husband that out of fear, but… No, we loved each other."

"She was so undone by your attack that she wound up killing herself. The shame became too much, finally. It happened a little over two years after you raped her. She'd have done it sooner, if it weren't for that bastard son of yours."

"Son?! Of *mine*?" Linus Schwartz had been caught completely off guard at the revelation. He stood up and paced with his hand to his forehead. When he returned to sit on the sofa, Dottie's older sister recoiled.

"She hated you more than she could deal with…"

Linus's mind was still racing. "That boy was mine!" he had exclaimed.

"How do you know about the boy?"

"The investigator I hired to find you told me," the visitor had lied.

"To make matters worse, that son of a bitch Marvin ran off. Never saw him again. Dropped your bastard son off at a church on his way out of town."

"It must've been Stovall's son. Dottie and I only made love the one time."

Deirdre was enraged. Even in her weakened condition that day, she pounded her frail fists on Schwartz.

"Stop referring to it like that. Stop making it sound like she wanted to!"

The sister had screamed until her voice wouldn't cooperate. Finally, she had been able to speak again.

"Marvin couldn't have kids. They had tried forever, and Dorothy never got pregnant. They had quit trying and the sadness of it all... they just never had relations anymore. Then she gets pregnant, so apparently the issue was his. And the boy could only have been yours. You ruined her life. You ruined Marvin's life, I suppose, if the drunk's even still alive. And you ruined my life."

Another coughing fit ensued.

"I had to raise the boy. He was a good enough kid, I guess. But I never got to marry and have my own kids." Linus Schwartz was hanging his head but raised it at the next words she spoke.

In a very quiet voice, Deirdre had said, "And now I'm dying. Can't be soon enough, I suppose."

Schwartz had started to speak, but the old woman continued.

"Please leave now. I can't take any more of this... of you."

The man who had just found out he was a father had gazed at a broken, worn out woman before taking his leave. On his way out to his driver, thoughts had besieged him – thoughts of an unknown son; the crushing truth about Dottie's suicide; the revelation that she didn't love him and had lied and said he raped her.

It had been too much to bear. He had remained silent all the miles back home.

And now, as he sat in the dark of his townhouse, consumed by the ghosts of his past, Schwartz held the picture of his son against his chest, laid his head on his pillow, and struggled to sleep away the memories.

CHAPTER 11

Josh had decided the information he had for Maggie wasn't of the type that he could deliver over the phone. He had lingered at the hospital for a short while, questioning doctors and nurses unsuccessfully about the circumstances of Trent's death. None would violate the confidentiality their positions demanded.

Finally, Morgan drove to The Four Seasons Hotel and made his way to the suite where Trent and Alicia – rather, where Alicia was staying. He put on his best game face, sitting with Alicia, Emma, Dr. Murray, and also Sir Albert McGinnis, who had flown from London and had driven straight to the hotel to see Alicia.

Morgan would've liked to visit with Sir Albert some, but that would have to wait. After he felt he had spent enough time visiting with everyone, he approached his fiancée.

"Maggie, would you come with me, please?"

The fiancé and fiancée moved to the bedroom where Maggie had stayed a couple of nights while Josh was in Russia trying to stop a showdown between his country and that one.

Maggie wasn't alarmed when Josh asked her to sit down on the bed. She figured it would be additional news about their friend's death. But when he sighed deeply and took her hands as he sat beside her, she knew it was something else.

"Josh?"

"Sweetheart, Curtis Jones was in a car wreck."

Maggie's hands raised to her mouth at the thought of her assistant at her public relations agency in Jackson being injured, or worse. Jones was the man she had left in charge when she moved to work at the White House.

"Is he…?" Her words stalled at the news of yet another tragedy hitting so close to home.

"No, sweetheart, he's alive, but he's in very bad shape. Tag called me earlier with the news."

The two sat in complete silence. Josh held Maggie and waited while she calmed down.

"It was a one car wreck. And he was the only one in his car."

"But Curtis is alive?"

"Remarkably. His car went over a – well, basically, a cliff. Tag doesn't know how he survived. The embankment was steep, though not a vertical drop-off. It appears some trees may have slowed the car down. In fact, two large trees, side-by-side, completely stopped it. It was sitting pretty precariously, according to Tag. If it gave way, it would've dropped another ninety feet – straight down."

Morgan gave Maggie time to speak. When she didn't, he resumed.

"What about family?" he asked.

"Curtis has no immediate family left. He had no siblings. Both his parents are dead. He only has some cousins that he's not close to at all. That's why I'm his emergency contact. I guess he didn't change it when I moved here."

"Maggie, sweetheart, there's more." Josh took another deep breath to gain some resolve. "It appears alcohol was involved."

A pair of blue eyes moved toward Morgan's.

"Alcohol?"

"Yes. The smell on his breath was obvious. There was a half empty bottle of…"

"Curtis doesn't drink."

"Well, Maggie, maybe not normally, but it appears…"

The auburn hair bounced as she shook her head.

"Curtis does *not* drink." She was adamant. "His dad was an alcoholic. He was abusive to Curtis' mom. He'd disappear for days at a time. He was driving one night – drunk – and ran into a stalled semi. It killed Curtis' mom. His dad lasted a day or two before he died, too."

Maggie shook her head again.

"No. Curtis was practically an evangelist about it."

"Sweetheart, maybe he had a drink for some reason and, since he didn't drink much, he couldn't handle it and dozed…"

"Dammit, Morgan. Curtis doesn't drink – *at all!*" She pounded Josh's chest and began to cry again. Morgan pulled her close. He had no idea what to say, but he believed her.

"There's more to this. I don't know what it is," she said through the lessening sobs. "He might've lost control, fallen asleep – I don't know. Something else. But he wasn't only not drinking and driving. He *wasn't* drinking."

Morgan had always liked Curtis. It was mostly because he was such a great friend to Maggie, but he was friendly, funny, and one of the bravest people Morgan knew. He was never anything less than who he was, and

115

never aspired to be more or different.

Maggie's agency couldn't have been in better hands than Curtis'. She would've never considered leaving Jackson Hole for any reason if she weren't confident that Image Quest would go on without missing a beat.

"Hmmm...," Morgan realized. "What's she gonna do about her business now?" He had been so caught up in the emotion of the day that most practical matters were pushed to the background. But Image Quest was Maggie's baby. The kinds of clients she had, which included politicians, made for a conflict of interest if she were to maintain even minimal involvement while she was serving in the White House Press Department.

Morgan would've liked for his fiancée to be able to save the decision for some point way down the road, but it was going to require an immediate answer. Curtis had only two on his staff, and while capable assistants, neither was of the caliber to run the place.

"I can wait to broach the subject with Maggie," he thought.

For now, Morgan held Maggie close until she fell asleep.

◆

Emma and her sister, the former First Lady of the U.S. and now widowed, sat at the dining table in the Four Seasons suite. Inside, along with Sir Albert, Larry Murray MD, Maggie, and Morgan, were Jack Johnston and Jeff Coulter. The Secret Service protectors were uncharacteristically sitting. In light of the determinations surrounding their protectee's death, other agents had shown up, not only to beef up Mrs. Weston's detail, but also to begin the process of interviewing and debriefing. That process included discussions with the two primary agents assigned to the Westons.

An additional agent stood by the front door of the suite. Two others were just outside in the hallway. A dozen or so were positioned throughout the hotel grounds. FBI personnel mirrored each of the locations.

Secret Service Director Keith Cortland was present, although, after offering his sympathies to Mrs. Weston, he had remained largely in the background, and on the phone.

It was the interviewers who had been front and center. However intrusive their presence, a former President had died, and the death was believed to be an assassination. The investigation couldn't wait. The questioners operated in pairs, one representative from the Secret Service and one from the FBI.

The deceased President's wife was first in the round of questions. The interviewer had been apologetic and as respectful as possible. Mrs. Weston had, of course, been very understanding of the necessity and was as forthcoming as she could be. The interviewer asked her and wrote down the answers to the same questions being asked of Johnston, Coulter, and every other person who had been near Weston in the last few days. Morgan and Maggie would get their turn.

The questions ran the gamut of locations, activities, and encounters. Where have you been lately? What and where have you eaten? Has anyone behaved suspiciously in your presence – overly aggressive, demanding of the President's attention? Had there been any physical contact that was unexpected – intentional or accidental? The queries were comprehensive.

The FBI agent interviewing Alicia Weston had expedited the process as much as possible without sacrificing thoroughness. She had left the ex-First Lady with another expression of sympathy and a request – though it really wasn't one – to interview her again the next day. Then she moved on to the next person, whom she would subject to the same line of questioning.

All of the Secret Service and FBI agents conducting the interviews were as efficient as they could be, but it was – and would be – a long process.

Morgan had left Maggie sleeping in the next room and was chatting with Sir Albert McGinnis. He had been part of the "rogue" team that also included Trent Weston, that had initiated the operation to intervene in the U.S.-Russia conflict. Each tried to speak about anything other than their friend, the pain of his passing was so raw, but they found themselves returning automatically to Trenton Weston.

Each had a uniquely personal bond with the man. The Brit had met the former President when he was CIA Director. Their relationship was purely professional until after Weston had left the Agency but before he had been voted into the White House. During that time, the two became fast friends.

Morgan had popped up on his friend's radar while he was President due to the young CIA officer's role in implementing and then preventing the assassination plot in Terrador. Weston had taken an interest in Morgan for the personal consequences he had suffered from the fallout. He had looked out for the man behind the scenes ever since. And when Morgan had saved Weston from the Saudi operative Al-Majeed, the two men forged a friendship that was at once like father-son and best of friends.

Josh Morgan and Sir Albert McGinnis had known their mutual friends from very different perspectives, but they agreed that he was a great man.

◆

Linus Schwartz had been in and out of bed since 8:30 PM. His restlessness, he knew, was because the day was the anniversary of the one on which he had found out about his son.

The wealthy businessman had made the decision almost immediately after learning about his illegitimate child to never confront him. The boy was already well into adulthood and Schwartz had decided he didn't need the complications that would come with learning that his supposed father wasn't the one who had apparently deserted him. Rather, his was a father he never knew existed.

The real father wondered at the time if that wouldn't be worse. Besides, the boy had prospered both personally and professionally, having served in the military and then risen through the ranks in his chosen profession. By all accounts, he was a fine man, honorable and giving. He was a man of faith. No, Schwartz had decided, it would be too much of a blow to intrude on the man's life.

However, buried deep in the psyche of Linus Schwartz were the two real reasons he had decided to never try to connect with his son: He was afraid of being rejected, for one thing. But the other reason was one that the father had only briefly considered before suppressing it. It was that meeting him would always remind him that the boy's mother had apparently not loved Linus and had even characterized their act of love as rape.

Over time, the billionaire had come to regret the decision, and was on the verge of reconsidering it. Perhaps it was that he himself was becoming a very old man. Or maybe meeting the grown-up boy might help him come to terms with the truth as it related to Dottie Stovall.

But the opportunity vanished forever when Schwartz lost his son. In much the same way as loving and losing his mother, it had shaped his life. And in the way strangling her husband had impacted his view toward anything that stood in his way, losing the man who was his child had further deepened the soulless man's resolve to destroy anything he hated.

When he had lost his son, he had developed a hatred for the world. That perspective was leading him to certain actions now. He cared little for what the consequences might be for himself, especially at his advanced age. And he really had no other person for whom his life mattered.

Schwartz had always kept a close eye on his adult son and even intervened on his behalf from time to time. He had worked to move him along professionally and to enrich him anonymously through projects the son initiated. The aging billionaire had considered reaching out to his dead child's wife and children but decided against it. It might prove too hurtful. Or worse, he might discover that, absent his son as an intermediary, he really cared nothing for them at all.

So, Schwartz only observed them from afar. They didn't deserve his riches when he died. What had they done for him? Schwartz had secretly set up a fund for the children's education, and that, he thought, was more than enough.

When Dottie's sister had told Linus of his son, she had called him his "bastard son." Yet she had raised the boy, sacrificing much, it appeared. She had even changed the boy's last name to her own, partly to shield him from the stigma of his mother's suicide and his father's desertion. It was a small town, and everyone knew.

When the woman had told the boy's father that he had ruined her life, he had dismissed it. For, beyond not caring a whit about her misfortune, Linus Schwartz believed that in many ways, Deirdre Blake had ruined his life, too.

In some ways, he wished he'd never learned of Everson's existence.

CHAPTER 12

Day 6 – Friday

The office of the District Attorney for the District of Columbia was abuzz with gossip. There were two MIAs. Siobhan Cassidy hadn't been to work since Tuesday. Ostensibly, she was sick. At least that's what Riley Maxwell had said. But now he was a no-show himself.

The "out sick" story was a bit suspect to begin with

A co-worker of Cassidy's had gone into the woman's office for a file and had noticed that some of her personal belongings were missing from her desk. Why would she have removed them? Did she somehow know in advance that she would be out of work for some extended period of time?

Riley Maxwell was a flirt. Most thought it was harmless and didn't quite reach the level that warranted reporting, although everyone who had eyes saw that he appeared to be especially friendly toward his Irish assistant. Those eyes also told everyone that Siobhan disliked the man intensely. At least that was how it appeared. Was it a front? After all, they were both AWOL.

◆

Metropolitan Police Detective Dillon Howard was called to the crime scene before he ever made it to the station. In most cases, knowing either a victim or a perpetrator would result in a police officer being removed from a case. However, in this instance, it would be difficult to find a local law enforcement official who didn't know the deceased, who appeared to be both a victim and a perp.

The body of U.S. District Attorney Riley Maxwell was found by a jogger at 8:00 AM. While there would be a formal autopsy by the medical examiner, the cause of death seemed pretty obvious. There was a single gunshot wound in his chin that took a substantial portion of the top of his head as it exited. There was a Smith & Wesson .38 Special in his hand. A single typed note beside the dead attorney said only, "I'm sorry."

The other element in the scene that was blatantly obvious was the disturbed dirt of a shallow grave. The female body found in it hadn't been dead very long. Crime Scene Investigators were about to complete their examination of the body when Detective Howard arrived on the scene. The police investigator had been informed during his drive to the site that the male corpse was the D.C. District Attorney, but that the female victim had yet to be identified. So, while prepared for the sight of Maxwell's body, he wasn't prepared for what he would be the first to recognize.

"Oh, damn," he said as the woman's corpse was lifted out of the eighteen-inch deep hole in the ground and onto an open body bag. "Dammit to hell."

The police investigator turned away and stroked his chin.

♦

Across town, Federal Judge Byron Caldwell sat in his easy chair at his stylish apartment. He was another no-show for work that morning. Both his landline phone and his mobile had rung incessantly until he ripped the cord of the first out of the wall and turned the second off. He had been due for a very early meeting with his staff and other judicial personnel to discuss his upcoming retirement. His departure had been accelerated due to the intervention of POTUS into what would have been his final trial. With the dismissal of the case on the basis of Hendrickson's pardon of Joshua Morgan, he was, for all intents and purposes, done. The calls were no doubt from the myriad of individuals with whom he was supposed to meet.

The judge looked down at the photos in his hands. They bore the graphic evidence of the deeds that had dragged him into the chaos he was in. After a few decades in honorable service to the citizens of the United States in matters occurring in the District of Columbia or having federal jurisdiction, Caldwell had been undone by the threat of exposure of his dalliances with young boys. It was hardly an appropriate word for sex with underage males, but it was how he saw it. His sexual preference had been rumored for a number of years, but people neither spoke of it nor cared. It simply didn't matter in the place where he lived. Both conservatives and liberals admired the fairness and dignity with which he presided over legal matters. So, they ignored the stories.

Caldwell looked again at the photos and let out a forlorn sigh. He dabbed at the tears that had thus far remained balanced on his lids. The disturbance by the tissue loosened them and they began to trickle down his cheek faster than he could stifle them.

The existence of the photos had been the leverage that ensured his cooperation in the trial of the *United States of America v. Joshua M Morgan*. He would guarantee that it would drag out. He would rule every significant dispute, every objection in the prosecution's favor. The outcome wasn't as important, the extorters had told the judge, as that it created as much torment for the accused as possible. When the White House had intervened, it wasn't only the outcome that was snatched completely out of his hands. The means to comply with his blackmailers vanished, too. Caldwell feared that they would publicize the photos then and there. But the takers of the photos appeared to hold someone else to blame. He didn't know who. Yet, they had made other demands of the judge. They had commanded that he delay his retirement in order to assist with other matters that might come before him.

The man headed to his bathroom tub and turned on the faucet; only the "C" handle. He had heard that cold water made these things easier.

♦

Detective Dillon Howard turned back to the Medical Examiner, who had stood from attending to the female's body.

"What is it, Dillon?" enquired Oliver Wood. "You know her?"

"Yeah. Siobhan Cassidy. That's Maxwell's assistant."

"The hell you say!"

"'Fraid so."

The two men stared silently at the body and shook their respective heads in unison.

"The hell you say," ME Wood restated, more quietly.

This time the detective only nodded.

"Damn," the examiner said, followed by, "Whew."

"How'd she die, Oliver?"

"Strangulation. Or a blow to the head. We'll do a thorough exam to make sure there aren't any other factors involved in her murder…"

Howard shuddered at the word, though he already knew that's what it had to be.

"There's no doubt she was choked. Ant the trauma to the head is obvious. I just need to figure out which was first." The ME handed a plastic evidence bag to Howard. "The head trauma appears to be a perfect match to this."

Inside the bag was a crystal award. It was in roughly the shape of a downward-facing arrowhead, heavy, and had a large wooden base. The left point of the "rear" of the arrowhead was broken off, though it, too, was in the bag.

"It was in the ground with her."

"Odd. So, what do you think, Oliver?"

The examiner knelt to point to the woman's head. The police detective leaned over and placed his hands on his knees.

Holding the detached piece of glass near the body's head, and the main section of the award – both still in the bag – near it to show how it would've fit together, the ME said, "This is how the blow would've landed. This is very heavy glass, so it did a lot of damage. It took a lot of force to break it off. But here's the other part," he continued, withdrawing the clear container holding the pieces of the crystal award.

"There's a lot of blood on her head and on the award. Most likely it wouldn't have bled this much if she were already deceased. It's entirely possible that the extent of the damage to her skull and brain could've resulted in her death anyhow, but…" The Medical Examiner used his free hand to push himself into a kneel, and then stood.

Dr. Wood handed the evidence bag to Howard and wiped the dirt from his gloves.

"…but I think the blow disabled Ms. Cassidy. The strangulation was the *coup de gras*. You know, to make sure she didn't get up."

Detective Howard examined the award through its clear container. He pressed the plastic flat over the engraved plate on its front to read the words.

"'Young Professional of the Year.'"

"Helluva thing," the ME said in agreement with the detective's unspoken assessment.

"Yeah. Shit."

♦

While he waited for cold water to fill his tub, Judge Caldwell had lit a fire in the fireplace in his bedroom. Laying the stack of photos on top of the fake, ceramic logs, he ignited the flow of natural gas. The jurist was hopeful that his blackmailer would see no point in exposing his transgressions after – well, after he had done what he was going to. The prints had been used as "motivation" to convince the judge to throw away his honor and succumb to the demands. Without them as proof of his involvement, Caldwell felt the matter would never be known. People, he hoped, would assume he ended his life because of his impending retirement. Whatever they thought, he knew he couldn't live with the threat of disclosure hanging over his head.

Once the salacious prints had begun to take flame, he undressed and laid his clothes on his bed, folding them nicely, and moved to his bathroom. He lifted his right leg over the edge of the antique bathtub. He flinched at the coolness of the liquid but forced himself to bring the left leg over to join it. He felt a significant chill as he lowered his butt into the water. Caldwell slid his rear to the middle of the tub and laid his torso backward against the end.

The judge lowered both hands into the water to let them chill. He had no idea how long to wait, so he left them submerged for a few minutes. While his extremities grew somewhat numb, he closed his eyes to contemplate his life. He reconsidered his past only momentarily before he opened his eyes, placed the kitchen knife in line with his wrist, and pulled backward. The sudden spurt of blood surprised him, and he found himself watching the flow of red liquid with some sense of detachment. He placed the knife's blade over his other wrist. This time, he closed his eyes before making the slice.

With both wrists bleeding freely, Byron Caldwell lay for a few minutes until he felt lightheaded. He was horrified when his thoughts suddenly turned to the stories of people who tried to take their lives in this way but survived.

The man opened his eyes in a start and was immediately aghast at the sight of his blood mixing with the water around him, turning his skin a pinkish hue. He decided to reclose his eyes, but he caught sight of his bedroom fireplace. The fire was still aflame, but he saw that a small number of the damning photos had slid off the pile he had placed on the fake logs.

Caldwell panicked. The increase in his heart rate accelerated the flow of his life's blood. He stood and lifted his left leg to exit the tub and return the pictures to the flames. Weakened by the loss of blood, Judge Caldwell fell to the floor. Determined, the man tried to crawl to replace the photographs. He made it only about ten feet before he passed out, never to awaken. The final trickle of blood left a streaked trail, smeared by his legs as he pulled himself along. The last sound he heard was the doorbell to his townhouse.

◆

Throughout the nation, flags were flying at half-mast for Former President of the United States Trenton Weston. He was well-regarded while he was in the White House, but he was adored in the recent two years. Though the public knew very few of the details of the past Chief Executive's abduction by Saudi operative Fadi Al-Majeed, the episode put Weston squarely in the spotlight. The entire world saw the resolve, the courage, and the graciousness of the man. After the ordeal, his approval ratings were higher than for any current or former elected official.

That Weston's death was almost without a doubt an assassination was withheld from the public. The "official" cause of death, for the time being, was a stroke. Undoubtedly, bystanders in the hallway outside the courtroom where Weston collapsed would all attest to that as the event that killed him. It was remarkable to all in the Weston circle of family and friends, and even more so to government officials, that the story seemed to be holding. No leaks to the news outlets; no slips of the tongue by people in the know; not one word had gotten out to the contrary that a cerebrovascular accident had caused Trent Weston's death.

At the Washington, D.C. Four Seasons, Alicia Weston was alone. There were still a number of people with her – her sister, Trent's personal doctor, Larry Murray, and Josh and Maggie, but she was utterly alone in the fog that surrounded a person when they'd lost their spouse of decades.

Morgan watched his newly widowed friend from a short distance away, giving her space to reflect and mourn. The sight of her broke his heart in a way equal to the loss of Trent. The strong, courageous spirit still dwelt within her, he was sure, but physically, she appeared fragile. Her posture lacked the uprightness it always had. And when she was able to persuade her lips to smile, her eyes lacked their characteristic twinkle.

He anguished as Alicia Weston busied herself in trying to attend to everyone, offering coffee and the breakfast pastries and fruit that had been brought up by room service over her objections. The woman had insisted she make breakfast, but Special Agent Johnston, in a rare display of the affection he felt for the couple, took her by the shoulders and moved her to the couch.

At that point, the former First Lady broke down again and laid her head against her protector. While she sobbed in his arms, Johnston gave his partner a look of uncertainty about the situation he found himself in. Secret Service Agent Coulter responded with a reassuring nod of the head. Both his and Jack Johnston's eyes glistened with the potential of tears that they were struggling to contain.

However, after the brief breakdown and once the breakfast items had been delivered, Alicia Weston was up and about again, alternating between moments of tending to her friends and times of solitary reflection. Everyone had reached the same conclusion. The busyness was how she was dealing with the deluge of emotions.

Because of Weston's position as a past POTUS, details of his funeral and related memorial activities had been worked out well in advance of his death. However, the actual implementation of the broader plan was still an undertaking of some magnitude. The officials in charge presented the former First Lady many details but took care of most of the arrangements unilaterally.

Morgan watched Alicia from his place at the dining table in the suite. From across the room, Maggie motioned her request that he join her. Josh followed his fiancée into the privacy of the extra bedroom.

Maggie put her phone away and sat on the edge of the bed.

"That was Tag."

Teton County Sheriff's Deputy Scott Taggart had allowed Morgan to break the news gently to Maggie about the car crash involving her assistant and friend, Curtis Jones. Maggie had called Tag directly this morning to get an update.

"And?"

Maggie rose and placed her arms around Josh.

"It's still touch and go, and…" She leaned away to look Morgan in the eyes. "Josh, they amputated Curtis' leg – his left one, I think."

Morgan was amazed that Maggie, who was so tender about the slightest things, was able to keep her tears in check. Perhaps she was simply "cried out," he speculated.

The couple remained locked in their hold of one another, until Morgan, hands on each of Maggie's shoulders, gently nudged her to arms' length where he could look her in the eyes.

"Curtis is still alive, Maggie. He's alive and that's what matters most." He lifted her chin until she was forced to look at him. "Right?"

She lowered her head, but Morgan lifted it lovingly back upward to regain eye contact.

"Right, sweetheart?" he reiterated.

Maggie's head bobbed slightly in agreement, and she rested her head on Morgan's chest.

◆

The suicides of two powerful legal officials in the District of Columbia's legal workings would've ordinarily been major news. But, in light of President Weston's death, the stories were in the second tier of journalistic disclosures this day. There was one man, however, for whom the deaths were of greater importance.

Billionaire Linus Schwartz sat at his desk, elbows on its surface and his fingers interlaced beneath his chin.

"This is an unfortunate complication."

"Yes, sir. It is," agreed Oskar Lammers, the man's fixer.

"Granted, there would possibly have come a time when we needed to tend to Judge Caldwell, but his own deed so close to your attending to Mr. Maxwell…" Schwartz considered where the scenario might lead; the suicides of two men who were not only prominent in the legal affairs of the District, but who were involved in the same case involving Mr. Morgan.

"Your delivery of the photos we had told him we possessed was only meant to reinforce the leverage we had on him. This was never the intended result. And regarding Mr. Maxwell, I assume there will be no evidence to suggest that the District Attorney's death was anything other than a suicide…"

Schwartz's troubleshooter's face never registered his thought, but he was greatly offended.

"No, sir. There will be none."

Schwartz's elbows remained on the desk, but his fingers were busily tapping against themselves in front of his chest.

Lammers rarely offered unsolicited comments in his encounters with his boss, but he felt some reassurance was in order.

"Sir, I believe the investigators will have no reasonable alternative to the notion that the 'suicides' were merely coincidental – however uncomfortable such a conclusion may make them."

"Perhaps you're right, Mr. Lammers," Schwartz said as he looked past him into the distance where his thoughts lived. "Perhaps you're right," he repeated, though he wasn't sure the man was.

"Mr. Maxwell's blundering administration of his assignment with regard to Mr. Morgan obviated the need for his elimination," the CEO continued. "It demonstrated that he could no longer be trusted to fulfill his obligations to me. He had become a liability. But his treatment of his assistant…" Schwartz shook his head. "You just don't treat women like that."

Lammers had never heard the story from his boss about his sexual encounter with Dottie Stovall decades earlier. But even without that knowledge, he was familiar with the man's treatment of the objects of his carnal desires over the years. The awareness provoked a fleeting recognition of the hypocrisy of his employer's last comment.

"And the matter in Wyoming?" he finally asked his employee.

"Well, sir…" Lammers was tense, though his demeanor never betrayed the emotion. "That's another bit of unfortunate news."

Schwartz likewise repressed his feelings, though he was greatly distressed at the second instance of hearing the word "unfortunate" in a revelation of the results of his plan.

"Curtis Jones is still alive, sir."

Schwartz's eyes bore into his fixer's.

"My man there executed the plan flawlessly, but in an instance of ill fortune, Mr. Jones' car was slowed and finally stopped by trees as it fell from the cliff. The fall was near-vertical from the roadside, but…. I don't know what to say… Just bad luck, sir. He may yet die. But I would allow that the pain to his friend is about as great as his death would've caused."

Difficult as it was, the founder and CEO of Schwartz, Cannon, and Raines stood and paced behind his desk.

"And what of the Loughlin woman?"

"After I tended to Mr. Maxwell, I staked out the townhouse she shares with Mr. Morgan. He showed up alone, so I did nothing. He left a short while later with some belongings. I followed him back to the Four Seasons, where it appears, they stayed overnight."

Schwartz eased himself back into his seat at his desk.

"Do you have any confusion about my instructions, Mr. Lammers?"

"No," came the immediate response. "I understand fully. Just the people around Morgan... for now."

◆

"I don't know what to do, Morgan."

Josh said softly, "Go to Curtis. He has no family; nobody in his life right now. You're on a leave of absence from the White House anyhow because of my legal problems. I'm sure Ginnetti would be happy to extend it. You built up a lot of goodwill during the whole Russia thing. Babe, you're a rock star right now."

Maggie's irritation at her guy's levity in light of all that had transpired showed in the flash of her blue eyes toward him.

"I'm just saying that this is important. The Press Secretary and President Hendrickson will both understand. They'll both be supportive."

Maggie voiced her only concern. "It's not that. I just need to be here with Alicia. And the funeral... How can I miss Trent's funeral?"

"Mag, the service won't be for close to a week. Go to Jackson to be with Curtis. Once he improves..." Morgan knew that was unlikely. "...you can return for the funeral. Okay?"

Maggie nodded and offered a faint smile.

"Love you, Josh."

Morgan wanted to say something flippant, as he often did, but he only had it in him to say, "Love you, too."

◆

CIA Director Elizabeth Parnell soldiered on in her duties in spite of the grief she felt at the death of her friend, Trent Weston. She had people working with other agencies to determine the actors in his poisoning and the exact nature and source of the toxin used. But other work had to carry on. Before her were a stack of file folders containing all sorts of reports that she could have easily read on her computer. But she preferred paper documents.

She had been prepared to perjure herself on Josh Morgan's behalf, declaring that he was acting at her behest in his pursuit of Fadi Al-Majeed and the rescue of President Weston. She would've hated it, but she would've. The pardon by President Hendrickson was a welcome reprieve for her as well as Morgan. Despite their conflict during the tensions with Russia, Parnell had developed an immense respect for her commander-in-chief. The courage it took to intercede on Morgan's behalf only heightened the personal regard. The public would never know anything of the entire scenario in which Morgan was first accused of murder, and then of treason. But people on the Hill would know he'd been in some sort of trouble, and her involvement would cost POTUS a great deal politically.

So, while Morgan was in the clear as far as any legal jeopardy went, the Director of Central Intelligence worried at the lengths his adversaries would go to take him down. She poured over the reports regarding the reestablishment of the U.S. base in Terrador – a fact that Parnell had withheld from Morgan. For the life of her, she couldn't come up with any persons of interest who might be acting against Morgan.

The DCI had taken the somewhat unusual step of allowing her Station Chief in Terrador, Art Flynn, to correspond directly with personnel in other agencies. She didn't have reason to suspect Flynn of any involvement with the conspirators against Morgan. He'd had no connection with the fiasco in Terrador in which Morgan was a central figure. But Parnell hoped that the appearance of unfettered and seemingly unmonitored communication might provide the proverbial rope with which the bad guys would hang themselves. She, of course, surreptitiously scrutinized every iota of interaction.

Parnell read and re-read every word of the pile of reports. And still there was nothing. None of it helped her ID the culprits who were out to get Morgan. Zero. She even scoured the communications that the National Security Agency had provided her between all non-governmental entities, such as contractors, that were involved with the restoration of the Terradoran military base. Again, *nada*.

The DCI leaned back in her chair and rubbed her eyes.

"Who are you guys?" she wondered aloud.

CHAPTER 13

Maggie Loughlin dreaded sharing her decision with Alicia Weston. How could she tell her friend that she was leaving for a few days, in light of the personal tragedy she had suffered? As she walked into the living area of the Four Seasons suite, the former First Lady took notice of her and met her as she approached.

"Maggie, dear." Mrs. Weston affectionately brushed her younger friend's auburn hair aside. "Maggie, you need to go be with your friend in Jackson."

Maggie was speechless at the overture.

"Josh told me last night when he returned from gathering some of your things at your place. You need to go be with him."

Suddenly, the certainty of Maggie's decision to leave her friend and head to Wyoming vanished.

"Alicia, I don't think I can lea…"

"Nonsense, Maggie. You go. You and Josh. I'm fine. Well, I'm not fine, but I'm not alone. Go."

Josh answered for Maggie. "Here's the compromise, Alicia. Maggie, you go, as we discussed, but I'll stay here."

Mrs. Weston tried to object, but Morgan held a hand up. "No discussion, Alicia. I stay or we both stay. Trent means so much to us…" Morgan realized he should've said "meant."

"And you mean so much to us. We need to be around. What do you say, Mag?"

Maggie Loughlin turned to Alicia Weston. "I'll be back in time for the memorial. Okay?"

The former First Lady's answer was a hug. "You be safe, dear. I hope your friend is okay. I'll pray for him."

"Alicia, I'll be back in a bit. I'm going to take Maggie to get packed. If there's anything you need while I'm out, call." Morgan knew that with the

Westons' regular security detail augmented by other agents at Alicia's beck and call, his offer would add little to her support, but he meant it, just the same.

"Thanks, Josh. Go take care of Maggie. And if you decide you want to go with…"

Morgan shook a smiling head and raised his index finger to his lips. "Not another word, ma'am. The subject is closed."

Josh and Maggie left for their home.

♦

Josh and Maggie's apartment was in The Wharf development not far from the West Wing of the White House, where Maggie worked. On the drive to their apartment, Maggie called her boss. White House Press Secretary Marie Ginnetti was more supportive than Maggie could've hoped.

As the couple reached their home, Maggie's phone rang. She recognized the private number and was concerned. President Hendrickson had called her personally a handful of times and each call was a pleasant one. But Maggie feared POTUS was going to raise some objection to her leaving for Wyoming.

"Yes, Madam President. How can I help you?"

"Good morning, Maggie. Secretary Ginnetti told me of your plans to go home to be with your business associate."

Maggie braced herself for the "but" that she was certain would follow.

Instead, "You take as much time as you need. I'm going to have Chief Chandler arrange a private fight for you."

"That's very kind, ma'am." Maggie looked at Morgan and arched her eyebrows. He was curious.

"Ma'am, I can't have the taxpayers foot the bill for…"

"They might not have to. I'll explain later. But even if they have to, for right now, I say, the hell with it. In view of the circumstances surrounding President Weston's death, we are, as you know, in a heightened state of security. Normally, an assistant to a Secretary wouldn't be afforded support or Secret Service protection for such a trip, but your high profile during the standoff with the Russians warrants it.

"Get ready for travel. And expect a call from Noah. You have a safe trip, Maggie, and don't worry about things here."

"Yes, ma'am. Thank you, Madam President." She disconnected the call and related all to Morgan.

"I told you that you were a rock star." This time his fiancée didn't mind the reference.

◆

Outside the apartment complex, the man in the nondescript dark sedan watched a black SUV park near the front entry. An apartment security guard approached to redirect the vehicle to a parking spot but reconsidered when a woman stepped from the passenger side and produced some sort of credentials that stopped him in his tracks.

As the guard stepped back a few paces, the driver of the SUV stepped out. Secret Service Agent Mac Marchman surveyed the area through his dark sunglasses, while his partner, Joy Griffith, put away her ID and opened the back door. Josh Morgan stepped out first and took the arm of Maggie Loughlin as she followed him to the entrance of the building.

Agent Marchman started the SUV's alternating red and blue flashing lights. He took a position beside the door to the apartments. The combination of the flashing lights and the imposing man should provide an intimidating deterrent to anyone who might want to intrude.

Agent Griffith escorted the couple to their townhouse

The development posed a dilemma for the sole observer in the dark sedan. He needed to leave. Doing so immediately might make him stand out among the handful of people who watched with curiosity and snapped photos with their phones. However, delaying his departure would provide more time for the agent standing guard by the door to fully take in his surroundings and make mental notes of every person and thing nearby.

"*Scheisse!*" came the muted, accented expletive.

◆

At his desk in the West Wing, the President's Chief of Staff Noah Chandler hung up his phone after completing his instructions to his secretary.

Among the resources available to the more prominent and powerful people in Washington were individuals in search of connections to that power. They often provided services to the power brokers, things that they hoped would buy them influence.

At Chandler's direction, his secretary had created a communication to a limited, but highly select, distribution list. A message to her boss confirmed that the request had been sent out. She hoped to have replies soon. The problem was that favors to the White House, in particular, couldn't appear to be performed solely for the benefit of the administration. They had to be in conjunction with something the patron was doing anyhow. For example, when a request for transportation was made, the obliging individual had to have been going to the specific destination anyhow. So, the government official accompanying them was essentially just hitching a ride.

Chandler knew that this request was unlikely to get any takers. He was unusually adept at spotting fabrications that people made up to justify providing a favor to his boss. And he was especially protective of POTUS with regard to the integrity of her office. Hendrickson was the first President in recent memory whose administration was scandal-free. Of course, the public was unaware that her being emotionally compromised nearly led to a nuclear attack on the Russian Federation.

So, knowing that the chance that he would find a ride for Maggie to the Jackson Hole Airport in Wyoming was miniscule, Chandler also had his secretary check the availability of small jets in the government's fleet.

◆

Personal Assistant Dexter Leach knocked lightly on his boss' door and entered when summoned.

"Sir, I believe you might be interested in this."

Linus Schwartz placed his glasses over his pale gray eyes and scanned the document. The man never smiled, at least not big ones, and only when in public to bolster an inaccurate image of himself as a friendly, benevolent man. So, for him, the presence of the barely present twinkle in his eyes was tantamount to an explosion of riotous laughter.

"Now *this* is the first stroke of good fortune that has happened for me. Mr. Leach, call Noah Chandler. Wait, never mind. I'll call him myself."

Knowing that to be his cue to leave, the billionaire's aide headed for the door.

"Well done, Mr. Leach."

◆

In the first few moments after taking up his position aside the door leading into the apartment building where Josh Morgan and Maggie Loughlin lived, Secret Service Agent Mac Marchman had taken in his surroundings – vehicles, people, anything that looked out of place. He was trained to be attentive and perceptive. However, in addition to that, one thing that was incumbent upon all agents in the employ of the Secret Service was a gut that told them, without any foundation or basis in fact, that something was significant. So, when the plain passenger automobile pulled away, it was only Marchman's intuition that led him to lift his phone and fire off a burst of photos that captured everything from the sedan itself to its license tags.

The agent couldn't get a photo of the driver, whose face was obscured by his left hand and the phone it was holding. The man behind the automobile's wheel seemed totally uninterested in the arrival of two agents of the U.S. Secret Service. That only served to amplify the tingling in Marchman's gut that he should take notice. He transmitted the photos to his office with a request to get the details on the ownership of the car and, if possible, anyone who might be driving it.

◆

"Noah. Linus Schwartz."

Noah Chandler took the call off speaker and held the phone to his ear. "Linus, how the hell are you?"

Chandler knew the billionaire to be a generous contributor to his boss' campaign war chest. However, he wasn't naïve. He knew the CEO of the construction company that had ties to all sorts of government projects hedged his bets, as most did, by contributing to the "other side," as well.

"Good, Noah. I'm good. How're things at 1600 Pennsylvania Avenue?"

There was some chit-chat of the sort not used by good friends, but more accurately, the type of men of like situation who owned and lived power. After a few exchanges about golf, sports, and the near-misses of the assassination attempts on President Hendrickson and the almost-war with Russia, the caller got to the point.

"I understand someone needs a lift to Wyoming."

Chandler was suddenly in verification mode. "Linus, you can't tell me you just happen to have a plane going there." He smiled, but it was a serious enquiry.

"I do. I swear. I've had one of my people out in Jackson Hole scouting a location for a summer home. I'm thinking of retiring and need a tranquil, beautiful place to park my weary body."

"You know you'll never retire," Chandler laughed. "So, your plane is heading out there anyhow?"

"It is. But if you'd rather not…"

"No, no. A ride would be most helpful."

The request said the passenger is… let's see…," Schwartz pretended to fumble around for the name.

"Maggie Loughlin," the Chief of Staff assisted,

"Ah, yes. Isn't that the young lady I saw on TV during all the attacks on your boss and the Russia mess?"

"Yes, that's her."

"Seems like a remarkable young woman. What's her reason for leaving Washington?"

"It's just for a few days. She's from Wyoming and has some personal matters to attend to."

"Just the one passenger?"

"Just her."

"And only one-way? I'd be happy to send my plane back for her."

"I couldn't ask you to do that, Linus. That's stepping over the line a bit. So, yes. Just one-way."

"Well, I'm happy to help, if you want it."

"Of course, my friend. You know I'll need to vet the pilot, attendants; anyone who might come into contact with Deputy Secretary Loughlin, or be involved with the flight in any way?"

"Already done. These are people I've used in the conduct of my business affairs, including those fulfilling government contracts. I'll have Mr. Leach provide their names to your secretary so that she can access their profiles."

There was additional small talk before the businessman and the right-hand man to the President concluded their call. Schwartz's smile was, for him, huge, but instead of a joyous countenance, the crease in his face was more ominous.

The billionaire had no concerns for the people that the White House would vet. Dexter Leach had long since been the subject of a thorough background check because of his association with a man who was involved in sensitive government contracts. So had Oskar Lammers. He'd had a few blips that caused some mild anguish among the interviewers. But in light of his role as security for Linus Schwartz, the vetting officials decided a few incidents might be expected. Lammers had been passed, as well. The vetting staffers didn't know that he had committed the most serious of his transgressions in the years after his initial background check. Those had escaped the attention of the interviewers in their regular updates of his profile.

Schwartz would rely on the services of assistants to his assistants for a couple of days. He knew he would be just fine.

♦

"Hinky?" said Agent Marchman. "What do you mean, it's 'hinky?'"

The agent at the office said, "Well, the car you asked about is registered to a company that is held by another company that is held by another company that I can't find any real information about. I'm still looking, Mac, but the whole thing is…"

"I know. 'Hinky.' Well let me know if you dig up anything. Probably nothing anyhow. Thanks, Doug."

As one agent ended his phone call, the other returned with Josh and Maggie in tow.

"Everything good?" asked Agent Griffith.

"Golden."

"Well, pard, we're taking these two to Reagan National so Ms. Loughlin can catch a private jet."

"Just her? Alone?"

"That's the word. Some corporate bigshot just happened to have a plane going to Wyoming to pick up one of his employees. He offered to let our protectee here tag along. He's apparently known to just about everybody in Washington. Word is he's trustworthy. Plane drops her off, picks up their guy, and heads home So, except for Ms. Loughlin, it's a round trip."

"Round trip?" Morgan's ears perked up. "Well, that changes things."

The quartet took their respective seats in the agency SUV and started for Ronald Reagan Washington National Airport.

◆

It was early afternoon in Terradora, the only city on the island of Terrador. Station Chief Flynn picked up his phone and looked at the display. "Hmmm," he muttered. He pressed the icon to connect.

"Director Parnell, good to hear from you. How are things inside the Beltway?"

"Fine, Art. Question, What's your relationship with Crawford?"

"Wilf Crawford? My NSA F6? It's good."

"Let me rephrase. What's your level of trust of him?"

Flynn thought a moment about why the DCI would be asking, but knew if he needed to know, she'd tell him.

"He's NSA, so, of course, I don't trust him one bit. But he is my friend."

"I'll get back to you." Then there was silence.

"Goodbye, Director. And thanks for calling," Flynn said to a disconnected line. He tapped a name in his Contacts.

"Wilf, let's grab a drink." He listened to the reply. "C'mon, man, it's 1:30. We can get lunch, too. Then we're not just going out drinking. Great. I'll head that way. See you in five."

Wilfred Lane Crawford was actually an NSA counterpart to one of the officers who reported to Flynn. With Seth Tierney, the two men formed a special joint unit of the Central Intelligence and National Security Agencies called the Special Collection Service. Codenamed F6, the service's teams are on the front lines of foreign espionage. Their primary task is to infiltrate high value hard targets to plant the most technologically advanced surveillance devices in the world. The data collections are transmitted to the NSA for intensive analysis.

The cooperative effort between the two spy agencies had successfully gathered intelligence from targets ranging from al Qaeda training camps to presidential headquarters in countries throughout the world. And with operations ramping up in Terrador, the SCS determined the need for an F6 team there. They would deploy into Latin America to surveil a variety of targets, from governmental offices to drug trafficking operations. Since Crawford had arrived a few weeks before Tierney, he and Flynn worked to lay the groundwork for the future partnership. The two became friends and often socialized together in the limited venues of Terradora.

Flynn was in the dark as to the nature of the Director's call. Perhaps, he thought, he could get some info from the other side of the coin.

The duo drove from the embassy in one of the base's Chevy Tahoes. Though everyone in the restaurant would realize the two Americans were involved with the revitalization of the military base, the Tahoe made them, if not less conspicuous, at least less threatening than they would've been had they driven one of the military Joint Light Tactical Vehicles. The replacement to the fabled Humvee was a formidable-looking transport with a distinctively military appearance.

"*Aclamaciones!*"

"Cheers to you, too, Wilf."

Tejas en Terrador was one of the favorite hangouts of expatriates on Terrador. But, despite its name, there was nothing "Texas" about the cuisine. At least, neither man could imagine that it was. Neither had been to Texas. The supposed "Tex-Mex" was more along the lines of native Latin food. However, the cheeseburgers were surprisingly close in taste to the American counterparts. But like all diners at *Tejas en Terrador*, Flynn and Tierney tried not to think about what the meat labeled "beef" on the menu might really be.

Just as Flynn started, "Have you...," Crawford began with, "I've been meaning..." Both of the friends started over, with the same result. Each man's attempt to speak interfered with the other.

"You go first," Flynn insisted.

Crawford leaned in a little closer. "Have you noticed how things are a little screwy right now? I've been getting requests from higher-ups at CIA for direct reporting. And I know you've been getting the same from NSA. Communication with our counterparts directly? What gives?"

Flynn wondered if his friend was as perplexed as he was, or if he was more in the loop than he was letting on and fishing for information to see what Flynn knew.

"I was gonna ask you the same thing, pal. Might be just a case of trying to expedite some things. You know, the old mantra of 'interagency cooperation' that never really happens."

"Yeah. Or the agencies are just getting tired of the BS of trying to abide by the proper channels," Crawford wondered.

Flynn decided his friend was as in the dark as he was. Contrary to the stereotypes, intelligence officers often told their friends things they weren't supposed to, especially if those friends were also operatives. They always rationalized it with the simple fact that each had the same clearances.

"Wilf, have any of your chiefs made any inquiries about me?"

The answer was a prolonged, "Nooo," as the NSA agent realized why his friend was asking. "But I'm betting some of your higher-ups have about me. Right?"

Flynn leaned in as though Director Parnell herself might have bugged the place.

"The DCI asked if I trusted you."

"Did she now? First of all, what'd you say?" the NSA spy said with a smile.

"I said, 'Hell, no.' I told her I didn't even like you."

The two friends clinked their glasses and laughed.

"Wilf, you know the history of this place, don't you? The base?"

"Only that it became the lightning rod for people's outrage over supposed military and intelligence overreach. That's what got the place shut down."

"I'm thinking that maybe the ghost of military bases past has gotten people a little nervous about reestablishing our presence here. All this supposed cooperation – you know, the blurring of the communications channels and everything – has just been a way to perhaps spy on each other."

"Without it looking like we're spying on each other."

"Exactly, Wilf."

The lunch companions dropped their conversation while the waiter delivered their burgers.

"*Dos mas, por favor,*" requested Flynn, holding up two fingers and pointing to the near-empty glasses of *cerveza.*

"Jeez, Art. I don't like being kept in the dark."

"Or used."

"Or used."

The NSA and CIA operatives ate their meals in relative silence. When they paid for their food and drinks and left, a rather shaggy-looking young American followed them out. He had likewise followed them into the restaurant when they had arrived. He considered all he'd heard from the two Americans through the sound enhancer in his phone. He decided the two men were uninvolved in any unsanctioned covert activities in Terrador.

Sitting alone on a park bench in the plaza outside, the man typed a text that merely said, "saw the sites you recommended not as interesting as you said"

In her office some three thousand miles away in Langley, Virginia, CIA Director Betsy Parnell was livid.

"Well, crap."

Parnell wasn't sure why she had set Flynn up in the way she had. Nor did she have a clear rationale for sending Roadrunner to Terrador to look around. But CIA Officer Trevor O'Bannon had just confirmed what her instincts had told her. There was at least one person on the island that she couldn't trust. But Roadrunner's message made it clear that he didn't think he was up to anything. Flynn just couldn't keep his mouth shut.

"enjoy your stay there's more to see."

Roadrunner's one letter response – "k" – indicated he knew he was to remain on the island and snoop around. Just as the woman who sent him there was uncertain about what she was looking for, her officer was similarly clueless about the nature of his mission.

♦

The Gulfstream G650ER was fueled and ready for departure when the two secret service agents arrived with the woman identified as the sole governmental passenger. Oskar Lammers was already seated in the plane with Dexter Leach. Both were fully informed of their boss' instructions.

The pilot of Schwartz's jet, on the other hand, was completely out of the loop concerning the real reason for the sudden order to fly to Jackson Hole. The fact that it was just a ruse to corral one Margaret Laughlin wasn't something he needed to know, so he didn't. And that was about to become a problem for his boss. He had been ordered on similar last-minute flights many times in the past, so it wasn't that unusual.

When Agent Marchman pulled alongside the Gulfstream, the pilot was standing beside the doorway with one of the two flight attendants to greet their passenger.

As they admired the beautiful flagship of the Gulfstream line, both Maggie and Josh forgot momentarily the tragedies of the last few days. Agent Marchman stood on watch outside the jet while Joy Griffith went inside to check the credentials of everyone on board.

Maggie and Josh introduced themselves to the flight crew.

"Yes, ma'am," said Captain Buck Edgerton, totally disregarding Josh. "I've seen you on TV a number of times. You were very effective in communicating what was going on about the assassination attempts and the almost war." Of course, being a guy, he was really thinking that Maggie was even hotter in person than on television. Morgan, also being a guy, realized that the pilot was having some less than noble thoughts about his fiancée, but he was happy to see Maggie get the recognition and the compliment.

He gave her a tiny elbow in the side.

"Say, Captain Edgerton…"

"Call me Buck, sir." He extended his hand to Morgan but didn't take his eyes off Maggie.

"He's certainly bold. I'll give him that," Morgan conceded silently. Then aloud, "Okay, Buck. Would you mind if I accompany my fiancée on your flight?" He could tell that the captain was disheartened at the word "fiancée" and the prospect that he would be joining the passenger manifest.

"Excuse me?" the pilot asked of Morgan, now giving him his full attention as Morgan pulled Maggie into an embrace.

"This is a quick there-and-back, isn't it? I thought I'd tag along to drop her off and then fly back with you."

"Well, I was expecting just the one passenger…"

"I bet you were," Morgan thought.

He told the pilot, "Agent Griffith has cleared it with her boss… Well, her boss' boss. If you feel you need verification, she might could get President Hendrickson on the phone. You know, to vouch for me."

Captain Edgerton was suddenly very matter of fact. "That won't be necessary. The more the merrier."

Morgan noticed that he didn't appear merry. Quite happy with himself, Morgan waited with his hottie until Agent Griffith reappeared to verify the pilot's and flight attendant's credentials. Once she had completed her validation of the identities of everyone on board, she addressed Maggie.

"Ms. Loughlin, everything appears fine, exactly as expected. An agent will contact you in Jackson. They'll come from one of our field offices; either Billings, Montana, or Cheyenne, Wyoming. Billings is about an hour closer, but it depends on the availability of an agent. Either way, you'll definitely arrive before one can get there."

"Thank you, Agent Griffith." Maggie offered her hand to her security escort.

"My pleasure, ma'am. You may stay at the airport until our agent arrives. Or he'll touch base when he does. Have a safe trip. Mr. Morgan, would you like us to meet you when you arrive back here at Reagan?"

"No, ma'am. I'll be fine."

After saying their goodbyes to Agent Marchman, the pair turned toward the gangway.

Maggie paused, "I'm glad you're coming, Josh, even if it is only to drop me off."

The engaged couple climbed the few steps to the cabin of the plane, with Maggie in the lead. The second flight attendant greeted her, and the two men aboard stood to introduce themselves, but each balked as Morgan appeared in the doorway behind Maggie.

Dexter Leach was less practiced than Oskar Lammers, so his face betrayed his dismay at the sight of the second, unexpected passenger. Lammers lost his usual poker face for a moment, but quickly collected himself and resumed his greeting of the two passengers.

Morgan noticed the hesitation in the men's approach. One of the pair seemed more visibly disturbed at his arrival, after initially smiling at Maggie's appearance. The other man? There was just some fleeting glimpse of what Morgan could only characterize as anger. His jaws had clinched, and his eyes had hardened. It was momentary, but it was there. Morgan was the type who noticed everything, and the men's reactions troubled him.

"Maybe every one of these studs is just disappointed that Maggie already has a guy," Morgan considered. For an instant, he locked eyes with the rougher-looking, but now smiling man.

"No, it's more than that," he decided.

CHAPTER 14

Somewhere over the Midwest – perhaps Nebraska; Morgan could only guess without the convenient lines on the ground that maps have – he tried to send a text to Sir Albert McGinnis.

"Are you able to use your phone, Maggie? Mine shows I'm connected to the plane's Wi-Fi, but I can't do anything."

"I'll try."

While Maggie tapped in a message to test her connection, Morgan retried his, to no avail.

"Nope. Nothing doing on mine, either. Must be some problem with the jet's network."

Morgan glanced at the sterner-looking man of the pair who was riding along to Wyoming.

"I'll be glad to be home. Even under these circumstances, and even if only for a few days. I hope Curtis... You're not listening to a word I'm saying, are you?"

"Huh? Sorry, Mag. You were saying."

"I was just saying that..."

"Uh, excuse me just a second." With that, Morgan rose and walked toward the passengers sitting behind them.

"Turd," Maggie mumbled to her fiancé, and turned to the view out the window.

When Morgan took a seat across from the two men, the younger became immediately uncomfortable. The older one smiled with a sense of confidence about something unknown to Morgan.

"Josh Morgan," the ex-CIA officer said.

"Oskar Lammers. This is Dexter Leach."

"So, what's taking you to Jackson Hole? I understood this plane was only headed there to pick up someone."

"Change of plans, Mr. Morgan. And I understood we were only going to have one additional guest."

Morgan smiled. "Change of plans." He sized up the other man, who was busily thumbing through some official-looking reports.

"So, Mr. Leach… Or Dexter. Can I call you Dexter? You seem nervous. Don't like flying?"

"I'm fine," Leach said, managing a weak smile.

"Maybe it's change you don't like, Dexter."

"I beg your pardon?"

"You were obviously bothered when I followed Maggie into the cabin at Reagan. So, was he – briefly," Morgan added, tilting his head toward Lammers. "He recovered in an instant. You never seemed to."

Leach turned to Lammers, as if pleading for help.

"What is your point, Mr. Morgan?" the German immigrant said.

"No point. Just making conversation. Oh, was I rude? Maggie says that sometimes I come across as being a little too nosy and direct. I'm sorry."

"No problem, Mr. Morgan," Lammers said.

Much to Leach's relief, their unwanted guest rose to return to his seat.

"Oh, one more thing. Has either of you been able to use your phone? We can't get either of ours to do anything."

"Honestly, we haven't tried."

"No, I haven't tried, either," echoed Leach.

"What was that about?" Maggie asked Morgan when he sat down.

"Just being neighborly."

"Right," Maggie said, clearly irritated.

◆

In his seat well behind the unexpected traveler, Dexter Leach was on edge.

"This is a problem, Oskar."

"I know it's a problem, Leach. Calm down."

Leach leaned toward Lammers. "Morgan's expecting someone to board the plane in Jackson Hole. With the Wi-Fi disabled, we can't touch base with Mr. Schwartz. And…"

"I don't need to talk to Schwartz."

"Do you have a plan?"

"Of course, I have a plan," Lammers lied. In truth, he had no earthly idea what he was going to do. When nobody showed up for the return flight to Washington, Morgan would know something was wrong. By all appearances, he suspected something already. "Either that, or he's the biggest jerk in existence," Lammers thought.

"So, it's under control?"

"It's under control, Leach. Get it together."

♦

Agents Griffith and Marchman were wrapping up dinner at the Shake Shack when the junior agent's phone rang. Joy Griffith pointed over her shoulder with a thumb toward the restrooms.

"Be back," she mouthed. Marchman nodded his understanding as he tapped his phone's display to connect the call.

"Hey, Doug, What's up, pal?"

"Say, Mac, I've got some more info on that car you were curious about. I don't think there's anything to worry about. I peeled back the layers and it turns out the vehicle belongs, ultimately, to a big-assed construction company called Schwartz, Cannon, and Raines – or SCR. The CEO is a real player. Knows everybody in the whole freaking universe. A lot of these types are pretty paranoid and try to hide their connections to their assets to help prevent opportunists from suing them."

"I get it, Doug."

"Yeah, this Schwartz guy has a reputation as a bigtime charity supporter."

Agent Griffith returned from the restroom.

"So, SCR is on the up-and-up. Well, nothing there. Okay, pal. Thanks for checking."

"Ready?" asked Griffith.

"Ready."

The agents buckled themselves into their agency vehicle

Griffith started the engine. "So, who were you talking to about the jet we put Ms. Loughlin on?"

"What do you mean, Joy?"

"The plane, Mac. Weren't you on the phone about the SCR plane?"

"I was talking to Doug Owens, one of the analysts in the office. He was tracking down the ownership of a car I saw in the parking lot when Loughlin was packing for the trip. What are you saying about the plane?"

"It belongs to a government-connected construction company named Schwartz, Cannon… something. Let me look." Before she could refresh her memory with a look at the info that she had received earlier on her phone, her partner completed the corporation's name.

"Raines."

"Yeah, that's it. How…?"

Agent Marchman explained his gut feeling about the dark sedan he had spotted in the parking lot of The Wharf where Morgan and Loughlin lived. "And the plane and the car belong to the same company?"

"Appears so," Griffith confirmed. "What do we do?"

"Let's try to get hold of Ms. Loughlin on the plane."

"Agreed, Mac." Griffith touched Maggie's name on her phone to dial the pre-programmed number. "Straight to voicemail. I'll try Morgan."

When she got the same result, Agent Griffith told Marchman, "This is probably nothing, but we've got to call it in."

◆

Alicia Weston felt somewhat left out of the planning for her own husband's funeral. Trent's identity was now almost uniquely *Former President Trenton Weston*. She felt that, with his last heartbeat, he was lost to her. He was now virtually absorbed into the pages of U.S. history. His legacy as husband vanished.

Of course, the organizers – my, how impersonal that sounded, she thought – ran all details by her, but that was less for approval than simply for the purpose of providing information.

"Have I lost my personal identity, too?" she wondered.

Trent and Alicia Weston had never been happier than when he left public service. Once he was over the initial shock and disappointment of losing his bid for a second term, her husband had settled into a very private, very happy and content life. It was only when the developers of the tourist train, *el Aguila de la Amistad,* invited him to be a guest of honor on its inaugural run, that the ex-POTUS had reemerged into the public eye from his self-imposed cocoon.

Of course, the excursion from San Antonio through northern Mexico was a tragedy on many fronts. Weston had been abducted and was very near to being spirited out of the country to be tried as a war criminal in the Holy Islamic Republic of Saudi Arabia. Trent's friend, Mexican President Francisco Javier Portillo, had been killed on that fateful journey.

Afterward, Trent had discovered a satisfying balance between his personal life and his renewed role as elder statesman, but now he was gone, too. And like his Mexican friend, his end was at the hands of an assassin.

Sitting before the former First Lady were FBI Director Gabriel Austin, Secret Service Director Keith Cortland, and Medical Toxicologist, Dr. Mia Palmer. Keith Cortland was the one in the trio whom Mrs. Weston knew personally. He had once been on her husband's detail.

"Ma'am, I can't express deeply enough how sorry I am for your loss. President Weston was perhaps the most decent man I've ever known. My feelings for him went well beyond that of an assignment. I had genuine personal affection for him. How're you holding up?" Cortland enquired.

145

Alicia Weston often wished she had the boldness to say what she wanted, rather than what was expected and socially acceptable. But, "My husband was murdered; how do you suppose I feel?" was neither. And it certainly wasn't the response Director Cortland deserved.

"It's almost more than I can bear, Keith. But the support of my friends, family, and the others around me is helping me get by. And the public outpouring of sympathy and support… Well, it's a tribute to Trent and it's been a rock for me."

"Mrs. Weston, we've only met briefly, but I want to tell you how much I admired your husband. And I want to assure you that my agency – the entire resources of the United States – we're all at work to uncover who's behind the President's death." The FBI chief was sincere.

There were more expressions of condolences from her visitors. All were heartfelt, she knew, but the widow was becoming impatient. She wanted to know how the investigation was progressing.

"Thank you all. Your words mean more than I can say. Now what can you tell me about what and who killed Trent?"

"We've brought Dr. Palmer into our investigation since she treated the President and also because she's one of the premier toxicologists in the world. Dr. Palmer."

"Ma'am, I'm not sure this will mean anything to you. Unless someone's in my field, it likely won't." The physician showed Mrs. Weston two diagrams of molecular compositions. They were similar, but the version on the right was more complex.

"Mrs. Weston, what you see on the left is the chemical composition of a very deadly toxin called methyl iodide."

"We talked about that briefly at the hospital, didn't we?"

"Yes, ma'am. You'll see a lot more chemical symbols on the diagram on the right. These symbols, in layman's language, represent the composition of two other chemicals. This…" The doctor circled a couple of chemical abbreviations. "…is almost identical in chemical makeup to an oral contraceptive."

Alicia Weston was stunned. "A birth control pill?"

"The chemicals in them. Yes. It's long been know that such hormonal contraceptives increase the risk of Ischemic stroke. This type of cerebrovascular event makes up about eighty-five percent of the total. The contraceptive's increase in risk is slight, but it's present, nevertheless. It's rarely a factor unless a woman has other risk factors. One conclusion of a study by Loyola Medicine stroke specialists in 2018 regarded the possibility that the contraceptives make blood hypercoagulable, or more prone to clotting. Clotting causes Ischemic strokes.

"Adding those chemicals alone wouldn't necessarily guarantee that the methyl iodide would mimic a stroke. But see these symbols…"

The toxicologist circled more letters on the chemical diagram.

"These chemicals together form a synthetic compound very closely akin to cocaine. One major difference is the introduction of fluorine. Cocaine can increase the risk of stroke six- or sevenfold in the twenty-four hours after its use through constriction of blood vessels. This synthetic form is so pure that the risk factor may increase by much more."

"I'm sorry. I'm confused, Dr. Palmer. What does all this mean?"

"I'm sorry, Mrs. Weston. I know this is difficult. Here's the bottom line. It's possible that methyl iodide can mimic a stroke, but it's likely to be lethal, whether it does or not. The addition of these other chemicals doesn't necessarily add to its likelihood of mortality, but it does almost guarantee a stoke – a real one – will occur simultaneously."

Reading the frustration on the widow's face, FBI Director Gabe Austin took over.

"Ma'am, the amount of methyl iodide in your husband's system was almost certainly going to kill him, whether these other compounds were added or not. What they did was to virtually guarantee that stroke symptoms appeared because President Weston actually did have a minor stroke simultaneously."

"Let me repeat what I think I'm hearing," said Alicia Weston. "The poison may or may not appear to be a stroke. A stroke may or may not be fatal. But this combination of all those things assured that my husband would die, and that it would look like a stroke."

The former First Lady's guests were all astounded and embarrassed by how succinctly she had restated the bottom line.

"Yes, ma'am," confirmed Dr. Palmer.

"Mrs. Weston," continued the FBI Director, "this compound has never been seen before. Its design is elegant, in the sense that getting the various pieces to bond together is a remarkable feat of chemical engineering. It isn't the kind of thing you can conjure up from online research and you can't make it in the equivalent of a meth lab."

"This was designed by serious chemists working in a very sophisticated, tightly controlled lab," Palmer emphasized.

"Trent was kidnapped by the Saudis, and then they tried to provoke a war with Russia. Could they have done this?"

Secret Service Director Cortland answered, "We don't think so."

"The technological requirements aren't something we believe they're capable of, ma'am," Austin continued. "Think of this as something on the order of developing a nuclear weapon…"

Toxicologist Palmer added the exclamation point. "And not just any nuclear weapon; the most advanced one that exists."

"So, if you don't believe Saudi Arabia has the technology to create this, who did? Russia?"

"They certainly have the technology, ma'am," confirmed Austin.

"So, this could be some sort of payback for our confronting them?"

"It could," admitted Cortland, "but why would they go after your husband. He was, after all, a big part of getting the tensions resolved."

The FBI Director took his turn leading the group down its logical assessment. "That leaves us with the uncomfortable conclusion that…"

"This was a domestic act."

"I'm afraid so, Mrs. Weston."

◆

Before meeting with Alicia Weston, Dr. Palmer, the FBI Director, and Secret Service Director Cortland had briefed the FBI chief about the information from Joy Griffith. They passed on that there was a connection between the flight carrying Josh Morgan and Maggie Loughlin to Wyoming and the car that drove leisurely away from the residential complex where the pair lived. Neither could contemplate that Linus Schwartz would be engaging in anything sinister. In addition to being a successful businessman and philanthropist, he had a reputation of being a patriot who crossed the line between political parties. His ideology, though well-known, had never seemed to be a factor in his business practices or his giving.

After conferring with his FBI counterpart, Cortland called the President's Chief of Staff. Chandler was equally incredulous as to any malicious motivation in providing transportation for a member of the West Wing staff. And likewise as to why there would be anything suspicious about having a car near where Morgan and Loughlin lived. Still, the coincidental nature was compelling enough to warrant a call to Schwartz – right after he informed his boss of the situation, which he did.

"Linus. Noah. How are you?"

"Very well, chief. Thank you for asking. Checking up on your passenger?"

"No, not at all. I have a coincidence for which I need your help in explaining."

"Of course, my friend. How can I help?"

"Earlier today, one of our Secret Service Agents observed a car at the residence of your passenger and her fiancé. He became a bit suspicious, so we tracked the registration down. After digging through a series of shell companies, we discovered SCR, Inc. owns the vehicle."

"We do?"

"Yes, Linus."

"What was it about the car that caught your agent's attention?"

Since he really couldn't identify any acts that were overtly suspect,

Chandler ignored the question."

"You've got to admit, Linus, that it's odd that your car was in the proximity of their residence and now your company jet is flying them to Wyoming."

Linus Schwartz was taken aback at the word "them." With outbound communications inhibited on his company's jet, the billionaire was unaware that Morgan had joined the passenger list. Nevertheless, he proceeded without pause.

"I must confess to being a little insulted by the insinuation, Noah, but I understand your position. You have to ask. Where was the car seen?"

"At The Wharf. It's a townhouse development..."

"Yes, The Wharf. I know it well. A few of our Washington-based employees live there."

"Of course, Linus. We should've thought of that," the Chief of Staff replied, even though he was well aware of that fact. It was the first thing the analyst checked after identifying the car's owner. It was the driver's disinterest in the sights and sounds of the presence of the U.S. Secret Service that had sparked a mild concern in Agent Marchman. It was, the agent had said, as though he was making a conscious effort to look away from the activity. The intent appeared to be deliberate indifference.

"Your men seem to be slipping? That's hardly encouraging, considering they're charged with protecting our President. But that really hasn't really gone well lately, either. Has it?"

The rebuke hit a nerve in Chandler. Like many in Washington, most particularly in the White House, he had keen instincts. He had been acquainted with Linus Schwartz for a couple of decades. The man occasionally launched a zinger when he thought he had caught someone in a misstep, but it was usually couched in terms that at least appeared good-humored. Chandler thought this one sounded different. It was aloof and the tone sharper. And that bothered him.

The Chief of Staff apologized for the call but reiterated that it was one he had to make. But when he hung up, he updated POTUS and immediately made a call to the Director of the FBI.

"Gabe, would you have your staff look into Linus Schwartz? See if they can find any connection between him or any of his associates with Maggie Loughlin or Josh Morgan. No, I don't have any reason to suspect anything's amiss. Just that my hackles are raised a bit. Yeah, you know the feeling. Thanks."

◆

A short distance away, Linus Schwartz was even more concerned.

The President's Chief of Staff's disclosure that a second passenger was on the plane had left him unsettled. It was another in a spate of complications in his plans.

He looked at his watch. The jet would be landing in Jackson Hole soon. He only hoped Mr. Lammers had a remedy for what could be a catastrophic setback.

Schwartz knew it was risky enough to have his plane in the middle of his plot. It could prove difficult to extricate his company, and by connection, himself from the fate of Margaret Loughlin.

◆

Aboard the Gulfstream, Maggie was getting some much-needed sleep. Her head against Morgan's shoulder gave him emotional support, merely by the closeness.

The ex-CIA spook's mental condition was less settled. After the end to the legal proceedings against him, he had been caught up in the death of his good friend, Trent Weston. The young man had racked his brain, trying to come up with a plausible theory as to who had killed him.

Unknown to Morgan, he had arrived at and subsequently dismissed the same scenarios that the investigators had, although not necessarily for the same reasons. The Saudis seemed the likely culprits, but he believed that they had pinned their conspiratorial hopes on their anticipated provocation of a war between the U.S. and the Russian Federation. Plus, intelligence agencies were reporting that their governing body was in shambles after their president, al-Hashimi, was killed in a tragic air crash. Publicly, the downing was still classified, but Morgan was sure that the al Qaeda party leadership in Saudi Arabia knew what had really happened and who was behind it.

The disarray there and Morgan's belief that an assassination such as this would require more planning had led him to count them out.

And as investigators had, he had considered whether the Russians would've killed the former President. In this case, Morgan had reached the same conclusion as the agencies investigating the assassination. The Kremlin had every right to be angry at the United States' actions toward them in wrongly blaming them for the attempted assassination of President Hendrickson. But why would they go after Weston? Despite the official story, the Russians knew that a small group of Americans had worked to prevent the escalation of tensions. And while they could never confirm that U.S. Green Berets had actually been outside of Moscow poised to strike, the Russian leaders knew that Weston had been one of those working unofficially to end the nightmare.

A working theory that Morgan was considering was one that the government's investigators had no reason to know about. It centered on the warning to him by Betsy Parnell. She had said that some of the actors in the conspiracy to take down the Terradoran president years ago had Morgan in their sights.

Weston was in the White House during that time. He had been a key figure in holding accountable the agency personnel and citizens who abused their authority around the world to set up lucrative and mostly illegal operations. Could the same people who were gunning for Morgan have killed Weston?

"Wouldn't they just have killed me instead of Trent?" Morgan theorized to himself.

Maggie began to stir and finally her eyes cracked open.

"Hi, sweetheart."

"Hi, Josh." Maggie pushed a few strands of her hair aside and sat up. "Mmm. I needed that… but my body aches."

She stretched and rubbed her eyes. "How long did I sleep?"

"Not long."

Maggie returned her head to Josh's shoulder. He was reluctant to bring up the thoughts that had been going through his mind. But after he had elected to run off to Russia to try to deescalate the friction between his country and that one, Maggie had made him promise that there would be no more secrets.

"Maggie," he started in a voice low enough that she could barely hear, "something's been bothering me. Why would someone – whoever they are – try to get me to prison rather than just killing me?"

The frankness and suddenness of the former spy's question startled the young woman in the seat next to his.

"Morgan…"

"I know. Not the cheeriest of topics but hear me out."

Maggie sat up straighter but inclined her head to a place in front of Morgan's face. He was almost whispering now.

"Think about it. They don't really have anything to gain by letting me live. And it's not like I would've been that difficult to take out."

Maggie's blue eyes turned up toward Morgan's though he couldn't see.

"Maybe they just wanted you to suffer."

"I thought of that. It's certainly possible, but I'm not sure that's how someone like that would think."

There was some silence while Morgan struggled to put the pieces together.

"I didn't tell you this, but while you were packing this morning, I got a call from Don Summers. We talked some about Trent's passing. Then he told me the oddest thing. Overnight, or early this morning – I don't know which – police found the bodies of Judge Crawford and D.A. Maxwell. Both apparent suicides."

Maggie pulled away from Josh.

"That's really weird."

"Yeah. It is."

"What are you thinking, Josh?"

Morgan bit his lower lip. He contorted his face and looked away. Finally, he spoke again.

"I'm gonna sound like a conspiracy nut. I'm sure those two guys had a lot more in common than just my case. But add in Trent. Make him part of the situation, and the thing they all had in common was me."

Maggie straightened up instantly. She glanced around the Gulfstream's cabin to see who might be near. Seeing nobody, she whispered.

"But as a former President, Trent would have to have a lot of enemies. There has to be any number of reasons for someone to kill him that don't involve the other two guys. And he was murdered. The judge and the D.A. killed themselves. Right?"

"That's what the investigators are saying. Virtual slam-dunks, as far as cases go." He paused to look at Maggie. "But what if they didn't?"

"Didn't what?"

"Commit suicide. Trent may not have anything to do with this at all. But you take two suicides on the same day by men in basically the same line of work. That's a big enough coincidence. And they both had a recent connection to me."

Maggie began to object. Morgan raised his hand.

"Please," he said, "bear with me. Mix Trent into the pot, and what are the odds that all three men had something in common besides me. Then, you have to consider that, since Trent was murdered, they might've been, too. At least, it's possible."

"But if it's even a little bit about you, Josh, what would killing two men who were out to get you gain them."

"I haven't figured that out... yet."

Maggie began to consider whether Josh could be on to something. The couple spent some time reflecting on the possibilities.

"You know, Josh, Curtis was nearly killed in a wreck; one that I'm confident couldn't have gone down the way Tag says it appears," Maggie added.

Morgan's awareness clicked as he got in sync with Maggie's speculation. "You think it wasn't an accident?"

Maggie's eyes showed the weight of her fears. "If we assume there are already three murders, then Curtis might've made four. But you don't know Curtis that well, really. He's more my friend than yours. That doesn't make sense, Josh."

Morgan dared not say what he was thinking. He tried not to stare at her but couldn't keep from it. The agony of his suspicions crystallized in an instant.

"Maybe it's precisely because he's close to Maggie. And she's close to me," he pondered silently.

Morgan nodded his agreement and lied to her, "No. No, Maggie, it doesn't make sense."

The purpose behind recent events was coming into sharper focus in Morgan's mind. His mind was racing with scenarios.

He asked himself if maybe the whole thing about putting him behind bars was simply to sideline him; take him out of action? The thought really wasn't a question. His speculation cascaded furiously. His internal theorizing continued. Was someone attempting to make him watch helplessly while they disrupted his life and picked off the people he cared about?

Morgan knew his last thoughts, in particular, were better left unsaid. He looked away from Maggie. When he looked back, he remained silent and pulled her close.

"I'm sorry, Maggie," he promised himself and her silently. "Nothing's gonna happen to you. I swear."

The pilot's voice crackled over the intercom.

"Hello, ladies and gentlemen. This is your captain. Just wanted to let you know that we're beginning our descent to the Jackson Hole Airport. If you'll get seated and begin stowing your personal items, I'll let you know when to prepare for landing."

Morgan thought about the men seated behind them, and their seeming discomfort in seeing him follow Maggie onto the plane. He didn't know how they could possibly be parts of a conspiracy against him and wind up on the same private jet.

And he didn't know what could await Maggie in Jackson. But one thing Morgan did know.

Maggie wouldn't be getting off the plane alone.

CHAPTER 15

Most workers in most places of the country would have ended their workdays by this time. But this was Washington, D.C Everyone knew that life was different here. Politicians and bureaucrats worked long hours, though most of their constituents would argue that they were seldom productive ones. But Detective Howard knew that anyone in his line of work could count on extended workdays, regardless of where they lived.

His case was the apparent murder of Siobhan Cassidy by U.S. Attorney Riley Maxwell, followed by his apparent suicide. However, since there was at least some possibility of overlap, he was also participating in the case of the death of Judge Byron Caldwell, also an apparent suicide.

Howard couldn't conceive of how there could be a connection between the suicides, short of some sort of bizarre pact. These two men, though related professionally, were found in different locations. Furthermore, nothing suggested that they knew each other outside of the courtroom. And evidence at each crime scene suggested wildly different motives.

Maxwell had almost certainly – though nothing was ever certain until it was – killed his assistant. Everybody in his office who was interviewed remarked that he apparently had romantic interests with regard to Cassidy, and that she didn't share them. He had killed her, most likely in her office, because the object of the attack had been a crystal award his victim had kept on her desk. Two of Cassidy's co-workers stated that they had noticed it was missing from her office about the time she began to be absent from work.

Then Maxwell, it seemed, choked her to ensure she was dead. If all that was true, he was somehow able to remove her from their office without anyone spotting him – that part troubled the detective – and bury her in a shallow grave in a park in the District.

Finally, a couple of days later, he killed himself beside that grave, likely out of remorse. The gun was in his hand. There was alcohol on his breath. There was a printer-written note on the ground beside the man reading, "I'm sorry." That bothered Howard, too. Why would a man, distraught and drunken, take the time to print a note from his computer? In these types of cases, a note is often not left at all. The personal rage and guilt would build and then, bang! The deed is done. And if a note were left, it would be handwritten.

Still, despite his couple of questions in the case, no other fingerprints were found. The note found beside his body was discovered as an open Word document on his home computer, and the printed characters of his suicide note matched his printer.

So why was he not one hundred percent convinced?

In the case of the judge, the police investigator had no serious reservations about a determination of suicide. Crime Scene Investigators had found photos in a burning fireplace of Caldwell with clearly underage boys. One puzzling element that was resolved, at least by conjecture, was why the man was out of the tub when he expired. He had clearly initiated the act in the bath water, so why had he attempted to leave? Howard agreed with the CSIs that Caldwell was attempting to get to the fireplace when he saw that not all of the perverted images were going to go up in flames. The bedroom fireplace was clearly visible from the tub, investigators had determined.

One of the judge's clerks had a key to the man's townhouse and went to check on him when he didn't show for an early meeting. After ringing the doorbell several times, she entered to find the man on the bathroom floor. The clerk admitted to seeing the photos in the fireplace, and even to considering removing them to protect her mentor's reputation. But she had left them there and called 911.

All the members of his staff had said in their interviews that he was looking forward to retirement. They all conceded to knowing that he was gay, and that there was the occasional rumor of his fondness for young boys. But he had been such a decent and honorable man in all other ways, none could remotely entertain the notion that the gossip was true. His clerk was horrified at the sight of the photos in the fireplace. She turned off the gas to the ceramic logs but left the scene alone.

Perhaps the most disturbing part of Detective Howard's job was looking at photos such as the ones he now held in his hands. The abuse of young children was more violent in his mind than a vicious and bloody murder. He abhorred the sights he saw in the images but examining them was part of his job. The investigator was returning the prints to their evidence bag, all of them charred around the edges and some with details almost obliterated from the fire, when a thought occurred to him.

He spread the printed photos across his desk for a reexamination. Howard and other investigators assumed, since Caldwell had tried to destroy the photos immediately before attempting to take his own life, that he was motivated by guilt. Either that, the lead detective on the judge's case supposed, or he feared the photos were about to be made public. In that case, his suicide might've been because of the potential embarrassment – maybe even jailtime. In either case, the photos were presumed to be personal keepsakes; trophies the pervert had made for himself.

"So, why aren't they better photos?" the D.C. detective said aloud. He picked up his cell phone and called his counterpart on the judge's case.

"Boz? Dillon."

Nelson Bosley was one of the few District police detectives who had been at it longer than Detective Howard. At one time, the two had served as partners, but as each advanced in their careers, they had gone their separate ways.

"Hello, Dillon. What's up?" The delay in Dillon's answer to the question led to one of his own. "Something bothering you, too?"

"Yeah, Boz."

"The pics?"

"Yeah. If these were trophy photos, why aren't they better? I mean, the quality is good, but the perspective is off."

"I agree, Dillon. I had the same thought but wanted to see if you came to the same conclusion independently. These despicable things appear to have been taken covertly; from odd angles; telephoto lenses, even. If the pervert had taken them himself, he would've had a better setup. Don't you think?"

"Exactly, Boz. He might've still wanted the cameras hidden, but they'd have been right on the… well, the action. And some of the photos were made in his apartment. Why didn't we find any equipment? Especially video? Wouldn't Caldwell have wanted video? I don't think he knew he was being photographed."

"Me neither, pal. Me neither."

♦

The Gulfstream G650ER completed its rollout northward on the sole runway at Jackson Hole Airport and slowly made the U-turn to starboard for the taxi to the terminal.

Oskar Lammers still didn't know how he would explain his departure from the plane. But the most troubling problem that loomed for him was that nobody would be boarding the plane for a return trip to D.C. And that was the story that justified having a plane going to Wyoming in the first place. Without Morgan on the plane, they would have taken his girlfriend in flight. Then Lammers would leave with her. It didn't matter that nobody got on. But now…?

One of the flight attendants picked up her microphone, even though it was hardly needed with the small group of passengers.

"Welcome to Jackson Hole, Wyoming. Please remain seated until we've come to a complete stop. As soon as we have, Ms. Loughlin and Mr. Lammers may exit the plane. For those of you who will be returning to Reagan, Mr. Morgan and Mr. Leach, we'll have a little time before we depart. You may remain on the plane where I and our other flight attendant will serve you drinks and food. Or, feel free to get out and stretch your legs. We'll send a text to your phones about thirty minutes before takeoff."

"So, Lammers is getting off here, too," Morgan considered with some trepidation. "And apparently my phone will work once I'm off the plane."

The luxury jet lurched slightly as it came to rest. Maggie was beginning to collect the items she had with her in the cabin.

"Hold on a sec, Mag."

The woman didn't understand, but there was a lot about Morgan that baffled her. Still, she had come to trust him without question. She watched as he walked forward in the plane to where the pilot was emerging from the cockpit.

Captain Edgerton, who had apparently gotten over his resentment that Maggie wasn't single, was much friendlier to Josh this time.

"Mr. Morgan, I hope you enjoyed the flight," said the pilot with a shake of his passenger's hand.

"I did. Very nice. Thank you for your hospitality. So, I guess it will be a little while before your return passenger boards."

Edgerton was puzzled by two things. The first was the notion of a return passenger. Not expecting an unscheduled passenger, nobody had thought to fill in the pilot on the cover story. The second odd thing was the sight over Morgan's shoulder of a rapidly approaching Oskar Lammers. As he continued to watch Lammers approach, he answered Morgan.

"I'm sorry. I don't understand." His head tilted and his brow furrowed as he glanced toward his equally confused co-pilot for help. His flight partner only shrugged. "We weren't expecting a return passenger," Edgerton stated with certainty.

"Shit!" Morgan thought. He immediately turned to the approaching man behind him. "Ah, Oskar. I was just telling Captain Edgerton how much Maggie and I appreciate the ride out here."

The passive expression on Lammers' face couldn't conceal that he was worried.

"And I was just about to tell him that I've decided to stay here with Maggie. After all, this is really our home and I can hang out here with her as easily as I can mope around alone back east."

Morgan locked eyes with Lammers. The intensity of the visual exchange dared Schwartz's fixer to object.

"That's not a problem, is it?" There was a lengthy pause, followed by, "Is it, Oskar?"

After three or four seconds, Lammers' answer arrived without expression, no smile; only a somewhat lowered head punctuated with likewise lowered eyebrows.

"Not at all... Josh."

Morgan cheerfully slapped Lammers and gave him the best deliberately fake smile he could marshal. "See, we're all on the same page now."

He tested Lammers' control by grasping his hand and shaking it energetically. He felt the bore of the German's eyes like laser pointers. And it felt good. The man's obvious inner rage was confirmation that he was a man with unfriendly intentions. Morgan felt the stare linger as he moved past his now unveiled adversary toward Maggie. Suddenly he turned to face Oskar Lammers again, raised an index finger and bobbed it up and down in concert with the wheels that were turning in his head. He stepped slightly back toward Lammers and slapped himself on the forehead.

"Now, here's a thought, Oskar. Why don't we get together in the next couple of days? I'll buy you a beer."

"I would look forward to seeing you again, Josh," returned Lammers, his lips curling into a smile that Morgan knew was a signal of some decision.

The ex-CIA spook stepped directly in front of the German and looked up slightly to the taller man. His eyes closed slightly, and his head leaned somewhat closer.

Morgan said, his voice barely above a whisper, "Me, too. It'll be great."

The stare-down lasted several seconds before Oskar Lammers looked away.

Morgan thought, "You're not so tough." Though inwardly, he knew that wasn't remotely true.

As Oskar Lammers turned to speak with Edgerton, Morgan moved to Maggie. She watched her fiancé, who was suddenly the one in a hurry."

"What was that about?"

"Just telling them how much we appreciate the ride." Morgan turned to Maggie and gave her a gentle kiss on her forehead. Then, "Let's go."

"'Let's?'"

Morgan was practically pulling her along now. "Yeah, I'm staying here with you."

Maggie was elated, but also had a knot building in her gut. With everything she knew about Morgan's life before they met and everything that he'd been involved in since then, she knew something was up. And she couldn't begin to imagine how bad it was likely to be.

♦

It was eight o'clock eastern time and the CIA Director was where she often was late in the day – in her office. Her private phone rang. It was FBI Director Austin.

"Hey, Gabe."

"Hi, Betsy, I know you can't go into specifics, but I need to talk about Terrador."

The DCI looked down at the stack of files she'd been scouring that concerned that very topic. Beginning with the initial rogue plot to kill its president to the current restoration of Joint Base Terrador, she was refreshing her mind with every detail. Parnell was reviewing everything from the perspective of Josh Morgan's involvement in the unsanctioned operation. She was trying to flesh out a present scenario that might lead to the person or group who might be targeting the ex-officer. The plan Morgan had disrupted occurred long before Austin was the FBI chief, so there was little likelihood that he was read in on any of it. But it also happened some time before she was CIA Director, so she didn't know for certain. Parnell had no idea what his interest might be, but she was curious. Could it have anything to do with Morgan?

"Sure, Gabe. I'll try to help. Let's do it this way. You ask the questions. I'll answer, if I can."

"Fair enough. It's about Linus Schwartz and his company, SCR, Inc."

"The billionaire?"

"Yeah, him," Austin said with a laugh. "That's the first word out of anyone's mouth when they identify him. Wish I had that problem."

The DCI laughed, too. "Ditto! But what 'problem?'"

"It's public knowledge that we're reestablishing JBT. I haven't been told this, but I would suspect your agency will have a presence there. A jumping-off place for operations in the region."

Parnell didn't reply. Austin hadn't expected her to.

"Schwartz's company has the contract getting things shipshape down there. Right?"

"Correct."

The FBI Director continued. "He also had the contract for the original construction on the island. I think it might've been before the merger with Cannon and Raines to become SCR. I guess it was just 'S' back then." Austin thought his quip funny and laughed. Parnell didn't.

"I don't know for sure, but that's probably also correct."

"Betsy, here's the part where I know you can't say much. I know there was a dustup down there years ago."

The Director of Central Intelligence was on guard now.

"Go ahead."

"I was in the field back then and was on a joint task force that looked into the debacle, so I know more than you probably think I do. From your end, was there any reason to think Schwartz was involved in the plot to kill Salinas and the rogue activities that were going on down there?"

Despite her FBI counterpart's assertion that he was privy to case files on the planned assassination of the Terradoran president and other facts, Parnell couldn't trust that to be true. She thought through how to respond.

"I can't speak to any details of operations anywhere, Gabe, but I can say this. As far as I know, neither Schwartz nor anyone in his employ was involved in any illegal activities in Terrador. Or anywhere else, for that matter. Why do you ask?"

Since he was asking for Parnell's help, the FBI boss decided to be more forthcoming than he would've otherwise been.

"It has to do with one of yours back then: Josh Morgan."

The relief that DCI Parnell had felt that Austin's line of questioning hadn't seemed to concern the Agency, in general, or specifically, Josh Morgan, vanished in an instant.

"How so?"

"I should probably have Secret Service Director Cortland on this call, too, but here's the background. A couple of his field agents were tasked for watching over Margaret Loughlin. Due to the assassination of Weston, they're providing extended protection to various administration officials. Anyhow, that means their overwatch includes your guy…"

"Former guy."

"Right. 'Former guy;' because of his relationship with her."

"And?"

"One of the agents became a little suspicious of a car in the area where Morgan and Loughlin live. He phoned in the plates. Took some research, but turns out it belongs, ultimately, to SCR. But, get this. Schwartz provided his private jet to get Loughlin home to Wyoming for some personal business. A weird coincidence, isn't it? They just landed in Jackson Hole."

Parnell was getting a tingling feeling.

"Cortland calls Hendrickson's Chief of Staff, who confronts Schwartz. He explains it away, but Chandler decides the matter needs some looking into and calls me. We can't find a connection of any kind between Loughlin and Schwartz. The only thing we could find in common between him and anybody was between him and Morgan. And that's only because Schwartz has this indirect connection with Terrador because his company originally built and is refitting the base. It's very thin. I mean, that whole episode was over with a long time ago. But it's all we came up with."

Director Parnell took a few moments to consider how far she would go in this discussion. She had warned Morgan that some lingering animosity from his involvement in Terrador had reared its head. And now, the FBI Director was expressing some concern, however minimal, about Morgan with regard to the Latin American country. She decided that since her investigation wasn't technically in the purview of her leadership of the Agency, she wouldn't break any laws by telling Austin. Besides, she needed to trust someone. And she might just get some help.

"Okay, Gabe. This is completely off the record."

"Got it."

"I know you know this, but Morgan was just arrested – twice technically – for murder and then treason. And you know POTUS pardoned him. I'm confident the arrests had something to do with Terrador. I've been looking into some rumblings about some of the bad players from way back then. Seems they're out to get Morgan. Don't know who or exactly why."

"That's news to me. Why don't they just whack him?"

"No idea. Then President Weston is killed. You may know some of the background, but probably not all. Beginning with the fallout after Terrador, Weston looked after Morgan. That's why Morgan went after him when he was kidnapped – moral obligation, and all that. And the ending to that wasn't what the official story said. The Deputy NSA Director didn't kill himse…"

Austin interrupted, "Sure, Morgan or Weston killed the bastard. My money's on Morgan. Blake deserved it. He was knee-deep in the corruption in Terrador, despite his squeaky clean, righteous reputation."

"Yes. That's what happened, Gabe." Parnell took a deep breath. "I'm thinking that Weston's death and Josh's legal troubles are related."

"Well, don't forget the deaths of the prosecutor and judge in Morgan's arrest."

"Excuse me?" The DCI had heard the news but, since the proceedings against Morgan were being conducted behind closed doors, none of the names of those involved were made public. Parnell didn't know the men who had killed themselves were involved with Morgan's case.

"Yeah. Maxwell was prosecuting your boy – sorry, *former* boy – and Caldwell was presiding. By the way, since both were on the public dole, the Bureau's participating in the investigation. Latest word from D.C. detectives is that they're not completely sold on the suicide rulings."

The silence was extensive this time as each director of their respective organizations tried to piece together what everything meant. FBI spoke first.

"Betsy, it appears that someone might have a very specific plan to simply make Morgan experience some personal tragedies."

"Right. Like you said, otherwise they'd just kill him. But, Gabe, that seems awfully personal. Could that really mean that Blake's cronies were so traumatized by his death that they want Morgan to suffer like they did? Seems preposterous to me."

"They wouldn't. In our task force's investigation of the criminal activity on Terrador, it was apparent that everyone hated the asshole. But he got things done, so they tolerated him. Shame we could never pin anything on him. He had some friends in very high places covering his ass."

"Just as Morgan did, Gabe."

"Yeah, Betsy. Shame about Weston. I really liked the man. And you can't find one thing he ever did that was out of line."

"Unless you count perjuring himself to cover for Morgan."

"I don't count that. That was righteous."

"Yes, it was, Gabe."

There was another prolonged period of silence. Parnell took a long, audible breath.

"All right, Gabe. New plan. Let's both continue to investigate. You can, of course, do so in an official capacity. I believe my work stills needs to be on the sly. I'm not sure who in the Agency might be involved. But no police. If things are as they appear to us, there could be someone on the inside there."

"But I tell Chandler, who will tell POTUS?"

"Of course."

"And Cortland?"

Betsy thought a moment. "Sure."

"Agreed."

"Oh, Gabe, before we hang up… I have one of mine snooping around in Terrador as we speak. Sorta spying on my personnel."

"That's interesting."

"Yes. Like I said, I don't trust anyone right now."

"Understood, Betsy. And thanks."

Both disconnected their phones without another word. Parnell reached into her desk for her bourbon.

"Hell, I'm about to go home anyhow."

She dashed off a quick message to Roadrunner, Trevor O'Bannon.

"you know that thing I asked you to get on vacation? very important to me"

♦

FBI Director Austin really wanted a drink, too, but his would have to wait. He had a couple of calls to make. First, he filled Secret Service Director Cortland in on his conversation with Parnell. Then he called the next number.

"Well, I can go ahead and pour it." And he splashed some Scotch into his glass while the connection was completed.

The voice on the other end said, "Hello, Director."

"Hello, Chief Chandler. There have been some developments concerning the matter you asked Cortland and me to look in to."

The call lasted a little over ten minutes.

♦

At 1600 Pennsylvania Avenue, the President's Chief of Staff put his phone away. He rubbed his weary eyes with both hands, pushed his left hand through his hair, and scratched the back of his head.

A small smile began to manifest itself, though Chandler really didn't find the situation funny at all.

"Josh Morgan," he said aloud. "Why am I not surprised? That boy seems to pop up in the middle of everything."

Like the two people who had come up with a possible motive for what was playing out, the Chief of Staff poured himself a drink. As he did, he resumed his assessment of what he'd just heard, and what it could mean.

Chandler threw back the shot of whiskey he had poured.

"This job would drive me to drink… if I didn't drink already."

With that, President Hendrickson's righthand man walked toward the Oval Office to fill her in.

CHAPTER 16

"Ms. Loughlin. Mr. Lammers," said the driver of the sedan who had picked up his passengers from the Gulfstream directly on the tarmac. He shut the door behind his passengers, who looked at one another with a fair amount of confusion.

Once the chauffer was behind the wheel, Maggie corrected him.

"I'm Maggie Loughlin. But this is Josh Morgan."

The mixed-up driver looked again at his orders.

"Hmmm. This says that you would be sharing a ride with Oskar Lammers."

Unaware of the extent of Josh's uneasiness, Maggie began her offer to wait on the delinquent man. "Oh, well, we don't want to leave him behi…"

Josh leaned toward the driver. "He's made other arrangements. We can leave."

Maggie turned to object but stopped when she saw Morgan's faint shake of his head and felt the squeeze of his hand.

The man in the front seat turned around fully to look toward the plane. With the other passengers and flight crew standing idly beside the private jet, he finally said, "Very well, then. Where can I take you?"

"Where were you supposed to take us?" Josh asked before Maggie could speak.

"Uh, says here… a private residence outside of the city."

Maggie was suddenly puzzled. She looked to her fiancé to try to gauge his level of concern. He appeared serious but not overly alarmed. She shrugged her shoulders and let Morgan speak for both of them.

"What address was it?" Morgan got his answer and said, "Oh, I guess you were going to drop Oskar – well, Mr. Lammers, that is – off first. We'd like you to take us to St. John's Medical Center, please."

Morgan figured Maggie would be safer at the hospital than hanging out at the airport for who knows how long until the promised Secret Service agent arrived. And perhaps checking up on Curtis Jones would occupy her mind and keep her from thinking about other things too much. After all, her friend was the reason she'd come in the first place.

The car pulled away. This time it was Morgan who looked through the rear window. He saw the flight crew together near the front of the fuselage. Dexter Leach stood with Oskar Lammers, who was on his phone.

"Phone!" Morgan said. Maggie rolled her eyes and shook her head at the not-unusual outburst. She looked out the window at the passing scenery. In the twilight she could see the familiar sights of home. It felt good.

Morgan was almost finished dialing his friend's phone. He was sure Teton County Deputy Sheriff Scott Taggart would come to the hospital to help keep an eye on Maggie. Suddenly, Josh stopped pressing the symbols on his phone's virtual keypad. He lowered the device to his lap. There was no way he could have the conversation with Tag that he needed to without Maggie overhearing. And he needed to keep her calm.

He replaced the phone to his pocket and said to Maggie, "You know, that can wait. Let's just enjoy the scenery."

When the car arrived at the hospital, the driver asked if he should wait. "No, thanks." Josh said. "We're good." The driver obviously wasn't in on the thing – if there even was a "thing" – or he would've never taken them to the hospital. Morgan had the address where he would've likely taken them. He needed his own vehicle to check it out.

♦

"You can't be serious!"

"I'm afraid so, ma'am."

President Sandra Hendrickson rose and paced behind her desk, reflexively smiling just as her Chief of Staff had earlier. She brushed her fingers through her hair, then turned to Chandler with her hands on her hips.

Noah Chandler had no words. He tried to speak but could only throw his hands up and shrug.

"Really!" reinforced POTUS. She walked to the loveseat in the center of her office and literally collapsed on it. She rested her face in her cupped hands and again shook her head. Finally, she broke the silence.

"Josh Morgan? Again? Do you think there's really some sort of threat to Morgan? Or that Trent Weston's death was somehow about *him*? And Linus Schwartz?" The reference to the highly regarded philanthropist was awash with incredulity. "You can't possibly believe he's involved in this... this, whatever!"

Chandler shrugged again, before finally shaking his head.

"No. No, ma'am. I've known the man for years. And while I've always seen a... Well, I don't want to say darker side of him – let's just say I've noticed a different side than his public persona. It was that sense of him that made me ask for a more thorough look into the seeming coincidence with the car and jet being owned by his company. But do I think he could be directing or even participating in anything nefarious? No way, ma'am."

The President's face showed some relief until her chief continued. "But is it possible that there could there be something else going on – something he wouldn't know about? There might be. I don't know why, but, yes. Maybe it's just because of all the drama of the last few months. And maybe it has something to do with Josh Morgan's propensity for winding up with his nose where it doesn't belong. Honestly, I don't know what to think. But something just feels off."

◆

Curtis Jones was awake – sort of – and improving – sort of. The emotional shock of waking up without his left leg was taking its toll on him as significantly as the physical injuries. The doctors treating him had upgraded his condition from "critical" to "serious, but stable."

When he saw Maggie, her friend tried to smile but it wouldn't come. Since she was his emergency contact in the absence of any direct relatives, hospital staff permitted his boss, mentor, and close friend into his room. She was alone with him. Staff had forbidden Morgan from going with her. Maggie successfully held back her own tears, although the sight of her assistant was crushing her.

"Hi, Curtis." She leaned over and kissed him lightly on his cheek.

"They removed my leg."

"I know, Curtis. I'm sorry."

Maggie turned away to lay her purse on a chair, but the act was really a means to allow her time to gather herself and wipe away the tear that had formed. Stoic again, she turned back and offered a melancholy smile.

The friends chatted to the extent the patient was able. Maggie wanted to ask about the accident but decided to wait. Instead, she gave every reassurance she could to Curtis about his recovery and her affection for him. She told him that Morgan was with her, but that the hospital rules kept him from coming in.

"Thought he was a rule-breaking, kick-ass kind of guy," the patient said with something close to a smile.

"He is," Maggie agreed, touching her friend's cheek. "But he's no match for the nurse at the desk."

"I don't remember anything about the accident," Jones volunteered.

"That's okay. Try not to think about that." Then she began again with the assurances that he would be fine.

Outside the hospital room, Morgan was surprised to see no police, no hospital security, nothing, until he realized that nobody suspected foul play in the car crash. Well, nobody but Maggie and him. The idea that the crash had been staged was beginning to seem more plausible to him now.

Morgan scanned the hallway and saw nothing he thought was suspicious. He sat down in a chair away from other people to make a phone call. The greeting surprised and disappointed him.

"This is Tag. I'm away fishing for a few days. I won't have cell service where I'm going. If this is a personal call, leave a message. If it's business, you can call the sheriff's office at..."

As Morgan hung up, the vibrating of an inbound call surprised him. He identified the caller by his phone's display and accepted the call.

"Hi, Betsy," he answered.

The ex-spy informed her that he had remained in Wyoming with Maggie.

"I think that's smart, Morgan." Then over the next few minutes, the CIA Director filled Morgan in on everything she knew and the discussion she'd had with her counterpart in the FBI.

"So," Parnell summarized, "we're not really sure anything is going on. And, if it is, we have no reason to suspect Schwartz is involved directly. Could be that some elements of the circle of bad guys benefitting from their illegal operations in Terrador work in his company. We just don't know."

"Okay." Morgan's one-word reply surprised Parnell.

"Okay," she answered. "Morgan, there's one more thing. In retrospect, I probably should've told you this already." She informed her ex-CIA friend about the rebuilding of the U.S. base in Terrador. "It's not exactly secret, but neither has it been front page news. The rebuilding of the facility could be the thing that has the old players down there getting active again. You know, thinking there might be an opportunity to resurrect their operations."

"Okay," was all Morgan said, for the second time.

Parnell asked about Maggie and her injured friend and they hung up.

Josh Morgan no longer regretted being unable to reach his deputy sheriff buddy. In fact, he no longer had plans to involve law enforcement or intelligence agencies of any kind.

The last couple of years had included a massive amount of trouble in his life. Despite that, it was the most content he'd been in a long time. His life with Maggie, his direction in life – there was so much that he felt blessed about. One more thing that had encouraged him about his future was that he thought the ghosts of Terrador had disappeared. Morgan had become convinced that the specter of lingering fallout from the people he had exposed for their corruption so many years ago had disappeared with the death of Everson Blake. Now it was growing increasingly likely that it wasn't true.

Yes, Josh Morgan had been happy. And it was precisely because he had been that planted a new resolve in him to remove the shadow of his past that continued to plague him.

Morgan didn't know how – he didn't even know if he was capable – but he was going to end this succession of crises. And he was going to do it alone.

When he had set out to find and rescue his abducted friend, Trent Weston, and when he had traveled to Russia to uncover the truth about the assassination attempts against the current President, he had done so because he felt he had to.

Now, somebody somewhere had killed Trent and maybe tried to kill Curtis Jones. And, if it was all because of him, then the most logical target to destroy him was his Maggie. So, if that was true, then, as he often read in the thrillers he enjoyed, this time it was personal. He would take care of matters himself; not because he had to, but because he needed to.

Morgan's phone vibrated again, and the caller was a surprise.

"Hey, Josh. It's Tag."

"Thought you were fishing."

"Nah. Haven't left yet. I put the greeting on my phone to screen calls; you know, maybe redirect some of them so I can get stuff packed to leave in the morning. Saw your name on my 'missed calls.' What's up, pal?"

"Nothing, really. I'm in Jackson. Don't know for how long."

"Aw, man. Wish I'd known. But this trip is all set up. Where are you now?"

"At the hospital. Maggie's with Curtis."

"Maybe I can come over there and visit for a while. I'm almost done packing."

"No, that's okay. Catch some for me, Tag."

The abrupt end to the call surprised Scott Taggart, but he wasn't that pissed. Over the years he'd known his fishing buddy, he'd had to come to accept some erratic behavior. Tag thought that was a polite way of calling his friend a son of a bitch. He looked at the phone and mumbled a good-natured expletive. The he smiled, put it away, and returned to his packing.

♦

Curtis Jones was encumbered with all sorts of tubes and cables. An IV and assorted monitors for his vitals were concentrated on his left hand and arm. So, with his right, he beckoned Maggie Loughlin closer with his curling index finger. She inclined her left ear to his lips.

"Would you call the nurse for me?" Curtis whispered. "I have to talk to Josh."

Maggie sat up abruptly.

"Oh, no you don't, Curtis! I'm not having any of this, 'Take care of Maggie, Josh.' You're going to be fine, asshole. Don't you give up on me!"

Maggie's friend's smile was broader this time.

'It's not that. Trust me. It's really not, *you* asshole."

Both friends smiled and squeezed hands.

"I'll see what I can do." With that, Maggie left for the nurses' station to pass on Curtis' request. His faced morphed from the smile at the sometimes-coarse banter he always enjoyed with Maggie into the expression that represented his persistent, unconquered pain.

After some argument, Nurse Tammy agreed to allow Josh in – *briefly*, she insisted.

"Hi, Curtis."

"Hi, Josh. Thought you were this big tough guy. You couldn't even handle Nurse Tammy. I had to take care of getting you in here." Josh smiled at the putdown.

"Well, I'm obviously not as tough as you." There was a pause. Then, "How're you doing, Curtis? I'm really sorry about this."

The car crash victim summoned Morgan closer with his index finger as he had with Maggie. Morgan leaned closer.

"You need to watch out for Maggie, Josh."

His current visitor had the same reaction as the previous one.

"Curtis, don't give up…"

"Shut up and listen, Josh," he whispered.

His voice was tiring and was barely audible. Josh returned his head closer to the patient's.

"Maggie's in danger, Josh."

Morgan's lips pursed and his eyes closed, though he kept his position in front of his friend's mouth.

"I lied to the police about not remembering anything about the wreck."

Morgan squeezed his eyelids together more tightly. Without moving from his listening position, he asked, "What do you remember, Curtis?"

"I was at a club with my friend, Anton. We left separately. As I was walking to my car…" His voice began to weaken.

"Do I need to call the nurse?"

Curtis shook his head. After a pause, he resumed.

"A guy grabbed me from behind. Normally, I might've enjoyed that."

Josh laughed to himself at Curtis' ability to maintain some humor despite the pain he was suffering.

"Bet you would've, Curtis. And don't try to kiss me while you've got me this close."

Jones managed a smile, although Josh couldn't see it from his position.

"Would if you weren't taken, dickhead. Maggie would kill me. Anyhow, he slapped some tape over my mouth immediately but nothing over my eyes. Made no effort to conceal his face from me. So, I felt like I was in real trouble. Guessed he wasn't real careful cause he figured I'd be dead soon.

"He dragged me into my own car and drove out close to where the doctors said they found me."

"Just the one guy?"

Jones nodded his affirmation. He wheezed some and rested a moment before continuing to recount what happened.

"Sometime along the way, he pulled off on a gravel road. Ripped the tape off. Got some liquor out..." Even in his obvious pain, Curtis' face registered his disdain for alcohol. "First he rubbed it around my lips and cheeks."

Using it like a solvent to remove the adhesive residue from the tape, Morgan knew.

"Then he forced the stuff down my mouth. Right before I passed out, I heard him say, 'This will take care of you. Then it's that bitch woman you work for.' That's all I remember."

Neither man spoke for a brief time, until Curtis said for the second time, "Maggie's in danger, Josh."

Morgan straightened himself and looked down at Curtis. He pulled his phone from his pocket and tapped the "photos" icon. He loaded an image he had discreetly taken of Oskar Lammers on the SCR Gulfstream.

The door opened. Nurse Tammy told Morgan he had to leave. Morgan never looked at her or spoke. He delayed her with a raised hand.

"Is this him, Curtis?"

Jones shook his head.

Josh swiped to the next image. "What about him?" It was a photo of Dexter Leach.

"No," was the extremely weak reply.

"Mr. Morgan, you have to leave!" Nurse Tammy approached as if she were going to physically remove Morgan. He thought she could, too.

"Yes, ma'am." As he was leaving, Morgan turned to promise Curtis Jones that he would take care of things, but the near-murder victim was already asleep.

◆

Regardless of how calm Linus Schwartz had sounded on the phone, Oskar Lammers could tell he was inwardly infuriated. He wasn't very happy himself, and it wasn't just because of the pressure of his boss' displeasure. The arrogance of that shit, Morgan, had fueled a *personal* craving to take care of him. The plan had always been to make him suffer before killing him by watching helplessly as those closest to him died. Lammers didn't know why things had to be carried out that way, because he didn't know of Schwartz's illegitimate son, Everson Blake. So, he couldn't understand the billionaire's determination to make Morgan endure loss in the way he had created it for Schwartz by killing Blake.

Lammers would prefer to just do away with Morgan now and skip all the foreplay. And he would, too, if his target gave him the slightest provocation, no matter his directions from his boss.

The German was at the residence that his associate – the one who had tried to kill Curtis Jones – had rented to use as a sort of safe house while in the area.

Like Lammers, Udo Stettin was of German descent. But unlike Oskar, Stettin was born in the U.S., his parents having immigrated shortly before his birth.

The two employees of Linus Schwartz had discussed the failure to kill Curtis Jones, but both were professionals who understood that things sometimes go wrong. Stettin didn't disclose his sloppy handling of the effort; that he'd let Jones see his face. He'd deal with that if it ever came up. He was still hopeful that his intended murder victim would die from his injuries.

Lammers had more of the details of Schwartz's plan than Stettin. The entire process was supposed to have taken longer. Weston was hit first. Then Jones. Stettin had gone after him to hurt Loughlin because she was close to Morgan. The death of her business partner would throw her company into disarray. Ryan Crenshaw, Morgan's former professor in Texas, was supposed to be next. Then Loughlin and Morgan.

However, the fucked-up court proceedings had failed to put Morgan away long enough to hear about the deaths of his loved ones from a jail cell. This had instilled Schwartz with a greater sense of urgency. The billionaire suspended his campaign of grief against the ex-CIA officer. He decided to move directly to the endgame.

Loughlin was, of course, the most significant target on the list. Dealing with her was more important than even Morgan's death, because he wasn't going to get off without seeing his lady killed. She had moved to the top of the list and now Morgan would be present to watch her tortured and abused before she died. He would be allowed to live a short time after Loughlin's death. Everson Blake's father wanted the man who had killed his son to have some time to experience similar grief.

Then, Linus Schwartz had ordered, his demise would be violent and prolonged. He would suffer a miserably slow, excruciatingly painful death.

The presence of the Secret Service had thwarted Lammers' effort to take both her and Morgan from their apartment. But when Loughlin decided to make the trip to Wyoming – alone, they thought – the opportunity to take her first was too good to pass up. She would disappear for a while, according to the quickly improvised plan, and Morgan would be notified where she was once he was out of jail, if he walked, regardless of how long that took. Then, they would take him when he tried to rescue the woman.

With there being no public mention of anything suspicious about the former President's death, the fallacy that it was a stroke seemed to be holding up. That was Schwartz's plan. Each person's death was to appear of natural causes or accidental, until Loughlin's. The opportunity to take her in Wyoming was a Godsend for the old man, until Morgan tagged along. That would've been fortuitous, too, putting him and the bitch he was living with back together for the taking; except that the man started getting suspicious.

The arrogant bastard's snooping had screwed up the revised plan. Lammers was trying to devise a way to take care of Loughlin and Morgan in the same operation. But regardless of how it unfolded, Morgan would have to watch her die, and then suffer a drawn-out, agonizing death himself.

Normally Oskar Lammers was devoid of emotion as he carried out his orders. But he was going to enjoy seeing Morgan watch Loughlin die, and then taking his time with the cocky son of a bitch.

♦

"Maggie, I'm going to get a cab to the house to pick up the Jeep. Do you need anything while I'm out?"

Morgan had taken his new SUV to Washington with them when they moved there. But the Jeep Wrangler that he mostly used for fishing was in the garage of his log home on Moose-Wilson Road north of the city.

"I might go with you, sweetheart."

Morgan's face didn't evidence it, but he couldn't have that.

"Sure, Mag. If you want to. I just figured you'd want to stay with Curtis. If something happened and you weren't here, you'd never forgive yourself." He felt like he was exploiting her friend's condition and her affection for him, but he knew that would keep her at the hospital. He needed to take care of some things.

"Of course, you're right, Josh. You go ahead then. And, no, I don't need anything. Thank you, though." She stood and gave Morgan a kiss.

"It may take a while. I want to look around the place."

"Okay. I'll call if I need you." Another quick kiss and Morgan was on his way – alone.

Morgan would've liked to use the time on the cab ride out of the city for phone calls, but he needed absolute privacy. He wanted to talk to Don Summers, Trent Weston's former legal counsel in the White House and the man who had represented him in his personal legal matters afterward. He wanted to touch base with Betsy Parnell again. Morgan realized the one person he wanted to call that he could do so in the presence of his taxi driver was Alicia Weston. It didn't require the privacy he needed for the other calls. The added bonus was that his call would put an end to the cab driver's efforts to engage him in small talk.

◆

Fortunately, CIA Officer Trevor O'Bannon had never met Art Flynn or the NSA operations guy, Wilf Crawford. So, when the pair took seats at the bar of the *Tejas en Terrador*, along with Crawford's CIA SCS cohort, Seth Tierney, Roadrunner simply sat down directly beside them. A barstool was conveniently vacant. He'd never met Tierney either.

It was nearly eight o'clock. The men clearly weren't going to be discussing anything terribly clandestine. Otherwise, they would've sought a more private location. Or, more likely, they wouldn't have come to the bar at all.

Tierney was on the stool closest to Roadrunner's. The men nodded at each other as the outsider sat down. Roadrunner noticed that Tierney was largely uninvolved in the conversation, so he thought he'd take a run at him.

"American?"

Tierney gave him an icy look, grunted a "yeah," and then returned his attention to his drink.

"I've never been here before. Much to see on the island?"

Tierney never turned to O'Bannon, as he said, "Not much."

"Well, I like it. Kind of reminds me of Cozumel. Of course, it's larger. I've heard the diving's pretty good here."

Before he had left for Terrador, Betsy Parnell had provided Roadrunner a profile of all embassy staff and intelligence operatives on the island. O'Bannon had noted that Tierney was a passionate SCUBA diver. Coincidentally, Roadrunner had brought diving gear as a cover for being in Terrador. It was about to pay dividends.

The other CIA operative's eyes lit up a bit, and he turned to face Roadrunner.

"As a matter of fact, it's really very good." The CIA half of the F6

Special Collection Service team put his hand out. "Seth Tierney."

"Marty Baechtel," Roadrunner said. "Good to meet you, Seth."

"Yeah, Marty, Terrador doesn't have the coral reefs like Cozumel, but lots of pelagics. If you're into sharks, mantas, and such, this is a super place. And I spearfish pretty often. At least when I can get away from work."

"Oh, what do you do?"

"I'm an electrician," Tierney said. His legend for his time on Terrador was well-practiced, so the "facts" of his life rolled off his tongue as if they were really true. "How 'bout you, Marty?"

"Marty Baechtel" pointed to his empty beer glass and motioned to the bartender. Then to Tierney, "Ready for another?"

"Sure."

O'Bannon-slash-Roadrunner-slash-Baechtel held two fingers up and signaled the bartender, "*Dos mas, por favor.*"

"Me? I'm not working right now. Got awarded some money from a lawsuit, so I'm just traveling around spending some of it." Baechtel's life story was as rehearsed as Tierney's.

"You don't say. That's a first for me. I mean, among people I know."

"So, tell me about the shark diving around here, Seth."

The two men chatted on at some length, sharing the same types of old war stories that American males are given to. During the course of their bullshit and bravado, Tierney and Baechtel switched to tequila and moved to a table. Both men had obviously received much training at maintaining their cover identities while drinking, but it was unavoidable that their tongues loosened a bit as the liquor flowed. And the expectation that they did presented the perfect opportunity for Roadrunner to advance the details of his legend that he wanted known. He returned from the *baño*, fumbled with his chair as he tried to seat himself, and let loose a big belch. "Baechtel" giggled.

Tierney laughed along with his new friend and the two men clinked their shot glasses together.

"Hey, Seth, we were speaking of sharks a while ago. Have you heard this? Baby shark, doo-doo, doo-doo-doo-doo. Baby shark, doo…"

Baechtel raised his hands to his face to fend off the napkin Tierney had thrown at him.

"Shut the fuck up, Marty. My niece drove me crazy with that song last time I saw her."

Both men laughed loudly. Marty pounded his fist on the table. He started again, "Baby shark, doo, doo…"

Tierney shook a fist at his drinking buddy with a huge smile, "Ahhhh!!! Stop it! You're killing me."

Roadrunner moved his pinched thumb and forefinger across his mouth as if zipping it shut. He momentarily moved the "zipper tab" back across and pretended like he was going to resume the annoying song.

The talk continued. The tequila tab mounted up.

Finally, Roadrunner said with a slur that was only partly faked, "Did I tell you how I got my money?"

"Yeah, a lawsuit."

"No, Seth. What the lawsuit was about?"

Seth shook his head.

"So – and this will surprise you. I was working for these guys. They were doing all sorts of illegal shit – drugs, money laundering..."

The humor fell off Tierney's face. "No kidding."

Roadrunner held his right first finger up to his lips and said, "Shhh." Then he giggled again and said, "Serious as a heart attack.

"I was collecting from one of their customers. It was a protection racket. I go into this upscale restaurant after hours to get their monthly premium and bam – just like that, they shot me." As "evidence," Roadrunner raised his shirt and displayed the wounds that he had received in the shootout with Everson Blake and Mark Sanders eighteen months earlier.

"Well, that brought some unwanted attention to my bosses. I was out of a job. The prosecutor wouldn't even charge the bastard. Get this, figured it was some sort of self-defense. Well, at least justifiable, they said. But, me, I sue the fuckers in civil court. And... I... won!" Roadrunner exaggerated the words.

"No way," Tierney practically shouted.

Roadrunner made the cross my heart sign. "Swear... to... God."

"Wow! How'd you stay out of jail?"

"My bosses' bigshot lawyer. I don't think they would've defended me except it impacted them. Convinced the prosecutor that the whole thing was a misunderstanding. That got me off. So, here's to lawyers." Baechtel saluted with an extended middle finger. "Oops. Sorry," he apologized before changing his gesture to a raised glass.

"That's a stroke of luck. Lots of money?"

"Yep. Course I spent most of it already. This is sort of my last hurrah, coming here. I'll be about broke, but, hell, what's money for? Right?" Marty affected a melancholy expression and said sadly, "I don't think my former bosses would kill me. At least, I hope not,"

"Baechtel" continued with another giggle. "They just mostly don't want me around." He sighed a prolonged, "Whewww."

There was some momentary silence. "Maybe you could spare a couple hundred grand."

Roadrunner pretended to break down a bit. He sniffled slightly. Finally, he held his glass aloft again and stood. He said loudly, "*Viva* Mexico. I mean... Wherever the hell I am."

Tierney laughed at his new friend as he watched him slump into his chair.

"Don't think I have that two hundred K you mentioned, but I can pay for your drinks." The CIA officer threw some money on the table and helped his drunken pal outside.

"And I might can help you with some work." He drove Marty Baechtel to his hotel, making note of his room number, and went back to his quarters at the U.S. base that he maintained in addition to one at the embassy.

Once in his room, Roadrunner jotted off a note to Betsy Parnell.

"had a good night. might have found work. night."

◆

Outside Langley, Virginia, Betsy Parnell had dozed off on her sofa. Her phoned chimed and she summoned her wits.

"Well, I'll be," she remarked at seeing her officer's text.

When the DCI and O'Bannon had created his backstop about being a corrupt errand boy for the mob, they knew it wouldn't hold up to serious scrutiny. They just hadn't had the time or resources to prepare. But, they'd hoped, perhaps it would hold up long enough to identify someone who might be in on the effort to relaunch the criminal enterprise in Terrador.

"Roadrunner apparently thinks he's found someone who might know what's going on down there. I hope so," Parnell thought.

◆

Morgan had spoken with Alicia Weston. He apologized to her for staying in Wyoming after promising he would be there for her.

"Your place is with Maggie," she had assured him.

He had decided against calling his attorney or the CIA Director. He wasn't sure how much he wanted to tell them.

As he walked into his Wyoming home, his fingers traced the outlines of the bullet holes that had been repaired in the logs that made up the exterior walls. They were reminders of the gun battle he'd had with two of Everson Blake's men. He walked to his bedroom and retrieved the Sig Sauer P226 that he kept there. It was the same one he had used against the intruders. He also pulled out a box of various electronic gadgets. Some were attachments for his smart phone. Others worked independently. Finally, he collected his shotgun and rifle and, looking around his home wistfully, he carried everything to his Jeep Wrangler. He pressed the button on the wall to open his garage door. After a few whirring attempts, his Jeep came to life. He backed out and closed the garage door with his remote.

Morgan rested both hands on top of the steering wheel, looked up and rolled his eyes.

"Well, here I go again, I guess." He turned around in his gravel drive and headed back to the hospital.

♦

It was almost midnight. Maggie was asleep in the chair by Curtis Jones' bed. She still held his hand.

Nurse Tammy's shift had ended. In her place was Nurse Roger, who had opened the door slightly and now whispered to Maggie.

"Ms. Loughlin. Ma'am." Unable to rouse her, he moved to her side and tapped her lightly on her shoulder.

"Ma'am."

Maggie awoke with a start and put her hand over her heart. Nurse Roger jumped back. He smiled and said, "Ma'am, there's someone her to see you. Would you come with me, please?"

Maggie stood and stretched. She followed the man in the scrubs.

Outside the room where Curtis lay, a man held up a blue and gold shield and an ID card.

"Ms. Loughlin, I'm Special Agent Wyman Hope of the United States Secret Service. I'm sorry for the delay in getting here. I came from Cheyenne and got here as fast as I could. Just wanted to let you know that I've arrived and am at your service. Whatever I can do to assist you while you're in Jackson, I'm happy to do, ma'am."

"Special Agent Hope, thank you for coming." Maggie had forgotten about the promise of Secret Service protection.

"Ma'am, do you have a moment to fill me in on the situation regarding your coming here? How long you intend to stay, etc.? Washington said it was for just a few days."

"Of course."

Maggie and Special Agent Hope moved to a small waiting room down the hall from Curtis Jones' room. She explained her and Morgan's qualms and Hope promised to keep a watchful eye for anything suspicious.

At the other end of the hall, Morgan walked to Curtis' room, where he expected to see Maggie. Seeing her belongings, but not her, Morgan assumed she'd gone to the restroom. He wandered around outside the room for a moment. He found a chair and picked up a magazine.

"Only five months old. Not bad for a hospital."

As the minutes ticked by, Morgan became more uneasy at Maggie's absence. He walked to the nurses' station.

"Excuse me…" He looked at the nurse's name badge. "…Roger. Do you know where Ms. Loughlin went?"

Nurse Roger stood and looked around a moment. "Oh, I saw her walking down the hall with some man."

Morgan looked up and down the corridor and didn't see Maggie in either direction. He grabbed Nurse Roger's scrubs with one hand. Roger's eyes widened as Morgan shouted at him.

"Where? Goddammit; where did she go?"

Over the medical attendant's stammering, Morgan heard, "Josh? What are you doing, Josh?"

Morgan turned, still holding onto the nurse's shirt. Maggie hurried to him and pulled him to the side.

"What's wrong with you, Morgan? Get a grip!" Her words were hushed, but the tone was harsh. Morgan hung his head slightly, as Maggie continued.

"I don't know how much more of this I can take."

The two remained silent. Finally, in a more even voice, "Josh, you seem to be lapsing into the funk and paranoia you had right before we got together. It's occasional, but it's showing up more frequently. Morgan, you're the smartest person I know. And I know how much you trust your gut. But, gee…"

Her blue eyes shifted away, and then rested on Morgan again. "These emotional fallouts… they're wearing on me."

Morgan expected the lecture to end in a hug and a word of understanding, but Maggie merely turned and walked back to the Secret Service agent who was tasked with watching over her.

CHAPTER 17

Day 7 – Saturday

The details of the activities associated with the memorial for Former President Trenton Weston had been finalized and made public. The events would begin with the former President lying in state at the Capitol Rotunda on Sunday. After that show of respect, there would be a service at the National Cathedral on Monday.

The tributes would conclude with a private service in the Westons' hometown of Frisco, Texas. Only a very small circle of friends would attend the Tuesday event. Trent had no family surviving him. Alicia had only her sister, Emma Gray. Their closest kin was Josh Morgan, who had been the first person selected as an honorary pallbearer. Of course, members of the armed services would serve as the real bearers of the former Chief Executive's casket.

With her husband, the widow and former First Lady had long ago prepared the personal touches that would be included with their respective funerals. Hers would also be a public affair, but less a spectacle than her husband's, Mrs. Weston knew. There would be but one service; in Texas. But owing to his time in the White House, Trenton Weston's memorial would be grander and more generally organized by others.

"So, that's the schedule, Josh."

"We'll both be there, Alicia." Mrs. Weston hadn't thought of the time zone differential when she had placed her call to Josh. It was six in the morning in Wyoming, but that was okay. He hadn't slept. It was partly out of his friction with Maggie from the night before, but mostly it was his worry for her.

"You know, Josh, Trent once said that, if it were possible, he'd be buried at that place where you took him fishing after you got him back

179

from that terrorist. Or, he'd at least be cremated and have his ashes scattered there."

"That's what I plan for myself, ma'am." His private thought was that he might wind up in eternal rest there sooner rather than later, considering how his life had been going.

"But when you've been President, there are expectations, even demands, that extend past your death."

"I understand, Alicia," he said, although nobody who hadn't been in that position could. "Civilians" had no frame of reference for the baggage that came with serving as the nation's Chief Executive.

"That was a great day, Alicia. You, Maggie, and Trent and I. Even Biscuit was back in good health and running up and down the bank while we fished and picnicked. At least for a brief time, I felt like all the ghosts of my past had been put away."

Each of the two on the call suddenly became unable to speak. Josh tried to resume.

"Alicia, ..."

"Trent thought of you as a son, Josh. He didn't just love you *like* a son. To him, you were more than flesh and blood."

Morgan was so overcome that he could only nod, as though Mrs. Weston could sense that over the phone.

"You go to Maggie now, son. I'll get back to you with exact times. I love you, Josh."

"Love you, too," barely squeaked out.

As much as Morgan would've liked for him and Maggie to spend nights at his house, he felt that she was safer in a public facility, and that she was safest with him around. But, in his mind, he had begun to consider that maybe she was right. Maybe this was all paranoia on his part. Maybe his gut feelings were just the result of the habit he had developed to always fear the worst. It was a well-earned habit, Morgan knew, but he had to consider that maybe there was nothing to his suspicions. But Curtis had expressed worry, too.

He rose from the chair he had slept in and moved to look into the hospital room where Maggie had remained by her friend throughout the night. He didn't know how much sleep she had managed, but she was asleep now. He nodded at Special Agent Hope as he left to go back to the small waiting area.

"How has he managed to stay awake?" Morgan asked himself. "And, without someone to relieve him, when will he rest?" Morgan wondered if, like some military pilots, the Secret Service used stimulants to remain awake and alert. "Who knows?" he mumbled.

Morgan got a Diet Coke and some chocolate-covered donuts from the vending machines. "Now, *this* is nutrition," he said aloud, rolling his eyes for his own benefit.

Back in his seat in the waiting room, he saw a familiar face on the television. QNN news anchor Cameron Neal was announcing the release of details of the coming events. Morgan found the remote and turned the volume up. Too loud, he guessed, seeing the reaction of a nurse he hadn't met – or manhandled yet – at her station. He lowered the volume to a more reasonable level and stood in front of the wall-mounted unit. He watched as he swallowed one of the little pastries practically whole.

"The White House Press Secretary has released preliminary details of the events that will allow the nation to mourn the passing of former President Weston. The President died of an apparent stroke…"

Morgan realized that he'd never met Neal or her senior partner at QNN, Tracy Adams, though the two had covered a great deal of the events in his recent life. Of course, neither of them knew he existed. His role in finding Weston when he was taken by the Saudi agent was unknown to the public. His role in preventing war with Russia was classified, too.

"The honorary pallbearers include individuals from President Weston's personal and public life. They are Sir Albert McGinnis, a longtime friend from the U.K., Weston's former legal counsel, Donald Summers, his personal physician…"

Morgan was mostly oblivious to the names. He watched the scenes in the background of Neal's voice. Various videos and still shots of Weston's life filled the screen, ending with a scene of military honor guards loading his casket into a hearse. Morgan had no idea where they would take his friend. The amount of time between death and interment would be considerable compared to non-presidents. Standing beside the funerary vehicle were what had to be special agents of the Secret Service. Morgan supposed the overwatch would only end when their protectee was laid to rest. He thought Special Agents Johnston and Coulter would watch over the President, but quickly realized they remained with Alicia Weston.

"That's a nice touch," Morgan thought, as he saw the black bands on the arms of the agents. His attention returned to the QNN anchor when he heard, "Concluding the list is Joshua Morgan, a photojournalist from Wyoming and visiting professor at Georgetown University. Morgan is said to be a fairly recent acquaintance." Josh smiled at the description.

"Morning."

Maggie's acknowledgment was short, and without the good cheer that usually accompanied her A.M. greetings, regardless of her personal mood.

Morgan stepped away from the QNN broadcast in the direction of his fiancée.

"Maggie, I'm s…"

She walked back down the hallway, with Special Agent Hope trailing her.

Josh's exhalation would've communicated volumes about his hurt, had there been anyone else in the waiting room to hear it. He lowered the TV's volume. Morgan felt like kicking something or throwing a chair but decided against it. He never demonstrated his outbursts physically. His "explosions" were marked by silence, mostly. Even when they manifested themselves verbally, they took the form of cynicism-laced sarcasm rather than loud, angry shouts.

But, despite his regret at his behavior toward Nurse Roger late last night, and even though he was trying to consider that his suspicions might be unfounded, the little voice in his head insisted something was going on. And that was what made him the angriest. That, and the fact that he couldn't figure out what it was.

He decided it was time to try to find out.

◆

It was very early in Terradora, the island's only city. Despite that his training allowed CIA Officer Trevor O'Bannon to remain mostly immune from screw-ups while drinking, it didn't help the physical aftereffects. He felt like shit. The sight of his appearance in the bathroom mirror of his hotel room was bordering on disgusting, he thought, but it was exactly what anyone who'd seen him partying with his new friend last night would expect him to look like.

A text announced itself on his phone with a chime.

"don't know your plans for today just hope you can finish your thing"

"Damn, Director," Roadrunner groused at the order to wrap up his task in one day. "Well, no rest for the weary – or hungover," he told the sorry figure looking at him from the mirror.

Another text followed immediately.

"btw went fishing yesterday had some bites"

"So," the CIA officer recognized, "someone's looking into my legend."

Parnell had instructed her analysts to monitor any queries into Martin Baechtel's personal history that had been created online as a backstop to Roadrunner's cover. Apparently, someone had done a search.

"We'll see if it holds," "Baechtel" hoped. They'd created his online presence in a hurry.

◆

Morgan had waited in the hospital overnight. It wasn't just because he wanted to be with Maggie, but that he felt safer there, too. Daylight might or might not allow him to spot tails better, but his movements would be more easily seen.

As he was considering what he would do, his phone buzzed again. Morgan looked at the ID of the caller.

"Don Summers. Crap. Doesn't anyone know it's only a little after six here?"

He tapped the green circle on the display.

"Hello, Don. I see we're both pallbearers."

Morgan's defense attorney ignored the opening greeting and launched into the reason for his call.

"Josh, something's bothering me. I know a lot of your background, obviously; first from Trent, and then through representing you. I need you to tell me if I'm just being paranoid."

Morgan chuckled. "You might be talking to the wrong person," he said dryly as he looked at Maggie. She was eating the breakfast that hospital staff had given her. His forehead wrinkled with jealousy. "I didn't get one of those," he complained silently. His attention returned to his caller.

"Go ahead, Don."

"Here's my dilemma. A friend of mine in the Metro P.D. here in D.C. gave me a heads-up that investigators are already close to wrapping up the cases of both Maxwell and Judge Caldwell, with rulings that each was suicide. And that Maxwell had killed his assistant, Siobhan Cassidy, first."

"Well, that's certainly how it appears, isn't it?" Morgan had already decided he wouldn't tell anyone of his own misgivings about the pair's deaths.

"It does. It's a no-brainer, in terms of the evidence. In fact, it appears so cut and dry that higher-ups ordered the detectives assigned to the cases to wrap them up and move on to other cases. They'll wait a few more days to prevent any accusations that they acted in undue haste. But they're done."

"And?"

"I can't really tell anyone this; the whole thing was highly improper. But Siobhan Cassidy got in touch with me. She said that Maxwell had assaulted her. Tried to rape her, she said."

"Why'd she call you, Don?"

"Said she might want me to represent her. I told her that it was premature for me to discuss it with her since we were on opposing sides of your case. It hadn't been closed then. But I told her that if she couldn't find anyone else, to get back with me."

Morgan continued on as though he was on board with the determinations of suicide. "Well, if Maxwell tried to rape Cassidy, and she was about to blow the whistle on him, that would be a strong motive for him to kill her. Wouldn't it, Don?"

"Of course, Josh, and there's even more motivation for him to get rid of her. She hinted to me that she was aware of someone buying off Maxwell."

"Well, there you go. Another reason to kill her."

"But here's my problem. My friend at the DCPD, who is the lead detective on the Caldwell case gave me the timeline of the deaths, including the woman's time of death. Siobhan Cassidy was deemed to already be dead when she contacted me. Either that's an awfully big screw-up by the Medical Examiner's office, or..."

"Or they're altering the evidence."

"Yes. And my friend, Detective Bosley, said that both he and the lead investigator on the Maxwell 'murder-suicide' felt a few things didn't add up. They both felt they were being forced to write their reports with that conclusion predetermined. That's why he called me; to blow off steam."

"Tell them what you know. Tell them that, according to them, you apparently talked to a dead woman."

"That's the thing, Josh. I just don't feel right doing that; especially when it's most likely nothing. Tell me I'm making a big deal over nothing."

"Don, I really do believe you're overthinking this thing," Morgan assured his attorney, although he knew he wasn't. "There are all sorts of things that could cause them to miscalculate time of death. I agree with you. No sense opening a can of worms when the official ruling is right on the nose."

The two men spoke a bit about the loss of their mutual friend and his upcoming funeral. Then Don Summers thanked Josh for listening and for providing advice. They hung up.

Josh had just received yet another piece of the puzzle that added to his uneasiness.

◆

Of course, Roadrunner could've walked right onto JBT in Terrador, with only a call from Betsy Parnell. But what would he find there? No, he decided. It was best to maintain his cover identity as Marty Baechtel. He had no idea if Seth Tierney would turn out to be a source about operations in Terrador. But two things had pointed the CIA chief's attention in his direction. First, he'd had some problems with the law in his younger days. That wasn't altogether uncommon for black bag operators in the Agency. But the main thing was that he had worked for Schwartz Construction some years ago, before it merged with Cannon & Raines to become SCR, Inc. And that corporation had taken on a role of some interest in the last two or three days.

O'Bannon's phone chimed.

"Speak of the devil." Roadrunner accepted the call and adopted a tone that made him seem as though he'd still been in bed. "Yeah? Who is it?"

"It's Seth Tierney, your ray of sunshine."

Roadrunner thought his drinking companion from the previous night sounded awfully chipper, given that he'd consumed as much tequila and beer as he had.

"Rise and shine, my boy. The day awaits."

O'Bannon, as Baechtel, slurred the word. "Seriously."

His caller's voice suddenly acquired a less jovial deportment.

"Breakfast, Baechtel. I'll pick you up in front of your hotel in fifteen." And with that, the connection ended.

◆

Morgan decided his first order of business would be to check out the address that the driver who showed up at the airport had given him. It was the place the chauffer was supposed to deliver Maggie and Oskar Lammers. That apple cart was upset when Maggie's co-passenger wasn't Lammers, but Morgan.

Well out of the town limits, Morgan was surprised to see that, instead of being situated in a residential neighborhood, the house was the only one in the area. It was about three hundred yards off the small highway, with a gravel road leading to it

"Well, if this is some sort of safehouse, you can look at the location in one of two ways," the ex-CIA officer decided. "You can try to lose your hideout in the mix of a number of other houses. Or..." He spoke aloud now, "You can put it smack dab in the middle of nowhere so that you can spot anyone who might be interested in it."

Morgan pulled back onto the highway from the shoulder. He hadn't the faintest notion of how to surveil or approach that house should he need to.

◆

A lot of "Marty Baechtel's" demeanor after a night of heavy drinking was fake, but not all of it. The coffee was welcome, but he wasn't sure he would be able to finish the *Chilaquiles* that Tierney had ordered for each of them. Just as in Mexico, the breakfast consisted of tortillas sliced into quarters and lightly fried until crisp. Roadrunner's was covered with green salsa, in addition to the *crema fresca*. The "fresh cream" was a mixture of buttermilk and heavy cream. The two dairy ingredients created a mild nausea in him.

It was good, but it was still food, and that was unwelcome on the CIA spy's stomach. He ate about a third and pushed his plate away. He signaled the waiter for more *café*.

Tierney, on the other hand, appeared to have never felt better. He wolfed down his entire breakfast, plus three additional *conchas*. The bread was identical to its Mexican version, soft and sweet and with an appearance like a conch shell.

"Showoff," Baechtel muttered to Tierney, eliciting the only smile the F6 operative had offered since they sat down at their table in *Mi Desayuno de Terrador.*

The undercover officer wondered to his pal, "So, what time is it when they change the name of this place from 'my Terradoran breakfast' to 'my Terradoran lunch?'"

Tierney smiled again. After the waiter refilled their coffees, the CIA spook being surveilled said to the one doing the surveillance, "Did a little checking up on you last night."

Roadrunner gave a bewildered look to Tierney. "What do you mean, 'a little checking up?'" He maintained his outward display of being hungover, but inwardly, his alertness increased. Silently, he wondered where this was going.

"Let's just say that, in my job at the base here, I have resources. I went online and found a smattering of information about you on social media. There were a few other references around the Internet."

"Yeah. Social media. Can't seem to stay off of it. So, what'd you find out about me?" Roadrunner's smile was an attempt to show disregard for the revelation.

"You remarked on your Facebook page that you'd won your lawsuit. You said you were gonna buy a new car and house and do some sightseeing around the world. I even saw some references to your dive trips. My professional resources, the more thorough ones, all supported your life story."

"What can I say? Not much of one, but, hey, it's my life."

"You know what I didn't find, though. I didn't find among my databases – and I assure you, they are exhaustive – I didn't find any legal filings about your supposed lawsuit. You know those would be matters of public record, don't you?"

O'Bannon tried not to gulp on his sip of coffees, but he knew he'd been made. He decided to bluff his way further down the crumbling tale.

"I'm sure you just missed it, Seth." He smiled.

"Oh, *I* might have, but the specialists I have at my disposal wouldn't have."

Roadrunner noticed that the two men at the next table were pushing their plates away and turning their attention very noticeably toward him.

"Hi, guys," he said.

"So, who are you? FBI? DEA?" Tierney asked.

Roadrunner instantly realized he was on the right track when Tierney voiced the Drug Enforcement Agency as a threat to himself and whatever he was involved in. The corrupt old organization in Terrador incorporated a number of illegal enterprises, including the drug trade. Made sense for that particular cash cow to be an integral part of any new operations.

"Maybe you're one of my own. Are you CIA?"

Roadrunner dropped his mouth open facetiously and leaned toward his breakfast companion.

"What? You're CIA?" O'Bannon whispered. He looked around the small café and whispered again. "That is *so* cool, Seth. Can I see your decoder ring?"

Silently, though, Roadrunner knew he was in trouble. Otherwise, Tierney would have never disclosed his profession.

The Special Collection Service operative smiled at the audacity on display. But the good humor didn't extend any further. Tierney looked over at the two men who were rising from the adjacent table and nodded.

Roadrunner didn't need any instructions on what to do next. He stood, too, and said to Tierney, "Looks like I'm going to see some more of the island." He reached for his phone, which was lying on the table. The display came to life as he did so.

"You won't need that."

"I won't need that," the phone's owner echoed. O'Bannon tossed it back on the table. Before he did, he discreetly touched an icon in the upper left corner that appeared to show the device's signal strength.

As the two men escorted O'Bannon to the door and their waiting car, the prisoner made a request. "Hey, would you mind getting breakfast?"

Tierney smiled another genuine smile and reached for his wallet and the Terradoran cash inside.

As the two thugs prodded Roadrunner toward the door, he enquired, "I don't suppose you're taking me to a job interview, are you?"

"I like you, Baechtel – or whoever the hell you are," Tierney thought. "Too bad I'm going to have to kill you."

◆

It was the beginning of CIA Director Elizabeth Parnell's workday. She had only just then stepped out of the car. Her driver was moving on to the parking area, when she heard the text alert on her phone. The DCI activated the display.

"Shit!" she said aloud. The message from Roadrunner was a simple exclamation point. The symbol was the result of an app that automatically generated the alert to her phone when an icon on Roadrunner's phone had been touched three times in rapid succession.

Parnell walked into the headquarters of the Central Intelligence Agency and stepped to the side of the doors. She waited. Five minutes passed. Then ten. No additional text. The first alert on her phone that was dedicated to her CIA officer in Terrador signaled that Roadrunner was in trouble. An identical, second alert would've indicated that, though there was a problem, at least he still had his phone. He didn't.

The Director of Central Intelligence walked through the security check without emotion and got on the elevator to her office.

As the doors closed in front of her, her head shook so slightly.

◆

Morgan needed some more things from his home. He would've preferred to just buy more of the items, but none of Jackson Hole's stores were open yet. Besides, he needed to see something. He drove warily up his driveway to the familiar sound of the gravel crunching beneath his tires. He stopped about halfway from its intersection with Moose-Wilson Road and took in the area. At the western, back edge of his property, a cow moose lumbered into the line of trees. He smiled in spite of himself. Ordinarily, he would've lingered to watch her, but now he scanned the grounds around his house.

With nothing apparently amiss in the scene he surveyed, he moved further up the way. He stopped short of his garage and touched the button on his remote. As the metal door began to lift, he noticed the damage on the front edge of the structure that remained from Maggie's Ford pickup. She had crashed into one of the mercenaries who, on Everson Blake's orders, was there to kill Morgan. Maggie had seen Morgan and the man fighting and had slammed into the man, pinning him against the logs of the garage, killing him.

With the garage door fully open, Morgan turned his attention to the interior.

"Just like I left it."

The former CIA officer looked around his property. Everything he could see was clear. He exited his Jeep with his Sig Sauer at the ready. Peering around each corner of his house, he was confident that no one was lurking about.

"Now, the inside." He took a couple of deep breaths and moved to the front door. His mind flashed back to the times when he and Maggie were just beginning to know one another. She always walked right past him boldly into his den each time he had opened the door on her visits.

First, the man looked at the boards of the floor of the porch just in front of the door.

Nothing.

Next, he gazed through the leaded glass of his door onto the floor of the entryway. Just a couple of feet away and slightly to one side, lay a small section of toothpick.

"Damn!" Josh Morgan said at the confirmation. Someone had been in his house since he left the night before. As he had closed the wooden door the previous evening, he had wedged a small section of the wooden toothpick between the top of the door and the frame. It had taken three or four tries to get it to stay there, but he had succeeded. When the door opened next, it would fall, either onto the porch or in the short hallway just inside.

Morgan exhaled so powerfully that he exhausted the air from his lungs. His breathing responded by accelerating to a near pant. It reached a point where he was exhaling more than he was taking in. On the verge of hyperventilating, he steadied himself. He inserted the key into his dead bolt and turned it. He twisted the knob. The door flew open at Morgan's powerful kick. He stepped back from the threshold, half expecting gunfire to erupt from some unknown intruder.

But nothing.

He examined his house. Nobody was there, but the small broken piece of wood made it clear that someone had been.

As far as he could tell, nothing was missing. And he couldn't determine what they might have been looking for.

"Maybe they just thought they'd catch me at home," was the only thing he could come up with.

He tucked the P226 back in his waistband. He really wanted a glass of ice water, but there was none in the fridge. Since he and Maggie no longer lived here, the appliances had all been turned off. He grabbed a glass out of the cabinet and opened the tap. The water was stale, but it wetted his dry mouth.

Moving first to the hall closet and then to the one in his bedroom, he collected the items he had come for.

Morgan moved around the house. His memories created a profound longing to still be living there, with Maggie. He wanted to be far from all the ordeals they had faced and were facing together since moving to Washington, D.C., for her job.

He saw the remote to his TV on the couch and turned it on, just out of curiosity. It crackled to life on the channel he often watched and the face of Tracy Adams, QNN's primetime anchor, appeared in a closeup. Adams was turning over some of the load to Cameron Neal, but he was still the senior person in that chair. So, Morgan wasn't entirely surprised to see him this early in the day. The sound was muted.

Morgan saw that the coverage surrounded the publicized funeral details for Weston. The picture switched to that of the U.S. Secret Service's chief of the New York Field Office. The graphic said he was the head of White House security during Weston's single term there. It also gave his name. Morgan didn't care. Ordinarily, as a news junkie, Morgan would be glued to the television, but today he had no time. He clicked his remote and the screen flickered and crackled as it began to fade.

Morgan immediately pushed the remote again and, before it had disappeared completely, the image popped back to life. The former officer in the Central Intelligence Agency stared at the image only a matter of seconds before dropping the remote and running for the door.

"Maggie!" he said.

He yanked the door to behind him. It didn't close. It didn't matter.

Morgan tossed the binoculars he'd picked up onto the passenger seat along with the camo he used while hunting, started the Wrangler's engine, and roared out of his driveway, spraying gravel behind him as his tires worked in vain for traction.

"Oh, Maggie!"

Morgan pounded the steering with his fist and let loose with a scream that carried no hint of humanity. His Jeep leaned and the tires spun onto the hard surface of Moose-Wilson Road, where the vehicle finally found purchase.

CHAPTER 18

CIA Director Parnell was at a loss. Her own private little operation was completely off the books and unsanctioned. Terrador had a way of bringing that out in people, she decided. But with no official justification for what Roadrunner was doing there, she had nowhere to go for support.

She and FBI Director Austin had consulted about their reservations around the credibility of Linus Schwartz. But that had been about alleged suicides and protecting Maggie. But this was well beyond that. She had known for months that things were heating up in Terrador; that unknown people in the military and intelligence communities were seizing on the rebuilding of the military base there to try to reestablish the illicit activities of years past.

Schwartz's connection to Terrador, both in the past and currently, was the only thing that the man, or his company, had in common with Maggie. And that tie-in was because of Josh Morgan's history with Terrador.

If the suicides of the prosecutor and judge were more than coincidence, then the unifying part of their lives was their participation in the legal proceedings against Morgan. If the assassination of the former President was part of the equation, then Morgan became even more the focal point. Weston was also involved in ending the corrupt activities in Terrador, even more than Morgan. He had fouled up their attempts to maintain the status quo. Weston's and Morgan's initial relationship was about Terrador. Schwartz's company was the contractor for the original buildout in Terrador and was currently bringing it back online.

"So, the D.A. and judge have Morgan in common. Weston and Morgan have Terrador in common. Schwartz has a connection with Terrador and seems to have an interest in Maggie."

The DCI pulled at her hair. A knock rang out from her door.

"Not now!" she shouted.

"This is all so circumstantial," she chided herself. "But things are starting to come together," she countered in her internal debate.

Her thoughts turned back to Austin. She wanted to ask him for help. She had already decided she trusted him.

"But, damn," she concluded, "his agency would be the very one in charge of investigating me for this clusterfuck."

She had few people she could trust. Parnell knew the Agency was out. She considered Sir Albert McGinnis, but immediately rejected involving a foreign intelligence agent, regardless of the help he'd been in dialing back the recent tensions with Russia.

The DCI hated it, but she only came up with one person she could trust. He was the only one who could fly under the radar. And it was familiar turf for him.

"Shit…" was barely a whisper.

♦

Morgan had turned off Wyoming Highway 390, Moose-Wilson Road, and was screaming east along Teton Pass Parkway, Wyoming 22. His phone chimed. He instinctively looked at it, though there was no way he would answer.

"Parnell," the ID read.

"Dammit, Betsy. Not now!"

♦

At the George Bush Center for Intelligence in Langley, Virginia, the Director of Central Intelligence was exasperated as she heard the voicemail greeting.

"Morgan; leave a message."

Parnell knew his line wasn't secure, so she had a momentary debate with herself about how much to say. Ultimately, she knew she would have to be more explicit than she would've liked. When she heard the beep, she made it quick.

"O'Bannon's in trouble on that island you love so much. He needs your help." The CIA Director was about to hang up when she added, "*I* need your help."

She hung up, wondering why he didn't pick up, and hoping he would call.

♦

The entire way to 2580 Teton Pines Drive was covered up with construction. The just over eight-mile drive took Morgan almost twenty minutes, even considering that he was speeding when the congestion allowed and darting in and out of lines of traffic when he was able. He locked his brakes and slid into a handicapped parking spot near the door of the hospital.

Josh raced to the room where Curtis Jones lay. He was awake and fairly alert. He looked pleased to see Morgan, but his visitor wheeled about and retreated to the nurses' station.

"Where's Maggie?" he demanded.

Nurse Tammy had apparently heard of Morgan's encounter with Nurse Roger. Her look of fright was instantly apparent. She pushed against the desktop surface of the modular furniture and her chair rolled backward – away from Morgan.

"This is important, Tammy. Where the hell is Maggie?"

"She just left with that agent guy."

Nurse Tammy stood and appeared ready to run if Morgan moved closer.

"Why is all her stuff still in Curtis' room?" he demanded.

Nurse Tammy had had enough. She put her hands on her hips and said, "Now how should I know that? And you…" She pointed a finger at Morgan. "You are way out of line. Roger may take it, but I'm…"

Before the medical aide could finish her sentence, Josh was headed back to where Curtis lay.

"I'm glad you're ok…"

"Where's Maggie, Curtis?" Josh demanded.

"Well, she's gone with Agent Hope. He said you'd had an accident and that…"

Morgan bolted out of the room into the corridor. He placed his right hand on his forehead and paced back and forth a few steps. Nurse Tammy had called security, but they hadn't arrived yet. As Morgan rushed down the hall, she stepped in front of him to try to delay his departure until the guards arrived.

"I'm sorry!" he said as he hurried around her. He rushed back to his Jeep, where a Jackson police officer was speaking on her radio, apparently requesting a truck to tow away the vehicle that had parked in the handicapped space without a permit.

At the end of the parking lot, an unexceptional sedan was pulling away. In the front passenger seat, Josh saw Maggie. He screamed and ran toward the car, but Maggie couldn't hear him with the automobile's windows up. And she was turned away from him toward the driver, so she didn't see him. The driver, on the other hand, was looking past Maggie directly toward her fiancé. He sped up his departure, turning left and away from the approaching figure.

Morgan put on the brakes and ran toward his Jeep. The police officer was walking toward him, speaking into her radio. As he had with Nurse Tammy, Josh moved around her with an abrupt, "Sorry."

The officer yelled after him "Sir, you can't..." But he was gone. She already had Morgan's license plate numbers and had called it in. He sped away in pursuit.

Though he needed to go the opposite direction, the Secret Service agent had turned away from Morgan. But in doing so, he had driven into the construction zone.

When Hope's progress was halted, so was Morgan's. Morgan remained almost a block behind.

Morgan considered leaving his Jeep and making a dash for the agent and Maggie. But he knew that if he failed to get there before they resumed moving, he would fall irretrievably behind. Maggie would be gone. So, he sat tapping the wheel of his Wrangler with both hands, hoping that the moment would come when Hope was ordered to stop, while he was allowed to proceed.

◆

Seth Tierney and his two thugs had blindfolded Roadrunner for the ride, so he had no idea where he was. But now, he was sitting in a small room, unshackled and without a cover over his eyes.

O'Bannon's drinking buddy sat across from him. The other two men stood by the doorway.

"Does this mean we're not going out for drinks later?" Roadrunner quipped.

Tierney scrolled through the items in his "guest's" phone.

"Well, I'm surprised. Really, your password is 1-2-3-4-5-6?"

"I'm not really good with technology," the prisoner answered about the simple password that a large number of people used. The ease of access was intended to bolster the idea of a user who had no technical sophistication. Of course, a few keystrokes on the device's calculator would open up an entirely different set of apps.

CHAPTER 19

To say that Maggie was confused would have been an understatement of colossal proportions. She had lived in Jackson Hole a number of years, so she knew the way to the police station. It was less than a mile away from St. John's Medical Center. She'd even thought they could have walked, considering the presence of the roadwork along the street.

Therefore, Maggie Loughlin did a doubletake when Special Agent Hope drove past the intersection of East Broadway Avenue with South Willow Street. He had convinced her of the need for this ride by telling her that Morgan had had some sort of confrontation with the police. It wasn't serious, the agent had said, but her fiancé needed her at the police station. However, a turn left onto South Willow, and then a right turn onto East Pearl would've taken them directly to the Jackson City Police Department.

"We're well past the police station, Agent Hope."

"I have a stop to make, ma'am."

"Okay," Maggie replied, but the Jackson native's intuition was telling her that something was badly off.

This agent was from Cheyenne. He came because there was no field office in Jackson Hole. What business could he possibly have here? And whatever it was, why would he let it interfere with his assignment to assist her?

Maggie would like to have thought that her escort knew what he was doing, but she didn't. Other thoughts were beginning to occur to her. Such as, why hadn't Morgan called himself? And why didn't this vehicle appear more, well, official? It was a standard sedan.

She noticed that the driver continually looked into his rearview mirror nervously. Maggie was growing increasingly uneasy.

The driver in the sedan finally cleared the construction zone, but he saw in his mirror that the Jeep behind him had, too. And the backup of the traffic from the interruptions prevented Hope from pulling away from the tail. Finally, at South Cache Avenue, where East Broadway became West Broadway, and where the street took on the added designation of Wyoming State Highway 191, the traffic began to flow more normally, and spaces were opening up to maneuver. The sedan gained some separation from the Jeep Wrangler. The extra ground Hope had picked up gave him some confidence that he would elude Morgan. It wasn't to be. Very near the Jackson Hole Lodge, where WY 191 veered southwest, the traffic stalled again. This time it was due to an accident, no doubt created by overanxious drivers trying to negotiate the fallout from the construction.

All vehicles were directed into the right lane. Hope saw that Morgan was only four cars behind. At least traffic was continuing to move, though at a snail's pace. Morgan wouldn't dare risk trying to overtake him on foot.

♦

CIA Special Collection Service Officer Seth Tierney continued his examination of his prisoner's phone.

"Just a few texts on here. Girlfriend?"

"Marty" dropped his chin in feigned embarrassment. "My mother."

"Are you serious?" Tierney and his cohorts all laughed. "We'll see."

The SCS F6 operative pressed the phone number in the contacts that was identified as 'Mom."

♦

Morgan's strategizing was interrupted as his phone chimed to announce a call.

"Parnell again. Shit!' Then it occurred to Morgan that, as unlikely as it was, she might have news about Maggie. He pressed the display to connect.

"What, Betsy?"

♦

Betsy Parnell was just beginning to explain the situation in Terrador to Morgan when the phone that was devoted to her officer on the Latin American island rang.

"Morgan, you have to hold on."

"Hold?" Morgan couldn't believe it. "Can't."

At the realization that Morgan had hung up, she uttered, "Crap!" However, her tone changed instantaneously when she pressed to connect the other phone.

"Marty, is that you? You were supposed to call me earlier. And last night, too. You know I don't like text…"

The person on the other end of the conversation terminated the call. How the DCI wished she could have the NSA track down the origin of the call. It might come to that, she knew, but, even if it did, it might be too late to help Roadrunner.

Parnell tried to reconnect with Morgan. No answer.

◆

Finally, Maggie said to her driver, "You're not really Secret Service, are you?" Her answer was an icy stare.

There was an extended time in which nothing was said. Maggie began to look around. She focused on the latch to unlock her door. Seeing her interest in it, and with the pace of traffic finally picking up, the driver began to accelerate south out of town.

At the increased speed, if Maggie jumped out, there would be a heavy cost physically. And if she were incapacitated after her escape attempt, Agent Hope – or whoever he was – would just drag her back into the car and head to wherever.

But Maggie also knew that the longer she stayed in the car, statistically, the greater peril she was in. She decided she would try to come up with some other plan and only jump as a last resort.

She turned fully around and saw a familiar Jeep darting in and out of traffic trying to catch up, it appeared. Morgan's Wrangler was identical to any number of others in the recreational playground that was Jackson Hole. But, considering the aggressive nature of the vehicle, she knew it had to be him.

Seeing his passenger previously check out the interior of the car, the driver observed that her attention now centered on the outside.

"Agent" Hope said, "Well, this little charade wasn't going to last forever. If you go quietly with me, no harm will come to you," he bluffed. "And who knows, perhaps that will give you enough time for that boyfriend of yours to save you."

Maggie couldn't think straight. The overload on her ability to sort things out was too much.

"But you jump out of this car or make any other attempt to escape. I will shoot you now."

The imitation agent pulled a gun and pointed it at his passenger.

Maggie hoped that Josh overtook them.

♦

The flow of traffic had become fast-paced. As things opened, Morgan had a clearer view of the sedan he was chasing. But, with no interference in front of him, he was losing ground. All hope that he would catch the car carrying his fiancée was evaporating.

♦

Hope saw that he was putting his adversary well behind him. Maybe he could use that to his advantage, he thought. He found a small Forest Service road and pulled onto it. The car fishtailed as it moved from the paved highway onto gravel. If Morgan pulled in behind him, he would be lying in wait and take him prisoner, as well. If not, if the pursuer stayed on the highway, Hope would slip in behind the man's Jeep and overtake him.

Either way he would have an advantage. He knew it – and Maggie knew it.

♦

Well ahead of him, Morgan saw a sedan begin to turn off of 191. It was a speck at that distance, but Morgan was sure it was Hope's.

♦

Wyman Hope hit the accelerator hard, intending to create distance from the road where his follower might soon appear, if it followed. The sedan's speed was up to nearly fifty on the dirt road, when, suddenly, a hand reached from the passenger side and yanked downward on the wheel.

Hope slapped Maggie's hand off the steering wheel with his right hand and tried to regain control of the car with his left. But the damage had been done. The car veered sharply right. Hope overcorrected with a hard move to the left. The vehicle slid sideways up the gravel surface before gaining traction on a smoother portion. When it did, the sedan shot leftward and hit the ditch that bordered the washboard road. The driver turned the wheel right and the car settled in the small ravine, still moving ahead until it turned up on its right side. It slid for several yards before coming to a stop. It teetered a moment and then rolled onto its top.

Hope was dazed, but not injured. He tried to brace himself, but when he unlatched his seatbelt in his inverted position, he dropped awkwardly and heavily onto the upturned interior ceiling of his auto. His passenger appeared conscious, though shaken. The weight of her body strained at the safety belt that held her in place. Hope put his gun directly against Loughlin's head, fully intending to pull the trigger, but in a moment of clarity, he realized that his pay depended on delivering the woman alive. He removed his finger from the trigger.

Collecting himself, the fake agent slid through his broken window and rolled to all fours. He began a slow crawl around the front of the upside-down car. Just as his torso made the turn around the fender, he felt a searing pain in his left buttocks. The impact caused him to flip onto his back. It was accompanied by an explosive report that was still echoing between the walls of the surrounding hills.

He knew that, in his addled state from the rollover, he had failed to notice that the man whose appearance he'd expected was already there. On his back, ahead of the upturned sedan, he pointed his gun in the direction from which he had crawled, the direction of the gunshot.

"Drop it!" came from the passenger side, to where Morgan had reversed. "So help me, God! I'll put a bullet in that fucking brain of yours!"

CHAPTER 20

Wyman Hope, the man who had pretended to be a U.S. Secret Service agent didn't have to think too hard to make his decision. The barrel of the Sig Sauer directed toward him, combined with the coldness of the eyes looking over it, convinced him. He dropped his gun to the grassy dirt adjacent to the Forest Service road.

Facing skyward and in excruciating pain, he raised both hands above his chest. He stared at the former spy who was walking toward him.

Morgan put his own Sig Sauer in his waistband and picked up the injured man's H&K handgun and held it on him. Morgan found the man's backup in an ankle holster and stuck it in his pocket. Further frisking assured him that the man had no other weapons, so he moved back to the passenger side of the car, where Maggie was struggling to free herself.

"Hold on, sweetheart. Slide your legs to the side; toward the steering wheel." When she had done so, Morgan placed his hands under her arms. "Now, unbuckle your seatbelt."

Maggie dropped downward to the ceiling of the sedan, her fall cushioned by the support of Morgan's grasp. The two hugged briefly, but Morgan noticed that hers seemed to lack any enthusiasm.

"Probably the shock of the crash," he decided.

He rested her against the car. She sat with head in hands. Then she moved her right hand to the back of her neck and began to rub it."

"Are you okay, Mag?"

Maggie shook her head and squeezed her eyelids tightly in an attempt to fight off the cobwebs. Finally, she nodded.

"I guess."

Morgan assessed her condition visually. Nothing appeared to be serious. Just some bumps that were already swelling and some minor scratches.

He returned to the man he'd shot in the ass.

"What put you on to me?"

"No armband," Morgan revealed.

"Huh?"

"All the Secret Service agents on the news wore identical black armbands in memory of President Weston. I realized you didn't have one."

"Clever."

"My turn. Where's the real agent who was supposed to show up for Maggie? Did you kill him?"

"Didn't have to. We just called the Secret Service office in Cheyenne and told them we were the Jackson PD." The man strained to look at his rear. "You shot me in the ass?"

"Does it hurt?"

"Like a son of a bitch!"

Morgan smiled his satisfaction. Maggie had risen and was standing directly behind him.

"Anyhow, we just told them that Ms. Loughlin had asked us – the police – to take care of her. She lived in Jackson and had friends there that she trusted."

"That easy?"

"Yeah. That easy."

"What were you going to do with her?"

"Me? Oh, I only had to deliver her to my employers. One actually flew in with you. He's at our safehouse."

"Employers," Morgan thought. Just business. He shook his head in disgust.

"And them?"

"They were going to mess her up pretty good. Then they were going to drop her corpse off to you. That is, if you weren't already there to watch."

Morgan shivered with rage and pointed the gun at the wounded man. A light breeze chilled him through the sweat that was beginning to form. He began to apply pressure on the trigger of the H&K handgun. But he realized he had one more answer to get.

"Who do you work for?"

The man held his hand against the left cheek of his rear. The pain was increasing, but he managed to laugh.

"Do you know how many times I've been threatened? Do you know how many times guys tougher than you have tried to get me to talk? You'll never…"

The counterfeit agent's voice was stopped in mid-sentence by a single nine-millimeter round through his head.

"Then I guess we're done here," Morgan concluded.

Maggie jumped at the thunderous explosion of the shot from Hope's own H&K. The sound terrified her. The sight of Hope's head being propelled upward from the cataclysmic impact of the bullet with the ground after it had passed through it brought a wave of nausea. Her hands rose to her mouth and her eyes turned to Morgan and then back to the soulless eyes of the man on the ground.

Morgan took out a knife and retrieved the forty-caliber slug from Hope's butt that he had fired earlier from his own gun. It wouldn't do to have it linger around as evidence. Ballistics reports existed from the rounds taken from his property eighteen months before. The bullet in Hope's rear could be tied to him.

There was no need to recover the bullet that had passed through the pretend federal agent's head. He had delivered that with Hope's gun, which he was taking with him but that wasn't traceable to him.

"Let's go, Maggie," Morgan said matter-of-factly. He took her by the arm and tried to lead her to his Jeep, which was still running with an open door about thirty yards up the road. Maggie yanked away and glared at Morgan, her blue eyes at once misty and cold.

"You shot him!"

"Yes, I did. Now, we need to go."

Maggie pulled away again and created some distance between her and Josh. She let loose a muted scream and spun around, her short auburn hair slightly trailing the whirl of her head. With her back to Morgan, she screamed again, and pulled at her locks.

Maggie finally faced Josh. She alternated her eyes from him to the body of the man near the crashed car. A pool of blood had formed around his head. The single circular dot beside his nose dripped red, too. Even though the ripped flesh and cracked skull of the exit wound in the back of his head weren't visible, tissue and bone fragments had ricocheted off the dirt beneath him and had sprayed outward from where it had come. But, against the horrifying scene, and even compared to the ghastly event itself, what disturbed Maggie Loughlin most was the emotionless expression on Josh's face. He seemed unmoved by the violence he had just committed. His eyes were vacant. She would like to have thought he was in shock, but she realized it was something else, something that terrified her.

Morgan wasn't bothered by his action at all. He was completely and totally void of remorse.

◆

"I guess you talked to mom. She's not gonna liked getting hung up on. Worse, she's going think it was me," CIA Officer O'Bannon, aka Roadrunner, aka Marty Baechtel, scolded.

As a result, for the first time since he'd been taken, his captors brought physical consequences to his smartass remark. The blow across the face from one of Tierney's associates sent Roadrunner onto the floor.

"Speaking of Mom," Roadrunner muttered, "she hits harder than that."

That brought a kick from the second man. The pair of thugs lifted "Baechtel" back onto his chair. Roadrunner was lifting his hand to his bruised face when one of the men seized it along with his other and brought both behind him. A large black cable tie wrap secured his hands.

Tierney moved to the side of the desk where his prisoner sat. He leaned against the flimsy wooden table and folded his arms. He held up Marty's phone, then tossed in onto the desk.

"Oh, I doubt that was really your mother." He nodded to his muscle, who began to pound the defenseless man in the face and stomach.

After a minute or two of relentless brutality, they paused.

O'Bannon could barely lift his head. He smiled as well as he could through bleeding lips. His words were soft but clear.

"Wow. I thought you were supposed to ask questions first."

"Would you have answered them?"

"Don't know anything," O'Bannon bluffed.

"Then there was really no point, was there?" Tierney pointed to his two thugs. They alternated blows to Baechtel's face. They stopped after three each.

Roadrunner was reeling. He widened his eyes a couple of times, trying to persuade them to focus. His left eye was starting to close. He sensed the taste of iron, as blood formed in his mouth. He could even feel wetness from his left ear, which he assumed to be blood, too. Sounds from that side were muffled.

"Now, we'll get to the questions."

♦

Morgan gathered up Maggie's purse from the upturned car and examined it for any other sign that she'd been in it.

"Maggie, you can be angry later." Morgan pulled at her left arm, leading her toward the idling Wrangler. "Right now, we *have* to go."

"It's not anger, Josh."

"What?" he said, stopped momentarily to absorb what she might have meant. He shook his head in frustration and resumed directing her toward the Jeep. "Well, whatever it is, we'll deal with it later."

Maggie jerked her arm away and trotted on her own to her seat in the vehicle.

Morgan spun his tires backing up. A quick turnaround and he was speeding forward toward Wyoming 191 and back to Jackson Hole. First, he knew, he had to figure out where Maggie would be safe. He didn't want to introduce anyone else into the equation that was his life. Tag knew much of his past profession due to the deputy's involvement in the events surrounding Morgan's role in rescuing Trent Weston those years ago. But his friend was away fishing.

"I wish I was fishing," he muttered. Maggie neither understood nor cared what Josh had said.

"He said he didn't have cell service, but I'll try anyhow," Morgan thought. He touched Scott Taggart's name and... straight to voicemail. Morgan got the greeting he had earlier. Tag was out of town. Wouldn't have cell service. And so on.

"Tag, I sure hope you get this. I need help. Well, Maggie needs help. Just call me if you get this." He disconnected from the call.

He really wasn't sure if his fishing pal could – or would – help. After all, he had just murdered someone – again.

Beside him, Maggie sat without a word. In her heart, she knew that Josh was justifying what he'd just done as being all for her. But she was frightened by the emotionless way in which he'd carried it out, his failure to consider other alternatives, and worse, his lack of hesitation in killing the man. It was as if she really didn't know Josh. Or, maybe there was just a side of him that was at odds with what she thought she knew about him.

She finally stared at him.

Josh retuned Maggie's gaze. He expected to see anger in her blue eyes. Instead, he read something else. He was puzzled at first. But then he understood that what was in her eyes was disappointment. Disappointment and a broken heart.

He held his breath and bit his lower lip as he pondered how to respond to what her eyes were saying. He didn't have the words. But at that moment, his heart was breaking, too, as he realized that things might never be the same for them.

Morgan felt he had to say something, but he didn't know how to begin.

Before he could form a response to Maggie's unspoken questions, red and blue lights flashed behind him. Were the law enforcers onto him already? He didn't have time for this, but there was no way he would outrun a police car – anyone, for that matter – in his worn-out Jeep. He pulled over and turned his flashers on.

He reached for his wallet and considered what he was going to tell the officer, who was approaching in a sort of circuitous route. His hand was on his gun, though it wasn't drawn. As Josh looked up with his license in hand, the officer stood more erectly and took his hand off his gun.

"Morgan?"

The Jackson Hole resident thanked God when he looked up to see a face he recognized.

"I thought you were back east now." Teton County Deputy Sheriff Eric Nash put his hand through the open window of Morgan's Jeep and shook the driver's hand.

Morgan grasped his hand and said, "Can I get out?"

"Sure. Sure, Josh." The deputy opened the door for him. Like Morgan, Eric was a displaced Texan who had moved to the Tetons area in pursuit of scenic nature and trout. He was an avid amateur photographer, though not an especially good one. In fact, he had been in the Community Education photo class that Josh had taught – the one where Morgan had first met Maggie. Morgan didn't know Deputy Nash as well as Tag, but they had all fished together a couple of times.

"Yeah, I am, Eric. Living in D.C. The deputy frowned and spat a brown string of tobacco at the reference to the seat of the national government. "Just in town for a couple of days while Maggie takes care of some personal business."

Nash stooped and looked into the Jeep toward the passenger.

"Hey, Maggie," he greeted with a slight wave. He was rewarded with something less than a smile.

And then to Morgan, "I remember her from the photo class. She's still quite the looker. Say, have you talked to Tag? He's off to the 'River of No Return Wilderness' in Idaho. It's a weeklong rafting and fishing trip. Asked me to go, but, of course, we weren't allowed to both take off."

Nash leaned against his friend's Jeep as though he planned to stay a while. Josh was growing increasingly impatient with the friendly banter. He didn't have time to waste. It had already been a terribly long day.

"Maybe we can do some fishing while you're here."

Just as Morgan was about to explain that he was only in Jackson Hole for another day or so and was wondering how he was going to extricate himself from this wretched conversation, Nash's radio mercifully squawked another call.

"Hate to skedaddle, man, but gotta run." Eric Nash shook Morgan's hand with the grip of a vise and turned to his patrol car. Morgan took his seat behind the wheel of the Wrangler. Suddenly, the deputy spun back around.

He walked back to Morgan's driver-side window. Morgan had started to raise it but lowered it again. Deputy Nash pointed to Morgan with one hand, with a puzzled look on his face, and scratching his forehead with his other hand.

"Almost forgot. What's the deal with you at the hospital? A police officer said you ran off – well, she used the words 'fled the scene' – from a handicapped parking lot."

"Sorry, Eric. I'd had a bit of a dustup with Maggie." He tilted his head toward her. "Forgot to pick up some stuff for her. You know, woman stuff. And she came with me when I ran off to correct the error of my ways. Was just in a hurry."

Josh patted Maggie on the leg, and even if it was probably unnoticed by the deputy, Josh felt the slight flinch.

At the mention of feminine needs, Nash cringed, without realizing that Morgan just had, too. It occurred to him that his explanation didn't account for why he was in the handicapped parking space to begin with, only the rushed departure. And the police officer, if asked, would say that he had left alone.

The deputy raised his hands. "TMI, my friend." Then he resumed the short walk back to his car.

"Fleeing the scene of an illegal parking incident." He laughed loudly. "Serious violation, Mr. Morgan." Another chuckle coincided with another call from his radio. "Hold your horses. I'm coming."

The Teton County deputy turned off his flashing lights and pulled alongside Morgan's Jeep.

"You're just lucky I don't have more time. I would haul your ass in. We don't allow that shit in my county. Nah, I'll talk to her and make it good. See ya!" Through the raised patrol car's window. Morgan could see he was laughing again.

"What the hell!" Morgan was about to boil over as the Sheriff Department's car began to back up again, but he smiled.

"Thought you had another call to attend to."

"I do. Just wanted to tell you that you were speeding. We'll forget that, too." Finally, Eric Nash drove completely away.

Morgan was shaking at the close call. Anyone else and he would've had to explain his actions. Part of the trembling, though, was because he felt sure that the deputy's other call might be about a murdered man, whose body was lying beside a crashed car not far away. He reviewed the scene in his mind and decided he'd left nothing that would incriminate him.

Morgan drove his Jeep slowly from the shoulder onto the state highway and toward the city he called home.

♦

Without any better plan, Josh drove back to the hospital. He drove around the parking lot slowly – twice – on the alert for anything suspicious, in general, or Lammers, in particular. All appeared clear.

He escorted Maggie to her injured friend's room. "Escorted" wasn't exactly the word for it. Maggie had refused his arm or even his hand when he offered it. She had walked briskly ahead of him until he grasped her arm in the hallway and turned her to face him.

"Maggie, you can't tell…"

"Don't worry, Morgan. I won't say a word."

Maggie pulled away from Josh's grip sharply and left him in the hallway as she completed her walk to see Curtis.

Morgan knew that the restoration of his relationship with Maggie would, at best, take a long time. But, he worried, "Might this event be the one thing she can't get over?"

One thing that Maggie was right about, though he didn't know she had thought it: He had absolutely no remorse about killing Wyman Hope. He'd had enough of being a target – from people whose plans he'd fucked up in Terrador years ago, to those that might be trying to get him now. He was done with waiting. He would take the fight to them and he would finish it.

And there were no rules anymore.

♦

CIA Operative Trevor O'Bannon never disclosed any information about who he really was or what he was doing in Terrador. But Tierney and his goons had beaten the "smartass" out of him long before he passed out, which he eventually did.

Tierney left him sprawled on the floor in the shack, guarded by one of the men, while he and the second heavy left for the U.S. base where they all worked.

The F6 operative had decided he would let his drinking partner stew overnight and take another run at him the following morning. If that failed to produce any information, "Marty" would disappear. In the meantime, he would do some more digging. And he'd get some help

When he reached the military base, he stuck his head into the cubicle of his Special Collection Service counterpart from the NSA.

"Hey, Wilf, old buddy, old pal." Crawford rolled his eyes and shook his head at the tired, old line Tierney used when he needed something.

"What do you need, now, Seth?"

"You know that guy I was drinking with last night? Well, he said he's looking for work. He has a checkered past, but I was still hoping to help him out on the base."

"Working with us?"

"Good lord, no! Somewhere else. Anywhere else," he proclaimed with a smirk. "I'm going to vet him a little from my side," Tierney told his friend. There was no need to tell him he had already done so. "Was hoping maybe you could do the same through some of your NSA channels."

"Don't see why not."

"Thanks. You know, before I go sticking my neck out for him, I'd like to know some more about him."

"*No problema.* What's his name?"

◆

Morgan was alone in the small waiting room down the hall from where Maggie sat with her friend. Occasionally he would walk past Curtis Jones' room and look in. Curtis, who was improving rapidly, would smile at him, but Maggie never looked up.

"Wonder when it's gonna sink in that you've lost a leg, pal?" Morgan wondered and returned to his seat alone.

He'd long since decided it was a good thing that he hadn't been able to involve his friend, Scott Taggart, in this latest mess. Tag might've covered for him, even at the risk of losing his job – or worse – but Morgan couldn't put him in that situation. So, he'd left another message for the deputy saying that everything was fine. He was fine. Maggie was fine. But nothing could be further from the truth.

Morgan had only one person he felt he could go to. He knew it was going to cost him.

"Betsy. Morgan. Sorry for not being able to talk earlier."

CIA Director Parnell's mood improved significantly at the sound of Morgan's voice. She had decided that she had to ask for FBI Director Austin's help and was just about to call him.

"No matter. I'm glad you called."

"So, tell me the deal with Trevor."

Neither Parnell nor Morgan wasted time engaging in pleasantries or small talk. She didn't ask about Maggie or her friend. Morgan didn't ask how things were in Washington. Without voicing it, both knew there was something more important and more threatening going on.

So, the DCI spent the next several minutes filling Morgan in on Roadrunner's mission to Terrador, and about his alert that told her things were off the rails.

"What's the deal with the Company and unsanctioned ops in Terrador?"
Parnell ignored the dig.

"I'd like you to go down there, Josh."

"Figured you might. Here are my terms. They're non-negotiable."

◆

FBI Director Gabe Austin was reporting his findings to Noah Chandler, the President's Chief of Staff, as it concerned Linus Schwartz.

"No, sir, Chief Chandler. We haven't found anything in the past or present behavior of Mr. Schwartz, or activities within or by SCR that appear suspicious."

Austin didn't pass along any of his conversation with the CIA Director. He felt like talk of suspicions of murders disguised as suicides, their links with Weston's assassination, and connections to Terrador all sounded like the wild speculation and conspiracy theories you'd hear about on cable TV. Neither did he tell Chandler of Parnell's disclosure that she had someone snooping around in Terrador. It wasn't germane to the Bureau's investigation. Besides, if she wanted to tell anyone, she would.

Austin personally felt that Schwartz was dirty as hell. He had a predisposition to think of billionaires that way, but there were a number of things that came up with regard to the man's business dealings. The details showed some occurrences over the years that had provided enormous advantages to him. They just seemed to be too coincidental, too out of the blue. But none of them had anything to do with the matter the Chief of Staff had asked him to look into.

"And Josh Morgan? Any connection to him?"

"Not that we found, sir. Please remember this was a rush job gathering the information, but we tried to leave no stone unturned. Bottom line is this: We found nothing to suggest that there is any direct connection between Schwartz and his company to Maggie Loughlin or Josh Morgan. The possible tie-in to the reconstruction of JBT – tenuous, at best."

"Okay, then."

"I'll keep digging, if you wish, sir."

"No, that won't be necessary, Director. But before we go, do you have an update on the assassination of President Weston?"

"We're making progress, sir. As you know, we've identified the specific toxin that was used. It was a cocktail of several things. We're trying to determine where it was manufactured, whether domestic or foreign. It was an ingenious blend, really. But no hits, so far."

"Gabe, any idea where Weston might've been exposed to it?"

"No, sir. We're tracing the President's steps over the last few days, but nothing yet."

◆

At twenty minutes, the task had taken longer than Parnell wanted, and she'd had to call in more favors than she could spare, but she phoned Morgan.

"A C-21 just left Hill AFB near Ogden, Utah. It's an Air Force version of a Learjet. It had carried a Congressional delegation there for a base inspection. They'll have to fly commercial back to D.C., but so what?

Anyhow, the base is less than two hundred air miles from you. It will be there in half an hour. It'll fly Maggie back to Reagan, where a protection detail will meet her on the tarmac. Is that acceptable?"

"Yes. And me?"

"You'll fly with Maggie to Peterson Air Force Base in Colorado Springs. It's a slight detour for her, but you'll pick up your ride to Terrador there, and she'll go on to D.C. Will that do?"

"Yes. And the other passenger?"

"He'll meet you at Peterson. Already approved and he'll be taking a C-21 to meet you there. Anything else?"

"Not right now."

Josh saw Maggie pacing the hall outside the room where Curtis Jones lay. He approached her cautiously.

"How's Curtis?"

Maggie never faced Morgan. "He's going to make it."

"Wow. Great news."

Maggie leaned back against a wall of the hallway with her arms folded. Morgan joined her.

Maggie, we have to talk."

"Morgan, I'm not ready."

"Not about us."

She stared at Morgan, disappointed that his first priority wasn't about "us."

"We have to get you out of town. You're not safe."

"Even with the mighty Josh Morgan protecting me – ready and willing to slay anyone in his way?" She saw the remark cut Morgan. She was glad. "I thought you'd taken care of things."

"Maggie, I think he worked for Lammers. You know, the guy on the plane with us. And I'm betting he's still around."

Morgan watched her turn away again. He pulled her back around.

"Listen! You said that Curtis is going to make it. You wanted to get back for Trent's funeral. Betsy Parnell has an Air Force jet landing at the airport here. It'll be here in half an hour."

"Oh. So now your presuming to make my travel arrangements for me, to schedule my itinerary?"

"Damnation, Maggie! Just shut up! Okay? You don't like what I did. I get that. But in your heart, you know you trust me. Right?" Josh raised his eyebrows and tilted his head toward Maggie hopefully.

Maggie said nothing but walked past Morgan toward her friend's room.

"Terrific," Morgan thought, and sat in a nearby chair.

About ten minutes later, Maggie emerged from the room with her belongings in her arms. She only looked at Morgan and waited.

Josh rushed in and said a quick goodbye to Curtis.

"I don't know what's happened, Morgan, but she'll come around."

"I'm not so sure, Curtis."

Morgan joined Maggie and the pair left the hospital and got into his Jeep.

CHAPTER 21

Oskar Lammers' associate had failed to deliver Margaret Loughlin. More concerning was that he hadn't checked in. And now, with news breaking about a murdered "Secret Service special agent" – the Jackson police hadn't yet discovered that he was an impostor – Schwartz's fixer had no doubt that Hope was the victim.

He was surprised at how formidable a victim this Morgan character was turning out to be. Lammers called his boss, who was unable to maintain the calm demeanor he always had, irrespective of the seriousness of the difficulties he faced. He was in a rage.

"Dammit, Lammers, what the hell is going on? Apparently, you can't get this thing done. Am I not able to rely on you?"

"Sir, I assu…"

"You can't assure me of anything, damn you! This was going to be practically impossible to keep me from being tied to this, but you assured me at the outset that you had a plan. You would carry out my wishes and would keep me safely disconnected. You can't even complete the list of targets. I'm beginning to wonder if I might go down, after all."

"I will get this done, sir."

"Are you sure, Mr. Lammers?" He paused to regain control of his emotions. "I am an old man, Mr. Lammers. I've lived my life. I am not so concerned with being held responsible for all of this, *IF* the objectives are reached. Mind you, I don't want to go to jail, but if my son's death is vindicated, I will face the music."

Lammers eyebrows furrowed.

"Son?" he thought. "He had a son?"

Linus Schwartz had never told anyone about fathering Everson Blake, not even the associates closest to him. He hadn't intended to now. It just spilled out. That's why the now-billionaire had disciplined himself to maintain such tight control over his emotions. They caused slips of the tongue, and he had many secrets to keep. From his murder and disposal of the body of Dottie Stovall's husband to the various acts necessary to build his business, there had been many things for which he held no regrets. However, authorities deemed a great many of those acts illegal.

Linus Schwartz took solace in the fact that, even in the midst of his recent inability to get the job done, Oskar Lammers was first and foremost a loyal and trusted employee. He would never mention his inadvertent disclosure to anyone. Nor would he ever bring it up.

"Mr. Lammers, whatever the cost to me personally, you must see this thing through. Protect me, if you can, but the goal comes first."

Schwartz ended with, "Rest assured, whatever happens, I have your back."

As Schwartz hung up, Oskar Lammers took no comfort in the last words. Having worked for the businessman for a number of years, he'd seen firsthand what punishment the billionaire meted out to whatever and whomever stood in his way. Lammers had himself delivered a significant portion of his messages.

"'Have my back?' More likely he'll have me shot in the back if this thing goes sideways."

♦

Anthony Drake was packing up to meet his driver downstairs. The FBI Deputy Director had much on his plate but had decided to get home and see his wife, and maybe share a late dinner. He paused and sighed, and hung his head at the knock on his door.

"Naturally," he said under his breath before telling his visitor to come in. He sat down so it wouldn't appear that he was leaving.

FBI Supervisory Special Agent Annchi Liu entered, followed by lab technician, Carl Smith. "Evening, Tony."

"Annie. Smitty. Have a seat."

SSA Liu spoke first, "You know the two suicides – the U.S. Attorney and the federal judge?"

"Of course."

"When our CSIs collected evidence from Riley Maxwell's office, they found a number of things. Of course, they sent everything back to the lab for analysis. Tell the Deputy Director what you discovered, Smitty."

The Crime Scene lab technician stood. He'd presented findings to Drake a few times. Each time, he felt like he was speaking to God.

Drake knew a little more about Smith than he did most of the technicians. The young man had played an instrumental part in the investigation of the bombings directed at President Hendrickson recently.

He smiled at his demeanor.

"Please, sit down, Smitty. If you stand, I'm going to feel like I have to, and I'm too tired."

"Oh. Yes, sir. Well, the field CSIs found a bottle of some sort of fluid. I analyzed the contents in a controlled setting." Smitty started to stand again as he handed his boss' boss a piece of paper. He caught himself and sat back down.

"It's a toxin, sir. That's the chemical composition."

Drake looked only momentarily at the lines and letters on the page before lowering his cocked head to stare at the technician.

"These might as well be hieroglyphics, Smith. I'm a manager; not a chemist. Besides, didn't Maxwell shoot himself?"

"Well, yes, sir. He did. No doubt about that."

"Then what's the big deal about this?"

"I only got one hit on what it is, Deputy Director. Just one. And it linked to something that came in just this week." The techie handed another printed sheet of paper to the deputy to the Director of the FBI, who looked at it and shrugged.

"Go on."

"The second sheet of paper shows a chemical compound that is identical to the first. It's the same toxin that killed President Weston."

♦

Despite its relatively small size, the craft was equipped with radar. Initially finding the larger vessel by its blip on the screen, once it had approached to within three-quarters of a nautical mile, no electronic assistance was necessary. Even with only its anchor lights glowing, the silhouette of the eighty-four-foot yacht was clearly evident under the glow of a nearly full moon.

The Pacific waters were calm, with only gentle swells lifting the craft at brief, regular intervals. Two men in the smaller boat rushed to toss fenders over the starboard gunwale to cushion it as it pulled alongside the one where the meeting would take place. Then, they tossed lines to men aboard the yacht, who pulled their guests' boat snug against the swim deck on the stern.

Two men stepped onto the *Bella Maga*, and their transport motored away to circle the host boat on the lookout for unwanted visitors. Past the outer lounge, the new arrivals saw their business partners in the dimly lit salon. In addition to the main deck, the *Beautiful Magician* boasted a lower deck and a flybridge, upon which armed men also watched for other boats, both visually and on the radar.

Seth Tierney was the CIA side of the Special Collection Service detachment in Terrador, but he wasn't here in that capacity. Neither was Porter McCall representing his employer, the National Security Agency, at the conference.

The men already on the boat had drinks in front of them. Several beautiful, young women in bikinis, or topless, sat on their laps or hung on their shoulders. But as the two *Norte Americanos* appeared, their counterparts from South America ordered their playthings away, slapping their asses and laughing at their power over them.

"*Buenas Noches, Señor* Tierney. *Señor* McCall" Five of the six men stood. The only one who did not was Carlos Castañeda. He nodded his superiority to the Americans.

Four of the men from Colombia were the leaders of the drug cartel that had operated freely in Terrador when Castañeda's brother Juan was dictator. The fifth man was the equivalent to a Chief Financial Officer in the illicit organization. Each was sophisticated and several American-educated.

During Juan Castañeda's regime, these men from the cartels had found a willing partner and the island became a hotbed of money laundering, human trafficking, drug trafficking, every vice-based activity imaginable. When the U.S. military and intelligence community expanded the small air strip into a major base, Castañeda found himself in the middle of a literal war. Though he benefitted financially from the payments from the U.S., the military was there to strike specifically at his partners. Ultimately, corrupt individuals within U.S. agencies injected themselves into the lucrative enterprise. When Castañeda was overthrown and the air base scaled back due to political pressures at home, operations on Terrador ended.

The men on board the *Bella Maga* were a planning committee, of sorts, to rebuild their corrupt organization. The recently approved initiative to rebuild JBT provided the background for the Americans to become involved, and it was their information that would enable the activities to thrive, despite the increased strikes against South American cartels.

Porter McCall would play a critical role. His job in the NSA would allow him to inform his cartel partners when and where strikes would occur. Of course, they would have to suffer some losses to avoid suspicion, but they could move their assets around to minimize them. Furthermore, since he was the lead man in identifying targets for the special ops warriors, he could in large part direct the operators' attacks against other cartels. This would provide a measure of protection for his associates, while directing most of the damage to competitors.

Seth Tierney's role would be to gather intelligence just as his CIA job required. But he would use the discretion that he and his F6 partner possessed to pick and choose the targets where they would plant listening devices and whom they would surveil.

He would pass on information through his job in the Special Collection Service that benefitted his partners while crippling their competitors. All the while, the United States would be racking up victories; just not against the members sitting at the table on the yacht.

The plan for Carlos Castañeda was to have him elected president. He had failed in his first attempt because of the electorate's hatred for his brother. But the economy had been struggling in recent years. Any positive effect from the revitalized Joint Base Terrador hadn't grown to its full extent yet. The citizens were unhappy. Throwing enough resources into Castañeda's second attempt to become Terrador's leader would help, just as money did in American politics, but it would be physical intimidation toward voters that would assure his victory.

Over time, he would solidify his support in his military through bribes and blackmail, and thereby secure unchecked leadership.

After the eight men concluded discussion of their organizational needs, Tierney spoke up.

"A problem had occurred."

"And what ees thees problem?" aspiring dictator Castañeda demanded.

"There's a man snooping around the island. He says he's just a tourist, but I suspect he's looking into things. I don't think he knows anything. Maybe it's just preemptive. You know, the government sending someone down here to keep things above board. Still, the collapse of our earlier organization years ago was undone by a covert operator turning on us."

The head of the cartel asked, "Why do you suspect him?"

"He started a conversation with me in a bar. At first, I was just going to blow him off, but I decided to check up on him. I did some research on him and his bullshit story, and... There's just not much information about him."

"Den keel heem," Castañeda ordered, with a dismissive wave of his hand. He leaned back in his chair and drew from his cigar.

Around the table, his associates' eyes demonstrated their disdain for him. None of them liked or even respected the brother of Terrador's former dictator. But he would be useful, so they tolerated him.

"It's not that simple," Tierney said. Castañeda shifted his eyes to the man who had dared to correct him and blew cigar smoke in his direction.

The F6 operative continued. "He might be just the tip of the spear. If he's trying to insert himself in our operation, it might be because somewhere, somebody's got their eyes on us."

"Go on, Seth," insisted the cartel boss.

"I need to know whether he's here because he suspects something, or just digging blindly. Hell, he might even just be a tourist like he said. But until I know – and I *will* find out – I'll keep him alive."

The men all agreed and ended their meeting. They demanded food from the staff and recalled the entertainment in the form of the women.

CHAPTER 22

Day 8 – Sunday

Takeoff to landing, the flight to Colorado Springs was just under two hours. Morgan and Maggie never spoke. The adapted Learjet landed not long after midnight.

Morgan thought long and hard about shooting the phony Secret Service agent. He remained unrepentant, except for having done so with Maggie there. She would've been profoundly disturbed to know that he'd done it, but he wished he'd have sent her some distance away so she wouldn't have had to watch.

And the fact that the sight of Hope's head opening up didn't bother him bothered him.

The Lear C-21 Air Force jet taxied away from the runway to an isolated location on the tarmac. Morgan stood to leave. He turned to Maggie and smiled weakly. Seeing none in return, he simply walked down the aisle and departed the plane.

As her eyes followed him out the door, Maggie was filled with inner turmoil. She still loved the man she thought she knew but was utterly crushed by the revelation of his colder, more brutal side. Was it something new, she wondered, birthed by the succession of personal crises? Or had it always been there, simply dormant until events rocked his soul sufficiently to bring it to life?

Maggie was jolted out of her speculation by her phone's ringing.

"Maggie Loughlin," she said, recognizing the number.

"Maggie, this is Betsy Parnell. I just received confirmation that you've landed at Peterson Air Force Base. I've made a slight addition to your protection. I'm texting you two photos right now. They are Special Agents out of the Denver Field Office of the Secret Service. They will be boarding the plane to travel to Washington with you. In light of what you just experienced, I wanted you to have absolute peace of mind."

"Hold on." Maggie looked at the photos in her "Messages" inbox. "Yes, I have them now."

The CIA Director's apparent involvement rattled Maggie.

"Betsy, where is Morgan going?"

"You should take that up with him. Have a safe flight. We'll have you home soon."

The line went dead.

The two men in the texted photos appeared in the cabin and introduced themselves with words and credentials. They offered Maggie assurances of their commitment to keeping her safe. One took a seat directly in front of her; the other, across the aisle to her side. The second agent got on his phone to report that they were with their protectee.

Outside the plane, Morgan was greeting a gentleman in Army battle dress. While the men shook hands, Josh looked at Maggie through the window of the military version of the business jet. But she wasn't looking back. He was devastated. But there was business to take care of, and he returned his attention to the man who would be traveling with him to Terrador.

As Maggie turned to look at Josh, his face was just turning away. She placed her hand on the window, as though it would send some sort of positive energy to him.

She recognized the soldier he was meeting as Master Sergeant Tom Lechler. She had met the Green Beret at Landstuhl Regional Medical Center near Ramstein Air Base in Germany just a couple of months ago when Josh was recovering from being shot in Russia.

MSG Lechler had led the team of Army Special Forces warriors known as SPIRITs, who were poised to take down the plane carrying Russia's president.

Knowing the types of missions Lechler's team was assigned to made Maggie even more fearful of what Morgan was about to do. She decided she had to say something more to Josh before he left, but the Air Force lieutenant attending to her for the flight was already closing the aircraft's door.

Maggie settled into her seat and looked out the window again.

Josh walked away with Lechler and never looked back.

♦

"You know you're delaying my retirement, don't you?" the Special

Forces operator said to Morgan.

"Yeah, I've found that circumstances can do that. They have a way of dragging you back into things – kicking and screaming. At least, for me."

"Well, friend, I'm happy to help. What's the plan?"

The civilian laughed aloud at the soldier's question.

"Plan? You actually thought I had a plan?"

Both men smiled as they walked to an Air Force vehicle that would take them to the transport that was waiting for them.

◆

It was 2:30 AM in Washington and Federal Bureau of Investigation CSIs had returned to the office of Federal Prosecutor Riley Maxwell. Since it was an active crime scene, no additional authorization was required.

One of the investigators looked at the copy of the report from the initial inspection of the office on her electronic pad.

Without looking up, she pointed to the desk that had belonged to the D.A. "Lower, left drawer."

An associate opened the drawer where the bottle of liquid had been that had turned out to be a toxin of the type that President Weston had ingested. He held up a coffee cup with the thumb and index finger of his latex-covered hand.

Despite the thoroughness of their investigation of the site, no thought had been given to the notion that a stained coffee cup would have any evidentiary value in a murder-suicide. They had only taken the bottle of fluid because they didn't know what it was. Now they had a cup that was stored near the bottle. Maybe it would shed additional light on things.

◆

In the Bureau's Crime Scene Laboratory, technician Carl Smith was pulling an all-nighter. He'd decided to take a deeper dive into the personal life of U.S. Attorney Riley Maxwell. He'd asked a computer tech whom he knew to help with the examination of the digital content that had so far stymied other FBI hackers.

Specifically, he wanted his geek buddy to take a crack at a file folder found on Maxwell's home computer. If anyone could open it, Lane could. He'd been at it a couple of hours while Smitty examined the new physical evidence that field personnel had brought in – a coffee cup from the deceased's desk.

Smitty carefully sampled the DNA he'd taken from the rim of the glass mug. It would take hours to prepare and profile the sample. It was never as quick as it was on television. But he would flag it for priority treatment, and that would mean an answer by noon, owing to the fact that the Bureau's capabilities far exceeded those of non-federal organizations.

"Got it!" Alonzo Lane announced with some amount of glee and an even greater degree of personal satisfaction. "Child's play, really."

Smitty walked to the slightly younger Lane and patted him on the shoulder.

"You da man!' They celebrated Lane's achievement with a fist bump. "Now, let's hope it leads to something."

The computer technician clicked one of the files residing in the newly-opened encrypted folder.

"Financial transactions," noted Lane.

"Yeah…," agreed Smitty, running his fingers across the lines of dates, notes, and dollar amounts, just as he would a physical, paper report. "And the account numbers appear to be from a foreign bank. That's a stroke of luck for us – well, at least if the information is relevant to our investigation."

Lane continued, "And foolish of Maxwell. One of the major benefits of offshore accounts, besides exploiting tax loopholes, is anonymity. We might've never found this account. And if we had, getting the name of the owner and the transactional details would've been a nightmare. Idiot."

The two FBI squints continued to explore the data before him.

Lane remarked, "The only transactions are deposits. Almost all are $5,000 and they occur biweekly." He did some quick mental math. "Wow, Smitty! That's $130,000 a year!" He whistled. "Wonder what he did to get this."

"Yeah, Lane. Me, too."

Lab Tech Smith moved to his own computer and pulled up a bureau database that would identify a company by its acronym. He typed in the letters he'd seen as the identity of the electronic depositor.

"P…T…H," he told Lane, as he pressed each letter's corresponding key.

Lane was looking over Smitty's shoulder now at results that covered over three digital pages.

"Dang! That's a ton of companies. Try sorting it, Smitty."

Smith was already using the filters at the top of each column of the results of his query. He sorted by location. Nothing jumped out. He tried market capitalization. Still no inkling of what company "his" PTH signified. Several other attempts yielded no meaningful direction, either.

"What about that?" Lane said, pointing to one of the last columns on the tabulated data.

The "File Activity" column provided a date for the most recent instance of data entry by anyone in the Bureau concerning the corresponding company. Clicking on the date would execute a link to the entire list of entries for that business. Some of the companies had no date because the FBI had never had the need to enter any content about them. Those companies fell to the bottom of the sorted list.

Smitty looked at the company with a PTH acronym that had moved to the top.

"This company's last entry was today – or, yesterday, that is," Smitty corrected at he looked at his watch. "Petroglyph Transnational Holdings." The two techies looked at each other and shrugged. Smith clicked on the link to examine the notes. He recoiled from the screen.

"I don't see this very often. The handful of case notes were all entered by Director Austin. The first one was last Friday. What's 'NFA' mean, Alonso?"

"No Further Action. Means he's basically closed the case. Although there might not have ever been a real case opened."

"Hmm…" Smitty was scanning the entries on the screen with his finger again. The first note says that some Secret Service guy wanted information about a car he saw in some parking lot." He continued reading subsequent notes.

"Next note says that the car belongs to PTH. Next one says that PTH is a shell company ultimately tied to Schwartz, Cannon, and Raines."

"The company that gets all the government construction contracts?"

Smitty nodded. Alonso Lane took over the narrative.

"'NAI' – That's No Additional Information. Means the Director didn't find anything else worth noting. The next to last note says he informed the President's Chief of Staff. That's when he NFA'd it."

"The Chief of Staff? That's sort of weird," Smitty observed.

Neither of the FBI technicians had any awareness of the questions Austin, CIA Director Parnell, or White House Chief Chandler had about Schwartz and his business empire, but they knew one thing."

"Maxwell was on the payroll of PTH, Smitty."

"And that means the money came from SCR, ultimately."

Lane sat down. Smitty rubbed his weary eyes and stretched with elbows out and hands interlaced on the back of his head. He pulled his left hand free and held it in front of his face. Four o'clock.

Carl Smith wasn't prepared to make the decision on the next step. He decided to call Supervisory Agent Liu. She could decide whether to wake up Director Austin.

◆

It had only been a few weeks since they'd last seen each other, but former spy Josh Morgan and Master Sergeant Tom Lechler spent a few minutes catching up.

"So, still planning on retiring?"

"That's the plan. Would've been gone by now but had one more op to run. Thought I was finally done till some sorry SOB I met in Russia called in a favor." The sergeant looked Morgan in the eyes. His smile was faint, and Morgan wasn't sure how to interpret it.

"Yeah, well, I'm sorry about that. I don't trust many people, even in usual circumstances."

"And these aren't 'usual circumstances,' I assume."

Morgan rolled his eyes and exhaled. "You could say that."

"So, how's your girl? Maggie?"

"She's good," Morgan replied and then hurried on to another line of conversation.

"So, that last op you mentioned – wouldn't have anything to do with the Saudi president's plane going down a week or so ago, would it?"

The sergeant's face contorted somewhat, as if he were genuinely perplexed. "No idea what you're talking about, Morgan." Then he winked.

Morgan's thoughts turned to Maggie as he leaned back to try to get comfortable. His travel companion had spent a great deal of time on these types of aircraft, Morgan knew. His only experience was his flight from Andrews Air Force Base to RAF Brize Norton, the British military installation west of London. It hadn't been that long ago, but it seemed like a lifetime. The Airbus-manufactured A400M Atlas employed by the Royal Air Force had been built for the same purpose as the C-5 he was flying in now. The cargo capacity of the RAF craft was over eighty-one thousand pounds, but that was roughly one-third of the standard payload capacity of the Galaxy at two-hundred-forty thousand pounds. The space differential hardly mattered though. Aside from crew, Morgan and Lechler were the only ones aboard.

What did matter was the cruising speed of the USAF plane compared to the RAF's. The GE turbofan jet engines generated a normal cruising speed of 540 MPH, and without cargo, the jet was moving at a somewhat faster pace. The British Atlas' turboprops only moved it along at 485 MPH. It might not have sounded like much to Morgan, but some quick math meant they were flying about twelve percent faster. Timewise, that meant a flight time of about five-and-one-half hours to cover the approximately three-thousand miles from Colorado Springs to Joint Base Terrador. That shaved about forty minutes off their arrival time, compared to the just over six hours that the British turboprop would've taken to traverse the distance.

The C-5 had left Peterson AFB at around 2:00 AM. They would land at the military outpost at around seven-thirty.

It was about 4:00 AM Mountain Time, which was the same as the Terradoran time zone. The satellite phone that Parnell had arranged for delivery to Morgan rang.

"Hi, Betsy."

"Morgan. I want to go over your cover story for this op."

The ex-CIA officer realized that, at the use of the word "op," he was back in the fold of the Agency. Maybe not "officially," in the strictest sense of the word, but he was indeed working for the Company again.

"Hold on, Betsy." He connected the earbuds that had been in the package containing the phone. He and Lechler each put one side in an ear.

"Go ahead, Director. I have the Master Sergeant on the line with us."

"Thank you for agreeing to do this, Master Sergeant."

"This is the Army, ma'am. They don't need me to agree to anything. But, you're welcome."

Over the next several minutes, DCI Elizabeth Parnell explained the operational details to her men. She had decided a straightforward approach was the best. The less "made-up shit," as she'd called it, the better.

"I sent a message to our station chief in Terrador, Art Flynn, a few minutes ago informing him that you would be arriving in a few hours. I had one of our guys manufacture an ID for you, Morgan. It's the pic you used on your passports when you travelled to Russia. But it identifies you as Matt Fenton. My message to Flynn said that you report directly to me and that he didn't need to know more."

Parnell's tech had also set up Morgan's legend in the Agency's database. It didn't need to have any backstory since anyone who tried to get into his file would get an "access denied" message.

"But even though you couldn't use your real name since you have some measure of notoriety for your journalism, the sergeant can. Lechler, you're yourself. So, I just sent the photo in your Army file.

"Morgan, you're there at my behest to assess the buildout and get the lay of the land for future ops. The Master Sergeant is assigned to the op to evaluate JBT in terms of proximity to targets known only to you. I told Flynn that all of what you two are doing is 'need to know;' that he doesn't need to know. I said he will be read in soon."

"So, we're not obligated to explain anything to anyone down there?" Morgan summarized as a question.

"Correct," answered the DCI.

"That should make things a little easier," added the Green Beret.

"That's our thinking, sergeant." Parnell started to provide a few more details about Terrador but realized who she was speaking to. "I guess you know all about the country, don't you, Morgan?"

"I'm sure a lot of things have changed, but I'll figure it out."

"One last thing," the CIA Director said. "Flynn will deliver some items to you before you disembark the plane. Nothing sensitive, because I've recently discovered I can't trust the twit. It'll be some civilian clothes, maps, stuff like that. You got the weapons I ordered to be on the plane at Peterson?"

"Yes, ma'am," answered Lechler.

Betsy's admission that she didn't trust her station chief disturbed Morgan. "Any chance Flynn's one of the bad guys?"

"Roadrunner doesn't think so."

"Okay, then."

"Get some rest."

"We'll be in touch."

Morgan and Lechler removed their ear buds.

"So, you've been here before."

"Yeah, a few lifetimes ago."

♦

Roadrunner was in pain. Having been shot before, he'd felt worse, but this was still substantial. He'd received no food or water. He'd been allowed to relieve himself. He figured it was because Tierney and crew didn't want to deal with the smell or mess. He occasionally felt himself slipping into sleep but had forced himself to remain awake.

O'Bannon had sat in the same chair that he'd been questioned in throughout the night. Through the plastic tarps tacked over the windows, he could tell that the sky was beginning to lighten, although the sun was still below the horizon.

The captive wondered if he was on his own. It was sure beginning to feel like it. He had struggled in vain to loosen his hands from the plastic binding, but to no avail. While he was passed out from the beating that he'd endured, his captors had used a cable tie to secure his hands to the chair. They had pulled his arms around the back, and not only was it extremely uncomfortable, the pressure of the wooden frame had caused his arms to go to sleep. Roadrunner worried that his numbed limbs would fail him at a critical moment if the opportunity for escape arose.

His single guard had dozed on and off in the chair on the opposite side of the desk in front of the CIA officer, feet propped up, handgun on his lap. He jolted to alertness as he heard a key turning the lock and the door beginning to open. He held his gun at the ready, but, as he expected, it was his relief who walked into the room.

"Up and at 'em, sunshine," the new arrival told his counterpart. He followed that by walking over and slapping the back of his prisoner's head.

"You, too."

He cut the strap tying O'Bannon's hands to the chair, and then the one that bound his hands together. While his partner kept watch, he placed another tie wrap on his hands, this time securing them in front.

"There. That should allow you to take a piss and a dump."

Overnight, Roadrunner's restraints had been removed entirely while he emptied his bladder in a coffee can in the room. There had been no chance for escape then. Now, however, thug number two led him out the door to the outside world. The CIA officer took in as much of his surroundings as he could in the brief walk to the tiny outhouse.

He was in the jungle, completely surrounded by trees. He realized that the sun had actually risen a little earlier. Trees had shielded the cabin from its rays, leading O'Bannon to think it was earlier than it was while he was inside. No sounds were apparent, other than the bugs and birds that always filled the background in movies with a tropical setting. Roadrunner saw no signs of human presence aside from the small, but well-built structure he was being held in. So, he obviously wasn't on the military base. But he was close.

The sound was the first thing that had caught his attention, but through the tops of the trees against the brightening sky of the dawn, he caught intermittent glimpses of a military transport descending toward a landing.

Roadrunner realized the scrutiny of the two men guarding him would make escape impossible now, but if an opening presented itself, at least he knew which way to run.

◆

The C-5 Galaxy transport completed its rollout on the newly resurfaced air strip at Joint Base Terrador. The base's original designation had simply been U.S. Army Base – Terrador, despite the fact that the Air Force had maintained a presence since day one.

The aircraft shook as it came to a complete stop. Outside, a Senior Airman and an Airman First Class secured the landing gears with chocks. CIA Officer "Fenton" and Master Sergeant Lechler walked down to the cargo hold from the troop deck on the second level and waited. The huge, hinged nose of the enormous craft began to rise. From the very bottom of the fuselage to a seam just below the forward cockpit windows, the giant opening to the cargo area climbed to a vertical position. A solitary figure walked up the ramp to the yawning entrance to the aircraft.

"Mr. Fenton, I presume." The CIA station chief in Terrador shook Morgan's hand. "Master Sergeant." He extended his hand again. "I'm Art Flynn. The Director informed me you were coming."

The men dispensed with small talk. The CIA officer and the Army Special Forces soldier weren't permitted to divulge any details about their visit to Joint Base Terrador. Flynn wasn't allowed to ask. So, there wasn't much to talk about.

"Okay, then," Flynn said. "Here are the items Director Parnell requested for you." He set a duffel bag and a small box on the deck of the plane. "Here are keys to the pickup truck outside. Don't worry. It's a civilian model. The DCI also had me confirm that Security received your information. They did, so you'll be able to come and go from JBT, as you please. Parnell said you weren't going to be credentialed, so, if you run into any trouble, here's my number at the embassy."

Morgan took the card.

"Sometime this afternoon, Mr. Fenton, come by the embassy and report that your passport has been lost or stolen. Embassy staff has already completed a DS-64 form for you to that effect. You'll only need to sign it. That should cover the fact that you don't have a passport."

Due to the DCI's information that Matt Fenton didn't have a passport, Flynn knew that wasn't his real name. He was also certain this was an expedited trip. There had apparently been too little lead time to prepare a passport for "Fenton." But, as Parnell had made clear, Flynn "didn't need to know."

"You have your passport, Master Sergeant?"

"Yes, sir."

"Okay, I'll leave you guys to your... whatever."

Flynn walked down the ramp to a waiting car.

Morgan and Lechler moved to a more private area in the aft section of the plane. A few minutes later, two tourists emerged from the C-5. Morgan had a "Hawaiian" shirt and white pants. Lechler wore khakis and a striped shirt.

"How come you got the cool white pants, Morgan?"

"'Cause I'm Crockett. You're Tubbs." Both men smiled at the recollection of the *Miami Vice* television show they had watched as kids.

Lechler took the seat behind the wheel. "Fenton" happily deferred to him.

♦

"So, tell me, Flynn. Who are those guys?"

"Hell if I know," the CIA station chief replied to Wilf Crawford. The NSA SCS officer worked with Seth Tierney, who was indirectly under Flynn's supervision. "I shouldn't tell you this, but they're down here doing some snooping around for Parnell. One's CIA. The other's an operator."

The Director of Central Intelligence was correct in thinking she couldn't trust her man in Terrador about even little things. But this "little thing" was about to become a very big one.

◆

Morgan – or Fenton – decided "first things first." He had Lechler drive to the embassy, where, as promised, a form was awaiting his signature. The staff gave him a document attesting to the fact that he had requested a replacement passport.

He walked to the lobby where Lechler was seated, reading a Spanish language *periódico*. He tossed the local newspaper aside and joined Fenton as he walked toward the exit.

"Well, that should keep me out of trouble if any authorities question me."

"Where to first, Matt." Morgan noticed that the sergeant didn't have to think before calling him by his cover name.

"O'Bannon's hotel room, I think."

"Makes sense."

◆

"As you asked, I did some digging about Marty Baechtel. Not much there." Crawford gave Tierney a printed summary of what he'd found through his NSA resources. It was no more than what Tierney had uncovered on his own.

Tierney was disappointed, but said, "That's okay. Anything's helpful."

"Sorry I missed you at breakfast this morning. Was giving Flynn a lift to JBT."

"Oh?"

"Yeah. He was dropping off a truck and some personal items to a couple of guys who just flew in. The CIA Director sent them down here to do some snooping around."

"Really."

"Some rush-rush, hush-hush factfinding trip. Apparently, they're assessing JBT's readiness as a forward base of operations. And get this. The two guys flew down here in a Galaxy. Just the two of them." Crawford paused to laugh. "If only the taxpayers knew."

Crawford's CIA partner in the Special Collection Service, or F6, group laughed along with his counterpart, but Tierney was instantly suspicious.

◆

Maggie hadn't gotten much sleep, but she rose early to visit Alicia Weston. The former First Lady had asked her to attend the private visit to her husband as he lay in state in the Capitol. The pair, along with Alicia's sister, and some close friends from Texas, would arrive at the Rotunda just after noon. Mrs. Weston would have some private moments, before the other members of her group joined her. Next, a few officials from the current administration, including President Hendrickson, would join the mourners. Finally, the Capitol would be opened to the public. It was only 10:30 and about fifteen hundred people were already lined up to pay their respects. More were arriving by the minute.

Maggie had found that it was easier to be angry and disappointed with Josh when he was right in front of her. With him gone, she could only wonder where he was – and worry. The presence of Master Sergeant Lechler had left Maggie convinced that Morgan was in the heart of something very dangerous.

◆

FBI Supervisory Special Agent Annie Liu had elected to not wake her boss when she had received word from Carl Smith that D.C. Attorney Riley Maxwell had undoubtedly been receiving payments from one of Linus Schwartz's companies. But neither did she wait until he was in his office.

Liu had called Deputy Director Drake at about 6:00 AM. They both hurried to the FBI headquarters and had huddled ever since, brainstorming about what that could mean. For a non-public employee, there might've been any number of rational explanations for the payouts. But since Maxwell was a servant of the people, his position prevented him from accepting payments of any kind from any source outside the U.S. government.

Tony Drake hadn't felt that he needed to inform anyone of the new information just yet.

That was about to change.

◆

Upon learning that both Loughlin and Morgan had left Jackson Hole, Oskar Lammers had taken the first available flight back to Reagan National. His meeting with his boss wouldn't contain any good news.

"I've gotten information that Ms. Loughlin is back in D.C. And she's surrounded by Secret Service."

Lammer's boss was dismayed but resisted the emotional outburst he delivered to his troubleshooter on the phone when he learned that things were falling apart in Wyoming.

"And Mr. Morgan?"

Lammers dreaded the revelation he was about to make about the man upon whom Schwartz was so fixated.

"I have no idea, sir." The employee saw the briefest flash of anger in his employer's eyes.

The billionaire philanthropist leaned back in his luxurious leather chair and began to tap his fingers against one another under his chin.

"None of our sources have heard anything at all concerning his whereabouts."

The eighty-two-year-old stopped his tapping and stared directly at his fixer. Momentarily, he resumed his nervous habit.

"Very well. I think it's time we abandoned any hope of pursuing Ms. Loughlin. Focus your entire efforts on Mr. Morgan. If possible, bring him to me. If not…"

Then Schwartz divulged the truth about his fatherhood of Everson Blake to his employee. Since Everson's aunt and guardian, Deirdre Blake, had passed, Oskar Lammers became only the second person on the planet who knew of the existence of his employer's son.

"If you must kill Mr. Morgan, tell him that it's for my son."

"Yes, sir. I will."

♦

FBI Crime Lab Technician Carl Smith's excitement at his discovery didn't allay the trepidation he felt at presenting it to his boss. SSA Liu was in her boss' office, so Smitty would be doing his reveal to the Deputy Director at the same time he announced it to her.

"Deputy Director, Annie. The DNA results from the cup found in D.A. Maxwell's desk are in. It's… uh, well… the…"

"Spit it out, Smitty," an impatient Liu demanded.

"The DNA belongs to President Weston. And I found traces of the toxin on it, too. It's conclusive," he emphasized, handing the supporting analysis to Drake.

Liu's mouth dropped and she jumped from her seat to look over her boss' shoulder at the report.

"How is that possible? How is that freaking possible?" She paced behind the Director, hand on her forehead, mumbling some curses quietly so that neither Smitty nor her boss could hear.

Drake ended the brief meeting. "That's all, Smitty. Don't say a word to anyone."

"I never do, sir."

Smitty closed the door quietly behind him.

It didn't require any discussion. Both Drake and Liu headed for the Director's office.

♦

"You don't seem surprised, Gabe."

Gabriel Austin stood and walked to the window of his office. "Oh, I'm astonished. I just know how it happened. At least, I think I do."

The FBI chief faced his deputy and Supervisory Special Agent and put his hands in his pockets. Leaning against his desk, he took some time to piece together what was forming in his mind.

"Tony, Annie, this may be the most sensitive bit of information I ever share with you." He took a deep breath. "Jeez."

Finally, Gabriel Austin began a disclosure of his own.

"This was never relevant to anything you were working on. Consequently, you never needed to know. But it seems to be a piece of our ongoing investigation into Weston's assassination."

The Bureau boss told Drake and Liu about the charges against Morgan; that the President had pardoned him, and that his case was the secret one that Maxwell and Judge Byron Caldwell were both involved in. He further explained that Weston and Morgan had a history that was the basis of their close friendship.

"So, Weston shows up with his former White House counsel, who would represent Morgan. It appears that, whether Maxwell did it himself or someone else did, Trent Weston was poisoned at the Metro Police Station where they were holding Morgan."

SSA Liu and her boss, the Deputy Director, were stunned.

"Maxwell, or somebody, assassinated a former President right in front of who knows how many people, and nobody knew a thing because the effect of the poison was delayed," remarked an astounded SSA.

"I suspect so. What's also troubling is..."

Drake looked at Austin's face while he listened to the tinkling of coins in his pocket as he fidgeted. He read his mind.

"It's that Linus Schwartz might be involved somehow."

Director Austin nodded. He returned to his seat.

"He might not. Or it might be unwitting. But we can't dismiss the possibility."

The FBI Director looked at his associates. "Is it too early to have a drink? A lot of them?"

He reached for his desk phone and called his admin. "Lexi, I need you to set up a conference call. *NO* refusals, okay. Tell everyone it's about Weston." Then he rattled off a list of names, including the President, the Secretary of State, and the Attorney General. Also included were the heads of the Secret Service and Homeland Security.

Lastly, Austin included Director of National Intelligence Chris Donleavy and CIA Director Betsy Parnell.

Austin knew he would have a private call with Parnell, but it would have to wait.

CHAPTER 23

Morgan, aka Matt Fenton, and Tom Lechler had no difficulty picking the meager lock on Roadrunner's hotel room door. Trouble was, they weren't finding anything of value because they weren't the first ones to toss the room. O'Bannon's belongings were scattered everywhere. His clothes were on the floor. They examined his toiletries spread over the bathroom counter. His SCUBA equipment was a mess.

"Pretty optimistic of him to think he'd have time for a dive, wasn't it?"

"Yeah. Probably part of his cover." The former CIA officer tossed the regulator rig onto the bed.

He turned and stared at the dive hardware he'd just dropped. "Still, it's a lot of trouble to go to for your backstory when you could rent equipment on the island. He retrieved the underwater life support system and examined it more closely. He worked the rubber cover that protected the dive computer back and forth and finally pulled the computer free. From behind the panel that looked like the face of a computer, he lifted a small cell phone.

"I thought you said whoever got him had his cell phone."

Morgan shrugged and shook his head. "That's what Parnell had said."

"Encrypted?"

"Doesn't look like it."

Morgan saw an icon he recognized. Discreetly placed, it appeared to be part of the device's "wallpaper," which was a scenic photo of some unknown ocean scene. Probably a stock photo that came with the phone. But the image didn't matter. In the lower right corner of the display, there appeared to be a problem with the image. A small grouping of "hot" pixels created a bright white flaw in the picture.

"The Agency still uses this?" Morgan was surprised.

Lechler didn't understand but said nothing. He figured he'd find out shortly.

Morgan pressed the white defect in the ocean scene and held it for three seconds until the display changed, and hidden icons appeared. He looked at the sergeant and smiled.

"I might have something."

Morgan examined the possible apps and pressed the one for "voice recording." At once, the prolonged conversation of two men becoming progressively inebriated began to play back.

"Good man, Roadrunner."

Morgan grew impatient at the recording, which lasted over an hour-and-a-half, so he pressed the fast forward arrows from time to time. Finally, he heard the slurred voice of "Marty Baechtel" say, "Seth Tierney, you are one fine fellow. We *should* go diving…" Morgan continued to advance through the conversation but came up with no other useful information.

"So, what's the story, Morgan?"

"Roadrunner apparently had two phones. He carried this one with him last night. That's the date of the audio file. Then he hid this one and switched to another sometime before he got in trouble. It's just a good thing nobody searched the room until after they got him. When he got picked up, whoever it was just assumed they had his only phone."

"Lot of talking for not much information," the Green Beret said.

"What?! Are you kidding? Maybe in your world things are more defined, but in mine, this is gold."

He pressed the keys to dial Betsy Parnell on the satellite phone. "Watch the door, Tom."

Momentarily, he heard, "What's up, Morgan. Got something?"

"Seth Tierney. Who is he?"

"One of mine. He was someone I put Roadrunner on. Why?"

"Roadrunner spent a great deal of time drinking with him last night. We found a recording of the two that mentioned Tierney by name."

Parnell gave Morgan all the details about the F6 operative, most of which she recited off the top of her head. But to make sure there were no gaps, she pulled up his file.

"So, why'd you zero in on Tierney, Betsy?"

"He used to work security for SCR, Inc., Morgan."

"Hmmph. That name just keeps coming up, doesn't it?"

Morgan hung up.

♦

Not far away, the subject of Parnell's and Morgan's discussion was on a call of his own.

"No reason to suspect anything specific, but you told me to let you know if anything unexpected shows up."

The man on the other end of the phone conversation couldn't believe what he saw. Tierney had messaged him pictures of the two visitors to Joint Base Terrador that he'd pulled from the outpost's security's files.

"Figured I'd give them to you before I have my guys run them through facial recognition."

"No need, Mr. Tierney."

"What? You know them?"

"One of them. He's Josh Morgan."

"Any reason to think he's associated with the guy we know as Baechtel?"

"Not that I know of. But it does give one pause. Spend some more time with Marty Baechtel before you take care of him. And keep me informed. I'll probably have you pick up Morgan, but I'll head that way to deal with him myself."

The two cohorts ended their call. Immediately, Lammers made a call of his own.

"Mr. Schwartz, I've located Mr. Morgan."

♦

The Master Sergeant and the former spy had only driven a short distance after leaving Roadrunner's room.

"I'm sure you see it," Morgan commented about the car that had fallen in behind them.

"Yes," confirmed the Army Special Forces soldier.

Neither knew who might be tailing them. Was it someone sent by Flynn to see what they were up to? Or was it someone who had staked out Roadrunner's hotel to see if anyone took an interest in him?

It would be difficult to be inconspicuous. At least it would be hard to remain unnoticed from the CIA station chief or anyone connected to him. After all, Flynn had provided the pickup Morgan and Lechler were using. They needed other transportation.

They stopped at a car rental business and Lechler drove away in a very plain sedan. Morgan kept the pickup.

The two-vehicle caravan drove through the streets of Terradora. Morgan was amazed and disappointed at the state of the city. When he had been there years before, the entire island was a thriving nation, with s surging economy and bustling with happy, prosperous citizens.

The major portion of the past financial and social success in Terrador had been due to the American dollars from the U.S. base. Therefore, it was unsurprising that, after the base was shuttered, one result had been a devastating impact on the Terradoran economy. As Morgan drove, he saw once-beautiful buildings in disrepair. Streets were messes due to lack of maintenance. Scores of apparently unemployed people wandered the streets.

"What a shame," the ex-CIA officer thought.

The pair found a rundown motel. After checking in, Morgan parked the pickup in front of his room in the sleazy, single-story building. Lechler parked the rental in front of his lodging, three doors down. The two put on a show for the benefit of their follower who had parked on the street at the edge of the motel's lot. It was unlikely that their tail had the ability to amplify their words with audio equipment. And who knew whether the single occupant of the car could read lips. But, just in case, Morgan added words to their charade.

Fenton said, "I'll go ahead and start the review. You get some rest."

The Master Sergeant agreed. "Excellent. I'm beat. Come by and get me up in three hours. We'll assess the island's possibilities together a while, then grab some grub."

"Sounds good."

"Fenton" entered his room with some of the less essential items they had brought with them on the C-5 and others that Flynn had delivered upon their arrival. He left the motel room's door open as he moved about briefly. Then he returned to where Lechler was waiting, closing the door behind him.

For his part, the soldier punctuated his need for rest by stretching and yawning. The two men looked at their respective watches.

"See you in three."

"Yep," confirmed the sergeant.

Morgan started the old pickup and pretended to read notes to give his partner a little extra time to execute his part of the deception.

Inside his room, Lechler hurriedly changed clothes – still civilian – and rushed to the bathroom and opened the window that they knew to be there from driving around the motel before they selected it and checked in. Sliding back the glass pane that represented half of the window, Lechler leaned out to survey the area beyond. Seeing nobody, he crawled through the small opening. After closing the window just short of completely, he trotted away.

To further complete the illusion, Morgan left the truck running while he walked to the door of his partner's now empty room. He said something through the door, waited, nodded, and spoke again. He nodded again at the "reply" from the long-gone Green Beret. As he returned to the truck, as expected, a second vehicle pulled up behind the one that had been following. He wondered which would tail him, and which would stake out the motel.

Morgan turned onto the street from the parking lot and observed the original car take its place behind him. The new arrival remained to make sure Lechler stayed put.

♦

It had taken MSG Lechler about forty-five minutes to cover the two miles to his destination. He could've covered the distance more quickly. He would've been able to run it in half the time. But, the need to avoid attention, coupled with the requirement to make sure he wasn't being followed, necessitated the more leisurely pace.

Arriving at a lot full of automobiles, the Master Sergeant retrieved keys from his pocket. He opened the door to the second vehicle that Morgan had rented along with the one that was currently being staked out in front of his vacant room at the motel.

Lechler drove less than a block from the rental agency and parked along the curb.

The sergeant's partner had killed time by visiting a couple of stores in the island city. In less than ten minutes after Lechler had parked, according to plan, Morgan drove by in the pickup the station chief had provided. Following an appropriate distance behind him was the car that had been following them since they left Roadrunner's hotel. Waiting until Morgan's tail was safely by, the Green Beret took up his position behind it.

The pickup arrived at the U.S. embassy and pulled into the compound after passing the scrutiny of the guards. The second car in the procession drove past the gate, turned around and parked to watch for Morgan's return. The last car of the three, driven by the U.S. soldier, likewise passed his target and parked and waited.

♦

O'Bannon/Roadrunner/Baechtel had undergone another beating. His ability to make wisecracks had suffered along with the rest of him. His resolve was waning.

Seth Tierney had neither the expertise nor the desire to use drugs in his questioning. He'd always been able to extract what he wanted without them. But this kid, as he thought of Roadrunner, was beginning to frustrate him. He had watched Baechtel take the best his thugs could dish out, and he still hadn't talked. He had decided the man might just be who he said he was. There was apparently no other motive for his presence than spending money, drinking, and having fun.

It no longer mattered. He would report his lack of discovery to

Lammers, and he was sure the man would order Baechtel's disappearance.

If Baechtel was some goof who was never a threat, it would be a shame. Tierney liked him. But that didn't mean he would have any hesitation about doing away with him. Caution was often at the expense of the innocent.

The rogue CIA operative stepped outside the shack when his phone rang.

"I don't have time for this," he griped to himself. He listened to the caller and went back to where the beaten man and his guard were. "I'll be back as soon as I can," he informed his heavy. Then, looking at the battered prisoner slumped and unconscious in his chair, "Leave him be. I think he's done. We'll take care of him when Lammers confirms that he has no further use for him."

"Understood. What's up?"

"That idiot Flynn has called me to a meeting at the embassy."

And with that, Tierney left.

Inside the shack, the "unconscious" Roadrunner had two takeaways from what he'd heard.

First, someone named Lammers was calling the shots. And secondly…

He didn't have much time left to do anything.

◆

At the same time that Art Flynn, CIA station chief in Terrador, was introducing Wilf Crawford, one-half of the Special Collection Service team in-country, the second half walked in.

"Sorry I'm late," apologized Seth Tierney.

"No problem, Seth. We're just getting started. Seth Tierney, this is Matt Fenton from Langley."

The CIA portion of the F6 team shook Fenton's hand. "A pleasure," he said, though it really wasn't. Neither was the introduction necessary; at least, not from his point of view. Tierney had already seen Fenton's face from the base security's database. And Oskar Lammers had laid waste to Morgan's alias.

Morgan didn't need an introduction either. Tierney's face was the one in DCI Parnell's message. And his name was the one on Roadrunner's secret recording.

The four men sat in a secure conference room. Morgan had decided Fenton was going to lay his cards on the table. And that meant that Morgan was about to go all-in, too. It was an enormous risk, he knew. But Roadrunner was bound to be almost out of time, if he wasn't dead already.

Morgan wasn't even certain that Tierney was behind O'Bannon's disappearance. If he wasn't, then no harm would result from the gambit.

But if he was, the risk would be worth it.

"Gentleman, I'm afraid we haven't been entirely honest with you. The real reason behind my visit is that one of our officers is missing. He was on a mission to investigate some evidence that a network is being established here to exploit JBT's proximity to Central and South America for personal gain. We suspect that the enterprise might involve human trafficking, money laundering, drugs... You name it. This man..." Morgan held up a photo of Trevor O'Bannon, watching for reactions from the men. He knew that at least Tierney had met him.

"...is Martin Baechtel," the CIA officer continued, sticking with Roadrunner's cover. Both Flynn and Crawford straightened in their seats at the missing man's photo. They looked first at each other, then at Tierney. Morgan noted that Tierney seemed calm, but intensely interested in the revelation of O'Bannon's real job.

"Damn!" said Flynn. "We've all seen him. Seth drank with him most of last night. Right, Seth?"

Tierney was quietly in a panic. Not only had he seized a fellow Agency operative, the man had been investigating an organization in which he was one of the principals. He realized immediately that he needed to get in line with what Crawford and Flynn knew. He stiffened and said, "Oh, shit!" at his feigned epiphany.

"Marty! That is Marty, or Martin. I didn't recognize him at first from your photo, and didn't recall his last name, but, yeah, that's him."

Morgan was mildly impressed with how well Tierney was playing his part, but it wasn't a total shock. Seth Tierney was SCS, meaning he performed some of the riskiest of all intelligence work. He had to have nerves of steel. His acknowledgement of meeting O'Bannon had to be made, in light of the two witnesses who were his friends.

"And he's missing? No shit? I mean, I even took him back to his room. He sure wasn't in any condition to drive. Maybe he went somewhere after I dropped him off. I don't know."

Morgan/Fenton questioned the men. Did they know of anywhere else Baechtel might have visited before showing up at the bar? Any further word from him after Tierney dropped him off at his hotel? All the questions were legitimate ones, but they were for show. Morgan was just making his concern appear genuine. His real goal was to get Tierney out of the meeting as soon as he could without it appearing suspicious.

Finally, Morgan ended the interview.

"Well, thank you, gentlemen. I know I don't have to say how sensitive this is. And Art, if you wouldn't mind staying behind."

SCS partners Crawford and Tierney each pledged to keep their eyes and ears open for any news about Baechtel. Both offered their help, if needed.

Once they left, Morgan continued with Flynn. "Fifteen minutes should be enough," he decided silently.

◆

"Wow! Who saw that coming?" an astonished Crawford asked outside the conference room.

"Certainly not me. And I sat with the guy for nearly two hours. Well, I gotta get outta here, Wilf. Maybe we can get together for drinks later."

Wilfred Crawford wondered what his partner's big hurry was but made his way back to the embassy office he kept along with the one at the base.

Seth Tierney waited until he was out the main entrance to the embassy before making his call.

◆

Master Sergeant Tom Lechler compared the photo that CIA Director Parnell had sent to him and Morgan to the face of the man rushing to the car he had tailed while it had followed Morgan.

"Tierney, all right."

The operator started his rental car and waited momentarily before pulling in behind the car where Seth Tierney now rode.

◆

It was early evening in Washington, D.C. and Oskar Lammers was about to board a plane to Terrador. Not normally given to expletives, he nevertheless hurled a string of profanity at the man on the other end of the line. However, he knew that, ultimately, he had set the events in motion in Wyoming and, now, in Terrador. They were crumbling into what might be an unsalvageable clusterfuck.

He concluded his string of epithets with a single question. "You are going to take care of Fenton, aren't you, Mr. Tierney?"

"Already on it, boss."

◆

Regardless of how unfazed Linus Schwartz appeared, he was raging on the inside. He was nearly undone at the news from Mr. Lammers that Mr. Morgan was investigating the disappearance of a CIA officer in Terrador; that the man was being held by the billionaire's surrogates there. He, too, sensed that his plans were unravelling.

"I need time to think, Mr. Lammers. Please excuse me."

Lammers nodded and took his leave.

Schwartz had followed his son's career and outside activities with great interest upon learning that he was Everson Blake's father. The interest grew into pride as he watched the NSA's Deputy Director help build a network in Terrador that had ultimately led to personal riches. It hadn't mattered to the construction magnate one bit that all of Blake's gains were ill-gotten; that they were the results of drug smuggling, human trafficking, money laundering, and the like. The creativity and resourcefulness had made Schwartz feel that his genes were indeed within the man. And the ruthlessness his boy had demonstrated whenever obstacles were in his path was nothing short of a carbon copy of the resolve that Schwartz himself had possessed throughout his life.

Blake might've been NSA and had the help of cohorts within the Central Intelligence Agency and other powerful organizations, but his success at concealing his network's activities hadn't extended to his father. Clandestine to the rest of the world, the deception was a mere inconvenience to a billionaire with unlimited resources. What Schwartz wanted to uncover, he uncovered. And his surveillance of his son's activities had enabled him to become an anonymous partner, of sorts. Many times Schwartz had silently intervened on Blake's behalf, removing threats or positioning individuals who would help.

Now that Joint Base Terrador was reopening, his familiarity with his son's operation in Terrador would make recreating it a simple matter for the father. He knew all the old players, in the U.S. and abroad. He had already contacted them through surrogates.

His plans to replicate Everson's success in Terrador was meant to be a type of tribute to him. And the tycoon's scheme to destroy Josh Morgan's life, and then kill him, was also a way to honor Blake by avenging his death. Morgan had almost certainly killed his son. And now he was standing in Schwartz's way at every turn.

To further complicate matters, the FBI had asked the construction CEO to come in tomorrow morning for what they termed an "interview." The Special Agent who called, Annie Liu, had assured him that it was just a friendly fact-finding discussion about some activities occurring within his company in its performance of government contracts. But in light of all the failures in carrying out his plans, he would be proactive.

Linus Schwartz pressed the button on his intercom. "Mr. Leach, please come in."

The door opened. "Yes, sir, Mr. Schwartz."

"Would you please inform my pilot and his crew to be on standby for a possible immediate departure?"

"Your destination, sir?"

"Qatar. But please don't advise anyone of that. It's uncertain that I'll be travelling there at all. If I do, the timing is undetermined. So, keep it between you and me. No flight plan. No announcement to the local staff. Understood?"

"Yes, sir."

"But, just in case, Mr. Leach, have my staff in Qatar ready the apartment."

"Yes, Mr. Schwartz."

As the billionaire philanthropist businessman watched the door shut behind his assistant, he pulled out the faded, wrinkled photo that he kept of a young Everson Blake.

The regret at the possibility that he would neither avenge his son's murder nor recreate the empire he had built was heartfelt.

"I'm sorry, son."

◆

It was five o'clock. The sun was still high in the sky.

Seth Tierney bolted from the car toward the cabin. As soon as he burst through the door, he told his partner, "It's time."

The muscle walked to the man slumped over in the chair and lifted his handgun to his head.

Roadrunner knew he had to make his move now. He also knew it would be futile, since he was still secured to the chair with a tie-wrap. But he wasn't going down without a fight. However, before he could surge, he heard, "Do it outside."

O'Bannon continued his pretend grogginess while the second of the two henchmen, the one who had driven Tierney to the shack, cut the plastic cable connected to the chair with his knife. He left the plastic tie that was on his wrists in place. Roadrunner offered no assistance in going out, forcing the men to practically carry a seemingly semi-conscious man. Tierney followed behind.

At the instant he reached the door, Roadrunner lowered his head and drove his crown into one man's chest. Unbalanced with his hands bound behind his back, he tumbled to the ground with the thug as he fell backward. The second man delivered a brutal kick to Roadrunner's ribs, causing him to roll to his back in anguish.

While Tierney watched, apparently content to let his men take care of the matter, the first one regained his footing.

CIA Officer Trevor O'Bannon looked up at the man pointing the Glock at him. He was determined to maintain eye contact until the end.

But the young operative's willpower to watch dissolved at the sound of

242

the reports. He reflexively blinked at the muffled cracks of the gunfire. Upon the realization that he was still alive, Roadrunner opened his eyes to see the man before him crumpling into a heap. A second pair of quiet cracks were accompanied by the thud-thud of nine-millimeter rounds burying themselves in the second man's chest.

Seth Tierney was scrambling to pull his handgun from its holster but decided against it as he saw a man approaching, his handgun at the ready.

Roadrunner strained through his swollen eyes to get a look at his savior. To his amusement, the man who had just saved him was dressed like any one of the tourists who still came to Terrador. He wore cream-colored pants and a brightly colored floral print tropical shirt.

Master Sergeant Tom Lechler was expressionless as he moved closer to Tierney.

The Green Beret knocked out Tierney with a single strike on the back of his head with his suppressed Steyr GB nine-millimeter. Tierney hit the ground hard and Lechler took his gun from his holster. The Army soldier held out his hand to the CIA officer he'd just rescued and pulled him to his feet.

Again observing the man's attire, O'Bannon said, "So, is there a party after this, or something? Or is that just the latest fashion for operators?"

"I guess you're Roadrunner, all right," Lechler remarked. "Morgan said you were a smartass."

"Morgan," O'Bannon thought. And suddenly he was overcome at the realization of just how close things had come. Lechler turned him around and freed his hands from the plastic tie. Roadrunner was trembling, but he was smiling with his head shaking. The Special Forces soldier helped him over to sit in Tierney's car.

"Morgan." This time it was aloud. "Where is he? I'd like to either thank him or belt him for cutting this so damned close."

One of Tierney's cohorts moved slightly. Lechler walked over and put a final round in his head. For good measure, he repeated the act for the second one.

"Oh, he'll be along shortly."

He handed Tierney's gun to Roadrunner and pointed at its owner. "Watch him."

The soldier walked to the cabin and returned with some tie-wraps. He knelt and pulled Tierney's arms behind him. He bound his wrists with a pair of the heavy-duty plastic straps. The man was stirring. Lechler zipped the cables tightly and slapped the man in his ear. Then he pushed his face into the dirt.

The sound of a pickup pulling into the clearing that surrounded the cabin startled O'Bannon. He turned with gun pointed. MSG Lechler gently pushed the barrel down.

"Morgan," he said.

The former CIA officer hurried from his truck to the spy currently in the employ of the Central Intelligence Agency.

"Were you followed?" asked Lechler.

Morgan gave Lechler his "are you serious" look, which consisted of a smirk and a tilted head.

"Sorry I asked," said Lechler. "Seriously, any trouble?"

"Well, not compared to you, it appears. Looks like you had more to deal with than I did. I only had to drive and follow your transponder signal on my GPS. But that *is* tougher than it sounds – a highly underappreciated skill."

While Morgan had stayed behind with Flynn at the embassy, Lechler had watched for Tierney. They hoped he would take the bait and go to Roadrunner. Lechler had carried a transponder in his rental car. It had been among the items that Parnell had ordered to be on the plane for them in Colorado Springs. Morgan had followed the beacon with the accompanying locator.

Morgan took in the scene around him. He saw two men, each with three bullet holes, and with blood pooled around them. Then he saw Seth Tierney, squirming and struggling to roll up on his side.

"Got him alive. Good."

"Yep."

Morgan finally walked to where O'Bannon had re-seated himself in Tierney's car.

"Morgan."

"O'Bannon."

"You know, Morgan, I don't fare too well whenever you're involved."

Morgan gave him an up and down assessment. He was bloodied and bruised. One eye was swollen nearly shut. The other was better, but still a mess. Morgan shook his head.

"You're never satisfied, Trev. Last time, you got shot. You only got beat up this time" Morgan raised his hands in obvious bewilderment. "It's getting better."

Roadrunner managed a smile.

"Glad you're okay, Trev."

"Thanks, man."

The drive back to Joint Base Terrador took the four men close to an hour. On the way, Morgan messaged Parnell. Though the secure satellite phone made it unnecessary, he made the message cryptic. It read, "enjoyed my vacation got you a gift something you've been wanting."

◆

It was almost ten o'clock and, at her desk in CIA headquarters, Betsy Parnell exhaled deeply and smiled. She didn't know how to repay Josh for all he'd done – now and in the past.

"But, for now…" Betsy raised the plastic cup that held the Scotch she'd already been drinking. "To you, Josh Morgan."

The DCI began gathering her things. She still had a lot on her plate, she knew, but, "I'm going home."

◆

Matt Fenton's profile in the base security's database was flagged, "NQA." So, when Morgan and Lechler arrived at the gate with two passengers, one battered and one of them with a bag over his head, the guard waved them through: No Questions Asked.

Morgan couldn't care less if Seth Tierney saw where they were headed. The precaution of the cover over his face was so that the guard wouldn't recognize him and enquire, despite the NQA order.

Lechler drove to the airstrip, where a business-style jet waited. It was of the type that had flown Maggie to Washington. It had been waiting since not long after the Army operator and former spy had landed in Terrador.

The C-21 Air Force version of the Learjet received priority clearance and moved to the head of the line. That really didn't mean much tonight. There wasn't yet much in the way of air traffic in and out of the joint Army-Air Force base. But Morgan couldn't get in the air fast enough.

He had hated leaving Lammers behind in Wyoming to come to Terrador. The man was his single focus now. Him, and figuring out how involved the man's employer was in everything that was going on. Was the billionaire head of SCR a partner – or even leader – in all of this? Or was he just in the dark, while underlings were carrying out their own ominous plan?

And finally, there was Maggie. Morgan didn't know where they stood.

CHAPTER 24

Day 9 – Monday

At first, Maggie was stunned. She'd found out from Alicia Weston that Morgan had arrived back in town last night. Why hadn't he called her? Why didn't he come home? She hadn't suddenly become comfortable with what he'd done in Wyoming, but she'd been worried beyond words while he was gone. The sight of him leaving with MSG Lechler, the man she knew was special ops, had unnerved her.

But Maggie finally realized that she'd given Morgan some very clear signals that she wasn't ready to talk yet. He probably took that to mean no talk "at all," rather than no talk about them. And she further realized that he could easily believe she wouldn't want to see him, either; that he wasn't welcome in their apartment.

♦

Josh had called Alicia to tell her that he would be at Trent's memorial service at the National Cathedral. The night before, he had delivered Seth Tierney to CIA interrogators who would try to get whatever information they could from him – about operations in Terrador, about his connection with Oskar Lammers; it was a long list.

A driver had taken Trevor O'Bannon to Walter Reed Hospital.

And Master Sergeant Tom Lechler? Morgan had no idea where he'd gone. Morgan couldn't help but chuckle to himself when he thought of the Green Beret simply vanishing into the night.

Josh had stayed at a hotel. He'd risen early but waited a while before going to his and Maggie's apartment to gather some things. He'd hoped she would be away. She was.

He put on his best suit – black with faint gray pinstripes – a dark gray shirt, and black tie with faint gray patterns. While he was at the apartment, Josh also took the opportunity to grab a number of other personal items and several changes of clothes.

Finally, he was off to the White House, where Alicia Weston and others had been invited to wait until the time came to leave for the National Cathedral. The thought of seeing Maggie left him conflicted, but he wouldn't consider missing Trent Weston's funeral.

◆

"I don't have much time, Ms. Liu."

"Supervisory Special Agent Liu," the woman corrected.

"I'll be attending President Weston's memorial and it begins in about four hours.

"We'll try to be brief," SSA Liu promised, though she had no such intention. She felt odd conducting business on a National Day of Mourning, but she told herself, "There's the possibility this man had something to do with the death of the man being mourned. It's outrageous to think of his being at the former President's service, if he did."

SSA Liu got right to the point.

"Mr. Schwartz, what was your relationship with U.S. Attorney Riley Maxwell?"

The man on the hot seat was mildly surprised at the question. He'd suspected the queries would be about more than merely business practices. And he wasn't intimidated at being questioned by the FBI. In fact, Schwartz saw the meeting as an opportunity for his own fact-finding. However, he didn't know they were on to the payments to the prosecutor from an SCR subsidiary.

"I thought the purpose of this conference was to discuss some possible irregularities in SCR's fulfilling its contractual obligations."

"It is," replied the supervisor. "This relates directly to that. Your contracts with the federal government state specifically that SCR will have no direct contact with any employee of the United States that is not publicly revealed. Furthermore, you and your companies are expressly forbidden from making payments of any kind without disclosure on the proper forms to appropriate regulatory and taxing authorities. Finally, you and any company or organization of which you are a part cannot make personal payments to any federal employee or representative individually."

Liu stared at the billionaire silently. He was nonplussed.

"So, Mr. Schwartz, I ask you again. What was the nature of your relationship with Maxwell?"

Linus Schwartz's attorney leaned in to whisper in his ear, but his client waved him off.

"I'll answer it. I have – or had – no relationship with him. I've never met the man." That was technically true. All arrangements were made through intermediates and the only personal contact between him and the prosecutor was by telephone.

Supervisory Special Agent Liu slid a document to her interviewee. The man took the paper and held it up. His legal counsel pulled Schwartz's hand toward himself so that he could see it, too. The personal contact earned him a rebuke in the form of a glare from a pair of old, sunken eyes.

"This is a list of payments from one of your subsidiaries to Maxwell; Petroglyph Transnational Holdings. Oh, it was buried under a few layers of shell companies, but it's yours. How do you explain them?"

Schwartz studied the printout only briefly before turning it completely over to his lawyer.

"Young lady…"

"Supervisory Special Agent or SSA… Either will do."

The irritation was manifest on Schwartz's face and he dropped any form of honorific.

"Do you know how many companies I own, or rather head up? Have you any idea how many business entities I'm associated with that are owned by shareholders? It is impossible for me to know of each one or, more specifically, the activities undertaken."

He continued, "I have no idea what this is." He took the two-page summary of transactions from his attorney and slid it back to Liu. "I would suggest that it might be part of some case Mr. Maxwell was part of. He was, after all, a federal prosecutor."

"No, sir. It took some effort, but the Bureau has verified that this was his personal account."

"Then I have no idea. Are we done here?" The construction mogul began to rise.

"No, sir." In her mind, the SSA continued, "Not even close."

The wealthy philanthropist actually looked to his lawyer for advice this time. When the attorney nodded, Schwartz returned to his seat.

The interview consisted of more questions about Maxwell and his suicide, and Schwartz's companies and activities associated with illegal payments, whether to the dead D.A. or others.

Gabriel Austin, the Federal Bureau of Investigation's Director was keenly interested in the dialogue between Liu and her associates and Schwartz and his attorney. He was watching through the one-way glass along with his Deputy Director, Tony Drake. Among the most serious of possibilities was that Schwartz or his company could be implicated with President Weston's death. A Special Agent entered the observation room and handed Austin a note from the agency's forensic accountants.

The interrogator listened to Austin's disembodied voice speaking through her hidden earpiece without expression, then repeated the suggested comment to Schwartz.

"We've been reviewing your holdings. So, as a matter of fact, I *do* know how many companies you 'own, or rather head up,' Mr. Schwartz," Liu informed him, referring to his earlier taunt. "It appears that one of your holdings is a chemical plant; one that manufactures pesticides. Is that right?" Liu studied the man's face and saw a brief hint of concern in his eyes. She suspected that the sudden change in topic from financial transactions and possible improprieties to a business that created chemical products had caught him off guard. And she was right.

Though the wealthy businessman was largely indifferent to his lawyer's advice, he leaned over to whisper into the man's ear, initiating a brief exchange between the two. Schwartz had done so to buy some time while he formulated his answer, but the almost unprecedented reliance on legal advice during the interview had made him appear more unnerved.

While Schwartz and the lawyer huddled, the man's personal assistant, Dexter Leach, stepped forward and handed his boss a sheet of paper.

Finally, Schwartz nodded and repeated what Leach had pointed to on the document, though the businessman had known all along.

"Yes, it appears so. In…" and he looked at the list of his holdings again as if the existence of the pesticide plant was news to him. "…in Oklahoma, it would seem."

The SSA and her interviewee locked in a visual showdown. Uncharacteristically, Schwartz blinked. Unable to maintain eye contact, he looked away, ostensibly to hand the document back to his assistant.

He was clearly rattled.

"Young lady…" Liu let it slide this time. "Please tell me what this has to do with my companies' financial dealings?"

"We'll get to that."

Since discovering that the liquid in the deceased prosecutor's desk was the toxin that had killed Weston and finding the former President's DNA on a coffee mug that was in Maxwell's drawer with it, the FBI had been conducting an intensive search. Only a few entities possessed the technical expertise to have created it. The result was a list of chemical labs around the world. Once investigators uncovered payments from one of SCR's subsidiaries to Maxwell, one company jumped to the top of the list.

Located outside of Oklahoma City, Volumetric Advanced Chemical Solutions was a research laboratory that boasted an impressive number of patents. With ties to government agencies and nearby University of

Oklahoma, the facility had developed an extensive array of specialty chemicals, including pesticides. The manufacturing arm of the subsidiary was located in Louisiana, but the R&D was carried out solely in the lab in the *Sooner State.*

As the questioning carried on, Linus Schwartz was becoming increasingly agitated, which was exactly the SSA's objective. She knew he was anxious to get to the memorial for President Weston. As one of the most prominent members of the private sector, he was on the list of VIPs. And personally, he found it satisfying with the private knowledge that his people's actions were behind the mourners' personal grief.

Finally, an exasperated interviewee leaned toward the agent sitting across from him. The hushed tone belied the intensity that it carried.

"What has any of this got to do with the bottle you found in Maxwell's office, woman?"

The mood immediately changed for everyone in the room. Schwartz's legal counsel put a hand to his chin and looked away. Dexter Leach's head dropped. On the side of the table where the questioner sat, the agent assisting the SSA barely managed to stifle his smile. Liu, despite her surge of adrenaline at provoking the error, only folded her arms.

Sensing the swing in the atmosphere in the interrogation room, Schwartz looked around at the various people in it. The only thing that could've added a greater degree of emphasis to his lack of understanding would've been if he'd thrown up his hands and said aloud, "What?," which he did not.

The sudden realization that he'd admitted knowledge of a fact that nobody had disclosed to him manifested itself in his widening eyes and scowl.

"I never said anything about evidence from the prosecutor's office," stated his questioner.

Schwartz realized that he at least had one way out of his self-inflicted legal wound. He rose immediately – or as immediately as his aged, stiff body permitted. The attorney at his side also stood. Struggling to regain the authority he had commanded before his verbal gaffe, the billionaire announced his attention to leave.

"Missy, as I have stated repeatedly, I have a memorial to attend. So, unless you plan to arrest me, I'll be on my way."

SSA Liu remained seated, thinking what an arrogant asshole the man was. She interlaced her fingers in front of her chest and leaned back in her chair to show her disrespect. But no matter how much she wanted to slap handcuffs on the bastard at that very instant and read him his rights, she knew she wasn't quite there yet.

The man whom she knew was complicit in a number of things,

including the assassination of an ex-U.S. President, waddled toward the door that his attorney was holding open for him. He threw his eyes backward over his shoulder in disdain and voiced a harrumph.

"Just don't leave town," the Supervisory Special Agent ordered, still seated.

But that was exactly what Linus Schwartz planned to do.

◆

Along with almost every politician, agency head, and bureaucrat in the District, DCI Elizabeth Parnell was travelling to President Weston's memorial in the Washington National Cathedral. In route, she made a call to Josh Morgan, who was with the President's widow.

"Hi, Morgan. I know you're with Mrs. Weston, so I'll keep this brief. Our interviewers have had some luck with Seth Tierney. I wouldn't call it spilling his guts, but they've been successful in... we'll call it 'coaxing' information out of him. I think we might be able to pull the plug on any future operations in Terrador."

The CIA Director listened as Morgan expressed his relief.

"Well, just thought you'd want to know. Didn't want to talk shop if I happened to see you at the service today. I do want to talk in the next day or two, though."

Morgan had already turned her down once recently, but she was undoubtedly going to make her request again.

◆

Billionaire business magnate Linus Schwartz's limo pulled up to the curb and he got in, along with his legal representative and Leach. As the black luxury car pulled into the traffic, another black car, significantly less extravagant, pulled onto the street behind it.

The FBI agent driving the car hung back a comfortable distance. When it was obvious that the limousine was heading in the wrong direction for a trip to the National Cathedral, he called his boss.

"SSA Liu, he's not going to the memorial. At least, not yet." A pause to listen, and then, "Yes, ma'am."

The two agents followed Schwartz's car all the way to the complex where his Washington townhouse consisted of the entire eighth floor. The driver rushed around to hold the door open for the wealthy man and his party, then returned to his place behind the wheel. He drove into the parking garage.

The FBI Special Agents parked about seventy yards from the entrance to the building and watched. A second vehicle took up a location at the other main entrance. A third parked outside the entrance to the parking structure and watched as the limo pulled in.

◆

Inside the parking garage adjacent to his townhouse, Linus Schwartz's fixer decided the man had waited long enough. Seeing no evidence that the anticipated surveillance extended into the garage's interior, he left his vehicle and opened the door of the limo that had pulled into the space beside his.

Linus Schwartz moved from the back seat of the car that had brought him from FBI headquarters and into that of his troubleshooter.

"Thank you, Mr. Lammers."

The white Lincoln Continental was an impressive luxury sedan, but it didn't have the look of a limousine. So, without earning more than a cursory glance from the FBI agents staking out the billionaire's residence, it pulled into the flow of traffic and away from the townhouse.

As it did, the passenger looked forlornly at the Washington residence he'd maintained for years. Then, he looked at the photograph of his son. He traced his finger lovingly across the young face with the crooked smile.

"How did it come to this, son?"

◆

The elevator stopped at the entrance to the townhouse, and all the occupants exited. Once inside, "Schwartz" loosened his tie and proceeded to the guest bedroom. There Max Kanady started to remove the suit that was identical to the one his boss was wearing for the day. At the same height, weight, and shape as his employer, and with a striking facial resemblance, he had often filled in visually for the man when he needed to be elsewhere.

On this day, Kanady had waited inside the limo while his boss underwent questioning in the FBI building.

◆

The FBI agents surveilling the business magnate's home exchanged a glance.

The driver looked at his watch and made a call.

"Looks like he's decided to sit the memorial out, Annie." He listened briefly and hung up.

"Boss thinks that's a good thing. This way, he'll be here when the team arrives with the warrant."

◆

Josh and Maggie hardly spoke while waiting with Alicia Weston to travel to her husband's service.

Maggie had told Josh she was glad he was okay but didn't ask where he'd been. In light of the emotional distance currently between them, she didn't feel it was her place.

Josh had thanked her and told her that he'd picked up a few things at their apartment at The Wharf.

Maggie's heart had sunk at the implication that he wouldn't be staying there.

After that, Maggie had mostly visited with Alicia's sister, Emma, and Josh had talked with Sir Albert McGinnis.

The time came and the closest friends and family to Former President Trent Weston departed the White House. The men and women separated into the various family cars and other vehicles that would transport them to continue the process of saying farewell to their husband and friend.

◆

Having successfully avoided any detection, Lammers arrived unfollowed at 2401 Smith Boulevard, Arlington, Virginia, with his employer in the back seat. Lammers steered the Lincoln parallel to the curb. In front of the Signature Flight Support section in the General Aviation area of Reagan National Airport, a valet opened the door for Schwartz while another moved to the driver's seat.

The mogul and his fixer walked into the terminal, and after a brief display of their credentials, proceeded outside to where the private Gulfstream was fueled and waiting for departure.

Lammers and Schwartz boarded the luxury jet and the flight attendant began to serve them. Momentarily, the pilot and co-pilot arrived from filing the flight plan.

Mere minutes after the aircraft marshaller had used his orange-filtered flashlights and radio to direct the pilot to the runway, the plane was lifting from the strip headed north/northwest and into the air.

The pilot initiated the required immediate left turn to avoid flying through the prohibited airspace designated as P-56. P-56A included the White House, while P-56B was an area in which the Naval Observatory, home of the Vice-president, sat.

Seated on the port side of the Gulfstream, its owner stared almost straight downward during the extreme bank. Once the pilot had completed the turn, Schwartz was able to look briefly back at Washington, D.C., which was rapidly disappearing from view behind the frame of the window beside his seat.

Linus Schwartz's purpose in travelling to Qatar was to buy time while his legal team tried to extricate him from the significant entanglements in which he'd found himself. He'd always believed the right amount of money in the right hands could bring about any solution to any situation in which he found himself. But as the last glimpse of the District disappeared behind him, he couldn't help wondering when – or if – he would be able to return.

Soon he was over the Atlantic and out of U.S. airspace.

♦

A procession for the State Funeral of a President or former President of the United States of America was a spectacle rivaled only, perhaps, by that of Inauguration Day.

A Capitol Police car's lights proclaimed the approach of the horse-drawn caisson bearing the flag-draped casket of Former President Trenton Weston. Ahead of the horses pulling the cart, a pair of servicemen escorted a saddled, riderless horse.

On each side of the caisson, a joint honor guard representing each branch of the armed services marched alongside, providing companionship for the fallen President. A single U.S. Army solder brought up the rear.

Next in the motorcade were the vehicles carrying those closest to President Weston. The first car was the presidential limousine with Mrs. Weston, her sister, and Josh and Maggie inside. President Hendrickson and First Gentleman Adam Hendrickson, Sr accompanied them. Other cars followed with additional friends from both the man's personal and political life.

Thousands of people lined the entire route of the procession, each expressing sympathy in various ways. Some held U.S. flags solemnly in front of them. Others held their hands over their hearts. Members of the U.S. Armed Forces interspersed with the mostly civilians along the way saluted their respects to the deceased commander-in-chief. The love for the man who had served his country was apparent in the myriad of gestures.

♦

At the townhouse residence of Linus Schwartz, a dozen investigators from the FBI and the local police packed into the elevator. Arriving on the eighth story, they announced their presence through its sliding, metal doors. Others waited on the ground floor for their time in the limited space of the elevator car. Once the complete team of detectives and Crime Scene Investigators had congregated in the residence, they would begin the search according to the terms of the warrant the lead Special Agent carried.

"FBI," one shouted in accompaniment to the pounding of another's fists on the polished gold-colored doors.

On the other side of the door, Dexter Leach turned a key and pressed a button. Without waiting for an invitation, the investigators rushed into the hallway of the townhouse and began to disperse. The lead agent handed the warrant to Mr. Leach.

"We have a warrant to search the premises."

Only four other individuals were present with Mr. Leach. The FBI Special Agent in Charge looked about for the apartment's owner and, not seeing him, said, "Would you find Linus Schwartz?"

Leach looked up from reading the warrant. "I presume I'm not required to say anything."

"That's right, but is that really how you want to handle this? What's your name?"

Leach considered the pros and cons of being forthcoming. Finally, he said, "Dexter Leach. I'm Mr. Schwartz's personal assistant."

"Okay, Leach, let your boss know we're here."

Leach's smirk caused the closest agents to wonder if he understood the seriousness of their arrival.

"I'm afraid I have to report that Mr. Schwartz isn't here."

The SAIC offered a smirk of his own, knowing that other agents had kept a tight lid on the place from the instant the property's resident had arrived from the Bureau's headquarters. Only Schwartz's attorney had left the premises, they believed. The agent's smug look disappeared when one of the investigators who had fanned out for an initial inspection of the residence, both to secure it and to find anyone else who might be there, returned with her report.

"He's not here."

"What do you mean, 'not here?' Of course, he's here!"

Dexter Leach's growing arrogance exhibited itself through his even larger smirk and folded arms.

"Is there another way out of here?" The question was directed both to Leach and to anybody else who could answer it.

"There's a fire escape, boss, but we've had that covered," an agent answered.

The SAIC thought about what he would tell his boss, Supervisory Agent Annie Liu. He evaluated the people standing before him. By their uniforms, three were definitely staff. He sized up the fourth individual, looking up and down the entire length of his body.

The Special Agent squinted at the man's face. Opening a file folder, he read the physical description of Linus Schwartz and looked at his photo.

The SAIC looked at the man before him again, who was now smiling. He exhaled and bit his lip. He slapped his forehead repeatedly before moving his hand to cover his mouth. Under his breath through lips hidden by his palm, he muttered.

"Dammit! Damn it all to hell."

Dexter Leach laughed aloud while the FBI agent reached for his phone.

♦

Inside the Washington National Cathedral, the FBI chief sat among the crowd of mourners waiting for the arrival of the motorcade. Had the service already begun, he would've turned off his phone. He would've never done anything as inappropriate as looking at a text, FBI Director or not.

In view of the first message, the second one came as a little less of a shock. However, the anger and disappointment resulted from the content of the most recent text from Annie Liu.

"flight plan filed for qatar already gone"

The first message from her that Schwartz hadn't been at his house, despite the intensive surveillance by agents, had astonished him. But the second message presented more of a complication. Their suspect – that's how the Bureau thought of him now – wasn't merely out of his house. He was out of the country. And Austin knew that the middle eastern country didn't have an extradition treaty with the U.S.

Director Austin considered leaving for headquarters, but the sight of members of the funeral procession entering the cathedral persuaded him to stay. Everybody stood as Mrs. Weston and her companions entered. Austin rose, too, and despite the stares of the people around him, he typed a quick message to Liu.

"check refueling points"

Gabriel Austin powered down his phone and attempted to put the matter out of his mind for a while. He couldn't.

♦

The Special Agent overseeing the search of Linus Schwartz's townhouse wasn't surprised that it had failed to turn up anything obvious about the acts he was suspected of. Perhaps the lab techs and analysts would turn up something from the computers and paper files. Agents loaded them for transport back to the Bureau's headquarters.

Agents had questioned the three members of Schwartz's household staff extensively and had decided to release them. The other two, Dexter Leach and Max Kanady, had tried to appear to be candid, but everyone involved knew they hadn't been.

Kanady had admitted to acting as his employer's stand-in whenever the man wanted to draw attention away from himself. He was surprised when his interrogator informed him that acting as a body double to permit someone to commit a crime made him an accomplice.

The Special Agent in Charge took both him and Leach into custody as material witnesses and persons of interest. Leach seemed to view the situation with some amusement. Kanady was more disturbed.

◆

Josh had followed his friend's casket into the cathedral with the other honorary pallbearers. Members of the combined honor guard performed the actual duty. The six men sat on the front row of one of the two central sections of the nave, while the former First Lady sat on the front row of the other. In what Morgan thought was an extremely respectful act, President Hendrickson sat on the second row behind Mrs. Weston, her sister, Maggie, and a few others.

It was a wonderful time of celebration for the deceased man whom so many loved. At Alicia Weston's request, the last of the eulogies was given by Josh. Of course, he couldn't reveal any of the details surrounding how he and his friend had met, so he just skipped over that part. Neither could he explain his role in the well-publicized abduction at the hands of the Saudi Arabian agent. So, he'd wondered as he prepared for his tribute exactly what he could say. He concluded that he would just speak from the heart about the only thing that really mattered in the end – the love for and from Trent Weston.

And so, he talked about spending time with the Westons, along with Maggie. He talked of their mutual interest in football, though he regretted that he'd failed to show him the light and convert him to a fan of the Texas Longhorns. He talked about introducing his friend to flyfishing and the ribbing Trent gave him on the first – and only, Josh emphasized – day that Weston had caught more fish than he.

His comments were brief but moving. He came to his closing remarks.

"I loved Trent. Pardon me, if I don't call him 'President Weston.' And I know that he returned that love. But the one love of his life was his wife, Alicia. To say that he saw her as his guiding light wouldn't do justice to his feelings for her. The word 'wife' is such an honorable one. And the best of what it embodies is a portrait of Alicia Weston. More than a companion, she was a true partner in every part of his life. She was his confidant and best friend.

"She was his comfort in the low points of his life and the assurance of her love brought him through those times. She was the beacon that brought him home when he was taken.

"Trent and Alicia were childhood sweethearts, and it's obvious that they never quite grew out of it. They weren't afraid to show their affection in public, holding hands and exchanging hugs and kisses. But during much of their lifetime together, they were never truly alone. The people of our country, whom Trent also loved, were ever-present. We watched, admired and criticized, praised and condemned. Always fickle, we were always looking over Trent Weston's shoulder. We didn't deserve him.

"So, thank you, Alicia, for sharing Trent with us. Thank you for your partnership with him in service. Thank you for being the steady support to him, so that he could be that to us.

"If any man deserved the rest that Trent now enjoys in his heavenly father's arms, he does."

As Josh stepped away from the lectern, Alicia Weston rose to greet him. The warmth of her embrace and love finally undid Josh. When he returned to his seat with the other honorary pallbearers, Sir Albert McGinnis, whose eyes were also moist, patted him on his leg. The others in the six-man group leaned forward and nodded their approval.

Maggie Loughlin realized that she was crying as much as Alicia Weston. Her tears were shed for Trent of course, but her soul ached within her at the despair that she knew Josh was experiencing. She knew that, for him, this was the loss of a father figure, as well as a cherished friend.

Maggie reflected on the full story of Josh's devotion to him. He'd risked his life for Weston before he really knew him well. His trust for the man was absolute, and she knew that Trent returned the love and the trust. As these things paraded through her subconscious, other things came into sharper perspective. In everything that her fiancé had done since she had known him, she had always thought of the danger he put himself in, and the bravery he had demonstrated in all his acts.

But now she realized, for the first time, the toll that these things must surely have taken on him. She had never fully considered the sacrifice he had made in his commitment to his friends – Trent especially – and to his country. How could he not be changed? How could he not be in some way "damaged?"

As the minister ended the service with some closing remarks and a word of prayer, across the throngs of people sitting in the main body of the Nave, the Directors of the Central Intelligence Agency and the Federal

Bureau of Investigation somehow made eye contact. Parnell spotted Austin and saw that he seemed distracted. When he returned her stare, she lowered her eyebrows and tilted her head slightly in the universal body language that asked, "What's going on?"

His very slight shake of his head gave the reply. "Not now."

Alicia Weston and her group followed the honor guard as they carried the former President's casket outside. Instead of the caisson that had brought him, Trent would ride in a hearse.

The ride to Andrews Air Force Base would be brisk. There, the presidential jet awaited. President Hendrickson had made the specially adapted Boeing 747 available to the former First Lady. Of course, without POTUS on board, it wouldn't carry the designation "Air Force One." The jet, however, would receive the same priority treatment as if it did. The aircraft would deliver Weston's remains to his home of recent years, Frisco, Texas, along with his wife and others closest to him.

After Mrs. Weston had departed the Cathedral, CIA Director Parnell sought out her FBI counterpart.

"Let's ride together. We'll talk," Austin said.

Parnell's aide left to inform her driver that she would be leaving with Gabe Austin. Her car would follow behind.

◆

FBI Supervisory Special Agent Liu was frustrated. Finding that Linus Schwartz's flight plan called for him to refuel in Paris, she had personally contacted officials there requesting that they detain him. Their position was that, since the man hadn't been formally charged with a crime, there was no justification for holding him. Liu was working her way up the organizational charts of France's aviation authority, *La Direction de l'Aviation Civile*, and other officials of their national government.

She'd enlisted the aid of the U.S. embassy in France. The ambassador was working on it but said a call from Director Austin might be the one thing to push French authorities into cooperation.

◆

"So, that's the story, Betsy. I'm only telling you because, if Schwartz is successful in escaping our jurisdiction to a place that won't extradite him, it begins to fall into your purview."

Austin's phone rang.

What Parnell heard unsettled her. As a problem that had expanded to other nations, her agency would be enlisted to provide intelligence.

"Mind if I start the ball rolling and get someone on it?"

"The sooner the better, Betsy."

The FBI boss answered his phone. It wasn't the news he'd hoped for.

"Damn."

Parnell saw the concern from Austin's reaction. He pushed his hair back and stared out the auto's window.

"Sorry, Betsy. I've got to start making some calls. Please listen in, as this mess now concerns you."

With Austin's permission, the DCI eavesdropped as he made a succession of calls attempting to get French authorities to detain Schwartz. He was largely unsuccessful. The only promising response was from the head of France's equivalent to the FAA. She said she would consult with her superiors and get back with him.

After Austin's last call, Parnell asked, "Think we should try to get the White House involved?"

The man's exaggerated exhalation gave her his answer. He dialed POTUS' Chief of Staff.

♦

Morgan sat on the 747 that used the callsign "Air Force One" whenever the President flew on it. He had never had the opportunity to travel on the jet, even considering everything he'd been involved with in the last few years.

In need of some alone time to decompress, he sat by himself while the others in Alicia Weston's circle of support visited among themselves. Mrs. Weston seemed to be relying heavily on Maggie, who was never far away.

His phone's caller ID announced the DCI.

"Hey, Betsy. What's up?"

Morgan listened silently as Parnell informed him in of the latest news. She had just returned to her office from the memorial service, she said. Then she filled Morgan in on everything she had learned – the discovery of the toxin that had killed Weston and where it had been found. The DCI named the suspected manufacturer in Oklahoma. She detailed the connection of Schwartz's company to Maxwell, which, in light of the other pieces that were coming together, made it inconceivable that he wasn't in on the assassination.

"Why are you telling me this?"

Parnell flinched at the question. She knew she had no legal justification in doing so.

"I thought you'd want to know."

"And?"

Morgan heard Betsy's sigh, even over the phone.

"And because I want to hire you, Morgan."

"I'm not coming back to CIA, Betsy"

"I'm not asking you to... exactly. You'd be sort of a contractor. You already know much about the people in Schwartz's organization. They're likely to be the same ones helping him now."

"You don't think I'm too personally involved?"

The CIA Director hesitated. "Ordinarily, I'd say 'yes.' But in this case, I think we need a personal touch. I want you to gather intelligence on Schwartz's activities in Qatar. Who knows, maybe you'll even come up with some plan to get the son of a bitch back into our jurisdiction."

"I'll leave for Qatar after Trent's funeral tomorrow."

With their call concluded, Parnell reflected on what she'd just done. There was no rationale for reading Morgan in on the circumstances surrounding Linus Schwartz, his company, the allegations against him – at least, not from the Agency's perspective.

And she had come to know the ex-CIA officer well enough that she knew that he would go after the man who'd had his friend assassinated. In fact, she suspected, he was already making plans. In light of all he'd done for the Agency and for the United States in recent years, the CIA Director had simply decided to give Morgan some help. And she knew that getting Schwartz back into the U.S. would be the last thing on his mind.

Parnell had wondered after Morgan returned from Terrador with Tierney how she'd repay him for everything he had accomplished. She just had.

"Well, Josh," she said to her empty office. "This should just about make us even."

◆

The Presidential jet landed at Dallas-Fort Worth International Airport at about 6:00 PM local time.

The casket carrying Former President Weston remained on the jet on an isolated part of the tarmac, where it would wait until taken to the private graveside service the next morning. As with any time that it was at any airport in the world, the aircraft remained under heavy guard. However, in addition to the armed soldiers keeping watch over it, four members of the joint honor guard at the memorial at the National Cathedral stood outside the blue and white jumbo-jet. Their shift would end during the night and others would take their place.

Morgan rode to the Weston's home in Frisco separately from everyone who'd travelled from Washington. All had been puzzled at his decision to rent a car, but none had enquired why.

Local friends joined the mourners from Washington, D.C. at a visitation at Mrs. Weston's home. She had insisted on having it there. She hadn't been home since before Inauguration Day, when the series of events began to unfold that nearly resulted in war with Russia.

Maggie had left Josh alone, for the most part. So, she was surprised – and hurt – when she saw him leave after a brief conversation with Alicia Weston.

The former First Lady came to where Maggie was watching Morgan through the front window as he left.

"Precious Maggie," Mrs. Weston said as she pulled her into an embrace.

"Whatever is going on between you and Josh, it might take some time to sort out."

Maggie nodded.

"Forgiveness takes time, honey."

"I'm not sure Morgan has done anything that I need to forgive him about."

"Oh, sweetie," the older friend said to her younger one, "I'm not talking about you forgiving him. I mean you forgiving yourself, and him forgiving himself."

◆

At FBI headquarters, Director Austin had gotten the word. Authorities in France, at the behest of President Hendrickson, would be willing to detain the billionaire businessman when he landed in Paris. As unprofessional as he knew it was, Austin hung up on his caller without a word. Linus Schwartz had already landed, refueled, and taken off. He was in the air heading for Qatar.

CHAPTER 25

Day 10 – Tuesday

It was a few minutes after midnight and Morgan was sitting in his rental car. He was among the few cars in a parking lot of a business adjacent to the one he was concerned with. His location was outside Oklahoma City, about seventy-five yards from the gate onto the property of Volumetric Advanced Chemical Solutions. Parnell had mentioned the name when she had brought Morgan up to date on the investigation into Weston's assassination. The ex-spy had simply Googled the address.

The DCI had also told him that Austin had said his organization would be raiding the place as early as this morning. Morgan hoped to get into the lab first, though he wasn't sure why it was important to him. Perhaps, he thought, he just wanted to make sure Betsy's details were accurate before he went into action.

In the twenty minutes that he'd watched the place, nobody had come or gone. Morgan had hoped his arrival time would coincide with a shift change, but so far, he'd seen no activity. Any employees signing out at midnight would probably take a few minutes to collect their things before making their way out of the building and off the property. Anyone arriving for the overnight shift might've already arrived before Morgan did. But the absence of cars led him to think there might not even be a night shift. As far as he could tell, only a single automobile was on the lot.

As he hoped, there was no guard at the gate. It had a keypad that the driver of any car could reach from the driver side seat to tap in the code. Anyone leaving would offer no opportunity for him to get what he needed. It had to be someone arriving.

Morgan's car faced the street that led to the research facility, which was to his left. He sat in the backseat to remain hidden, especially from anyone coming to or leaving the building he was parked in front of.

Eventually, the former CIA spook saw a single man leaving the Volumetric building, enter the solitary vehicle and drive toward the gate. The two pieces of the chain-link opening in the fence separated automatically as the vehicle approached.

Provided it remained open long enough for the employee to get out of sight, Morgan prepared to try to bolt from the car and through the gate before it closed. He knew it was unlikely, but he would attempt it. He'd try to figure some way into the building once inside the fenced perimeter. But as he reached for the door handle, headlights of an approaching car appeared on the street. He let go of the latch.

The employee pulled to a stop just outside the gate, which closed behind him. A medium-sized sedan passed in front of Morgan. On its front door and along the rear on the trunk were the name and telephone number of a private security service. The security guard pulled alongside the car of the departing employee. The two men lowered their windows and carried on a brief conversation that Morgan couldn't hear.

When the two men waved a casual goodbye, Morgan knew an opportunity was about to present itself.

He put on a hoodie he'd bought on his way from Texas. The he tied a bandana around his face. Finally, Morgan retrieved a device from the bag he had gotten from his house in Wyoming while Maggie was at the hospital with Curtis Jones. He inserted the plug into the lightning connector of his iPhone and waited.

The security guard pressed the correct combination of keys and the two-part gate began to roll open. While he waited for the guard to drive through, hopefully to a place some distance from the gate, Morgan looked at his Sig Sauer on the seat beside him.

"Can't," he decided. He set the handgun in the floorboard and stepped out of the car to prepare for his dash. The guard parked twenty yards inside the fence and, to Morgan's relief, immediately exited his vehicle and began to walk around the corner of the nearest building. The longer the delay, Morgan understood, the more the accuracy of his device suffered.

He sprinted to the keypad that controlled the gate. He cursed himself for not already having the app launched. As he fumbled through the icons on the display, he looked up to make sure the guard hadn't spotted him.

With the device's operating app launched, Morgan snapped three quick photos of the keypad and ran back to his car. Returning to the back seat, he pulled up the thermal images his phone had just produced of the twelve keys of the pad that controlled the gate.

"Only four. Good." On his mobile phone's screen was a brightly colored image of the keypad. It wasn't a typical photograph and showed nothing that would make sense to the casual viewer. But among the blue background, four ovals with colors of varying intensities stood out. Each had a lime green outline, filled with hues ranging from light orange to a deep reddish orange.

The about-to-be burglar was grateful that the code was short. Then he realized that some numbers might have been repeated. That would make the images useless. He wouldn't have time to sort out all the combinations of numbers that might work, if that were the case.

Morgan gauged the intensity of each oval, from lightest to darkest and noted which key each would've been on. The heat signature transferred to the keys from the guard's fingers would last a little over a minute. Each impression's strength would determine the order in which they were pressed. The lightest indicated the first key touched, having lost the most of the transferred heat from the guard's finger. The darkest oval would be the last one touched, retaining more of the thermal signature.

"7061," Morgan concluded. He slipped the phone into his back pocket and crouched beside a car in the farthest space from where he was parked.

With no sign of the guard, the former spook bolted for the gate. He hurriedly pressed the keys.

7 – 0 – 6 – 1.

The sections of chain-link fabric started to separate. He squeezed through and ran toward two large metal boxes that he assumed to provide electrical access. He paused to catch his breath and looked toward where he'd last seen the guard.

♦

At the Federal Bureau of Investigation field office on Memorial Boulevard in Oklahoma City, a string of six agency vehicles were parked with agents standing beside them. A final vehicle pulled alongside the lineup of sedans and SUVs.

Inside the last arrival was the manager of a local research facility. They had executed a warrant at his home to pick him up. They would need his assistance gaining access to the premises. Calling him to meet the agents there would've provided the chance for him to warn people at the lab that the FBI was on its way.

The manager of the facility was tired, grumpy, and confused. He had no idea what the feds might be looking for.

♦

Morgan's wait was lengthened. No sooner had he knelt in his hiding place than the guard reappeared. The man was moving from building to building, entering one for a look around, then moving on to the next structure.

There was only one building that interested Morgan. It was clearly marked, "Lab."

Finally, the gray-uniformed man moved to the laboratory. Morgan had counted off seconds while the man was in each of the three buildings that he'd already seen him enter. The shortest time in a structure was just under four minutes. The longest was about six. Morgan should have plenty of time.

The private security guard entered the lab's code onto the keys beside its door.

As soon as the door had closed, the burglar sped to the keypad, snapped off a burst of images and returned to his hiding place.

Morgan almost laughed when he examined the thermal images.

"Are you shitting me?" he whispered. "7061."

He waited until the guard left the lab. He only toured one additional building before driving off, presumably to the next business that had contracted his company's services.

Morgan waited until the gates were fully closed and the watchman's car well out of sight. He hurried to the lab's door,

Touching the 7,0,6, and 1 keys resulted in a soft click. He was in.

♦

In one of the abundant futuristic buildings making up the skyline of the capital city of Doha, Linus Schwartz had settled in after a long flight. Of course, in the confines of his Gulfstream, the man had enjoyed a far more comfortable flight than the average traveler would have. He had managed to get some sleep, though not much. Now he was on the eastern shore of the Arabian Peninsula in the State of Qatar. The fugitive was safely out of the reach of American authorities.

The construction magnate would miss his home country, he was sure. But though this nation was largely arid desert, the capital afforded all the luxuries he could want. Schwartz couldn't imagine a better safe haven.

♦

The former CIA officer nearly fainted when his phone vibrated.

"Maggie," he saw. He hated it, but he pressed "ignore" and let it go to voicemail.

Fortunately, the interior of the laboratory was illuminated by the dim tray lights along the edges of the ceiling. The soft glow from the rope lights hidden in the open-air soffits was more than sufficient for Morgan to make his way about the lab. He sprayed the lens of the single security camera with paint he'd bought when he purchased the hooded sweatshirt. Then he removed the bandana from his face.

It looked exactly like he'd imagined. Glass beakers, vials, and test tubes were everywhere. He saw computers, microscopes, and more. He didn't recognize most of the electronic equipment. There were several computers about the main room, but he dared not waste time with them. They were certainly going to be secured more strongly than the gate and door he'd just entered. Besides, hacking wasn't in his skillset.

During the little over three-hour drive from Frisco, the ex-CIA officer had tried to come up with some way he would recognize what he had come for. After all, the container wouldn't have a label with the words, "Assassination Toxin." Morgan had failed to come up with anything.

There was one thing he knew from the information Betsy Parnell had given him. The base component of the deadly liquid was a chemical compound commonly used in pesticides. He had done an internet search for methyl iodide while on the jet to DFW. It was extremely dangerous whether ingested, inhaled, or absorbed. Therefore, there were two details he'd decided would help him. The containers would certainly have one of a number of symbols identifying the contents as hazardous. And it made sense that the chemical would be quarantined, either in a locked cabinet or maybe a separate room or closet.

Finally, the most useful thing he discovered during his web search – at least, he thought it could be – was that the chemical name for methyl iodide was ICH_3. The former CIA spy hoped the thing he was looking for would have that somewhere on its label.

Morgan's greatest problem was that the methyl iodide-based substance might not even be here.

◆

Josh hadn't answered, so she had left a voicemail. Nothing too personal. Maggie simply explained that she noticed he had left Trent and Alicia Weston's home and that she hoped he was okay. She didn't ask for details in her message, but she did say that, knowing him, she was sure he was up to no good. She had winced at her attempt at humor.

She ended her voicemail by saying. "Goodnight, Josh. I'll see you in the morning.

◆

After a brief interview with the manager of Volumetric Advanced Chemical Solutions, the Special Agent in Charge of the planned search of his facility ordered everyone into their cars.

The line of unmarked vehicles pulled away for the thirty-five-minute drive.

♦

Morgan eliminated – he hoped correctly – several collections of containers in various parts of the main room of the lab. Some were powders. He was fairly certain that he was looking for a liquid.

Some of the liquids in different types of glass vessels had ordinary screw-off or pop-off lids. Hardly what you'd employ for a dangerous toxin, he figured.

Morgan was down to three locked cabinets. They had seemed like obvious choices, but he'd wanted to examine the remainder of the room before resorting to smashing locks. He'd hoped to get lucky. He hadn't.

One of the gray cabinets had a Master padlock. It was formidable. Morgan shook his head, though, at people's inability to recognize that securing a place or thing was only as strong as its weakest link. He looked past the lock at the flimsy hasp through which it was inserted. He found a small fire extinguisher and placed it above the hinge of the latch. He raised the extinguisher about six inches and slammed it down. The piece was loose but not fully detached. He repeated his assault on the hasp, and it dropped to the floor.

Morgan scanned the items on the eight shelves. It would've been helpful, he thought, if they'd at least had a single shelf labeled "pesticides." In light of the facility's purpose, though, maybe all of them were.

All of the items in the storage cabinet had different types of symbols marking them as hazardous. And many had the contents' chemical abbreviations clearly marked. Some included "I" and some included "CH$_3$." Two even had both, but neither of the labels had them in the sequence he'd seen online. He wondered if that mattered.

Turning to the second of the cabinets, he dispatched its combination lock as easily as he had the padlock. The lock held up, but, as with the first cabinet, the hasp gave way easily.

The sight inside this cabinet encouraged Morgan. Every container in it was dually protected. Clear, thick Plexiglas cubes enclosed other vessels of different types.

Morgan's gut was telling him that he was taking way too long. The security guard or any other person might arrive at any moment.

He hurriedly scanned the labels of the boxes, all of which had the words "very toxic" below whatever version of graphic warning it used.

Finally, "ICH$_3$" jumped out at him from one of the imprints stuck on its container. It had other chemical abbreviations, too.

In his mind, that was the confirmation he needed to ease his conscience with regard to his plan. Morgan looked around the lab. Hanging at various places on the walls were boxes of plastic gloves. He pulled a pair from one through a hole in the box.

Donning them, he took the container that had interested him and set it on a stainless-steel table nearby. Morgan began shuffling the various containers he was leaving behind to disguise what he'd taken. He ultimately decided that was a pointless exercise. There was bound to be an inventory.

He momentarily considered taking several other containers in the hopes that the methyl iodide derivative would get lost in the myriad of items that were missing. But these were dangerous compounds. How would he dispose of them? Finally, he took the single container. He found a heavy-duty plastic box to further insulate him from it. Placing it inside, he walked to the door's window. Seeing nobody around, he left the lab.

When he got to the gate, though, it didn't open. Apparently, it took something as substantial as a car to trigger the motion detector that activated it. He looked to the side of the gate. Much to his relief, he saw a keypad.

He typed, "7-0-6-1." Nothing.

He repeated, "7-0-6-1." The gate didn't budge.

"Great. So this one you use a different code."

The former spy looked around for some other means of exit but saw none. Worse, around a curve down the street, through the few trees that lined it, the flashing blue and red lights of a parade of several cars were coming into view. He ran to his previous hiding place behind the electrical access boxes.

The lead car reached the gate. The driver listened as a passenger was obviously giving him the code. The gate began to part at its center.

When the final car had pulled through, there was a pause, and the gate shut behind it.

Morgan was stuck.

♦

FBI Director Austin had been sleeping on the sofa in his office for some time but had ordered his agents in Oklahoma City to inform him of the beginning of the raid on the chemical lab.

Putting his phone on his desk after getting the news, he walked to his private restroom, and splashed water on his face.

◆

Maggie couldn't sleep. She was grieving not only the loss of her and Morgan's friend but also the damage their relationship had suffered. She wondered where Morgan had gone, and what he was doing. She assured herself that he was simply spending the night at a hotel somewhere and that she would see him in the morning.

◆

Morgan watched the men spread out to the various buildings in the Volumetric compound. Right now, their focus was on the insides of the structures. But, he knew, once they discovered the break-in, they would scour the grounds. Hopefully, he had delayed that inevitability.

He watched with some satisfaction at the growing frustration of one of the men, who appeared to be a civilian, at his inability to open the door.

"I'm telling you that it's the same code as the outside gate," the lab manager was telling the lead agent.

"And I'm telling you that you've got one minute to open the door, or we'll break it down," the SAIC yelled.

When Morgan had entered the lab, he had noticed that, when he typed in the code, as the door unlocked, the display on the keypad illuminated with the word, "Settings."

On his way out, he had entered the code again and at the prompt, pressed the number "3." There had been an arrow pointing to it beside the word "Settings."

He had progressed through a couple of options until he saw one that said, "Change code?"

He entered the current string of numbers at the prompt, then pressed "0-8-2-7" as the new code, confirmed it at the next prompt, and left.

He had changed the key to delay people arriving for work the following morning in order to postpone discovery of his theft. He'd had no way of knowing how quickly his decision would benefit him.

Morgan watched as the lead agent pointed to one of the others, who walked toward a car. Apparently, the fed had reached the limit of his patience.

Before the agent reached his car, the agent in charge began waving toward the gate. Simultaneously, the edge of the beams of another approaching car splashed across the ground. Morgan slid further around the obstacle that hid him.

♦

In his car, the guard for the private security service wondered at the activity inside the chemical company's property.

He said aloud, "Uh-oh. What the hell did I miss?"

He reached the keypad and entered the numbers. As the gate began to roll open, he saw a man running urgently toward him, waving his arms. The private watchman began to drive in. That is, until the man held both arms directly in front of himself and shouted, "Stop!" One hand carried opened, double-flapped credentials. The guard couldn't read the ID, of course, but the glare off the gold shield that accompanied it was unmistakable.

The agent walked to the sedan and shone his light in the driver's face. A short discussion took place. The private security firm's employee explained that he was returning for his second round of the night. He also asked what was going on. He didn't get an answer.

As he backed up to turn around for his departure, he muttered, "Wow! The FBI!"

The gate was nearly shut when a car with additional agents arrived. The same one who had prevented the guard from entering walked to the gate and shouted the code. The driver of the newly arrived car keyed it in and drove forward. No sooner had he parked than another carful of agents appeared on the street. The agent inside the gate prepared to provide the code to this car but came up with a better idea. He returned to his own car, started it, and backed toward the gate.

The gate's motion detector responded, and the chain-link sections began to part. The agent left the vehicle where it was to keep the gate open. He retrieved a battering ram from his trunk and proceeded toward the lab. The arriving SUV parked inside, and two agents exited. All the agents turned their focus, guns drawn, to the door that one of their own was about to force open. They yelled a chorus of "FBI" and "federal agents."

With their attention squarely on the door that had refused to cooperate with its known code, Morgan slid out the gate and to his car.

He started his engine, turned on his lights, and drove slowly away. He was shaking at the thought of how close that had been. He also wasn't very comfortable with the cargo he was carrying.

As soon as he was out of sight of the chemical research facility, Morgan picked up the pace, though he stayed within the speed limit. He made a beeline toward the edge of Oklahoma City in an effort to lose himself in the congestion of the city. If the federal agents set up a roadblock – they had no doubt discovered the break-in now – he wanted to be in the midst of as many cars as he could.

♦

FBI Director Gabe Austin got the word from the team executing the search warrant. None of the news was good. There had been a break-in at the lab. No way of telling when, but an employee had left shortly after midnight. He'd said by phone that everything was fine when he left, but agents were on their way to pick him up for questioning.

Agents said the manager didn't know what was missing. He was "management, not a worker bee," he'd said. One of the "worker bees" was on his way from his home to do an inventory of items. Two cabinets had been broken into, and another left untouched. The three were the storage units for the most hazardous substances.

"Any video surveillance there?" the Director asked an agent.

"Outside and inside. The one in the lab had been painted over. We're pulling the tapes now, but we're not hopeful."

The SAIC asked if Austin wanted him to tell the manager specifically what they had come to look for.

"No," the Director had said. "Let's see if the methyl iodide blend shows up on the list of missing items. If it doesn't, it may mean someone there is trying to hide something."

♦

It was almost 6:00 AM when Morgan got back to the Frisco area. He hadn't had the chance to get a hotel room there. He'd gone straight from the rental agency at the airport to Alicia Weston's home for the reception. From there, he'd driven directly to Oklahoma.

He knew he wouldn't sleep, but he had to get out of his car. He pulled into the lot of the Comfort Suites on North Dallas Parkway. It was northwest of the original town of Frisco that had exploded in recent years to an upscale mini-metropolis.

No availability.

Morgan certainly couldn't go to Alicia Weston's home at this hour. He drove a short distance north on the North Tollway to a McDonald's that was open twenty-four hours. He ordered the pancake platter and drank coffee – lots of coffee. He needed the caffeine, and his weariness was only going to get worse as the day wore on.

Back in the privacy of the rental car, he made a call.

"Hello, Morgan."

"Betsy." He struggled to begin. Finally, "I think I have proof that Schwartz's company developed the poison that killed Trent."

"Oklahoma?"

"Yeah."

"Wondered if that was you. Got a call from Gabe Austin just now. He's keeping me in the loop about his investigation since the Agency might need to join it, with Schwartz in Qatar. Said they raided his company's chemical research lab overnight. It had already been broken into. And they just discovered that an experimental pesticide, a derivative of methyl iodide was taken."

Morgan said nothing.

"What am I going to do with you?"

"Damn you, Betsy. Don't give me that shit! You knew exactly what I would do when you gave me all that information. So, just stop it!"

"Fair enough. What's your plan?"

"First, I need to figure out how to get this to you. You can give it to the Bureau. I'm assuming they can do some sort of chemistry magic and link this sample to what got Trent."

"What will I tell Austin that will allow this thing to be admissible in court?"

"What does it matter? Schwartz is in the wind in a non-extraditable country. But you'll think of something. Besides, I don't plan to ever let the son of a bitch get to trial."

"Okay, Morgan. You're headed for Qatar?"

"After Trent's service. I am *not* missing his funeral."

"Okay, Josh. Call me when the service is over. I'll figure out some way to get the toxin. And I'll pave the way for your trip."

Morgan returned to the McDonald's carrying a garment bag and small case of toiletries. The workers all stared at the customer who'd just eaten breakfast there, but nobody stopped him.

Reemerging in his suit and tie, Morgan tossed everything haphazardly in the back seat of the rental. His face stung from shaving in cold water. His hair was oily from not being able to wash it.

Josh arrived at Alicia Weston's home. He wasn't sure he'd ever get used to not saying *Trent and* Alicia's home. The street was blocked off, but, after a call to Agent Jack Johnston, the Secret Service Special Agent standing watch let Morgan proceed. Fortunately, Mrs. Weston's and her guards' familiarity with Morgan made them feel a search of his car was unnecessary. Josh hadn't considered that possibility until he was already there. He had both a gun and a dangerous chemical with him.

He had to park some distance away, but when he arrived at the front door, Maggie opened it.

"Agent Johnston told me you were here."

Maggie looked at her fiancé's appearance. His normally perfect appearance when he dressed up was something far less. His hair was slicked down. His face had a slight rash.

"Would you like a do-over, Josh?"

He knew exactly what she meant and nodded.

He returned to his car and got his bag of toiletries. In the bathroom, he decided his face was beyond hope, but he took off his shirt and tie and leaned over the tub to wash his hair. The hot water felt wonderful.

When he arrived in the living room, Maggie said, "Much better." His hair was still damp, but it was combed more neatly and would dry out.

Alicia appeared and gave him a warm hug.

CHAPTER 26

Trent's – he was simply 'Trent,' and not President Weston, to the group of friends here – private memorial was more intimate. Compared to the Washington service, there was more crying. There was also more laughing than at the National Cathedral. The weather was beautiful and there was only a graveside event.

At its conclusion, everyone gathered again at the Weston's home. The atmosphere was lighter, though the grief wouldn't disappear for a long time, if ever. Stories abounded. Some were humorous, but all wound up back to the conclusion that Trenton Weston was the most honorable, decent man that any of the mourners had ever known.

Maggie's heart rate picked up when Morgan approached.

"Hi, Josh."

"Maggie, I wanted to let you know that I'll be away for a while." And that was it. He left her and moved to Alicia, who had witnessed the brief interaction between her two young friends who were like her own children. For a moment, her heartbreak shifted from her loss of Trent to a concern for Josh and Maggie.

Alicia took Morgan by the hand and led him to Trent's study. She closed the door.

"Josh, what's going on?" she asked. But when she saw a cold look in Morgan's eyes, unlike any that she'd ever seen, she knew exactly what he was planning to do.

"No, son. Don't do this."

"I don't know what you mean, Alicia."

"You're going after whoever killed Trent, aren't you?"

Morgan lowered his head and said nothing.

"You've got Maggie to think about. And yourself. You've done enough, Josh."

"But I've…"

Alicia Weston took his hands in hers. "You've done enough."

Josh Morgan leaned over and kissed his friend's widow on the forehead. As they hugged, she knew there would be no talking him out of whatever he was planning.

Morgan left the house, passing Maggie on his way out.

◆

"You leave DFW Airport for Qatar at 7:20 PM."

"Thank you, Betsy. And the package?"

"There will be a U.S. Army Rangers Sergeant First Class arriving in Dallas before you leave. He's already on his way from Fort Hood, which isn't too far from there. He'll pick it up from you and bring it to me personally on a military transport."

"Good."

"Well, couldn't exactly send it FedEx, could we?"

Elizabeth Parnell gave Morgan the address of a convenience store that would be on his way to Dallas-Fort Worth International Airport, and a coded exchange to use when meeting SFC Steele.

◆

At 5:00 PM, Morgan drove into the parking lot of a Seven-Eleven convenience store, where he saw a man who, although he was in civilian clothes, unmistakably had the bearing of a professional warrior.

"Excuse me, any good barbecue places around here?"

The sergeant gave the reply Morgan expected. "It's Texas. There's good barbecue everywhere."

"Sergeant Steele."

"Sir." Parnell hadn't provided Morgan's name to the soldier.

Morgan leaned in to whisper. "I'm not shitting you. This package has some nasty, nasty stuff in it." And with that, Morgan handed over the plastic box containing the methyl iodide derivative that he believed had killed his friend.

"Yes, sir."

◆

The departure was a little late, but by seven-fifty Morgan was in the air headed for the Arabian Peninsula to find Linus Schwartz and, he hoped, Oskar Lammers.

CHAPTER 27

Day 11 – Wednesday

Maggie hated to leave, but she knew Alicia Weston was in good hands with her sister, Emma Gray. Emma had arranged an extended leave from her missionary post and would stay with the newly widowed woman for almost the entirety of the time, four weeks.

So, Maggie boarded a mid-day flight to Washington Dulles. She had called her boss, Press Secretary Marie Ginnetti and told her that she would be back at work tomorrow.

Ginnetti had tried to insist Maggie take another few days, but Maggie refused. She'd already missed too much time, she'd said. But the truth was, Maggie didn't want to spend time in the apartment she shared with Josh. It was bad enough when she knew he'd be coming back. But right now, she didn't know if he even wanted to.

♦

DCI Elizabeth Parnell had arranged for a driver to take her to meet SFC Steele at Andrews, where she took custody of Morgan's discovery. She wasn't disturbed at the contents. She had always been one to figure when her time was up, it was up.

She had asked the FBI chief to meet her on the National Mall without explaining why. Austin had already arrived and was waiting on a bench beside the Reflecting Pool near the Lincoln Memorial.

"Is it my birthday?" he asked at the sight of a box wrapped in plastic.

The CIA Director said, "Be careful," as she turned over the package that contained the lethal toxin.

"What is this, Betsy?"

"Gabe, you're going to have to trust me on some things, and not ask too many questions."

"No promises."

"The package contains the methyl iodide that killed President Weston – we think."

The FBI Director opened the plastic bag that surrounded the plastic box with the toxin. "Kinda like Russian nesting dolls," he joked, as he proceeded through the layers. Through the clear plastic of the box that contained the Plexiglas that contained the vial that contained the liquid, he made out the word "Volumetric."

"Betsy. No."

The Director had monitored the raid on the chemical lab, which had finally resulted in the disclosure that a container of the derivative of the pesticide was missing.

"No questions, Gabe. Please."

Austin handed over the package to his aide, who was standing nearby.

"How?"

Parnell didn't answer and stood to leave.

"You know I'll figure it out, Parnell."

"But you won't have heard it from me." Parnell knew he'd piece together that Morgan had been in north Texas for Weston's funeral. She could only hope that the head of the FBI had as much appreciation for what Morgan had done in the past as she did.

♦

The FBI hadn't had anything to charge Dexter Leach with since they hadn't charged his boss. They'd given him the same warning they had Schwartz but weren't surveilling him. So, when he scheduled a commercial flight to Doha, Qatar, no alerts went out.

♦

The FBI lab wasted no time in analyzing the fluid in the vial that the Director had brought. The techs gave priority, of course, to anything requested by their ultimate boss, but even his requests would drop to second place behind anything related to the assassination of a President, current or former. In this case, the evidence filled both elements of prioritization.

The chemical DNA of the variant of the methyl iodide was a perfect match. Not only did it possess the exact chemical composition, but the chemists within the Bureau had assigned a ninety-five percent likelihood that it had come from the same batch as the sample found in Riley Maxwell's desk drawer.

Elsewhere, in the D.C. headquarters FBI cyber-specialists were busy unlocking the files found on the personal computers taken from Linus Schwartz's home.

The billionaire construction CEO had given orders to his personal assistant to destroy the files on the PCs. Leach had made it through a number of the digital records, but not all. The federal agents had gotten their warrant much more quickly than even Schwartz had planned on.

Leach had prioritized the order of his destruction of the records on the networked computers. Before agents arrived to seize the property, he had already placed a magnet next to three of the four computers in the dwelling. They held data related to their owner's financial dealings and those of his companies.

Unfortunately for Leach and ultimately, his employer, the magnet wasn't powerful enough nor did he leave it near the hard drives long enough for complete erasure. Data had been severely corrupted, but not sufficiently to prevent the world-class experts at the Bureau's lab from recovering the files. It would just take some time.

Other data was stored in the cloud. The FBI had already obtained the warrant for that search and were accessing the information stored there.

◆

Not far from Schwartz's luxury townhouse in Washington, agents had raided a much more modest apartment belonging to Oskar Lammers. The owner wasn't there. Neither was much of anything else. Lammers' residence was austere, to say the least. He had few conveniences. Even the television was small by current standards, a twenty-incher. The CSIs found no computer of any sort. In fact, there were no digital devices of any kind. The men and women searching the place had found a wireless router, so the man apparently owned a computer, probably a laptop. He must have taken it with him when he left.

In the course of the search, the agent in charge received a call from Annie Liu. Lammers had passed through customs at the Doha Airport with Schwartz. He was beyond the Bureau's reach, too.

CSIs gathered everything that wasn't nailed down, and even some things that were. But there was hardly anything in the take that could yield any clues to the man's activities, or his role in the service of Linus Schwartz.

◆

Some of the Bureau's internal hackers were working through the recovery of the files on three of the four personal computers found in Schwartz's townhouse. Others had gone to work on the final one. Its encryption was sophisticated. It was "elegant," to use one of the techies' words, but it was ultimately no match for the human and digital resources at the FBI's disposal. In no time, analysts were reading what turned out to be mostly personal files.

Supervisory Agent Annie Liu had finished a series of meetings and dropped by the lab to check the progress of the cyber-specialists.

"How's it going, Smitty?"

Lab tech Carl Smith was quite capable at hacking PCs in his own right, but even he knew his skills were no match for his friend's. His coworker, Alonzo Lane, pulled data from the computer and dropped it into a shared folder for Smitty to assess.

"Good, Annie. The guys in the other room are even making good progress on the corrupted files."

"Well, keep me posted." The SSA headed for the door.

"Will do," Smitty promised. "Say, boss, did you know Schwartz had a son?"

Liu returned to Smitty's work area. Her face was twisted as she thought back to the details in their suspect's personal file. "I guess I missed that," she was embarrassed to say.

"Well, he was illegitimate. There's this big-ass file that contains a lot of documents about private investigators, data analysts – all sorts of people he hired to track him down. And judging by the dates of the files, Schwartz started looking for the guy right after he found the son's aunt."

"You don't say?"

"Yeah. And the son was a bigshot in the NSA."

Liu leaned over Smitty's shoulder to view the side-by-side twenty-four-inch monitors. "What's his name?"

"You should say, what *was* his name. He's dead."

Liu waited, but Smitty didn't continue. He simply looked at her.

"And?" Sometimes Liu was frustrated by some of the squints' lack of continuity in their revelations.

"Huh? Oh! Let's see." Smitty found the right digital report. "Hmm… Okay, here it is: Everson Blake. He was a Deputy Director."

"Yeah, I remember the name from a couple of years ago. Apparently, he was killed rescuing President Weston from that Saudi agent. A hero, really. Nothing like his old man, it appears."

Supervisory Agent Liu didn't know the entire story of Blake's corrupt dealings in Terrador. Neither did she know that he had only pursued kidnapped Former President Weston with the intent to kill him. Few people knew the truth.

"Do me a favor. Compile a summary about Schwartz finding out he had a son. Just a brief rundown of the basics that I can give to the Deputy Director."

"You got it, boss."

Annie Liu left the lab without any inkling of the magnitude of the discovery Carl Smith had just revealed.

◆

It had taken some time, but a couple of hours after taking off from the Dallas-Fort Worth Airport, Morgan had cleared his mind well enough to get some sleep. What had kept him awake was his awareness that, once again, he was going into action without a strategy.

Somehow, these things always seemed to work out in the end, but it was hell in the meantime.

He'd had the foresight to bring the satellite phone that Parnell had provided for him when he went to Terrador. But he had no weapon. He didn't even have a suitcase. The garment bag he'd had with him for Trent's funeral was all he had brought. It contained some casual clothes – one change, to be precise. He also had his small bag of toiletries. That was it. So, when he reached Qatar, he'd have to go shopping.

"I'm gonna have to go back to work," the former employee of the Central Intelligence Agency thought. "I'm spending way too much money."

Finally, he forced himself to quit worrying and start planning. With the change of mindset, Morgan had fallen asleep.

◆

SSA Annie Liu knocked on Director Austin's open door.

Austin motioned her in as he hung up his desk phone. He looked at his phone.

"Six-thirty. Seems later."

Turning his attention to his visitor, he said, "It's been a long several days, hasn't it?" He forced the bland "I'm so tired" expression from his face and gave his associate a smile.

"Coffee?"

"No, thanks, but you go ahead."

While he poured the hours-old black beverage into his cup, he asked, "So, what's the latest?"

Liu placed a folder on the Director's desk. "Deputy Director Drake asked me to bring this directly to you. The lab techs are starting to get some data from the corrupted files, but, in the interim, here are some summary reports from what we've got from the others."

"I'll read 'em in a bit. Highlights?" Austin walked over to the window and wished he were on a Caribbean beach somewhere.

"Really just some personal stuff. It will probably help our profilers is all."

"Anything else?"

"Not really. But, say, you remember Everson Blake, the guy who rescued Weston?"

Director Austin was glad he was facing away from Annie. His face immediately turned to a scowl at the mention of the dead NSA Deputy Director. And to hear Liu reciting the public version of the bastard's involvement in the episode with the now-deceased former President and the Saudi Agent – well, that turned his stomach.

"If you only knew the real story, kiddo," he thought. Aloud, he just said, "Yeah, I remember the son... him. What about him?"

"Turns out he's Linus Schwartz's illegitimate son."

Gabe Austin stopped in mid-drink and lowered his coffee cup. Several seconds went by before he turned to his SSA. She saw that his face was pallid.

"Say that again."

"The man's computer files detailed a search for him – well, Blake's aunt first, and..."

"It's all in here?" the Director enquired, taking the files Liu had brought from his desk and sinking into his chair.

"Yes, sir, Director."

Unless he got a phone call or was late for a meeting, the head of the FBI had never rushed Liu out of his office. So, she was utterly dumbfounded when he said, "Would you excuse me?"

The supervisor of a team of agents rose slowly. "Uh. Of course. Anything else?"

The Director never looked up. Nor did he acknowledge Liu's question, so she left his office.

"Shut the door," stopped her in her tracks. She closed the office door quietly and left. Under her breath, she mumbled, "What was that about?"

♦

Morgan felt better – and worse. The sleep had done him good. Waking into the same world he'd drifted off in hadn't.

The worries flooded back. He knew no one in Qatar. He'd never been there in his photojournalist espionage days. He considered going to the U.S. embassy, but what would he say?

Furthermore, it was more than a theory now that the man he was after, Linus Schwartz, was behind Trent's assassination. Lammers had tried to kidnap Maggie… Morgan realized he hadn't thought of her the entire flight. "What does that mean?" he wondered.

"After he kidnapped Maggie, the plan was to torture her for no other reason than to hurt me," Josh pieced together mentally. "Then they would come after me."

"Now here I am," Morgan thought of the irony, "trying to turn the tables on an entire organization trying to kill me."

He wondered if Schwartz would somehow know he was coming. Billions of dollars can buy lots of information and tons of resources.

◆

FBI Director Austin pushed the folder away and tried to come to terms with what he'd read.

"Blake's his son." Austin could hardly comprehend the significance of the revelation. He rubbed his eyes. He took a sip of his coffee, which had gotten cold. He rubbed his forehead, then pushed his hand through his hair.

As several thoughts began to crystallize, a great number of things were becoming obvious.

"Shiiiiit."

The Director had a decision to make. CIA Director Parnell had shared her theory that Morgan was at the center of all this. Now Austin knew she had been right. "But, should I tell her about this?"

CHAPTER 28

Day 12 – Thursday

British Airways operated American Airlines Flight 78. At London Heathrow, Morgan had connected with AA Flight 6413, also flying under the BA flag. Despite 78's delayed departure from DFW, the last leg's flight was arriving right on time in Doha, twenty-five hours after he had boarded for the first portion.

"4:30. Crap!" Morgan griped.

He had slept about half the hours of the combined flights. Only half of those hours had been restful.

Given that the former CIA operative was traveling so light, he passed successfully through Customs in a very short amount of time. Of course, not many planes were landing at Hamad International Airport at this time of the morning.

By 5:15 AM, Morgan was past the secure part of the airport. He went into the men's room to relieve himself. It was also a great place to think.

Standing not far from the door to the restroom, a trim man in his mid-fifties waited patiently. Seeing his fellow countryman emerge, he started toward him.

When Morgan saw the man approaching him, his mind flashed back to his arrival in Russia not that long ago. A Moscow local had similarly greeted him. Vladislav Proskurkin was a member of Russian intelligence. His director had sent him to help defuse the situation that was propelling his country and Morgan's toward a nuclear confrontation. Slava had been an invaluable ally. But Morgan was suspicious of the figure approaching him now. One thing was certain. He wasn't a local.

The man wore light-colored linen pants, an equally comfortable shirt, and a sport coat.

"Hello, Josh. Geoff Ricketts. I'm your ride." The man handed a business card identifying him as an employee of the U.S. delegation to the State of Qatar. But the American who had just arrived knew he was more.

"Thank you, Parnell," Morgan thought.

"A friend of yours said you were going to vacation here. She asked me to greet you. You couldn't have gotten a flight that arrived later?"

Ricketts laughed and slapped his guest on the shoulder. "This way."

Morgan studied the small card introducing the man as an employee of the United States State Department and considered the spelling of his first name. As if sensing the unspoken question, Ricketts said, "My mother is British."

Once the CIA station chief and Morgan were in his car, he handed the ex-spy an envelope from the inside pocket of his jacket.

Inside was a stack of bills. Some were denominated in U.S. dollars. The rest of the bills were Qatari Riyals. "Parnell said you should also feel free to use your personal credit card. Your limit has increased to a generous amount."

Morgan smiled. "Do I have to keep receipts?"

"You've met Parnell. I'd advise you to." Ricketts laughed again.

Morgan checked the time on his phone. "What time do stores open here?"

"Mostly nine or ten. About like back home."

"I need clothes."

"We have a few things at the embassy you can look through. We'll be there in less than half an hour."

Morgan watched the scenery zipping by. He had noticed when he was landing that the sun was already rising. It had peeked over the horizon in Doha a little after 5:00 AM, so it was well on its upward journey.

Breaking the silence, Morgan put forth the question he needed to ask.

"Do you know why I'm here?

"No clue," answered the man with the Foreign Service cover. "Don't need to. All I know is what the Director gave me, and that was just a laundry list of things to do for you."

There was no further conversation until they reached the embassy. Once inside the gate, Ricketts parked the car and told Morgan, "I don't need to remind you, Morgan. You have no official cover here. Getting you registered as an employee of State would've taken a lot longer than we had time for. You get caught doing anything illegal, we can't offer you any protection. Some assistance, yes. But protection, no."

Ricketts knew nothing of his guest's background. Morgan had spent his brief career at CIA as a NOC officer. "Non-Official Cover" meant he had no diplomatic immunity if arrested in a foreign country.

"I understand," he said with a smile.

◆

It was a little after midnight, District time, when the DCI got word that Morgan was safely at the embassy in Doha. She'd thought he might call himself, but it was a text message from diplomatic staff.

Parnell had gotten the word from her FBI peer that Schwartz was Everson Blake's father. Not hearing from Morgan personally upon his arrival at the embassy had given her more time to decide whether to pass the news of the relationship along to him or not. The CIA Director wasn't worried that the information would push the ex-spy into doing something foolish. He was already determined to do whatever it was he had in mind for the billionaire. Her fear was that the impact of the revelation could make Morgan too emotional about his target, and that might cause him to become careless from the distraction.

Morgan's motivation right now appeared to be clearly rational in nature. Of course, he *was* angry, but this whole thing was solely about retribution. At least that's what Parnell thought. The man had seemed cold and calculating the couple of times she had spoken with him on the phone. He was all about revenge for what Schwartz had done to Maggie Loughlin and Trent Weston. How would he respond to finding out that everything that had happened was about vengeance for Schwartz, too – against Morgan, for killing his son?

The CIA Director had realized that she had been mistaken about the reasons that people were out to get Morgan. Because of the suspected tie to Terrador, she had assumed that it was some sort of vendetta against him by some of Blake's old friends. She had thought that to be oddly personal if the perpetrators just wanted to revitalize an old organization in Terrador. Learning the news that Schwartz was Everson Blake's father had cleared everything up.

"It *is* about revenge against Morgan for killing Blake," she said to herself, "but it's by his father."

◆

Morgan returned from the small room that contained an assortment of clothing. He'd found matching linen slacks and sport coat, and a golf shirt. The items fit well, but the main thing was that they were clean. He'd been in his suit since before Weston's Texas memorial, and that had been well over a day. Before changing clothes, the ex-CIA officer had also taken a shower and shaved. He would've thought getting cleaned up would improve his attitude.

It didn't.

"So, here are the things the DCI asked me to get for you." He slid a tray of items across the desk to Morgan.

Most of the items were obvious. First, a handgun.

"I hope you're okay with an HK."

Morgan sized up the .45 caliber-chambered semiautomatic. The German-made Heckler & Koch HK45CT had a standard eight-round magazine and two extended magazines that held ten bullets each. The gun's case also had a suppressor that fit on its extended, threaded barrel. Morgan had never carried a gun during his shortened tenure with CIA and had rarely seen a suppressor since weapons training at the Agency's training facility at Camp Peary, Virginia.

"Kinda James Bond-ish," he assessed silently, as he placed the compact gun in his waistband.

"Here's a GPS unit. I know your phone will have one, but this is programmed with a huge amount of detail about Qatar; Doha, in particular. Plus, it will also track the beacons that are in the case with it."

Morgan returned the unit to its case.

"Here are the keys to the car I picked you up in. It's one of ours, but it has local plates. I considered giving you one with an embassy sticker on it; you know, thinking authorities might leave you alone. But ultimately, I decided it might call attention to you.

"Here's a key card to a hotel room. The details are on the sleeve it's in. The location is near here."

He handed Morgan a handwritten note.

"What's this?"

"Linus Schwartz's address. Parnell said you would want it."

Morgan nodded. "Thanks."

Station Chief Ricketts went over a few other items. When he was finished, he said, "Now, if you've got time, let's get some breakfast in the cafeteria."

The former CIA officer's first instinct was to hit the road, even though breakfast sounded very inviting. Finally, realizing that he still had no plan, and that Schwartz wasn't going to leave the non-extradition country anyhow, he gave in to his hunger.

◆

FBI lab rats worked through the night to recover the data that had been corrupted by Dexter Leach's attempted destruction with his magnet. Most of the information they were able to restore held no significance with their investigation.

However, the files they found on the cloud-based storage were another story. Analysts uncovered deposits corresponding to those found on the dead prosecutor's home computer. It would've taken some time to determine the nature of the offshore deposits, if not for the fact that the amounts and dates exactly matched the ones Maxwell had recorded. That alone corroborated the working theory that Schwartz's company, at least, was used to funnel under-the-table payments to the U.S. attorney.

But, the most meaningful piece of data, one that was especially damning, was that the online records' internal activity log identified various users who had accessed the financial file. One of the user IDs was that of Schwartz himself. That didn't eliminate the possibility that another person had logged in with his credentials, but it was unlikely.

The Bureau was building a very strong case against the tycoon. Now, if investigators could just get him back into their jurisdiction.

◆

Morgan's and Ricketts' breakfast conversation was mostly personal in nature. Ricketts was from Arizona and, like Morgan, joined the Company right out of college.

Just before going their separate ways, the station chief related his orders from the Director.

"Morgan, I can provide all the logistical support you need. Other than that, I can't be involved."

"I understand."

The two men shook hands, and the former CIA officer thanked the present one. "I'll see you around, Ricketts."

"Yep. Take care, Morgan."

Ricketts remained at the table, finishing his coffee.

"I hope he knows what he's doing." He got a refill and headed for his office.

CHAPTER 29

Located on the top floor of Forty Four West Bay Tower in Doha, the Penthouse was as luxurious as any in Qatar. The atmosphere was brighter than his townhouse in Washington, D.C. Schwartz preferred the darker mood but at over eleven thousand square feet, this apartment provided the space he required and possessed the level of security features that he demanded.

The apartment boasted a commanding view of the Arabian Gulf from the bedroom, lounge area, and bathroom. It also had the latest in electronic entertainment components, including a plasma TV, none of which the business magnate cared about.

Linus Schwartz's only concerns were the security and comfort it provided him. Like his place in the District, the penthouse had a private elevator. He'd hired his own staff when acquiring the place five years earlier but had spent little time here. And now, newly arrived, he could already see that he was going to have difficulty settling in.

Seated in the lounge, the construction tycoon found it challenging to concentrate on his business affairs. The only things on his mind were his failure to avenge his son's death and the likely collapse of the network he was reestablishing in Terrador. It was mostly about restoring it as a tribute to his late son, but it also had the potential to make millions through the various illicit activities it entailed. And, even when you were a billionaire, there could never be enough zeroes at the end of your net worth. It had been profitable while Everson was alive. It could've been so now.

While his boss stared mindlessly over the waters of the Gulf, Oskar Lammers interrupted his mental rehashing of what had gone wrong over the last several days.

"Sir?"

Schwartz said nothing. He only turned with an empty expression toward his fixer.

Lammers asked, "Would you like me to come back later?"

The wealthy businessman shook his head and pointed to a seat on the sofa in the penthouse lounge.

Lammers appraised his boss' look and decided that the man did indeed looked frailer, weaker than mere days before. Perhaps it was only jetlag from the long flight to Qatar.

Finally, "What is it, Mr. Lammers?"

"I have some interesting news. Our source in the embassy has identified a new arrival to the country that should interest you."

Linus Schwartz had never considered himself a patriot. He'd never had an overly intense love for his country. He thought the military was run by fools with a rigid hierarchical structure that was overly large – too many chiefs. But the nature of his companies' projects involved government contracts, so the better the United States fared, the greater the number of opportunities for his enrichment.

The source within the embassy was never asked to provide any information for the purpose of subversive activities. The reports were only important to give Schwartz edges locally with regard to his business activities. He had similar arrangements with U.S. embassy staff throughout the world.

Part of the information coming from the Qatari woman who worked in an administrative capacity for the State Department was to report visitors to the diplomatic compound.

"Sir, Mrs. Khan sent the daily list of visitors to the embassy from yesterday and there is one from today already." Lammers held out a piece of paper.

"Set it on the coffee table."

"Josh Morgan is here."

The revelation immediately changed Schwartz's attitude. Lammers hadn't been sure what his reaction would be. Would the man be fearful? Might he be nervous? But in his employer's smile, the German saw the reaction he'd finally decided he would see.

"He's here!" The billionaire suddenly sat up straighter. And he raised his hands in front of his chest and tapped his fingers together as he frequently did when in thought.

"Well, what could he possibly be doing here?" Schwartz's smile at his own sarcasm broadened at the prospect that the opportunity to exact revenge for his son's death might not have vanished, after all.

◆

Morgan's drive to Forty Four West Bay Tower had taken about twenty minutes. It was located on Diplomatic Street, owing its name to the presence of a number of embassies. The street ran parallel to the shoreline. Between the street and the beach were the diplomatic headquarters of Jordan, Kuwait, and the Republic of Korea, among others. He parked and walked around to assess the place. It was a fortress, he saw. The note that CIA Station Chief Ricketts had given him said that Schwartz lived on the top floor.

As he cased the place, Morgan saw multiple entrances. He knew that a penthouse would have a private elevator, and that it would likely go to the underground parking garage. It would probably stop in the lobby, too, but wherever passengers boarded, it wouldn't be able to go anywhere unless a key were used.

The ex-spook pulled out his phone and read about the place online. It had twenty-four-hour security. There was no way he had the skills to get in there. He sort of wished he had Seth Tierney here. This was precisely the kind of place that the black bag operatives of the Special Collection Service could breach. Morgan realized that the U.S. embassy in Doha would unquestionably have an F6 team of its own. But the hope of assistance disappeared as soon as the thought had occurred. Parnell had told Ricketts not to get directly involved.

"But she said he *could* provide logistical support."

He retrieved Ricketts' business card from his shirt pocket. The local CIA boss had scribbled his personal number on it.

"Ricketts? Morgan. Could you get me some license plate numbers and vehicle information?"

◆

It was only four-thirty in Washington. Maggie had been awake since three. A million thoughts rattled around in her weary, restless mind.

She wondered if D.C. was the right place for her and Morgan to live. Her job in the West Wing demanded so much of her time and energy. Of course, during most of her time there, she'd been filling in as Press Secretary while Marie Ginnetti recovered from the injuries that she'd suffered at the bombing at St. John's Episcopal Church. Now she was back in her own position, so maybe things would lighten up somewhat.

On the other hand, Maggie thought about when Secretary Ginnetti had told her that she intended to retire in the coming months. She had voiced then that the consensus in the White House was that Maggie should replace her.

Maggie tossed around in her bed, settling on her back with her hands clutching Morgan's pillow to her chest.

Her concern moved to Morgan directly. She didn't think he really had an interest in serving as a visiting professor in the School of Journalism at Georgetown University. She knew he'd just taken the job to have something to do and bring in some income.

Maggie turned up on her left side and stared at the clock on her nightstand.

"Is the damned thing broken?"

Her misgivings about her job and Morgan's were real, but she finally admitted to herself the real reason for her anxiety about remaining in Washington.

As long as they were here, there was the chance that Morgan would be pulled back into some sort of crisis by Betsy Parnell.

The knot in her stomach convinced her. "I'm not going back to sleep."

Principal Deputy Press Secretary Loughlin got up and dressed for work, having made two decisions. The most important was that she would talk to Morgan and offer to leave her post at the White House, if he wanted her to.

The other verdict she'd arrived at was to call Betsy Parnell as soon as it got to be a decent hour. She would find out where Morgan was and how to get in touch with him. He wasn't picking up his cell.

She wouldn't mention her thoughts about moving back to Wyoming to Josh yet, but she needed to clear the air about her behavior toward him lately. An apology and an expression of her deep love might or might not make a difference to him, but she needed it.

◆

It had taken longer than he'd expected to hear back from Ricketts, so Morgan had grabbed lunch at one of the eateries near the high-rise condominium complex. He'd kept a sharp eye out for Schwartz or Lammers, but knew it was absurd to think they might luckily walk right in front of him.

Finally, his phone rang.

He jotted down the information. Ricketts had only found one vehicle for which Morgan had requested a check for license plate numbers. It was registered to Lammers.

It was a white Rolls-Royce Phantom. A car like that would stand out in most places, but not here. Qatar was a wealthy country with wealthy citizens. Most of the riches came from oil and natural gas. Luxury cars abounded. Morgan wasn't even sure that Lammers', or Schwartz's, would be the only one at Forty Four West Bay Tower.

He sat on a stone ledge not far from the entrance to the parking area for the high-rise. One car after another came and went. A great many of them were luxury cars. He'd even seen one Rolls-Royce returning to the underground lot's entrance, but it was dark gray.

The footprint of the Tower was huge, so businesses nearest it were some distance away; especially restaurants. It was only four in the afternoon, so Morgan wasn't ready for dinner yet. He could use a beer. Alcohol was available in Qatar in licensed restaurants and bars. But the distance to the nearest ones would put him too far from his car. If he did catch sight of the Rolls, he'd never make it back to his car quickly enough to follow it.

The former spook kept looking at the entryway to the underground car storage. The tower's website said the parking was free. Problem was, there was still a guardhouse.

Morgan's plan so far was to wait for as long as it took to spot the white Phantom exiting. He would try to follow Schwartz somewhere and hope to catch him alone, when Lammers wandered off on some errand. But no luck. He was losing patience. And worse, people were beginning to take note of his hanging around the area for several hours. Morgan had changed locations from time to time, but he got the sense that he was being noticed.

He'd kept the GPS beacon that had been among the items Ricketts had given him in his jacket pocket. But he was beginning to see no way to get it on the white Rolls.

It was 4:40 PM. The man pursuing Schwartz decided to be bolder.

♦

It was half past nine and Maggie had struggled with whether she should call the CIA Director or not. Finally, she dialed the number. She didn't know if she was relieved that Parnell had picked up, or whether she would've preferred to miss her and leave a message – or not.

♦

Parnell saw the name on the display and hesitated. She opted to answer.
"Hi, Maggie."
"Hi, Betsy."
The chit-chat was brief. Betsy took the conversation straight to where she knew it was headed.
"What can I help you with, Maggie?"
She listened as the caller, voice shaking somewhat, told her how Morgan hadn't been answering his phone. Then Maggie had asked the DCI if she knew where her fiancé was.
"No, I don't, Maggie."
On the other end of the line, Maggie was very calm, but she explained

that she thought she deserved better than a lie. She was certain Parnell knew where Josh was.

"Anytime Josh goes on one of his trips, I'm the one who suffers. I don't know where he goes or what he does. And I think I have a right to know. Based on the last few days, I suspect he's going after that Lammers guy."

Maggie didn't know the full involvement of Schwartz. She was almost furious when she heard Betsy say she couldn't tell her.

"Fine. Don't tell me. But at least tell me how to get in touch with him. I need to hear his voice. And, more than that, I need him to hear mine!"

"I'm sorry, Maggie. I can't. Josh doesn't need the distraction right now."

Maggie hung up with Betsy Parnell. Her anger had transformed to hurt. "Is that what I am now? A distraction?"

♦

Forty Four West Bay Tower, in addition to leasing apartments long-term, rented suites for nightly lodging. Morgan waited until a group carrying luggage entered the curved, glassed entrance to the lobby. He strode up the few steps and followed the hotel guests in. As he expected, the travelers moved directly to the front desk where, fortunately, others were ahead of them.

Morgan stood in line behind them momentarily, before walking away. He moved around the lobby briefly, as though taking in the impressive décor of the Tower. He moved to the elevator and pushed the "down" arrow. Inside, he found others who were apparently heading for their cars. The "P" button, identified in Arabic and English, was already illuminated. The conveyance lurched slightly and began the short trip downward, bypassing the guard at the garage entrance.

Morgan stepped out and paused to allow his fellow riders to move some distance away. As he expected, the area was filled with a huge number of vehicles, covering multiple levels. A quick look around the ceiling and columns revealed security cameras everywhere. He knew that, if he appeared to be snooping around, a guard would confront him in short order. So, to buy himself time in his search for the Rolls-Royce Phantom, he pulled the keys to the embassy car he was driving from his pocket and walked around leisurely.

He hoped that any one in some small back room watching the video feed from the garage's cameras would buy into the notion that he simply didn't remember where he had parked. The pretend hotel visitor went so far as to hold the keys up and press the "unlock" button. He trusted that he would appear to be trying to locate his vehicle by hearing the beep of its horn and seeing the flash of its lights in response to the command from the remote.

But, the entire time, Morgan was scanning the cars for the white luxury car belonging to Linus Schwartz and registered to Oskar Lammers. He assumed that the occupant of the penthouse would have a preferred spot not far from the elevator. Some distance into the recesses of the huge lot, the "lost" car owner saw a sign. Below the scribbles of characters in Arabic, he saw the word, "Reserved." The former employee of America's CIA walked as briskly as he felt he could without attracting unwanted attention. To his relief, among the vehicles with designated spaces, he found a Rolls-Royce with the plates Ricketts had passed along.

Morgan retrieved two things from his pockets, his phone and the GPS transponder. Lifting the phone to his ear, he feigned a phone call to disguise the fact that his real focus was the expensive automobile. He wandered around as he "conversed" with his caller. Next, he acted as if he had taken something from his shirt and dropped it. As he bent to recover the nonexistent item, he slipped the GPS beacon under the right front fender. Mission accomplished.

Morgan continued his ruse of preoccupation with a phone call as he turned toward the elevator. From the direction of the parking area's exit, he saw the security guard who had been watching guests come and go, marching toward him. It was pretty obvious that he was coming to enquire if Morgan needed help, and possibly to find out whether he had a legitimate reason to be there.

Morgan decided to complete his gambit with bravado. He pivoted to intercept the watchman. As he did, he smiled and waved. As the gap between the two men closed, Morgan paused and raised a single index finger. He hoped what meant "just a second" in the U.S. was likewise understood in Qatar.

The guard stopped. Morgan lifted his phone to his ear and lowered his head and turned to the side, seeming to have difficulty hearing the words of his pretend caller. The uniformed man came closer and waited respectfully a short distance away for the presumed hotel guest to complete his phone conversation.

Morgan smiled again, shrugged, and pointed to his phone. He was beginning to get nervous, and that made faking a phone call more difficult. He raised his hand in the direction of the guard again.

Finally, the Tower security officer grew impatient. He smiled and nodded and, leaving the friendly guest to his call, retreated to his guard shack.

With his back to the departing guard, Morgan closed his eyes. His chest heaved with relief. All he had to do now was to exit by way of the elevator and the lobby. Watching the exit from the parking garage was no longer necessary. He could just monitor the GPS locator from the safety of his auto. When the beacon began to move on the display, he would follow.

The former spy checked behind him to confirm that the guard had indeed left. Seeing him in the guardhouse, Morgan decided it was safe to end his "call." As he headed for the elevator, it dinged its pronouncement that it had arrived at this level of the parking area. He picked up his pace slightly to try to catch it for the short ride back to the lobby.

Morgan stopped in his tracks and turned one-hundred-eighty degrees. For stepping out of the penthouse's inter-floor conveyance was Oskar Lammers. Morgan put the phone back to his ear with one hand to repeat his previous ploy. He placed the other hand on his forehead so that it partially covered his face. He knew a man with Lammers' obvious training would survey the area as he left.

Morgan remained in place to avoid additional attention. He expected to hear a voice or feel a touch on the shoulder from behind at any time. Neither materialized. He found himself holding his breath. The German troubleshooter for Linus Schwartz had gotten a good look at him during the plane ride from Reagan National to Jackson hole. Morgan could only hope that remaining virtually motionless would preempt a good look now.

He desperately wanted to sneak a look at Lammers, but he dared not chance exposing his face. Yet, he also knew he needed to move. Lammers' car's route toward the exit would take him directly by Morgan's location. Feeling that enough time had elapsed that the henchman hadn't spotted him, Morgan turned away from where the man was probably heading – to the Rolls – and walked at a moderate pace toward the elevator.

The American had a dilemma. His car was quite a distance away. Lammers would get a sizeable head start. The GPS locator Geoff Ricketts had provided in his bag of goodies performed the same function as the one he had used to find Lechler and Tierney at the shack in Terrador. But it was a different model. Morgan had no way of knowing its range. Would he be able to home in on the Rolls from the greater distance it would be with the jump it was getting?

Morgan stood with a quartet of two men and two women before the closed door of the general elevator. He felt he couldn't afford the time for the ride to the lobby now. He would prefer to bolt out the parking garage's exit, guard or not. But he needed the cover the two couples provided. More than anything, he needed to know what was going on behind him.

He launched the camera app on his phone and touched the icon that reversed the lens' view as though taking a selfie. The image of the area behind him wasn't as focused as he would've liked, but the whiteness of the vehicle of interest stood out on the display. Morgan lowered his head as the vehicle passed directly behind him and made its turn toward the opening that led to the street.

Just as the former CIA operative prepared to sprint toward the exit, the white auto stopped.

"Shit!" Morgan thought, as he wondered if Lammers had spotted him. With the ding indicating the arrival of the elevator car, he knew he had no choice but to get on.

The ride to the lobby was blessedly quick. As Morgan stepped out, he paused to take in his surroundings. Seeing no sign of Lammers, he walked cautiously toward the lobby exit. Through the glass doors was the sight of the white Rolls-Royce Phantom pulling onto the street.

"No time to be discreet now," Morgan thought, and he raced for the lobby exit.

◆

Always aware of his surroundings, Oskar Lammers had paused to survey the area just beyond the exit of the parking garage before moving on. Pulling onto the small street adjoining the outer parking area of the Tower, he was forced to make a series of left turns to comply with the one-way direction of his route. With Diplomatic Street so near, it was annoying to have to take such a circuitous route to get there.

In addition to the extraordinary inventory of accoutrements that came standard with a $450,000 luxury automobile, Lammers had ordered additional features that added to the security of his employer. It had taken until he had negotiated his way from the Forty Four West Bay Tower's property, but he finally noticed the small light beaming from below the dashboard. He'd never seen it illuminated before in his five or six visits to Doha with his boss.

"Someone's bugged the car," he realized.

◆

Morgan covered the distance to his car as rapidly as he could, but it was some distance from the Tower. Before he had even reached the sedan, he was pressing the remote's button to unlock it. He saw the headlights flash. He muttered a curse when the keys fell from his hands. He reversed from where his momentum had carried him, grabbed the keys from the pavement, and cursed again.

He scrambled into the vehicle, not knowing how far ahead of him Lammers would be. He grabbed the GPS locator from the floorboard and turned it on.

Morgan grew increasingly frustrated as the display provided one prompt after another in the start-up sequence. It gave him warnings and alerts. It even said the unit had an update available and asked if Morgan wanted to install it now.

"No, dammit!" the device's operator said.

Finally, the Global Positioning System tracker entered its initialization phase. Morgan needed to be moving, but it would be pointless if he started out in the wrong direction. Suddenly, he recalled from his first look at the area around the hotel earlier that day that the flow of traffic from the Tower was one-way.

"Lammers would have to follow this route no matter where he's headed." Morgan jerked the stick into "D" and tore out from his parking space.

Finally, the GPS device that Morgan hoped would still be in range of the white Rolls beeped its readiness.

"Hell, yeah!"

When the map finally materialized, a blinking red dot appeared with it. Morgan looked at the map to try to make sense of the streets. On a hunch, he tapped the dot. A menu opened with options. One of his choices was "Directions." He selected it.

Instantly, a synthetic voice instructed, "In 300 ft., turn left on…"

Morgan followed the command. On the display was the statement, "Arrival time: 11 minutes."

"How'd Lammers get that far ahead? Well, at least it's located him."

The problem with the arrival time to his destination was that his target was moving, too. He had to close over ten minutes worth of head start. He could only hope Lammers stopped along his route.

As Morgan followed the directions, he noticed a level of sophistication he hadn't expected from the GPS tracker. It appeared to adjust with the changing position of the target he'd selected,

"Cool. Missile lock."

He struggled to keep his eyes on the road and simultaneously steal glances at the digital map to see if there might be a way to shave time off the route. Ultimately, he decided that the computer could think faster than he could. He would continue as instructed. Realizing he was speeding, he slowed to the legal pace. If he were stopped, he would be found to be in possession of a number of curious objects. And while the car and its contents belonged to the State Department, he didn't.

His only hope was to catch Lammers when he stopped. Morgan figured he had to be going somewhere specific. The old man wasn't with him, so the ex-CIA officer changed his plan. He hoped he could take care of Lammers first, while he was alone. And that, he believed, would make his ultimate objective easier.

"He can't just be out for a joy ride. Right?" Morgan asked himself.

Finally, the Rolls-Royce represented by the blink on the map stopped. But he only closed the separation around thirty seconds before it moved again.

This time it drove only a matter of yards before it stopped again.

"Traffic backing up?" the follower wondered. But he realized that each time the dot quit moving, its location was off the street slightly. The erratic stop-and-go continued. Morgan was closing in, but he was confused.

"Is he delivering papers?" he quipped aloud.

Finally, he was within a few hundred feet, at least according to the GPS. But no Rolls.

The red icon moved again. Morgan followed. After another effort to find the white luxury car at the location indicated on his monitor, the befuddled ex-spy panicked.

The only thing constant in his pursuit over the last couple of stops was the garbage truck in front of him – the one that obviously carried the transmitter. Before he could put the car in reverse, the passenger door opened.

◆

The FBI and the Treasury Department were working in tandem to seize the accounts of Linus Schwartz. They had no illusions that they would account for all of the fugitive's assets, but the amount of money they had already blocked was enormous. Assuming that much of his riches was tied up in real estate or other investments, they were hopeful they had made a serious dent in his cash positions and therefore his liquidity. Whatever other resources the billionaire had, the approximately four-hundred million dollars that the agencies were making unavailable to him would surely hurt.

Upon being served warrants for all of Schwartz, Cannon, & Raines, Incorporated's records, the Deputy CEO of the company notified his Board of Directors. The men and women had held an emergency conference call and had removed the man who had built the company from his position as CEO and Chairman of the Board.

Schwartz's empire was crumbling.

◆

The uninvited passenger took his seat beside Morgan, handgun pointed directly at him.

"Hello, Mr. Morgan."

"Lammers."

"You know, it's funny how even experienced operatives can get so focused on their own objective that they forget to check their six."

"I suppose it is," Morgan replied, though he found little humor in his circumstances.

"You were so intent on following what you believed to be my signal, that you didn't spot something as obvious as a white Rolls-Royce following you. Please hand me your…"

Before the German completed his request, Morgan handed over his compact handgun.

"Thank you." Lammers tucked the H&K into his waistband. When he made eye contact again, he saw the question on his captive's face.

"You're wondering how I pulled this off? Simple, really. Among the wonderful options on the Phantom are several counter-surveillance devices. I must admit to having been a bit on the sloppy side myself. You see, I had driven a couple of minutes before I saw the flashing light beneath the dashboard of the car. Well, in my defense, it *is* partly obscured by the steering column."

Lammers tilted his head, smiled, and shrugged.

"Anyhow, the car has a signal detector. Think of it as a larger, more powerful version of the wand you would use to sweep a person for bugs. The flashing alerted me to the fact that something was transmitting from the immediate area of the car. I made a couple of turns and, when I saw nobody following, I pulled over to find the beacon. I found the homing device immediately. And I wondered, 'Who could've put this on the car?'

"Then I realized, 'Mr. Morgan is in Doha, too!'" The Schwartz employee put a hand to his forehead in a display of fake astonishment.

Morgan smirked.

"Well, I couldn't have you following me, so I tossed the homing beacon into the passing waste management truck. But I also thought, 'I can't forego the opportunity to see you again.' What was it you said to me at the end of our flight to Wyoming together?"

Oskar Lammers tapped his chin, as though deep in thought.

"Oh, yes. I remember. You offered to buy me a beer."

Lammers' phony good nature morphed into a scowl. His eyes were cold. He tilted his head forward slightly and said in a near-whisper, "I think I'll pass on the drink, but I would enjoy a nice drive with you."

Morgan put the car in drive and followed where Lammers pointed with his gun. His captor called his boss.

"Mr. Schwartz, I have an early birthday gift for you."

CHAPTER 30

At less than ten miles away, the drive to Lusail still took about fifteen minutes. The city was on the coast of the Arabian Gulf, in the northern part of the city of Al Daayen. It was planned from the ground up to be a combination of residential and commercial zones, with a number of entertainment districts throughout. Qatari Diar, a state-owned entity, had developed it in conjunction with Parsons Corporation and Dorsch-Gruppe.

Like all Qatari cities, there was a heavy concentration of energy- and construction-related companies. One of the offices in Lusail belonged to Schwartz, Cannon, and Raines, Inc. It was a satellite office to the larger SCR presence in Doha. The facility was on the southern edge of the development.

During the ride, Lammers had been disinclined to talk. Morgan had to think, so he refrained from making the snide remarks he often offered in tense situations. When Lammers had called Schwartz, he'd only heard his passenger's side of the conversation, but it was enough. Part of it was the employee's explanation of his plan to his employer. He would secure Morgan in the small office building at their Lusail facility, then return to the Tower to retrieve Schwartz, who apparently wanted a ringside seat to whatever his fixer had planned for Morgan.

The billionaire's glee was apparent from the numerous replies Lammers had given in response to what must have been utter praise.

"You're welcome, Mr. Schwartz."

"Thank you, Mr. Schwartz."

"You're too kind, sir."

"It's my pleasure, Mr. Schwartz."

Morgan wondered how the man kept from blushing at the adulation. He wanted to puke.

Oskar Lammers directed his driver past the main door to the SCR office and through a small gate that passed between a warehouse and the main building. Morgan guessed at the code for the keypad.

"7-0-6-1. Right?"

Lammers squinted and frowned.

Morgan smiled and waited for the real code and pressed the corresponding keys. The gate swung inward and the construction magnate's troubleshooter ordered Morgan to a parking area at the rear of the primary building. They entered from the back door to a somewhat modest room of cubicles with two full offices. Morgan wondered at the lack of workers, not knowing that Schwartz had called and ordered all of them to leave.

"I would put you in the warehouse. You'd be more miserable in there. But drivers sometimes come and go, and you might be found. Nobody ever comes into the offices unescorted."

Morgan made mental notes of the details of the site.

"Sit down," Lammers demanded. Morgan lowered himself onto a contemporary-styled chair and watched. One of the things he had learned in SERE training was that a prisoner might only have one opportunity at escape, so he had to be prepared at all times.

For case officers, the primer on Survival, Evasion, Resistance, and Escape at The Farm in Virginia was abbreviated, compared to what ground soldiers, pilots, and special operators experienced. Unless you were part of the black ops side of espionage, the world of spies often skipped the "S" and the first "E" in the acronym. Capture for someone who operated in the Clandestine Services side of intelligence, as Morgan had, were usually taken into custody without the opportunity to evade.

Lammers went to the front windows of the office and closed the blinds. The glass front door had no such covering.

The German pulled a chair in front of his prisoner, careful to stay far enough away that Morgan couldn't attempt anything.

"You killed a good man in Wyoming. Wyman Hope was a friend of mine."

"He was a rock gut bastard."

When Lammers rose and stepped toward Morgan, the captive thought he might have a chance to act. But, before he could, his abductor snap-kicked him in the chest. The blow sent Morgan and the chair reeling backwards to the floor.

Morgan struggled to catch his breath. He was sure no ribs were broken, but it was still extraordinarily painful. He gasped and propped up on an elbow.

"In retrospect, Hope was a sweet and compassionate soul," he said through his gasps, hoping the sarcasm would draw the man closer. It didn't.

"Get up."

Morgan was weak from the blow, and had genuine difficulty getting to his feet. He used his attempt to try to inch closer. Lammers retreated a couple of steps.

"Pick up your chair and sit down."

The ex-spy did as instructed.

"You're pretty good against somebody in a chair. Care to go a round, man to man?"

His kidnapper laughed. "I have no interest in fair play. And your attempts to goad me into some foolish act won't work."

The man took his seat again.

"But I *could* take you." The German smiled.

Morgan remained expressionless, but, at the reply, he realized that he had gotten to his opponent, if only slightly.

"So, what's the plan, Stan?"

The prisoner's quip brought some annoyance. He observed that Lammers had ground his teeth.

The two men stared at one another. Finally, Morgan ended the quiet game.

"You know, now that I think about it, I was right the first time. Your friend Hope *was* a bastard." Almost before the last letter of his final word came forth from his mouth, a reverse roundhouse from Lammers' left leg sent Morgan and his chair tumbling again.

Josh Morgan rolled onto his back. The blow to the left side of his head had stunned him. His ear rang, and his entire face stung. He realized he must've bitten his cheek upon the impact, because he tasted blood. As he fought to clear the fog from his mind, he rubbed his face, feeling puffiness as swelling was setting in.

"You're really quick," Morgan uttered weakly. And he meant it.

His tormentor waved his gun at him.

"I know. Pick the chair up. Sit back down."

Morgan knew he wouldn't be able to cover the distance to Lammers quickly enough to avoid being sent to the floor, bleeding from a bullet wound.

Once his prisoner was back in his chair, the tycoon's employee tossed a pair of cable tie wraps to him.

"Fasten one loosely on each of the chair's arms."

Morgan picked up the hefty plastic straps from the floor. He wrapped one around the metal arm and fed one end through the other, just tightly enough to catch. He repeated the process on the other arm of his seat.

"Now slide your right hand through its cable and pull it tight."

Morgan did.

"Tighter."

Morgan tugged at the flat end with his left hand. The clicks of the tiny slots passing through the other end assured Lammers that the right hand was locked.

"And the other. Slide your other hand through the loop on the other arm and tighten it."

"Now, how am I supposed to do that?"

"Use your teeth. It's a long strap."

Morgan stared at him, appearing to refuse.

"Do you want another kick to the head?!" Lammers shouted.

Morgan stuck his hand through its plastic cable. He leaned over but couldn't reach the plastic strap. He removed his hand and held the makeshift handcuff so that the loose end was pointing up. He bit down on the plastic. Then he placed his hand back through the loop and, with significant effort, leaned back. The cable zipped taut.

Morgan felt he'd just lost his one chance at escape.

When Lammers sized up his prisoner, he mumbled, "Fuuuck…"

Morgan had no idea what his disgust was about.

"Cross your legs. At the ankles."

Morgan complied, as he understood Lammers' frustration. He should've made him secure his legs before his hands were immobilized.

With no way to gain leverage with his legs, Morgan could only watch as the German moved closer. He raised his leg up and placed the bottom of his foot against Morgan's chest. A forceful push with his sole sent the chair and its occupant toppling backward. The back of the chair slammed to the carpeted floor. Morgan's head whiplashed with such force that it nearly knocked him out. It still left him in such a fog that he had no intention of moving.

Suddenly, he felt two fingers pressing against the side of his neck.

Relieved to feel a pulse, Lammers stood and cursed himself for his foolish action. He watched nervously for some sign of activity from the man on the floor. When he saw none, he reached a second time to check for beating through the man's carotid artery.

Satisfied again, he put his hand down to support his standing.

The "unconscious" man secured to the chair swung a leg violently, catching Lammers' outstretched arm and his left leg.

The German fell face first to the floor. The carpet cushioned the impact, but his head was near Morgan's feet. Morgan took another powerful swipe with his right foot, this time for the head.

His foot caught his captor flush in the face. Lammers blinked at the tears forming in his eyes. Blood was pouring from his broken nose. He tried to stand, but Morgan's foot caught him again. The German could hardly see. He looked briefly for his gun. Not finding it, he turned toward the man inflicting his punishment. Before he could move away, Morgan's right foot caught him in the side of the knee. It buckled and Lammers collapsed.

Morgan saw the handgun under the edge of a desk, but it didn't matter. He knew he couldn't retrieve it with his hands still fastened to the chair's arms. His only hope was to make sure the German didn't get it, either.

The former CIA officer tried to stand, but he was so unbalanced that his opponent sent him back to the floor with a meager push.

Morgan pushed with the bottom of his left foot and missed. He swung his right leg around, but Lammers blocked it from his place on the ground. Morgan finally connected with a kick to the man's balls. It wasn't especially strong, but it hurt enough that Lammers stumbled. As he fell forward, the German henchman's face came near enough to Morgan's legs that he was able to deliver another kick to his face.

The chair-bound man was able to push toward a sofa against a wall. He swung his torso around so that he was in a more or less seated position. The chair stretched behind him, still attached to his wrists. Pushing the chair against the couch for leverage, he walked backward with his feet. His back was now above the seat of the sofa, and he was able to stand. Lammers was also rising, though he was unsteady. His face was bloody, and he still had trouble with his vision from the repeated kicks.

Morgan rushed the man before he could collect himself, head-butting him in the chest. Lammers stumbled but didn't fall. Despite his shakiness, the German tried to take the initiative. Morgan spun, striking him with the chair, but he fell to one knee in the process.

Morgan rose again. He moved to a wall and began to spin, swinging the chair as brutally as he could against the wall. Each time almost sent him to the floor. He looked at Lammers, who had apparently spotted the handgun.

On his third attempt, the chair came partially apart. Its left arm separated completely from the rest of the frame. Morgan pulled his left hand free. As Lammers was crawling toward his gun, his adversary swung with his right arm. The pieces of the chair came around, secured to Morgan only by the plastic cable fastened to his right wrist. The pain of the strap cutting into Morgan's flesh almost undid him, but the impact with the henchman broke apart the remaining pieces of the chair.

Fueled by adrenaline and free of the metal frame, Morgan rushed his opponent. The pair crashed to the floor, and Morgan slid across the carpet. The impact of his head against the wall addled him, but he managed to regain his footing. As he did, though, Lammers found his wits and caught him with a right hook. He delivered a roundhouse, but it lacked the force of the man's previous kick, and Morgan deflected it.

Nevertheless, a right cross stunned the now tiring ex-CIA officer and he fell to a knee, where he caught the impact of another kick. He knew he was fading fast. He charged from his kneeling position and caught Lammers with his shoulder. The pair of men slammed into the front door of the office, cracking, but not breaking it. The men grappled for superiority in the encounter and rolled across the floor.

Morgan had caught the worst of the impact with the door and succumbed to the pounding of the man atop him. He was done.

Lammers fell off his adversary toward the handgun. He picked it up and tried to stand. Completely devoid of strength himself, he stumbled backward.

The tycoon's fixer held the gun as Morgan was rising. The former CIA spy was determined to be on his feet when the end came.

Both men were panting. Lammers wiped at the blood still dripping from his nose with his forearm. The defeated man stared at the other's silhouette against the faint twilight coming from the door.

Morgan saw the German's chest heaving as he lifted the gun for a precise aim. He placed his finger on the trigger.

"I thought your boss wanted to watch."

"He'll understand."

Morgan winced and flinched at the crashing of glass that came from behind Lammers, whose face had a puzzled look. He shook his head from pain and also a lack of understanding. He blinked several times. His entire body shuddered. Then he raised his free hand to his forehead. Finally, while trying to lift the gun again, he strained at his eyes as they were beginning to close.

Lammers fell to his knees. Then both hands felt limp to his side. The gun dropped to the carpet. He tried one last time to force his eyes open. They closed, and he fell forward to the floor.

Morgan saw two round, bloody holes in his back, and then looked up to see a man he didn't know knocking out the rest of the glass in the front door. He stepped carefully from the front parking area through the jagged hole in the pane, putting away his gun.

Following the rescuer into the office was Geoff Ricketts.

"Thought Parnell told you not to get involved."

"She changed her mind."

CHAPTER 31

Josh Morgan sat in the parking area in back of SCR's office in the car he'd driven to Lusail while Ricketts' case officer looked at his cuts. He placed a pair of butterfly bandages from a first aid kit onto the deeper ones.

"You'll live," the operative declared.

"You sure? I feel dead already."

"Was that Lammers?" Ricketts enquired.

Morgan nodded. "How'd you find me?"

"You remember the embassy car I loaned you? They all have tracking devices. Would've thought you knew that."

Morgan laughed.

His thought was interrupted by the ringing of Oskar Lammers' phone, which was lying on the seat next to him. He'd brought it with him from inside. The caller ID read, "Mr. Schwartz." Morgan considered answering it but decided not now. He pressed "Ignore."

Shortly, the phone rang again. A second time, Morgan sent it straight to voicemail.

"Fuck him."

Ricketts laughed. "Yeah, I'd think so." He looked over the bruised man before him. "The Director called and authorized direct support. It took a few minutes to get outfitted. By that time, you'd apparently already been here a while. Sorry for the delay."

"You know, my life is just like a spy movie. Everything always happens just in the nick of time. Whether it's me getting my ass rescued, or I'm bailing someone out, it's always real close. Just once, it'd be nice for the cavalry to maybe get here *before* I get the shit beat out of me. Or maybe, just stop crap from happening in the first place."

"You're welcome," offered the case officer who'd shot Lammers.

Morgan smiled and shook the hand of his rescuer. Then he offered his hand to the local station chief. "I owe you."

"Nah. Buy me a beer sometimes."

◆

DCI Elizabeth Parnell placed her phone back on her desk. Her Doha station chief had called to report that, despite some trouble, Morgan was fine. Ricketts had said he would give her a full report soon.

Parnell had elected to withhold the information about Schwartz's fatherhood of Everson Blake from Josh. She would tell him soon, but not now.

She dialed Maggie's number. The greeting was cold. Parnell understood.

"Call to apologize?"

"Maggie, I'm sorry. I still can't tell you where Josh is. And, whether you believe me or not, it bothers me that I can't, but it doesn't change anything. Regardless, I wanted to tell you that I got news from Josh and he's fine."

"Fine" might've been an exaggeration, but in the context of what she suspected had transpired, it was close enough.

◆

The former CIA case officer rode with the Qatar station chief back to Doha in the car the man had loaned him. Morgan sat mostly silent with his head in his right hand. It was very dark now. The sun had set around six o'clock, just about the time the man driving had arrived in Lusail to bail him out. It was well below the horizon now. Twilight had disappeared and the sky was black. The city lights washed out all but the brightest stars.

The drive was short, so Morgan had little time to come up with a way to approach Linus Schwartz. His original plan hadn't been much of one. He had intended to catch the man out in public, probably when Oskar Lammers had driven him somewhere, and... that was it. The former spy had nothing further planned.

Now, with Lammers out of the way, Morgan had to come up with something more specific.

The German henchman's phone had rung twice more in the short time between Lusail and Doha. The caller ID showed that each of the calls was Schwartz. The man must be going crazy at the lack of response from his employee, Morgan figured. Surely, he had realized something was amiss. But what would he do? Morgan had no knowledge of another goon at the billionaire's disposal. But that didn't mean there wasn't one.

After the last attempt by the employer to reach his fixer, Morgan had studied the phone again. It was passcode protected. Morgan knew none of

Lammers' personal data to use to try to open the device's files. It probably didn't matter, though. Josh guessed the man wasn't the type to use his birthday or other personal information as his password. Nevertheless, it was still worth a try.

"1-2-3-4-5-6," Morgan mumbled as he pressed the keys. Not surprisingly to him, the attempt failed.

"You say something?" asked Ricketts.

"No. Nothing."

"You sure you don't want me to stick around?" his new friend asked as they arrived where Oskar Lammers had left the Rolls-Royce.

"Thanks, but I'm good. I'll take it from here. However this turns out, I'll handle it."

The case officer who had shot Lammers through the office building's door had followed in their car. He pulled alongside Ricketts.

"We staying?"

His boss shook his head. "Says he's got it."

Morgan leaned over to where he could see the driver of the second car. He lifted his hand in acknowledgement for the deed he'd done, and simply said, "See you around."

The man nodded without another word.

Ricketts shook Morgan's hand and wished him luck. "Call if you need anything," he said. Morgan gathered his personal belongings from the car. He'd never made it to the hotel that Ricketts had booked him in.

Morgan's nerves got the better of him for a moment as he watched the cavalry drive away. With the Rolls-Royce's key fob in hand that he'd lifted from Lammers pocket, the luxury car sprang to life. Its lights flashed and front doors unlocked. Morgan tossed his things into the back seat and got into the white Phantom.

He rested his head on the steering wheel. His shaking was slight, but uncontrollable. Finally, he gained enough composure to look around the car's interior. He found a laptop. He couldn't get past its security code either.

"Well, if I live through this, I'll take it to Langley," he decided.

He found an expensive bottle of bourbon, half empty, and took a drink. The one item that might have value was a passkey. Morgan could only pray that it would give him access to the elevator to Schwartz's condominium.

Satisfied that none of the remaining items in the Rolls was significant, Morgan fired up the engine and headed for Forty Four West Bay Tower. He still didn't know what he would do there.

"I'll just make it up as I go," he guessed and pulled onto the street. "Seems like that's how it always works out anyhow."

Arriving at the Tower, Morgan continued around the high-rise instead of pulling into the parking area. The one-way circle took him back away from the complex.

"I need a drink – and more time," he decided. He remembered seeing Z Lounge a short distance back and decided that would be as good a place as any. On the sixty-first floor of Kempinski Residences & Suites, the view afforded a good look at where he presumed his objective was sitting. Perhaps Schwartz was gazing in his direction right now, too, Morgan thought.

"But how to pull this off?" he wondered, placing his hand over the snifter when the bartender asked if he wanted another.

The hunter had ordered two drinks that, in conjunction with the quick sip of bourbon from the bottle in the Phantom, had provided the courage and confidence – perhaps foolishly, the drinker considered – to proceed with his mission. Another might push him into the area of clouded judgement and recklessness.

He sipped from his bourbon again. As he did, his eyes narrowed at the contents of the glass, though the brown liquid was too near his eyes to focus on it. He set the snifter on the bar and, arms folded on the surface in front of him, leaned forward and simply stared at his beverage.

"How to pull this off…" This time the thought was less a question and more an epiphany. Morgan considered his nearly empty drink and smiled.

Even with a high-speed elevator, it takes a while to reach the ground floor from the sixty-first. Morgan was in a hurry now. With something close to a plan, he felt some urgency to move forward. Perhaps he feared he would chicken out. On the other hand, losing his nerve might save him a lifetime behind bars – or perhaps even his life.

The valet returned with his car – rather, his intended victim's. The drive back to the Tower was brief. This time he waited until another car was entering the parking garage. As the blue coupe stopped at the guardhouse for approval to enter, Morgan passed it on the outside lane. His left hand was casually against the left side of his face. He raised his right index finger from the hand on the wheel and nodded. The guard, seeing the tenant's Rolls, paid it little mind, giving only a cursory nod as it drove past.

The ex-CIA officer made a righthand turn at the corner of the level where the elevator was and moved past the row of vehicles along the wall to the far corner and its reserved parking spot. Whereas Lammers had backed into the spot for an easy exit, Morgan pulled in facing forward to hide his activity from anyone walking by. He needed privacy.

He placed Lammers' phone and pass key in his pocket. He took the bottle of fine bourbon. Feeling his nerve slipping, he took one last swallow to bolster his bravado. Then he sat in the dim light of the parking space and prepared to execute his strategy.

Josh Morgan would've preferred stealth. A clandestine approach would've provided an element of surprise, but he knew that was impossible. The billionaire philanthropist's home in Doha was a virtual castle atop a hill and the elevator was its moat. It was tens of floors up and the only way in was by the elevator dedicated solely to the man's condominium.

Morgan's only hope was to arrive at the top floor of the Tower and catch Schwartz by surprise. Oh, he knew the tenant would know someone was riding to his residence. Morgan just hoped his adversary wouldn't realize it was him. He wasn't sure how he was going to hide his identity. The elevator car would certainly have a surveillance camera.

However this unfolded, he knew he had to approach it with the same boldness as when he had confronted Seth Tierney in the United States embassy in Terradora.

Morgan took his jacket off. It was hot and he was sweating. Of course, not all of the perspiration was due to the high temperature. Still, he would need his coat. He took a deep breath and inserted Lammers' pass card into the slot adjacent to the elevator's doors. They parted. Josh spotted the curved glass portal. It would require him to jump. With his hand wrapped in his sport coat, he leaped vertically and pounded the lens of the elevator's security camera with a hammer blow. It appeared to be dislodged, but nothing more. He jumped for a second strike. This time the force of the base of his fist drove the camera backward and into the wall of the elevator.

Now he could only hope Linus Schwartz wasn't already looking at the video transmission when Morgan disabled it.

The button that would begin his ride upward had no label. After all, it only went to the penthouse. It shot upward, and in a matter of seconds, proclaimed with a "ding" that it had reached its destination.

CHAPTER 32

It was 2:30 PM at the George Bush Center for Intelligence. DCI Elizabeth Parnell had cleared her calendar and instructed her administrative assistant to block all calls and all visitors. She had received a call from Geoff Ricketts in Doha. He had given her a full report of the shooting at Lusail.

Despite movies' portrayals of CIA officers as gunslingers whose first instinct was to take out any adversaries, a shooting involving one of her officers was extremely rare, and a very big deal. With no opportunity to clean the scene at the SCR office and warehouse, Oskar Lammers' body would be found. The only positive news related to the event was that nobody had witnessed the shooting. According to Ricketts, who was repeating Josh Morgan, he saw none of the company's employees in the offices or outside. The Qatar station chief had speculated that they had been sent home to ensure privacy.

It was half past nine in Lusail. Perhaps, she hoped, nobody had discovered the crime scene with Lammers' body and wouldn't until the following morning – Friday – when workers arrived for their day at the office.

Her chief of station and his associate had cleared the remaining glass from the edges of the door, hoping that it wouldn't stand out to a passing driver on the street.

Parnell's hope that no surveillance camera had recorded the presence of her men in the area was extremely slim. Doha and the surrounding area were covered with digital eyes. Once the corpse was discovered, the local law enforcement would begin to collect images from the cameras' feeds and examine them.

But the CIA Director hadn't heard from the Doha CIA boss that any call had come from officials.

So, in the absence of any such report from the embassy, she only waited for other, possibly more dire news. Ricketts had said he had dropped his passenger back at Schwartz's car. Parnell knew that meant that Morgan was moving toward his target.

◆

Maggie couldn't concentrate. At her desk in the West Wing, she went through the motions of performing her job duties, but her mind wandered frequently. She caught herself making and correcting stupid errors in her work product.

Press Secretary Marie Ginnetti stopped by to provide instructions for some press releases she wanted Maggie to handle. While she was there, she mentioned her upcoming retirement.

"Maggie, you can't imagine my excitement in knowing I'll be leaving this department in your hands. You're one of the best things to happen to it in – well, since I've been here."

Maggie knew she wouldn't mention that she might be resigning to move back to Jackson Hole with Morgan. First of all, she didn't want to shatter her boss' hopefulness. But, more than that, she hadn't discussed the option with Josh. So, she merely smiled and moved to another topic.

"You appear to be getting around better, Marie."

"I just wish I could get rid of this thing," she answered, waving in the air the cane she had used since her injury in the assassination attempt on President Hendrickson. "It's a nuisance. I've tried getting along without it, and I can. But I'm worn out when I do."

With the small talk out of the way, the pair got back to their discussion of the requirements for the White House press department.

◆

FBI Director Austin looked at the draft of the report of the investigation into the death of Former President Trenton Weston. It wasn't yet complete, but it was close. There was virtually no doubt that U.S. Attorney Riley Maxwell had laced a cup of coffee with a pesticide-based toxin and passed the cup to Weston.

Analysis of the lethal potion had found it to be an extremely potent cocktail composed of methyl iodide, a chemical commonly used in contraceptives, and a cocaine derivative. The FBI lab staff had never seen it before and logged it into the Bureau's database of toxic substances.

The methyl iodide alone had been synthesized to such a strength that it would've killed in even the smallest quantity. But murdering Weston apparently wasn't enough. It was intended to appear to be a stroke. That was the purpose of the other ingredients. And it did appear to be a cerebrovascular accident. In fact, it was the conclusion that would have been reached as the official cause of death for anyone other than a person of the importance of an ex-President. The extraordinary attention to Weston because of his stature had led to suspicions of foul play. And the unmatched expertise of Medical Toxicologist Mia Palmer had uncovered the truth.

So far, the public COD remained a stroke. Austin would discuss his organization's findings with Weston's widow soon.

The draft summary concluded furthermore that Linus Schwartz was behind the assassination. He was in Doha, Qatar, and therefore, ineligible for extradition, due to the country's lack of a formal agreement with the United States.

"I have a feeling that the issue may be about to be resolved," Austin speculated, aware that Morgan had boarded a flight for Hamad International Airport.

Schwartz's assets – at least the ones the Bureau was aware of – had been frozen, and steps were being taken to try to uncover any remaining personal resources.

The only remaining area of the investigation that was still open surrounded the peripheral matters to Weston's activities. Investigators were taking another look at the suicides of the U.S. Attorney for the District of Columbia Riley Maxwell and Federal Judge Byron Caldwell.

There was also the matter of the unexplained death of an as-yet unidentified man on a forest service road near Jackson Hole Wyoming. He'd been shot in his buttocks, then killed with a single round to the head. No guns were left at the scene. His apparent impersonation of a U.S. Secret Service special agent had given the FBI a reason to investigate.

◆

While waiting for a call that she knew could come at any moment with news about Josh Morgan's actions – or his fate – the Director of the Central Intelligence Agency reviewed reports of the interrogation of CIA Officer and Special Collection Service Operative Seth Tierney. He had proven to be very *cooperative*.

His revelations had led to the arrests of a dozen individuals in Terrador and the U.S. In cooperation with her organization and the DEA, the Bureau had taken into custody CIA officers, contractors, and two Drug Enforcement Agency agents. Parnell was confident that there would be more arrests. Hopefully, the roundup had put an end to the attempt to reestablish the old network that had collapsed when Morgan had disrupted the plan to kill the Terradoran president years ago.

It appeared that Linus Schwartz had been instrumental in attempts to revive that organization, too.

Parnell's cell phone rang. She held her breath as she greeted her caller. Whether about the shootout with Lammers or new events involving Morgan, the report had to be bad.

"Hello, Geoff."

◆

Maggie had tried everything to get her mind in gear and focused on the tasks at hand. She'd had another cup of coffee, but the additional caffeine had left her shaky. At least, she assumed it was the caffeine. She had started to check on Alicia Weston but had stopped before completing the number. She felt the chances of a discussion about her and Josh were too great.

Finally, she dialed the number of the St. John's Medical Center in Jackson.

"Hi, Curtis," she said.

◆

DCI Betsy Parnell hung up her phone. Ricketts' news hadn't been of the devastating nature she had feared. But he had informed her of two recent arrivals in Doha.

When she had asked her station chief if he'd alerted Morgan, he'd said, "Tried. My calls go straight to voicemail. I think his phone is turned off. I left a message."

"Hopefully he'll check it," Parnell had returned.

◆

Her conversation with Curtis Jones had been brief, but it had lifted Maggie's spirits. He had said that the doctors had told him that he was fully out of the woods. His good cheer seemed to be, in part, due to the fact that his friend Anton was visiting in his hospital room.

Maggie hoped Curtis fully understood the tough road ahead of him. As she considered that, she realized that most of his recovery would be mental. Fortunately – if you can refer to any aspect of losing a limb that way – her friend's had been a transtibial amputation, or below the knee. Having that joint intact would make his prosthetic at least marginally like the real thing.

Her associate would be in the hospital for another five or six days. The staff had already commenced physical therapy and counseling.

Jones had assured Maggie that he could keep on managing Image Quest during his recovery. She had smiled at his enthusiasm, but knew it was unrealistic. Curtis' assistant at the company Maggie had founded would just have to get by until a solution was found.

◆

A set of eyes had watched Morgan board the private elevator to the penthouse at Forty Four West Bay Tower. The observer had made a phone call as he watched the former spy move toward the doors with the key card. He would await instructions from Linus Schwartz.

CHAPTER 33

The ex-CIA case officer was in near panic in the elevator outside the penthouse at the Tower. The doors had opened to reveal a second door, one more like the front door to a house. He had smiled when he saw that it, too, had a slot for a pass card, but when he had inserted the one that he had taken from Schwartz's Rolls, the wooden door wouldn't open. He'd heard the soft click of a lock disengaging, but when Morgan had turned the knob, the door wouldn't budge.

The would-be intruder realized immediately that the door must have had a dead bolt, or something like it. And, whether digital or keyed, it could only be unlatched from the inside.

Morgan was breathing heavily. On the other side of the door was the man who had killed Trent Weston – at least, arranged it. He had sent a phony Secret Service Agent after Maggie. And he had used surrogates in the legal system to come after Morgan himself.

After all the former CIA operative had been through, he was so close. But as he lacked the means to enter the bastard's apartment, he began to wonder if he even had the will to continue.

In the midst of his internal debate, the speaker in the elevator car crackled briefly.

Then he heard, "Good evening, Mr. Morgan." The sudden voice alarmed him. He was instantly on-guard. Josh looked about the car for a second camera that he might've missed. He didn't see one.

The speaker's timbre was obviously that of an elderly gentleman. So, despite never having met the man, Morgan knew he was speaking with Linus Schwartz.

"Good evening… you sorry bastard."

"Now, now, Mr. Morgan," the speaker lectured. "There is no need for that kind of language."

When he got no reply, he continued. "May I assume Mr. Lammers won't be joining us?"

"You may, indeed. Ever."

There was a pause on the part of the man behind the microphone. Morgan was sure he had suspected his fixer's demise but was probably still unnerved by the confirmation. Morgan heard the soft sigh, even with the rather poor quality of the transmission.

"That's unfortunate. He was a fine gentleman."

Morgan laughed aloud at the characterization. "We must define the word differently," he answered. He added, "He was as much a bastard as you!"

"Again, Mr. Morgan, I object to your language. There's no reason we can't behave in a civilized manner."

Morgan was grinding his teeth as he thought, "Just open the fucking door. I'll show you civilized." But even as his anger raged, he knew that Schwartz held all the cards.

"Come now, Mr. Morgan, did you think I had only the one employee to, shall we say, watch over me? In fact, one of Mr. Lammers' associates watched you enter the elevator. At my direction, he didn't intervene. I am in my office, but another of my employees is waiting for you in the foyer."

Morgan pursed his lips. Under his breath, he mumbled, "Dammit!"

"You may come in for a visit – I assume that's why you're here – or I can order the elevator back to the parking garage, where you will be shot on sight. What is your pleasure?"

Morgan's mind raced. He realized at that moment that he was out of his element. In his days at CIA, he had done nothing like this. He'd met known assets, delivered messages, planted the occasional listening device. Mostly, he'd used his cover as a photojournalist to recruit individuals who were potential agents. He'd had explosives training, weapons training, and the like at Camp Peary, but it was largely to assure some means of protecting himself if things got out of hand.

When he'd had his showdown with NSA Deputy Director Everson Blake and when he'd found himself in the middle of gunfights in Russia, they were spur of the moment. There had been no time to think.

"But now I'm in this elevator," he thought. "My plan's gone to shit and I'm getting ultimatums."

"Shit!" he said aloud.

It entered his mind to return to the parking garage and take his chances with Schwartz's man there. But two things prevented his selecting that option. As a practical matter, he felt that surviving a shootout would be virtually impossible.

But more importantly, Linus Schwartz was a few feet away. All that separated him was the door.

"Is this about your little elevator camera that I broke?" Morgan asked dryly. "I'll replace it."

A soft, cracking voice replied, "Ah, I do enjoy a sense of humor."

Neither man spoke for several seconds. Morgan knew he had no options; certainly, none that worked to his benefit.

"Time is running out, Mr. Morgan. I have my finger on the button that will send the elevator on its way."

Josh Morgan had no idea what to expect on the other side of the front door to the penthouse. In contrast, he was certain he knew what awaited him in the parking garage. He'd pressed his luck far beyond what he should've many times already, and he'd been fortunate to still be alive.

"Yes. Thank you, Mr. Schwartz," Morgan said through clenched teeth. "I'd love to have a meeting with you. And, you're right. That *is* why I came."

"Very good. You may open the door when you hear the buzz. Oh, do place any weapons on the ground and kick them out ahead of you before you enter my home."

Morgan put his jacket back on and straightened it. Momentarily, an annoying buzz informed the elevator occupant that he could enter the penthouse. Seeing nobody in front of him when the door swung open, Morgan decided to oblige his host. He set his gun on the floor and kicked it forward.

"Is that the only one?" someone nearby enquired.

"Yes." Silently he continued, "Unfortunately."

"Come out."

When Morgan stepped into and through the foyer into the main living area, off to one side, he saw Dexter Leach. Schwartz's personal assistant held a gun on him, rather shakily, Morgan thought.

"Mr. Schwartz is in there," Leach indicated, punctuating the direction with a wave of his handgun.

Morgan walked into an office, stark and with contemporary styled furnishings. Behind the desk sat an elderly man in a three-piece suit, with a look that seemed at odds with his modern surroundings. There were no photographs on the walls or his desk. A personal computer sat on a second counter to one side of where the man sat. His chair was a short distance away from his desk.

Linus Schwartz sat, leaning back in his chair, tapping a cane with his left hand in the palm of his right. The cane's handle was the head of a lion. The shaft was black, and the collar and ferrule were gold – real, Morgan suspected. Despite the intended aggressive nature of the pounding, the guest's impression was that his host wasn't nearly as threatening as he was trying to appear.

319

"Sit down!" The remark had a sharp tone, lacking the polite rhetoric that the billionaire had used until now.

Morgan took a seat.

"Very well, thank you. How are you, Mr. Schwartz?" Morgan said in response to the unspoken courtesies.

The man stared from his throne, the scowl accented with the wrinkles of years of hard work and stress.

"Sorry. It's just that you were much nicer when I was on the elevator."

The man leaned his cane against his desk and, resting his elbows on the arms of his elegant chair, folded his hands in front of his chest.

Though he remained silent, the intensity of his gaze communicated a sense of malice toward Morgan that the former U.S. spy didn't understand. What had he ever done to this man? he wondered.

With the silence extending further, Morgan said, "Well, this is awkward." He turned to the man with the gun.

"You know, Dexter, when we met on the plane to Wyoming, I didn't peg you for this kind of guy."

Leach shifted his stance.

"Oh, don't be nervous. That was a compliment. I'm impressed."

Schwartz finally spoke. "Mr. Leach prefers not to become involved with the more unpleasant duties my needs often require. But he *is* quite capable."

"Well, good for you," Morgan said with an accompanying, obviously insincere smile. "And here I thought of you as just some flunky."

Leach's hands shook. Morgan didn't know if he was getting to the assistant, or if he had already been that ill at ease. The personal assistant looked at his employer, who waved his hand up and down, as though petting a dog.

"Settle down, Mr. Leach. Don't let him get to you."

"Oh, before I forget, I have some things that belong to you." He retrieved some objects from his jacket pocket. Morgan turned to Leach and whispered. "I took them from his car," he confessed, pointing his head toward Schwartz.

"Here we have Oskar's key card for the elevator. I don't think he'll be needing it anymore." Morgan raised both eyebrows up and down.

"Here's his phone. You don't happen to know the passcode, do you? I mean, it's no use to me without it." The smartass ex-spy dropped it on Schwartz's desk with the plastic card that enabled entrance to the elevator.

"And here is the bourbon from the Rolls." Morgan held it in front of his own face and whistled softly. He tapped the paper label on the almost full bottle and said, "You know, I can't afford this stuff myself. I must confess to stealing a drink."

Linus Schwartz leaned forward and slammed his fist on his desk.

"You little shit! Is this a joke to you? Do you want to get shot right now?"

Morgan squinted and stared off into space, before turning his head back to his host.

"Is that a trick question? I mean, obviously, no." Morgan lifted his palms upward and gave Schwartz a slight shake of the head, accompanied with his best implied, "Duh."

When Morgan began to rise, Dexter Leach stepped back and raised his handgun swiftly.

"Relax, Dexter. I'm just getting glasses."

Leach looked to his boss for directions. The man shook his head and gestured toward his assistant with a wave of his hand.

Morgan walked to a modern-looking stand that held a decanter and serving glasses.

He returned to his seat with two snifters, one for his host and another for himself. He poured bourbon from the bottle he'd stolen from the white luxury vehicle. The ex-CIA officer held up his glass to toast.

"Here's to... Oh, I'm sorry, Dexter. Would you like one?"

"No, thank you," Leach said. His boss rolled his eyes and harrumphed.

"Now, where was I? Oh... here's to..."

Schwartz never lifted his glass.

"Well, now I'm really offended," Morgan objected. "Threatening to kill me; that's one thing... but refusing to drink with me before you do..."

"Enough of this foolishness!" Schwartz pounded his desk again.

"All right, then," Morgan agreed, dismissing his sarcasm, and leaning toward the construction tycoon. His brown eyes drilled into his counterpart's. "What's on your mind? Why are you so hell-bent on ruining my life and killing the people I love?"

The two men's eyes locked in a standoff. Morgan saw that his host was breathing heavily. Finally, Schwartz flipped a cracked and faded photograph toward the man he so utterly despised.

With his eyes still fixed on Schwartz, Morgan retrieved the photo of a young boy. After an examination, still holding the picture, Morgan looked back to the man opposite him.

"So?"

"That's my son!"

Morgan shrugged and looked at the crooked smile of a somewhat sad-looking expression on the child. He set it respectfully on Schwartz's desk.

"And...?"

He watched the elderly magnate lift the photo, trace the outline of the image's face with a finger. The sudden shift from rage to melancholy confused the younger man. The businessman misted slightly but when his eyes returned to Josh, the rage returned and manifested itself past the moist eyes. In yet another turnabout, his tone softened again as he began to relate his personal tragedy.

"His mother and I were in love, but she was married. Dottie and I worked together. We only made love once…" Schwartz paused and sighed. When he turned to Morgan, it was as though he were telling the story to a friend.

"You know, I would've done anything for her. I guess it was her sense of honor that made her stay with her husband."

Josh Morgan was still confused about what the tale meant for him.

"Dottie's husband dragged her away after our encounter. I think she told him of our love, and he wouldn't release her and took her away." This was the version of the events that Schwartz, over time, had convinced himself was true.

"I tried to find her. I did everything I could. When I finally found where she had moved to, I went there. But she had killed herself some while before. Not being with me, and her experience with the bastard who kept us apart…"

The old eyes were streaming tears freely now. "I… well, I took care of her husband. She'd had a child. I didn't know the lad was mine at that time. Of course, I had compassion for him and took him to a minister." He didn't clarify that he'd simply dropped the boy off at the doorsteps to a church.

"I was lost. Over time, I knew I had to find out more about Dottie's life after we were torn apart. I had the money then to try to track down any relatives. I found her sister and went to her.

"Deirdre was thrilled to see me. She said that Dottie had loved me deeply." This truth was only Schwartz's interpretation. "She told me that she had raised the boy and given him her name. Finally, she admitted that the boy was mine and gave me his name and this picture. She was relieved that I knew and hoped I would find him." The man had actually gotten the photo after the aunt died. Schwartz had sent men to break into her dilapidated house and search it for anything that concerned his illegitimate son.

"I felt I couldn't upset the boy's life by reaching out to him. He was an adult by then. He was a fine person – religious, you know. He was successful, too, climbing the ladder of the organization he worked for."

The tears started again, enough so that this time the man brought out his handkerchief and dabbed at his eyes.

Morgan couldn't help himself. "What happened to him? How did he die?"

"He was murdered." The man's red, puffy eyes turned to Morgan again and the younger man found himself with some sympathy for the old man.

"He was killed in cold blood while he was carrying out his duties." The glare in the eyes was intensifying again.

Morgan could see the wrath returning, and with it, Morgan's coldness toward the man came back, too. The wheels were turning in his head, but he couldn't understand what the tale had to do with him.

Morgan finally said, "Sad story."

With that comment, the old storyteller erupted. He grabbed his cane and slammed it onto the surface of his desk. He struggled and finally rose.

A crooked finger pointed toward Morgan. "You... you did this!" Schwartz raised his cane and swung over the desk at the younger man. The head of the cane glanced off Morgan's arms as he blocked the blow. Schwartz dropped the cane and sat again. He was panting furiously, stuttering uncontrollably, trying to get the accusation out.

He finally screamed at full pitch.

"EVERSON BLAKE WAS MY SON!!!"

CHAPTER 34

Former CIA Case Officer Josh Morgan felt the blood drain instantly from his face at the name of the man who had tormented him for years. The threat of his appearance had been almost as bad as his actual presence. He had led him into the assassination plot that ultimately resulted in Morgan's expulsion from the Agency, despite Morgan's role in upsetting the plan.

Blake's ghost had tormented him in the years after he left CIA, too. And when the Arab agent had abducted Trent Weston, Blake and a crony had gone after him; not to rescue him, but to kill the ex-President himself.

He had sent two men to kill Morgan at his home. He had ordered the murder of Morgan's best friend, Ben Reid. And finally, when Morgan had him on the dock on the Texas coast and was prepared to turn him over to authorities, Blake had threatened Maggie, the Westons, and everyone he loved.

And now, in this posh penthouse in Qatar, his father stood screaming his hatred. He had already fulfilled one of Blake's threats by killing Weston. And he had tried to kill Maggie and him. He was unknowingly carrying out the threats his son had made that had caused Josh Morgan to finally end the man's life.

"YOU KILLED MY SON!!!"

"YOU'RE GOD DAMNED RIGHT I KILLED HIM!!!" Morgan screamed with a rage equal to Schwartz's. Morgan stood to reach for the man and received a blow across the back of his skull. The force of Leach's handgun didn't knock the former spy out, but his legs collapsed under him. He fell past the seat of his chair onto the floor.

At finally hearing Morgan's confession, the old man's countenance became pale and he collapsed into his chair. His face was a mixture of fury and sorrow. The release from Morgan's words had justified his need for revenge. But it had left him devoid of energy. His exhaustion tempered his urgency and he regained some of the control that he'd possessed earlier. Staring at Morgan, the tycoon wiped his brow.

"Get up!"

Morgan rose, but wasn't quite able to get to his feet. He managed only to regain his seat in the chair. He rubbed the back of his bleeding head. He struggled to shake away the remaining fog that had enveloped his mind.

"You killed my son," Linus Schwartz said again, this time almost in a whisper. "Now I'm going to kill you."

"You must know I have friends; people who will come after you. Extradition be damned. They won't need to take you home. They'll kill you right here."

Schwartz lifted the glass Morgan had poured earlier, held it for a moment, then set it down. He pointed his gnarly finger at his son's murderer again.

"And you, young man, must know that I don't care what happens to me. I'm an old, old man. From afar, I watched Everson's life, his career, his Godly work, his family – all with a father's pride. I helped anonymously when I could. I remained at arm's length so as not to disrupt his life.

"But I came to love him. When he died – when *you* murdered him – my life ended, too. The only thing that kept me going was my mission to find out what really happened in Texas. Everson would've never killed himself. He was strong; not like his mother. He would've never done it. That left only one possibility. *You* killed him." The final statement was filled with sadness.

"Yes, I did. And I'm going to kill you, too, just like I did that bastard son of yours." Morgan saw the glint of fury in the man's eyes again, but it failed to erupt.

"I think not, Mr. Morgan. And whatever your so-called friends do to me won't matter. You'll already be dead." The man's satisfaction was manifest in his smile.

"And you're going to do this? I don't think you have it in you."

"You can't provoke me, Mr. Morgan. I've won. And I don't need to actually pull the trigger to kill you. The last thought you'll have in this life will be that I killed you – that *I* killed you."

"So, then, Dexter here is going to do it?" Morgan turned to Leach. "You seem like a pussy, Dexter. Show some balls. Make this asshole do his own dirty work."

The billionaire, philanthropist, and corporate CEO smiled as he once again waved off his personal assistant.

"He won't need to," Schwartz said as he saw the indicator above the distant door leading to the elevator.

"You'll recall, Mr. Morgan, that I said I had an employee observing you as you got on the elevator. He only permitted you to do so because I ordered it. Udo Stettin was with Mr. Lammers in Wyoming. He arrived with Mr. Leach and has already proven invaluable in his service to me.

"Mr. Leach doesn't enjoy direct involvement in disposing of my enemies. As I said earlier, he will do whatever I ask, but would prefer not to. I always try to keep my employees happy. Mr. Leach may not have the inclination for such work, but I assure you; Mr. Stettin has no such misgivings. He will find great satisfaction in eliminating the man who killed his friend."

The elevator dinged its arrival and the gold-colored sections of the door began to separate.

"That should be him now."

As the doors opened entirely, a man advanced through the open wooden door into the foyer. His handgun was raised and pointed forward as he moved briskly into the office.

Dexter Leach had relaxed his coverage of Morgan with his handgun. It was drooping at his side. Seeing the man entering the room, he jerked his gun upward. A double-tap hit his chest. He slumped to the floor following the center mass shots. His executioner walked calmly over and put another round into his head.

Linus Schwartz scrambled to pull open the desk drawer that held his gun. Before he could grasp it, Morgan vaulted over the desk and pushed him in the chest. The billionaire's chair rolled backward on its casters. Morgan slid the rest of the way across the surface of the desk, and with no hint of remorse, slapped the old man across the face. He turned to the man who had dispatched Leach.

"Just in the neighborhood, I guess?"

United States Army Special Forces Master Sergeant Tom Lechler nodded. He walked to where Morgan and Linus Schwartz were.

"This is sorta getting to be a habit with us, isn't it?"

CHAPTER 35

Except for Everson Blake, Josh Morgan had never felt true hatred for anyone.

"Must run in the family," he said. The man in the chair had no idea what that meant.

"Don't mind me, Linus. I'm a little unbalanced right now. I have this aversion to being threatened and having my loved ones targeted by some monster. So, excuse me if I give some thought to putting a bullet through your skull."

Morgan felt a tap on his shoulder and turned to see MSG Lechler handing him Dexter Leach's Glock. Morgan watched Schwartz's eyes widen.

He peeked down at the man's lap. "Well, at least you're not soiling your pants. One guy I killed pissed his pants." Morgan looked at Lechler, who wondered if his friend was enjoying this a little too much. Or maybe Morgan's self-assessment was right on the mark. Lechler thought that maybe this had unhinged him. But it was understandable.

"Master Sergeant, you've seen that, haven't you?"

The least that Lechler could do was let Morgan play this thing out on his own terms. "Yeah, a couple of real bad asses pissed their pants." It was the truth.

Morgan pressed the barrel of the Glock nine-millimeter hard into Schwartz's forehead.

"Now, your son... he didn't piss his pants. But he didn't know what was coming. I just walked up to him and put a round through his heart. The ass was even smiling. He really didn't think I could do it, so it caught him off-guard."

The billionaire wanted to be angry at the declaration about his son, but he couldn't manage it. He was shaking, perspiring, his heart was racing. He was holding his breath.

"But you know what's coming. Don't you, Linus?"

The man tried to answer, but his stammering made his efforts unintelligible. He finally looked at the Green Beret and managed to utter a coherent sentence.

"P... p... please. D... d... don't let... don't let him do this."

Lechler appeared amused. "I just offed your guy here. I hardly think I'm the guy to go to for help."

"I... I'll p... pay you."

"Really? How much?"

Morgan delivered a cold look at his partner.

"Sorry. My bad. It's just that I'm about to retire and..." Seeing that Morgan found no humor in his remarks, he raised both hands and placed his handgun in his waistband. He turned for the foyer.

"Where are you going?" Morgan asked.

"I'll just wait out here. I think you've got this."

"Please don't leave me!" This time Schwartz's words were clear and sharp.

Morgan pressed the gun harder against the tycoon's brow. Schwartz closed his eyes. He tried to reach for the younger man's hand, but he slapped it away.

"Please don't," the man pleaded. Linus Schwartz's tears ran down his face. He opened his eyes and looked up. "I don't want to die."

Josh pulled the gun away. "I thought you didn't care what happened to you."

The construction magnate lowered his face, unable to look Morgan in his eyes.

The younger man moved around the desk and took the seat he'd had earlier. He set the Glock on the desk. Schwartz looked at the gun. He didn't understand why the man had backed off.

"Your son tormented me for years. Oh, he wasn't around, but I couldn't get him out of my mind. You see, he'd made threats against me. My friend, Trent Weston, had my back. He kept your son from carrying out any of those threats by making some of his own. I learned that some time afterward."

Schwartz dabbed his eyes with the handkerchief he'd used earlier.

"Maybe that's what you need – to have to always look over your shoulder; to always have the knowledge that I'll show up one day and finish what I started here."

The standoff was tense. The ex-spook leaned back in his chair and tapped his fingers on the desk. Then he pushed the Glock with his index finger, spinning it this way, then that.

Schwartz made the same offer he'd made the Master Sergeant.

"I'll pay you."

Morgan lifted the gun and pointed it toward the old man.

"Be reasonable, Morgan. How much do you want?"

Josh pointed the gun directly at his counterpart's face and began to squeeze the trigger. Immediately before the nine-millimeter round discharged, he pivoted the gun to the right. The thunderous blast deafened Schwartz. The bullet slammed into the bookshelf behind the businessman's desk with a slap.

The billionaire known around the world for his generosity shivered at the near miss. He rubbed his face with both hands. He loosened his tie.

"If you're going to kill me, just do it!!!" the corporate powerhouse shrieked. He propped his elbows on his desk and buried his face in his hands. He was sobbing uncontrollably now. His gasps for air were becoming increasingly pronounced and frequent. He pounded his forehead.

"Say something, damn you!"

Finally, Linus Schwartz grabbed the snifter holding the bourbon and slammed it down to steel himself for the inevitable.

The former officer for America's spy agency set the black handgun on the desk again. He put his hands together and rested his chin on the tips of his outstretched index fingers. His mouth was tightly closed, neither a smile nor a frown. But his eyes seemed to twinkle.

Morgan retrieved the Glock 17 and pointed it at Schwartz, who raised his hands in front of his face, as though they would stop bullets.

"Relax," Morgan suggested. He pressed the button adjacent the trigger guard on the front left side of the handgrip with his thumb. The magazine released and dropped to the desk. Next, he racked the slide and the chambered round flew out from the ejector port. Lastly, Morgan deftly released the slide and disassembled parts of the gun fell onto the desk.

"You're not going to kill me?"

"I already have."

Billionaire businessman Linus Schwartz stared at his tormenter, struggling to understand the meaning of what he had said. He rubbed his eyes with the heels of his hands. He ran his fingers through his thin hair. Morgan, he saw, was perfectly relaxed.

"I need a drink," he disclosed. But rather than taking the bourbon before him, he walked to the stand that held the crystal set. Taking one of the glasses, he filled it with liquor from the decanter.

Sipping at his bourbon, he walked behind Schwartz to the bookshelf. The old man swiveled in his chair, eyes fixed on Morgan. The younger man scanned the books until he found the one with the nine-millimeter slug in it. He took the book and set it on the desk.

He started to set his drink on the desk, but paused, and with an index finger lifted as though he'd had an epiphany, he returned the glass to the stand with the serving ware. Then he went back to Schwartz's desk, retrieved the glass of bourbon he had poured for himself earlier from the liquor bottle from the Phantom.

The tycoon was still quivering from Morgan's threats. He had no interest in provoking him by trying to get his gun. But he was baffled at the man's behavior and leisurely pace as he went about his tasks.

Morgan collected Schwartz's empty glass and took it along with the snifter holding the drink he'd originally poured for himself into the small toilet adjoining the office.

"You know, I visited one of your business facilities a couple of days ago," he informed Schwartz, who failed to grasp the significance of the comment.

Josh Morgan poured the contents of his glass down the sink and ran water from the faucet behind it. Then he rinsed both crystal snifters out. Finally, he wiped his prints from the faucet handle with a hand towel. He reached to the trashcan and lifted the plastic garbage bag from it.

Returning to his seat across from Schwartz, he placed the book and the two glasses he had filled from the bottle from the car in the trash liner.

"Yes, sir. I don't know much about chemistry, but seeing all the vials, and test tubes, and such – it made an impression."

Linus Schwarz was still confused but his stomach began to churn with the increased anxiety.

"Hold that thought," Morgan requested with a lifted finger.

He moved to the foyer where Tom Lechler sat calmly on a window ledge.

"Heard the shot. You shoot him?"

"Didn't have to," Morgan replied.

Holding out his hand, the ex-CIA officer made a request.

"Give me your gun."

The Master Sergeant didn't understand but handed it over without question.

Back at the desk, Morgan seated himself and pulled a handkerchief from his pocket. As he wiped down the gun, remembering to remove the magazine and clean it and the bullets remaining in it, he continued his narrative to Blake's father.

"So – and again, not being a chemist – all those letters and numbers on all those labels... well, it made my task pretty damned difficult."

The storyteller saw the light bulb click on in his listener's mind. The spark of awareness provided additional satisfaction and emotional release for the former CIA officer.

"You see, Linus, I wanted to kill you like you killed my friend. I could've just shot you. Thought I was going to have to, too, when you wouldn't drink the liquor that I offered you." Morgan took the bottle that had come from the Rolls and placed it in the plastic bag with the other items.

Suddenly, a panicking old man reached for his phone. Morgan slapped it away.

"Now, Linus. I can't have you calling for help. Besides, it wouldn't matter. I gave you a pretty big dose. I heard that Trent Weston must've only had a small sip for him to have lasted the amount of time he did. Anything more, he would've died in a matter of minutes. *Minutes.*"

Morgan took the various components of Leach's gun – the handgrip, slide, magazine, bullets – and wiped fingerprints from them, too, before tossing everything back on the desk.

He walked to Leach's corpse, where he collected the gun he had come in with. He placed it in in his jacket pocket. Lastly, he tossed Lammers' phone and passkey in the plastic bag as well.

"Here," the guest told the host, sliding Lechler's gun across the desk to Schwartz, "Take a nice, solid grip on it."

The business magnate hesitated, but finally reached for the gun. He picked it up gingerly and aimed at Morgan and pulled the trigger. Nothing happened.

The ex-CIA spy shook his head.

"Really?" he complained at the man's assumption that he would be so stupid. He held up the gun's magazine.

"Your fucking son failed to recognize what I'm capable of when it concerns the people I love." He shook his head at the pitiful sight of the man bawling before him. "Look at what you did for a son you never knew. Did it never occur to you that I'd be capable of the same sort of violence when my friends were threatened?"

Josh Morgan saw a sudden change in Linus Schwartz's appearance. The bloodshot eyes became glassy. Holding it with his handkerchief, Morgan returned the magazine to Lechler's handgun, chambered a round, and dropped it onto the floor near the poisoned man's chair.

Returning to his seat, he watched patiently as the "bourbon" began to take its toll.

"The morning of Trent Weston's funeral in Texas, after I'd been to your research lab, I had stopped at a McDonald's. I guess breaking and entering can make you hungry enough. Before I left the parking lot, I opened the various layers of protection for the container of the stuff you poisoned my friend with. Then I poured some into a bottle of cologne and more into a bottle of mouthwash that I had emptied."

Schwartz was rubbing his arm now.

"Have to admit, it scared the crap out of me. I hear you can absorb the stuff through your skin. Each bottle I filled contained less than the maximum amount of fluid that airlines allow."

Schwartz was reeling. He alternately squeezed his eyes shut severely and strained to open them as wide as possible.

"The thing that could've unraveled my plan was if some sniffer dog at an airport got onto my contraband. But I guess the concoction wasn't something they'd been trained to be alert for."

Now Linus Schwartz was sweating profusely. His left arm had fallen limp at his side. He slumped against the arm of his chair. He tried to plead for help, but the words were unintelligible. Drool spilled from his lips, the left corner of which was drooping significantly. The garbled sounds continued. Schwartz's attempt to make himself understood, combined with his gasps for air, made him look like a fish smacking its lips when it was out of the water.

Morgan kicked the Sig Sauer that Lechler had shot Leach with, now covered with Schwartz's fingerprints, across the floor a little closer to the shaking man. Linus Schwartz tried to gather in the gun but was incapable.

The ex-case officer watched the dying man for a few seconds. Then he turned to leave.

Lechler fell in behind Morgan as he walked toward the elevator. Morgan stepped inside and turned to face the man askew in his chair. As Master Sergeant Lechler stepped inside with him, the former CIA officer lingered before pressing the button.

A few yards away, Linus Schwartz shook vigorously. The tycoon tried to yell toward the men leaving his penthouse. Finally he tried to stand.

Morgan pressed the button to begin his ride to the parking garage. As the doors closed, the last image Morgan saw was the figure of Everson Blake's father falling to the floor.

CHAPTER 36

Day 13 - Friday

Neither man spoke on the way down from the penthouse. With nobody waiting for the public elevator as the pair emerged from the private one, Lechler hurried to the spot behind one of the parked vehicles where he'd left Udo Stettin with a bullet in his head.

Then he caught up with Morgan, who had never stopped walking toward the white Rolls-Royce Phantom.

The two men got into the luxury sedan. As he took his seat behind the wheel, Morgan tossed the garbage bag filled with incriminating items into the rear floorboard. It was nearly 1:30 AM.

"How'd you get here?" Morgan asked, starting the car.

"Military transport. Director Parnell asked me to come."

"And Stettin?"

"Parnell had sent me photos of Lammers, Schwartz, Leach, and him. When I recognized him standing around in the garage, I popped him and hid the body."

Josh put the Phantom in reverse.

"Lammers is taken care of?" Lechler guessed.

Morgan nodded. Nothing more was said for some time as Morgan drove toward his destination.

"Turn here," ordered the Master Sergeant.

Morgan objected. "The airport's that way." Morgan's intention was to get there and buy tickets for the first flight out, regardless of where it was flying to.

"But al-Udeid Air Base is this way. We get there and we can hide out as long as we need to until we can catch a military flight back stateside."

Morgan made the turn. al-Udeid Air Base was the largest U.S. military

333

installation in the Middle East, housing around eleven thousand military personnel.

"What do we do about the car and the things in the bag in the back?"

Lechler assured the driver, "Oh, they have people at the base who specialize in disposing of things. Special operators often bring back things that, when they're no longer of value, need to go away."

◆

The Director of the Central Intelligence Agency looked at the clock on her phone. It was 9:00 PM Thursday. She did the quick mental calculation.

"So, around 4:00 AM... tomorrow," she said, adjusting for the time zone difference.

Elizabeth Parnell had just gotten off a call from Josh Morgan. He and Master Sergeant Tom Lechler were settled into quarters at the air base outside of Doha that the U.S. shared with the Qatari Air Force and Royal Air Force, among others. She was beyond relief that the men were safe and, while she wanted to know the entire story of what happened, she had told Morgan to get some sleep. They would speak later, and he could give her a full report. With the ex-officer from her Agency safe, she knew what the outcome of his actions must have been.

Parnell considered the time in Qatar but decided to make a call to the U.S. embassy in Doha anyhow. Geoff Ricketts answered immediately. Like Parnell, he'd been waiting for word on the fate of the American citizen he'd helped.

"They're fine, Ricketts. I can only imagine what transpired. Thanks for your help. Any news of a body being discovered in Schwartz's office in Lusail? No? Well, it's early there. The news will break in the morning, I'm sure. But I do need one more thing."

The Director explained her requirements. "Now, get someone on it and call me when it's done."

◆

Both Morgan and the Green Beret had slept well. That the Master Sergeant had didn't surprise Josh. After all, he was a trained operator with a long career in the Special Forces. But his own ability to sleep surprised him, though it didn't bother him. He felt no regret for what he'd done.

Morgan and Lechler had risen at around eight-thirty. While Lechler was busy making transportation arrangements, Josh sat in a base recreation area and watched the TV. It was tuned to QNN. He didn't recognize the newscasters. It was, after all, two-fifteen in the morning in the U.S. so the anchors weren't the prime-time men and women he was used to seeing. The "Breaking News" graphic splashed across the screen. The blond making the announcement relayed it in somber fashion.

"Billionaire philanthropist Linus Schwartz has died. The cause of death appears to have been a stroke. Household staff members arriving for work early Friday morning found the construction tycoon and CEO of Schwartz, Cannon, and Raines already dead in his Doha, Qatar, penthouse.

"Adding confusion to the tragedy is the discovery of two deceased employees of Mr. Schwartz, both victims of gunshot wounds. One man was found in the room with Mr. Schwartz. The other victim was found in the parking garage of Forty Four West Bay Tower, where the wealthy construction magnate lived.

"One source, speaking on condition of anonymity, told QNN that the scene was puzzling to authorities. A handgun was found near Schwartz with his fingerprints on it. Ballistics analysis will determine if that gun was the one used to kill the two employees. And video is being collected from security cameras throughout the area."

Josh Morgan's pulse raced, and his stomach churned. He knew that video cameras were everywhere throughout the Forty Four West Bay Tower, but in his rush to leave the place, and with adrenaline charging his emotions, he forgot about it. He knew it would only be a matter of time before he was identified. He hoped his being on the base would provide some protection from arrest. Even if it didn't, Maggie should be safe now. He would accept the consequences.

The QNN reporter continued. "But, whatever the results of the investigation into the shootings, sources believe that Mr. Schwartz died of natural causes. An autopsy will be performed by authorities in Doha."

Despite his sudden concern about security cameras, Morgan smiled at the news as the reporter rattled on about the man's life story.

"In another part of the world, a luxury yacht has exploded off the Pacific coast of Colombia, killing all passengers on board. An anonymous source has identified the cruiser as the *Bella Maga* and has told QNN that it belonged to high-ranking members of one of that country's drug cartels."

Morgan had no inkling that he was indirectly tied to the victims of the explosion on the vessel. As the QNN talking head moved on to other news items, the ex-CIA officer dozed off on a sofa in the rec center.

By ten-thirty, the special operator had arranged transportation to the United States. He tapped his partner on the shoulder.

"Wake up, Sleeping Beauty."

Lechler sat in a chair across from Morgan.

"We leave at 5:00 PM. The flight will take us to Pope Air Force Base near Fayetteville, North Carolina. Then we'll catch another transport; a direct flight to Andrews in D.C."

"Good. Thanks. It'll be nice to get home." Morgan rolled over and pulled a throw pillow under his head and resumed his nap.

"Wuss," assessed the sergeant.

♦

It was 9:15 AM in the White House's West Wing. Principal Deputy Press Secretary Margaret Loughlin had been at her desk for close to an hour-and-a-half. She continued tapping out a press release on her keyboard, ignoring the chirp from her phone announcing another text message. In the course of her workday, Maggie received scores of messages. She never perceived any as being urgent. Otherwise, the sender would have called. She would check the backlog when she had time.

However, one text-tone stopped her in her tracks. She grabbed her phone immediately when she heard the custom combination of beeps she had assigned to a small circle of friends. It wasn't Morgan's personal alert, but she hoped it would be news of him.

The text from the CIA Director was brief.

"fine, on his way home"

Maggie didn't have to wonder who "his" referred to.

"thx," she replied.

The auburn-haired woman laid her arms on her desk and rested her head on them.

"Thank God."

♦

It was only eight-thirty in Frisco, Texas, but Alicia Weston, Former First Lady of the United States of America, already had visitors.

"And that's what we know, ma'am," concluded FBI Director Gabriel Austin. The Bureau's lead investigator into President Weston's death nodded her agreement.

"We know it's a lot to take in, but we felt it was important enough to tell you in person," Supervisory Special Agent Annie Lui added.

The pair had taken one of the Bureau's private jets to visit with President Weston's widow. They had planned to explain the results of their investigation personally anyhow, but after learning of Linus Schwartz's death in Qatar, they had moved their flight up. Leaving Washington at 5:00 AM, they had driven directly to the Westons' house immediately upon arriving at Addison Airport.

"So, he was behind everything, including my husband's death."

Both agents nodded. "We're certain Mrs. Weston."

Alicia Weston moved to the bay window that looked out over their backyard, lovingly rubbing the back of the leather recliner where Trent often napped.

"And with him gone, we may never have all the answers."

"No, ma'am."

The visitors from the FBI waited respectfully for the woman to digest all she'd just heard. Mrs. Weston turned to face them.

"I don't understand. Trent and I met Linus many times. We've been acquainted with him for years. What could possibly have led him to do such a thing?"

Liu looked at Austin to see if they were on the same page. "There is one other detail, Mrs. Weston. During our investigation, we discovered that Schwartz had an illegitimate son. It was Everson Blake."

Their host's bewildered, sad look transformed into a hard stare at the sound of that name. Her eyes rose to meet theirs.

"Blake was his son?"

Austin had struggled with whether to trouble the widow with that news. Of course, she would know the true story of the NSA Deputy Director's part in the threat to her husband. The Bureau's Director had disclosed the story to Liu, partly because he felt she needed to know. But also, he wanted to use her as a sounding board in deciding whether he should burden Mrs. Weston with Blake's being the reason behind her husband's assassination.

The Director and his agent gave all the details they had about Schwartz's vendetta; that it had centered on striking out against those who were close to Josh to avenge Blake's death.

♦

For the second time in his life, Josh Morgan rode on a C-5 Galaxy. Of course, Tom Lechler had been aboard one many times before. But unlike the other time the two men had shared a ride on the giant transport, they weren't alone. The cargo area was filled with assorted materiel and members of the U.S. military sat in the rear section of the upper deck that was designed to carry seventy-three troops.

"How you doing, Morgan?

"I'm fine," the man answered with a smile and a thumbs-up.

Lechler wondered if the man who had been his partner on two separate occasions was truly "fine." He'd acted heroically in Russia. This time had been personal, but he'd still shown more balls than most men the Master Sergeant had known in his life, including many fellow warriors. Lechler knew he was once a CIA officer, but that was wildly different from special ops. He wondered if his friend's comfort with what he'd done was a front, or if he had truly compartmentalized his actions. Operators often took some time to acquire professional detachment. And they'd had intensive training and psychological assessments to identify and deal with anything that might get in their way emotionally.

The operator decided he'd just have to take the man at his word.

Morgan felt the vibration of his phone ringing, and the caller ID showed the name: Parnell. He quickly connected the call and said, "Hold on."

Josh fumbled around but finally found his AirPods and inserted them into his ears.

"Hi, Betsy."

Lechler left to go to the head and wander around the troop compartment while his friend took the call.

Parnell spent a few minutes checking on Morgan's mental state, although she didn't state that she was doing so. Then she filled him in on her most recent phone discussion with her station chief in Qatar.

When they spoke, she said, he'd still heard no news concerning the discovery of Lammers' body. The Director and her man in Doha both suspected that Schwartz had sent someone to check on the man before suffering his "stroke" and that the person doing so had disposed of the body to cover it up.

Parnell finally asked how Linus Schwartz had died. Morgan answered, "What did you hear on the news?" Of course, he knew he'd tell her the entire story when they met at Langley sometime within the next few days.

"There is one thing, Betsy; one thing I overlooked. Video surveillance at the Tower will show some pretty damning things."

"No, I'm pretty sure it won't."

"I don't understand," Morgan said.

"I had Ricketts send his Special Collection Service guys to take care of it. F6 is made for these exact types of things."

The former CIA officer's chin sank to his chest and he closed his eyes.

"Thank you, Betsy."

Then the DCI got to the real purpose of her call. She'd asked the same question just a few weeks ago and Josh had immediately refused her request.

But this time, when she asked him to come back to CIA, he agreed to think about it. In fact, he'd already given it some consideration, suspecting she would bring it up again. And as he always did with Betsy, he presented her with a list of demands – nonnegotiable.

They hung up, and Morgan wondered who would've found Lammers' body, moved it, and cleaned up the scene. If Schwartz had other fixers, would he have anything to fear from them?

Lechler returned to his seat.

"So, you're retiring, Tom."

"Supposed to have already happened. Things keep coming up." He looked at his travel companion and grinned. "Mostly involving you. Or at least related to something you did."

Morgan smiled, too, and closed his eyes. "What are you going to do?"

"What am I going to do for work? Or, what am I going to do without you always needing to get bailed out?"

The sergeant leaned back and closed his eyes, too. "If I *never* see you, or even hear your name again, it won't be soon enough!"

Both men smiled and fell asleep.

♦

"What can you tell me about his death?" Alicia Weston asked her visitors from the Federal Bureau of Investigation. The four had moved to the breakfast area and were drinking coffee.

"Mrs. Weston, I know I don't need to say this, but this is off the record."

Then Director Austin passed on to her what his Bureau had been told privately; that it appeared that Schwartz had killed the two men whose bodies were found in the parking garage and in his office. Then he'd had a stroke. Perhaps the stress of his actions caused it.

"Any idea of why he killed them?"

"None at all, ma'am," Austin said.

"It's hard to believe that a man older than I am could get the drop on younger, and probably more violent, men."

"Yes, ma'am. It is. Authorities in Doha were certain that the extensive network of surveillance cameras where Schwartz lived would clear things up. But when they reviewed the recordings, all of them were solid static. They're baffled. It appears that the entire system had some sort of network problem – a glitch, they suppose. It basically overwrote the feeds while they were happening. Like I said, baffling."

Trenton Weston's widow lifted her cup to her lips to hide her bittersweet smile from the agents, but her eyes twinkled above the rim.

Her private thought was also of mixed emotions.

"Trent really loved you, Josh."

"There is one more thing, Mrs. Weston," the Bureau's Director said. "We're consulting with various agencies and with the White House. We haven't reached a decision yet and want your thoughts. We've managed to keep the truth about your husband's death a secret so far. Would you prefer we go public with the fact that he was assassinated, or try to keep it classified?"

Alicia Weston set her cup down and folded her hands in her lap. As she thought about her answer, SSA Liu offered some insight.

"Ma'am, a lot of people know about this. They're all bound by nondisclosure agreements, but it's likely to come out eventually. Maybe it will just sound like a bunch of conspiracy nuts popping off about their latest theory, or..."

"Or maybe it will be someone with sufficient credibility to spark public concern."

"That's about the size of it," Austin admitted.

The widow thought more about it and said. "I trust you to do what you think is best, but I think the country has been through an awful lot over the last few months. As far as I'm concerned with regard to the public, my husband died of a stroke."

CHAPTER 37

Day 14 - Saturday

The United States Air Force C-5 Galaxy covered the 6,218 nautical miles from al-Udeid Air Base in Qatar to Pope AFB in North Carolina in about twelve hours. The huge jet touched down a few minutes after midnight and taxied onto the tarmac, where the ex-CIA officer and the soon-to-be ex-Green Beret disembarked with about forty military personnel from the troop compartment.

"I trained just down the road from here," noted Lechler, referring to the John F. Kennedy Special Warfare Center and School at Fort Bragg.

"Will you miss it? Serving in the military?"

"I'll miss my brothers, for sure. And honestly, I'll miss the action. But I won't miss being deployed ten months or more every year."

Morgan nodded. "I can't stand being away from home for a week."

"You get used to it. Or, more accurately, you simply accept it. You focus on the mission and put it out of your mind."

"So, what's your plan? You're married. Right?"

"Sort of," Lechler said, smiling. "Things have been rough for several years now. You know, the stress of being married to an operator. But, yeah. We tied the knot when we were both twenty-one."

"Well, you'll be around the house more real soon."

The retiring Master Sergeant laughed. "I don't know if that's a good thing, or not." He gave his friend a sideways glance. "My wife might decide the stress isn't from me being away, but from when I'm home. Ava might figure out that she really can't stand me."

Morgan noticed the Special Forces warrior wasn't smiling.

"Yessir. Ava said I've given her fifteen of the best years of her life."

"Well, that sounds good."

"We've been married twenty."

Morgan had to stifle a laugh. "You've got three daughters?"

"Best thing I ever did. They're one-year apart – sixteen, seventeen, and eighteen."

Morgan whistled and laughed. "Wow! Rapid fire."

"Ava said for those three years, I was just home long enough to knock her up. Then I was off, leaving her to deal with it. I intend to change that. Well, it's too late to change anything, but I'm definitely going to reengage my daughters."

"Reengage?" Josh thought it was funny that, even when talking about his kids, the sergeant used a military term.

The former CIA case officer's thoughts turned to his phone conversation with the DCI. He stopped. Lechler took another couple of steps before turning to face him.

"Tom, what if you could keep your toes in the water?"

The soldier tilted his head, and said, "I have no earthly idea what that means, Josh."

"What if you could keep operating? Just in a different role. And with less time in the field."

The sergeant's expression made it clear that he still didn't know what the hell his friend was trying to say.

"Just expect a call." Josh Morgan resumed his walk toward the building ahead.

Master Sergeant Lechler rolled his eyes and shook his head and stood on the tarmac another five seconds. Finally, he picked up the pace to catch Morgan.

"You need to work on your communication skills."

Morgan smiled and knew he would need to add one more demand to the list he'd given Director Parnell. That is, *if* he returned to the Agency.

◆

After a few hours at Pope, the pair hopped onto another transport for the flight north. Compared to the flights to and from Doha, the trip to Andrews felt like a walk in the park.

By 7:00 AM, they were back on the ground. The men exchanged a hug and a handshake and went their separate ways.

By 8:30 AM, Morgan was in Betsy Parnell's office at Langley. He gave her Lammers' laptop and phone. He also gave her a full report on all the events in Qatar. He said he was in debt to Ricketts and his associate. And equally so to Tom Lechler.

"Thanks for sending them, Betsy."

"You're welcome. You're pretty badass on your own, Morgan, but everyone needs a little help now and then." DCI Parnell only got a nod in response.

"I'd like to talk some more about your coming back to…."

Morgan shook his head and lifted both hands.

"Not now, Betsy. I promised to think about it, and I will. But right now, I need to step back and take care of some things in my real life."

"Fair enough."

"But I do have one more request."

"It sounds so nice when you say 'request.' But I won't really have a choice, will I?"

The CIA Director and the prospective CIA employee both smiled, and Morgan gave her his latest nonnegotiable demand.

"I'll look into it. Anything else?"

Morgan put a finger to his lips, deep in thought. Finally, he laughed. "Probably. I'll let you know."

"So, what are you going to do, now that you're home?"

Morgan became very quiet. His answer was just above a whisper.

"First, I have to get things sorted out with Maggie. She doesn't know what I've been up to. For all she knows, I might be dead."

"She knows you're home. I texted her when I found out you were headed this way."

"Thanks, Betsy. I'll have to think of what to say."

Josh Morgan and Elizabeth Parnell rose. Instead of a handshake, Morgan hugged the woman who'd had his back when he was chasing Trent Weston when he'd been abducted. She'd been a lifesaver when he went to Russia, risking her career. And over the last two weeks, she'd saved his ass more than once.

"Thanks, Betsy. For everything."

"Thank you, Josh."

The friends separated.

"You know, if I come back, I won't be able to hug you anymore. You'll miss it."

"No, I won't. Besides, I don't think you've ever hugged me before. Now go get things right with Maggie."

"I will, just one thing first."

♦

Josh Morgan walked out of the George Bush Center for Intelligence, thinking this time that he might be back.

He walked a short distance from the building's entrance and sat on one of the benches. He took his phone from his pocket and pressed a name from his contacts.

◆

"Hi, Josh," greeted Alicia Weston, upon seeing her friend's name on the display.

"I'm sorry I haven't called since the funeral." Morgan realized with some finality that his friend was really dead. He had been in such a frenzy, with so much on his mind, and so many things to do, that he'd largely put it out of his mind.

But as soon as he heard the sound of Alicia's voice, it came crashing into his world, and he knew he finally had to come to terms with it, and to grieve.

The friends chatted. The widow made Josh promise to settle things with Maggie. He promised to come to Texas to see her soon.

They were about to hang up when, out of the blue, Alicia asked, "Have you been to Qatar?"

The enquiry caught Morgan completely off-guard. It took several moments before he could even speak. When he did, it was a return question.

"Why do you ask?"

To the wife of Trenton Weston, it was answer enough.

"Thank you, Josh. I love you, son."

Morgan couldn't speak. If he tried, he would only cry. He simply nodded, as though Alicia would hear the nonverbal reply through the phone.

She did. Mrs. Weston said softly, "Bye for now, Josh."

EPILOGUE

It would be the first time that Josh and Maggie had talked in days. And it was the first time that both of them had ever felt awkward at an encounter.

Maggie had arrived at McCormick & Schmick's, not far from the White House. Lunch or dinner, the steak and seafood restaurant was a place where powerful Washington insiders often dined. Maggie had used her position as Principal Deputy Press Secretary in the White House to move higher on the reservation list than she would've been. She had an idea of what she wanted to say to Josh. Well, there were a number of things she was going to say, but some of the minutiae surrounding those expressions weren't fully formed in her mind. She'd intentionally gotten to the restaurant early to brace herself with an early glass of wine, which she virtually inhaled.

Outside the establishment at 1652 K St. NW, Josh paced the sidewalk, flowers in hand. He was deliberately a short distance down from the restaurant's entrance to avoid the possibility that Maggie would see him through the windows. He needed to think.

Like Maggie, he had a framework of what he needed to say. But, also like her, the full scope of those words wasn't yet in his grasp. He and his fiancée had never had any arguments beyond minor disagreements. Never anything serious, and certainly not approaching the magnitude of this.

Josh was ready to move forward. He knew it would be difficult. He had been calloused in taking care of the fake secret service agent outside Jackson Hole while Maggie watched.

She had seen him taking on the attackers outside his home less than two years earlier. She had even killed one of them herself with her truck. But that had been kill or be killed. The scene she had witnessed in Wyoming was that of her fiancé standing over a wounded, defenseless man, and mercilessly shooting him.

Josh knew Maggie would remember that for as long as she lived.

When she had called him to have lunch, he wondered whether she was ready to carry on with their life together? Or was she going to break up?

There was only one way to get his answer.

He was nervous.

♦

Maggie was nervous.

The waiter enquired whether there was anything more that Maggie needed. She said there wasn't but pointed to the bottle of Chardonnay she had ordered. It was a favorite of Morgan's. The server obliged by refilling her glass.

As the man walked away, Maggie pressed the home key of her phone.

One-fifteen. Morgan was late.

She set the glass on the table and moved it in small circular motions. She watched the whirlpool of wine in its crystal container.

Occasionally, and more often than she supposed, she would look up to see if Josh was approaching.

♦

Outside the eatery, Morgan, too, needed a drink. But, more than that, he needed to think of some way to tell Maggie how he felt and beg her to forgive him. He took a deep breath and started for the entrance.

Josh had taken about two steps when his phone rang. He started to ignore it, but instinctively looked at the display. Despite his better judgement, he pressed the screen to connect.

"Yes."

His caller's voice carried a slight accent, and it was instantly recognizable to Morgan. He closed his eyes and put his hand to his face.

"Lammers."

"You should've checked me more closely. Or, put a bullet in my head."

"Apparently so. Where are you?"

"I'm sorry to say that I'm still recovering in the hospital. It's very secure and, of course, I'm not using my real name."

"Any chance you'll die?"

The weak voice hid the owner's genuine appreciation for Morgan's ability to maintain his sarcasm.

"No. I'm afraid I'll have to disappoint you. My doctors say that I'll make a full recovery – slow, but complete."

"That's too bad. What do you want?"

Josh heard the German cough and clear his throat before answering.

"I just wanted to let you know that my actions toward you and anyone else were purely business."

The ex-CIA officer knew Lammers was waiting for a response. He didn't indulge him with one.

"At any rate, Mr. Morgan, I see you as a professional like me." Josh's pulse raced at what he perceived to be an insult, but, in his soul, he wondered if it were true.

"You may not see yourself in that way, but your response to our activities, your entire course of action, they were the skills of a man meant to operate."

"Not true," Morgan answered curtly.

"No matter," Lammers replied. "I really called to say you won't be hearing from me again. I had no personal stake in this matter. My boss is dead. I presume that was your doing. Nice work, by the way. But with no financial incentive to carry on, I wanted to tell you it's over."

Josh Morgan's eyes closed halfway. It surprised him that he was holding his breath. A thousand thoughts flew through his mind, but he couldn't speak.

"It was simply business. It was never perso..."

Morgan touched the red circle on his phone's display and the German's voice stopped abruptly.

He stood motionless in the center of the sidewalk along K Street for several seconds. People grumbled for having to walk around him. His arms were limp at his side. One held his phone; the other the bouquet. Josh raised the flowers and smelled them. A few of the blossoms reminded him of what he might've seen along the road to his grandparents' home in Texas.

Finally he moved out of the way of the passersby and considered the conversation he'd just had.

"Never personal?" he said in a whisper. "It was for me."

Josh Morgan started for the door to McCormick & Schmick's. As he did, he passed a trash can. Without hesitation, he dropped the colorful arrangement of blooms into it.

♦

Maggie looked at her phone again. It was 1:30. She wondered if Josh was going to be a no-show. Then, she looked up, and there he was.

Maggie stood and the pair exchanged an embrace, awkward at first, then transforming into a deeply felt moment. Maggie's blue eyes leaked a tear or two. When she tried to look at Morgan, he refused to make eye contact.

Josh held Maggie's chair, then took his seat. No sooner had he sat than the waiter arrived and offered to pour a glass of wine from the bottle resting in the chiller.

"I'm fine with water. Thank you."

Suddenly, Maggie felt uncomfortable drinking alone.

The pair sat without a word. Occasionally they made unintended eye contact. Each would smile and look away. All Maggie could think was how she had treated Josh since their encounter with the phony Secret Service Agent, Wyman Hope.

As the period of silence grew longer, Maggie decided she would go first.

"Josh, I'm sorry for how things have been..."

"I am, too," he agreed.

"What never occurred to me," she continued, "was that everything you were doing, you were doing for me. To protect me."

She saw that Morgan lowered his head.

"I know you, sweetheart. What you did wasn't part of the Josh I know. It had to be difficult... no, agonizing, for you."

Maggie reached across the table to the man she loved and took both his hands. He appeared as though he were going to cry.

"I love you, Josh. More than I can say. I want to be together. I want to pick up where we left off. I know that I've been the one who has put off setting a date for our wedding. I want to get married... as soon as we can. I don't care if it's a big wedding, or in front of a justice of the peace. I love you, and I want to spend the rest of my life with you."

Maggie looked at Morgan. Her blue eyes communicated a look of immeasurable love and commitment.

Morgan squeezed her hands gently and returned her gaze. When he said that he loved her, too, Maggie knew things were going to be all right.

But then Josh pulled his hands away.

"Maggie, I do love you, beyond my ability to express it. I'll always adore you."

Maggie's heart sank. The words were exactly what she had hoped to hear, but, all of a sudden, the tone was wrong.

"I can't imagine my life without you, Maggie, but when I think about what I've put you through..."

Tears welled up in Maggie's eyes.

"Maggie, I've changed. Or maybe I haven't changed. Maybe this is just the real me that I've managed to hide from you. But I'm colder, more cynical than I want to be."

"No, Morgan, you're the most decent, honorable..."

Morgan held his hand to silence her.

"Maggie, I love you, but I can't put you through what my life seems to be. I'm a lightning rod for trouble."

"But that's all over, sweetheart." She tried to take his hands again, but as before, he pulled them back.

"Is it? Maybe it is. I'm not sure. Some disaster, some crisis pops up at every corner. I just now had a reminder of that. I can't risk your happiness... your safety... I just can't."

Maggie Loughlin finally conceded to herself that this was going to end much differently than she'd hoped, and more sadly than she'd expected. She hung her head and fiddled with the cloth napkin in her lap.

"Maggie, I'm afraid of who I am. I don't even know who I am. But I believe I'm the same troubled, emotionless, selfish bastard that you found when you moved back to Wyoming from Dallas."

"But I fell in love with that guy."

Morgan smiled, but his eyes said something else. He stood and began to walk away. After only a couple of steps, he turned his head and spoke to Maggie over his shoulder.

"I'll always love you, Maggie. I'm sorry."

Morgan remained motionless a second and then left.

The other diners whispered. They pointed, but only with their eyes.

Maggie finished her wine and signaled for the waiter. "Would you bring my check, please?"

Morgan walked west from the restaurant to Farragut Square, sat on one the many benches, and cried.

Three Weeks Later

Josh Morgan's routine was the polar opposite of the way he'd lived his life for the last several years. He rarely drank anymore. He ate regular, healthy meals. He had moved all the junk out of the workout room in his home, and lifted weights every day.

Josh had returned from a two-mile run. Each day he ran north on Moose-Wilson road for a mile, and then back.

After his shower, Morgan made breakfast. It was an omelet from egg whites, with ham and peppers. Half a grapefruit and a banana-blueberry smoothie completed his meal. He moved to his sofa and turned on the TV. The graphic announced breaking news.

Cameron Neal gave her QNN viewers an update on old news.

"We have breaking news. The autopsy on philanthropist and

businessman Linus Schwartz has confirmed that the man died of a stroke. Also, ballistics tests on the gun found beside the billionaire's body have identified it as having fired the shots that killed his employees, Dexter Leach and Udo Stettin. Whether Schwartz fired in self-defense may never be known. A technical glitch had apparently disabled surveillance cameras in the complex where he lived, so the hoped-for recordings were nonexistent."

Morgan smiled and breathed a deep sigh of relief.

Neal completed the brief from Qatar and moved on.

"In other news, the White House is set to announce the details of a new trade deal with the European Union. We now take you to a live briefing from the White House press room."

The image shifted to a view Morgan had seen many times before. He watched as an auburn-haired woman took her place behind the dais. The graphic identified her as Principal Deputy Press Secretary Margaret Loughlin. Morgan watched only momentarily and sighed. Then he pressed a button on the remote and the image disappeared with a crackle.

He finished his meal in silence.

In the afternoon, Morgan followed another structured routine. He had used his John Deere tractor's blade and front-end loader to push soil up to form a berm behind his log home. In front of the dirt bank, at intervals of a few yards, wooden frames held the black and white shapes of human silhouettes. Shooting benches stood at various distances from the targets.

In another part of his property, Morgan had designed a 3-gun range, a course where he could hone his skills by moving through stages, engaging targets from various positions. With an AR-style rifle, a shotgun, and a handgun, he shot from behind barriers and around obstacles.

When the ex-CIA officer had finished his regimen for the day, he rested on the swing on his front porch. The iced tea was the perfect reward for a successful day of training. Biscuit, his Golden Retriever, sat at his feet. Memories flooded his mind. He recalled the morning Everson Blake's operators had attacked him at this very place. He had dispatched one. Maggie had taken care of the second.

Morgan recalled his friend at the Agency, Ben Reid, whom Blake had also ordered killed.

Mostly he thought of the love he'd had – that he still had – for Trent Weston. He felt guilty for not calling Alicia Weston more often.

Joshua Matthew Morgan tossed the ice from his empty glass toward his driveway and removed his phone from his pocket. He touched a contact's name and waited.

"Morgan. Was wondering when I'd hear from you. So?"

"Did you talk to Lechler?" Josh asked the CIA Director.

"He's on board."

"Then I'm in, if you accept my demands."

"And they're non-negotiable. Right?" Betsy Parnell chuckled.

Morgan continued. "I won't come back as a Case Officer. At least, not right now. I'll be a sort of contractor."

"Agreed."

"I'll have a certain amount of discretion over the ops I take on."

"Also acceptable."

"And I'll have a lot of autonomy over my actions – how I handle things. And I can quit without warning, anytime I want."

"Go on."

"Finally, I get to pick my first op."

"Lammers. I figured as much. The FBI was able to get into his laptop that you brought us. There was a lot of information about places he frequents. Lots of other personal info on the man, too."

"I'll need that. Do we have a deal?"

"We do, Morgan."

Current CIA Field Operator Josh Morgan pressed the display and disconnected the call. He scratched Biscuit behind the ear.

"Come on, old boy. Let's go fishing."

The end.

Hearing from my readers is one of the best things about writing. And your honest review is one of the most helpful things you can do.

If you enjoyed reading *Hell in the Meantime*, I'd be very grateful if you would take a few moments to rate it and post your comments on Amazon, Goodreads, or any other site where my books are sold or discussed.

Please visit my website at www.rodjohnsonauthor.com and follow me on Facebook at Rod Johnson Novels. You can contact me through either site.

Thank you for reading and reviewing. Now I have to get back to work on Book 4 of the Josh Morgan Novels series!

ABOUT THE AUTHOR

After a career in the Financial Services industry, Rod Johnson retired to devote his time to his family and writing.

Hell in the Meantime is the third novel in the *Josh Morgan* series that carries the protagonist's name. It follows Rod's debut work, *Half of Faith*, and the sequel, *SPIRITs of Retribution*.

Among the author's influences are great novelists in the thriller genre such as Clancy, Ludlum, le Carré, and others. Nelson DeMille's *Charm School* is an all-time favorite novel, along with anything by thriller rock star Brad Thor.

Rod works hard to ensure his plots are filled with a myriad of moving parts, lived out in characters with compelling blends of virtues and flaws and complex personalities who struggle to balance their hypocrisies and better selves.

When Rod isn't writing, he enjoys flyfishing and photography and his family spends as much time as possible on their thirty-seven-foot sailboat, *No Regrets*.

The author resides in a small north Texas town with his wife and daughter.